# THE HORSEMAN ON THE ROOF

JEAN GIONO was born in 1895 in Manosque, Provence, and lived there most of his life. He was sent to the front in early 1915, an experience he refused to repeat in the second world war when he was briefly arrested for declaring himself a pacifist. For eighteen years he supported his parents, Jean-Antoine and Pauline, by working as a bank clerk before his first two novels were published, thanks to the generosity of André Gide, to critical acclaim. He went on to write thirty novels and numerous essays and stories. Placed in 1944 on the black list of national writers, Giono was later awarded the Prix Monégasque for his collective work. He died in October 1970.

D1494053

*Jean Giono*

# THE HORSEMAN
# ON THE ROOF

*Translated from the French by*
*Jonathan Griffin*

THE HARVILL PRESS
LONDON

First published in France in 1951
with the title *Le Hussard sur le Toit*
by Librairie Gallimard, Paris

This edition first published in 1995 by
The Harvill Press
84 Thornhill Road
London N1 1RD

1 3 5 7 9 8 6 4 2

A CIP catalogue record for this title is
available from the British Library

ISBN 1 86046 086 0

Typeset in Bembo at Libanus Press

Printed and bound in Great Britain by
Selwood Printing Ltd, Burgess Hill

*To the memory of my friend*
*Charles Bistési*
*and to*
*Suzanne*

# I

DAWN FOUND ANGELO mute and yawning but awake. The brow of the hill had protected him from the slight dew that falls in these regions in summer. He rubbed his horse down with a handful of heather and rolled his saddlebag.

The birds were stirring in the valley into which he descended. It was not cool, even in the hollows still covered by the darkness of the night. The whole sky was lit by shafts of grey. At last the red sun, smothered in a thicket of dark clouds, emerged from the forests.

Despite the already stifling heat, Angelo longed for something hot to drink. As he descended into the middle valley separating the hills on which he had spent the night from another, higher and wilder range, two or three leagues ahead of him, where the first rays of the sun were burnishing the bronze of the tall oak woods, he saw a small farm building by the roadside and, in the field, a woman in a red skirt, picking up the washing that she had spread out in the evening dew.

He drew near. Her shoulders and arms were bare above a coarse linen bodice, which also displayed enormous, deeply sunburned breasts.

"Excuse me, madame," he said, "but will you let me have a little coffee? I'll pay for it."

She did not answer at once, and he realized that he had adopted too polite a manner. "That 'I'll pay for it' is clumsy," he thought.

"I can give you some coffee," she said; "come in." She was tall, but so nimble that she swung around slowly in one place, like a ship. "The door's over there," she said, pointing to the end of the hedge.

In the kitchen there were only an old man and a great many flies. But on the low stove with its roaring fire, alongside a cauldron of bran for the pigs, the coffeepot emitted such a good smell that Angelo found the soot-blackened room altogether charming. Even the pig-bran spoke a language of magnificence to his stomach, poorly satisfied by a supper of dry bread.

He drank a bowl of coffee. The woman planted herself in front of him, giving him a good view of her brawny shoulders, full of dimples, and even of the huge pink blossom of her breasts. She asked him if he was an official gentleman. "Careful!" thought Angelo. "She's regretting her coffee."

"Oh no," he said (taking care not to say "madame"), "I'm in business at Marseille; I'm going to see clients in the Drôme and I thought I'd get some fresh air on the way."

The woman's face grew more kindly; especially when he asked the way to Banon. "You'd like an egg," she said. She had already pushed the cauldron of bran to one side and put the frying-pan on the fire.

He ate an egg and a piece of bacon with four slices of coarse, extremely white bread, which seemed to him as light as feathers. The woman was now bustling maternally around him. To his surprise he didn't mind the smell of her sweat at all, nor even the thick tufts of red hair in her armpits when she raised her arms to adjust her bun. She refused payment and even began to laugh when he insisted, roughly pushing his purse away. Angelo felt painfully awkward and ridiculous in her presence; he would have liked to be able to pay and depart with that dry, detached air which was his timidity's usual defence. He rapidly murmured his thanks and pocketed his purse.

The woman showed him his road rising on the other side of the valley into the oak woods. Angelo walked his horse for a while in silence along the little plain, through bright green fields. He was under a spell from the food, which had left a most pleasant taste in his mouth. At length he sighed and set his horse to trot.

The sun was high; it was very hot but there was no violence in the light. It was white and so diffused that it seemed to butter the earth with dense air. Angelo had been climbing for a long time through the oak forest. He was following a narrow road covered with a thick layer of dust, and each step of his horse raised a cloud that did not settle again. Through the ragged and withered undergrowth he could see, at each turning, how the signs of his passing remained upon all the windings of the road below him. The trees brought no coolness. Instead, the small hard oak leaves reflected the heat and light. The shade of the forest dazzled and stifled.

On these banks, burned to the bone, a few white thistles cracked as his horse went by, as though the metal earth all around were vibrating under the iron-shod hoofs. There was nothing but this little thorny noise, crackling with extreme clarity above the sound of the hoofs, dulled by the dust and a silence so total that the presence of the great mute trees became almost unreal. The saddle was scorching. The movement of the girths raised a lather of sweat. The animal sucked its bit and from time to time cleared its throat by shaking its head. The steady rising of the heat hummed like a boiler mercilessly stoked with coal. The trunks of the oaks cracked. Through the undergrowth, dry and bare like a church floor, flooded by the white light that had no sparkle, but a blinding powderiness, the horse's gait set long black rays slowly turning. The road, hoisting itself in stiffer coils up over ancient rocks covered with white lichens, sometimes headed straight into the sun: then, in the chalk sky, there opened a sort of abyss of unbelievable phosphorescence, and out of it came a breath of furnace and fever, sticky, the slime and fat of it visibly quivering. The huge trees dissolved within this dazzle; great stretches of forest engulfed in the light showed only as a vague foliage of cinders, shapeless forms, almost transparent and suddenly coated by the heat with a slow sway of shimmering viscosity. Then the road would turn westward, instantly shrunken to the dimensions of the mule track that it had become; it would be hemmed in by living, violent tree trunks supported by pillars of gold, with branches twisted by crackling twigs of gold, and still leaves all gilded like little mirrors set in thin gold threads that closely framed their every outline.

\* \*

After a while, Angelo was surprised at seeing no life except that of the light. There should have been at least some lizards and even crows, who enjoy this burning chalky weather and keep watch from the tips of branches as they do in times of snow. Angelo remembered the summer manoeuvres in the Garbia hills; he had never before seen this crystalline landscape, this effect of a glass globe over a clock, this mineralogical phantasmagoria (even the trees were faceted and full of prisms like rock crystal). He was stunned by the proximity of these inhuman caverns.

3

"I've hardly," he thought, "left the bare shoulders of that woman who gave me coffee! And here is a complete world more remote from those bare shoulders than the moon or the phosphorescent caves of China, and quite capable, too, of killing me. Well," he continued, "this is the world I live in. At Garbia I had my little staff and I had to keep my mind on the manoeuvres if I didn't want a dressing-down from General San Giorgio with his beautiful moustaches and cowherd language. All that protected me from the world and saved me from seeing these groves of tetrahedra. Which is perhaps the last word on the subject of these sublime principles: simply to provide oneself with a small staff and a foul-mouthed general, through terror of realizing that one is encased under a domed glass clock-cover in which a slight touch of the light may kill one. There are warriors of Ariosto in the sun. That is why anybody who counts tries to fortify his importance with sublime principles."

But still these baffling and tenuous trees, which must, he reckoned, weigh the least of them a hundred tons and yet hid and slid in the light with the agility of trout, continued to worry him. He was impatient to reach the top of the hill in the hope of catching a breath of wind.

There was none. It was a heath on which the light and heat pressed more heavily than ever. One could now see the whole of the chalk sky in its utter whiteness. The horizon was a distant stirring of faintly blue hills. The part of it towards which Angelo turned was filled by the grey bulk of a long mountain, very high though hummocky and rounded. The country in between bristled with tall rocks like lateen sails faintly tinged with green, with villages clinging like wasps' nests to their edges. The slopes, from which these rocks rose almost bare, were clothed with brown forests of oak and chestnut. At their feet, with capes and gulfs clearly distinguishable, ran little valleys, either yellow or even whiter than the sky. Everything was a-quiver and distorted by intense light and oily heat. Clouds of dust, smoke, or mist, exhaled by the earth under the beating of the sun, were beginning to rise here and there, from stubble where the harvest had already been gathered, from little flame-coloured hayfields, and even from the forests, where one could feel the heat frying the last fresh blade of grass.

The road would not make up its mind to go down again, and ran along the crest, which itself was very broad, almost a plateau, undulating and embedded to right and left in the gently sloping flanks of higher hills. At last it entered a forest of small white oaks barely eight or nine feet high, with a deep carpet of savory and thyme. The horse's hoofs kicked up a thick scent, which, in the motionless, heavy air, eventually became sickening. Here there were, however, some traces of human life. From time to time an old track covered with chalk-white summer grass branched off from the road and, twisting at once into the thick of the wood, concealed its course, but at least intended to lead somewhere. Finally, through the stocky trees, Angelo saw a sheepfold. Its walls were the colour of bread, and it was roofed with *lauze* – enormous flat stones of great weight. Angelo turned into the lane. He thought he might find a little water there for his horse. The sheepfold, whose walls were buttressed like a church or a fort, had no windows; nor, since it had its back to the road, was any door visible. In spite of his rank having been "bought like two-penn'orth of pepper" (as he used to say bitterly in fits of honesty), Angelo was a genuine soldier, and he had the instincts of the forager. He noticed that, as he drew near the sheepfold, it echoed to his horse's hoofs. "It's empty," he thought, "and has been so for a long time." Indeed, the long troughs of polished wood resting on stones were dry and white as a skeleton. But the wide-open doorway gave out a breath of coolness and a delicious smell of old sheep's-dung. As he moved towards it, however, Angelo heard a humming, almost a roar, coming from inside, and saw in the shadows a sort of heavy drapery moving. The horse understood, a second before he did, that the sheepfold was inhabited by swarms of wild bees: it turned about and made off at a sharp trot towards the wood. A bend in the lane brought him around to a distant view of the front of the building standing on a slight elevation above the short white oaks. The bees had come out in thick, floating ribbons. In the light they were black, like lumps of soot. They streamed from the broad doorway and from two oval windows above it, as though from the jaw and eye-sockets of some old skull left lying in the woods.

For a long time the need to find water kept growing more and more urgent. The track kept on along the parched crest. In his morning high spirits Angelo had forgotten to wind his watch. He reckoned he must have covered at least four leagues. He tried to tell the time from the sun, but there was no sun, only a blinding light coming from all parts of the sky at once. At last the track began to go down and suddenly, rounding a bend, Angelo felt on his shoulders a coolness that made him look up; he had just entered beneath the bright green foliage of a tall beech, and beside the beech stood four huge, glittering poplars. He wouldn't believe in them until he heard the rustling of their leaves, which, despite the absence of wind, trembled and made a sound like water. Behind these trees lay yet another stubblefield, not merely harvested but cleared of shocks and already showing some furrows that had been opened just that morning. As Angelo automatically reined in his horse, which was champing and straining at the bit, he observed that the field continued past a group of willows. And through these willows he saw three donkeys approaching, harnessed to a plough. His horse carried him at a brisk trot towards a grove of sycamores, poplars, and willows, and he hardly had time to notice that the ploughman was wearing a robe.

The fountain stood in the grove by the roadside. Out of a fat spout, water (coloured like aubergines) flowed noiselessly into a basin red with thick-growing mosses. A little stream ran off from the fountain to irrigate the fields. In the middle of the fields a long one-storey building rose from the grass, austere and extremely clean, newly roughcast, with fresh-painted shutters, and even more silent than the fountain.

As his eyes became used to the shade, Angelo noticed, a few feet from him on the other side of the road, a monk sitting at the foot of a tree. He was thin and ageless, his face the same rusty colour as his robe, and his eyes were burning.

"What a magnificent place," said Angelo with a false air of ease, shifting his heels in his boots.

The monk did not reply. He stared with his luminous eyes at the horse, the saddlebag, and particularly the boots, until Angelo felt embarrassed and found it too cool under the trees. Leading his horse by the bridle, he walked out into the sun. By way of excuse he told himself: "Staying under there one might easily catch a chill. The water has done us good, and we can perfectly well cover another league or two before eating." The man's head, thin as a wild beast's, had impressed him, especially the tendons of the neck, standing out like cords binding head to robe. "Besides, who knows what swarms of bees . . . !" he was thinking when he saw, two or three hundred paces ahead, a house that was plainly an inn (there was even a sign) and, overhead, a huge flock of crows making northward.

"Good morning, soldier," said the innkeeper. "I've got all you need for your horse, but you won't do so well, unless you can put up with my dinner." And with a wink he lifted the lid of a saucepan in which stuffed quails lay simmering on a bed of onions and tomatoes. "The luck of the woods . . . Are you very fussy about your coat?" he added, glancing at Angelo's elegant summer riding coat. "My chair coverings have been worn away by the fellows in skirts, and the straw will bite into that fine cloth of yours like acid."

This shirtless man was wearing a red postillion-vest over his bare skin. The thick hair on his chest took the place of a cravat. But he put on an old helmet, in order to go out and dash two pails of water over the horse's legs.

"That's an old soldier," said Angelo to himself. After the raging heat nothing could have put him more at his ease. "These French," he went on, "will never get over Napoleon. But now that there's nobody to fight but weavers demanding the right to eat meat once a week, they go off and dream of Austerlitz in the sticks rather than sing 'Long live Louis-Philippe' at the expense of the workers. This man with no shirt, given the right circumstances, would make himself King of Naples. That's the difference between the two sides of the Alps. We have no precedent, and that makes us timid."

"Know what I'd do in your place?" said the man. "I'd unstrap my saddlebag and put it inside on a couple of chairs."

"There are no robbers here," said Angelo.

"What about me?" said the man. "Opportunity puts fat on the pig."

"Trust me to keep your bacon lean," said Angelo drily.

"You're a joker too," said the man. "I don't mind merchants of sudden death. Come and have a glass of *piquette*," and he gave Angelo a hearty slap on the shoulder.

The promised *piquette* was a light red wine, but quite good. "The boys in skirts at the monastery trot their half mile through the woods to sip a half pint of this," said the man.

"I thought," said Angelo innocently, "they wouldn't drink anything but the water from their beautiful fountain by the roadside under the trees. Besides, are they permitted to come here and drink wine?"

"If you look at it that way," said the man, "nothing's permitted. Is an ex-noncom of the 27th Light Infantry permitted to set up as an innkeeper on a road that only foxes use? Is that written in the Rights of Man? These people in skirts are good fellows. They ring their bells every now and then, and they have a parade with banners and trumpets on Rogation Days, but their real work is farming. I can tell you they don't lie down on the job. And what farmer ever spits on red wine? Besides, their own commander said: 'Drink, this is My Blood'. All I did was to send away my niece. She worried them. Because of her skirts, I guess. It's annoying, when you wear them through conviction, to see someone who wears them by necessity. Now I'm all alone in this hole; what does it matter if they wet their whistles from time to time? Everybody's happy; isn't that the main thing? Anyway," he continued, "they do it like gentlemen. They don't come by the road. They make a big detour through the woods (which means something when you're thirsty), by way of penance and all that, which is their speciality, not mine. And they come in by the back – I always leave the stable door open – and that's a mortification too for anyone with a proud heart. All the same, who'd have told me that one day I'd be a barman?"

Angelo enjoyed some deep reflection. He could see how, living alone in these silent woods, one couldn't help needing company and talking to the firstcomer. "With my love for the people," he told himself, "I'm like this noncom by his road where only foxes pass. Love is absurd. 'Devil take you!' people will say. 'Truth lies in the bare shoulders of that woman who gave you coffee. They were beautiful, and their dimples smiled charmingly in spite of sunburn. What more do you want? Did you turn up your nose just now at the fountain, or even at the cool shade of that beech and those poplars? They too sparkled very charmingly.' But with the beech, the poplar, and the fountain one can be an egoist. Who will teach me to be an egoist?

There's no denying that with his red waistcoat over his bare skin this man is perfectly at peace and he can discuss what he wants to with the firstcomer." Angelo had been much affected by the silence of the woods.

"I don't have a dining-room," the peaceful man said to him at last, "and usually I take my grub on that marble table over there. I think it'd be silly for us to feed at two separate tables. Especially as I'd have to be getting up all the time to serve you. Would you be put out if I laid the same table for us both? My manners are all right if you agree, but I'm alone, and . . ." (This word decided Angelo.) In the end he managed to get paid for what he drank of his own wine.

His manners were indeed all right: he had learned in camp to eat without dirtying his neckerchief of hair. "Inns like the one you have," said Angelo, "are generally running with blood. In such places there's always an oven for roasting corpses and a well down which to throw the bones."

"I've an oven but no well," said the man. "Mind you," he added, "the bones could be buried in the woods, where it would take the devil to spot anything."

"In my present state of mind," said Angelo, "I'd like nothing better than an adventure of that kind. Men are queer fish: it's superfluous to tell that to a noncom who has had the honour to belong to the 27th Light Infantry. But I'm up to my neck debating with myself problems of such difficulty that it would be a great relief to be attacked by some really determined cutthroats, out for my purse and with no chance of avoiding the galleys or even the guillotine except by desperately threatening my life. I think I'd take them on with real joy, even on that little narrow staircase I see over there – though it would make swordplay difficult. I'd even like being in a garret with a door that wouldn't shut and hearing the murderers coming upstairs in their stocking-feet, telling myself that I could only fire my pistol twice and would then have to settle things with the well-sharpened dagger that is always at my side . . ." Then he made a very melancholy declaration. He was wholly serious. "This," he said to himself, "is the only way to talk of love without having people make fun of you."

"That's easy to say," said the man, "but I don't think such moments are very amusing."

9

But when Angelo persisted with a sort of sad ardour, he poured him out a glass of wine and spoke philosophically and with good sense about youth, which everybody goes through, thus proving that its dangers are not mortal.

"I'll settle down as a hermit," thought Angelo. "Well, why not? A little orchard, some vines, maybe a robe – after all, it's a sensible costume. And very thin cords to fasten the robe to my head. That does at least look extremely impressive, and makes a perfect protection for a man who fears ridicule above all things. Perhaps that is a way of being free!"

When it came time to settle the bill, the man lost all philosophy and literally begged for a few pennies. He said no more about the 27th Light Infantry but made great use of the word "alone". He was aware that at this word, every time, Angelo's eyes lost their sternness. He very easily got what he wanted, and put on his helmet for the pleasure of taking it off and holding it in his hand while he walked with Angelo to the mounting-block.

*　*

It was about one in the afternoon, and the heat was sharp, like phosphorus. "Keep out of the sun," said the man (with what he thought was profound irony, since there was no shade anywhere).

It seemed to Angelo that each step of his horse was taking him into the oven of which he had just been speaking. The valley he followed was very narrow, and choked up with clumps of dwarf oaks; the rocky walls sloping down to it were at white heat. The light, crushed to a fine irritant dust, rubbed its sandpaper over the drowsy horse and rider, and over the little trees, which it gradually spirited away into worn air, whose coarse texture quivered, mingling smears of greasy yellow with dull ochres, with great slabs of chalk wherein it was impossible to recognize anything familiar. Down high anfractuous rocks flowed the odour of rotten eggs from nests deserted by the hawks. The slopes poured down into the valley the stale reek of everything that had died within the vast radius of these pale hills. Tree stumps and skins; ants' nests; little cages of ribs the size of a fist; skeletons of snakes like broken chains of silver; patches of slaughtered flies like handfuls of dried currants; dead hedgehogs whose bones looked like chestnuts in their burrs; vicious shreds of wild boars strewn over wide threshing-floors of agony; trees devoured from head to foot, stuffed with sawdust to the tips of their branches, which the thick air kept standing; carcasses of buzzards fallen into the boughs of oaks on which the sun beat down; or the sharp stink of the heated sap bursting out of the fissures along the hawthorn trunks.

All this barbarousness did not exist merely in Angelo's red sleep. There had never been such a summer in the hills. Moreover, that day, the same black heat began to break in sudden, brutal waves over the whole south: over the solitudes of the Var, where the little oaks began crackling, over the doomed farms of the plateaus, where the wells were at once besieged by flocks of pigeons, over Marseille, where the sewers began to smoke. At Aix, at noon, the siesta silence was so great that, on the boulevards, the fountains sounded as loud as at night. At Rians, by nine in the morning, there were two people sick: a carter who had an attack just as he entered town – he was carried into a wineshop, set in the shade. and bled, but had still not recovered the use of speech – and a young girl of twenty who, at about the same time, suddenly fouled herself standing by the fountain where she had just drunk; she tried to run to her home nearby but fell in a heap on her doorstep. At the hour when Angelo was dozing on his horse, they were saying that she was dead. At Draguignan the hills reflected the heat back into the bowl where the town lies; it was impossible to take a siesta: the tiny windows of the houses in ordinary times keep the rooms cool, but now it was so hot that people longed to hack them open with pickaxes to get a little air. Everyone went out into the fields; there are no springs, no fountains, so people ate melons and apricots, which were hot, almost cooked; they lay down on the grass on their bellies.

Melons were being eaten at La Valette also and, just when Angelo was passing under the rocks down which flowed the smell of rotten eggs, young Mme de Théus was running in glaring sunlight down the steps of the château to go to the village where, it seems, a kitchenmaid, who had gone there an hour before (just when that old scoundrel of an innkeeper was saying to Angelo: "Don't go out into the sun"), had suddenly become very ill. And now (while Angelo, with eyes shut, was still following that burning trail through the hills) the kitchenmaid was dead; people imagined it was an apoplectic fit, because her face was quite black. The young lady was sickened by the heat, the smell of the dead girl, the black face. She was obliged to go behind a bush to vomit.

There was much eating of melons in the Rhone Valley. This valley on its eastern side skirts the greenish country that Angelo was crossing. There, because of the river, there are quite tall groves of sycamores, of planes more than ninety feet high, of sumptuous beeches whose drooping foliage is very fair and fresh. This year there had been no winter. The pine caterpillar had devoured the needles of all the pine groves; it had stripped the *thujas* and cypresses; it had even changed its feeding-habits so as to eat the leaves of the sycamores, planes, and beeches. From the heights of Carpentras, across hundreds of square leagues of tree skeletons, of leaves reduced to lace and cinders that the wind carried away, one could make out the ramparts of Avignon like the carcass of an ox picked white by ants. The heat reached there the same day, and its first blasts ate into the sickliest trees.

At Orange station the passengers in a train from Lyon began to pound as hard as they could on their carriage doors to get someone to come and let them out. They were dying of thirst; many had vomited and were writhing with colic. The engine-driver came along with the keys, but after opening two of the doors he could not open the third: he went away and rested his forehead on a railing; after a time he fell against it. As he was carried off, he had the strength to say that they should uncouple the engine as soon as possible, since it might catch fire or explode. In any case, he said, they should at once turn the second lever to the left, as far as it would go. Meanwhile the passengers in the third compartment kept pounding with their fists against the locked door.

There was a huge crop of melons in the towns and villages of this entire valley. The heat had ripened them. It was impossible to think of eating anything: bread, meat – the very idea turned the stomach. People ate melons. That took the place of drink: there were great tongues of scum hanging from the spouts of the fountains. People felt a furious longing to rinse their mouths. The dust swirling from the flaked branches of certain trees, or rising from meadows as white as snow, where the hay dust that came from the snow-white fields was baked dry and disintegrated under the weight of the air, tickled their throats and nostrils like plane-tree pollen. The little streets around the synagogue were strewn with the peel, seeds, and pith of melons. They ate raw tomatoes, too. It was the first day and, as time went on, this refuse quickly rotted. On the evening of this first day it began to rot, and the ensuing night was hotter than the day. So far, the peasants had brought into Carpentras more than fifty cartloads of big watermelons. By one in the afternoon, thirty of these carts returned empty to the melon fields just outside the walls. At the moment when, thirty leagues east of Carpentras, Angelo, half asleep, was letting his horse carry him as it pleased, through gorges sickening with heat and the smell of rotten eggs, the melon peel was beginning to litter the main street and even the approaches to the *sous-préfecture*, the library, the royal *gendarmerie*, and the Lion Hotel, the best hotel in town; fresh cartloads of melons were arriving; a doctor was taking some drops of paregoric elixir on a gramme of sugar; and the *diligence* for Blovac, which was due to leave at two, did not harness its horses.

In the towns and villages, as in the open fields, the light from this heat was as mysterious as fog. It made the walls of the houses invisible from one side of the street to the other. The reflection from surfaces struck by the sun was so intense that the shade opposite was dazzling. Shapes were distorted in an air as viscous as syrup. The people walked as if they were drunk; their intoxication came not from their stomachs, in which the green flesh and water of the hastily chewed melons gurgled, but from this blurring of forms, which kept shifting doorways, windows, latches, portières, raffia curtains, altering the height of pavements and the position of the cobbles. Added to which, everyone walked with half-closed eyes and, as with Angelo, under their lowered eyelids, dyed poppy-red by the sun, their desires came crowding, forming images of boiling water into which they stumbled.

So it came about that, in the first days, many victims passed unnoticed. Nobody bothered about them until, lacking the strength to reach their houses, they collapsed in the street. And not always even then. If they fell on their bellies, it could be supposed that they were asleep. Only if they rolled on the ground and ended up on their backs, did people see their black faces and become concerned. And not always even then, for the heat and the furious thirstiness made people self-centred. That is why, in actual fact, there were on this first day – precisely as Angelo was musing under his red eyelids about the carcasses of buzzards fallen into the branches of the tall oaks – by and large very few cases of sickness. A Jewish doctor, summoned by a rabbi who was chiefly worried about pollution, came to examine three corpses crumpled up just outside the little door of the synagogue (it was presumed that they had meant to go into the temple to be in the cool). There were only two alarms that afternoon in Carpentras, including the coachman of the Blovac *diligence*. In his case, moreover, it was difficult to distinguish the effects of absinthe from those of the heat (he was a very fat man of inordinate thirst and appetite and, after a meal at the inn – he was probably the only person to eat a midday meal in the whole town – during which he devoured a whole dish of tripe, he had drunk seven absinthes in place of coffee and liqueur).

At Orange, Avignon, Apt, Manosque, Arles, Tarascon, Nîmes, Montpellier, Aix, La Valette (though here the death of the kitchen-maid had created a long, ominous silence), Draguignan, and as far as the coast, hardly anybody yet (but only at the beginning of the afternoon, it is true; at the moment when Angelo in his sleep, shaken by the horse's gait, felt like vomiting), hardly anybody was moved to worry about a couple of deaths in each place and a few people taken more or less seriously ill, all attributed to those melons and tomatoes that were being eaten so ravenously everywhere. These sick were treated with paregoric elixir on lumps of sugar.

At Toulon, around two in the afternoon, a navy medical inspector insisted on seeing the Duke of T., the base commander. He was told to come back at seven in the evening. He acted in a very unmannerly way, and even raised his voice unsuitably in the antechamber. He was finally sent away by the midshipman orderly, who noticed that he looked haggard and seemed to have an irrepressible desire to talk, which he restrained by clapping his hand over his mouth. The midshipman said he was sorry. The doctor said: "Can't be helped," and went off.

At Marseille there was only one question: that frightful smell of sewers. In a few hours the water in the Old Port had grown thick, dark, and the colour of tar. The town was too crowded for people to notice the doctors, who began to make their rounds in cabriolets in the early afternoon. Some of them looked extremely serious. But that terrible stench of excrement gave everybody a sad and thoughtful look.

*  *

The road that Angelo's horse was following made straight for one of those rocks shaped like lateen sails, and began to zigzag up it towards a village concealed among the stones like a wasps' nest. Angelo felt the horse's change of gait; he woke up, and found that he was climbing among small terraced farms, held in place by little walls of white stones and bearing very mournful cypresses. The village was deserted; the walls of its narrow street were stifling; the glare of the light made one giddy. Angelo dismounted and led his horse into a sort of shelter created by a tumble down vault near the church. There was a violent smell of bird droppings; the ceiling of the vault was plastered with swallows' nests from which a brownish juice was oozing; but the shade, although gritty, brought peace to Angelo's burning neck, which felt almost bruised: he could not keep his hand off it. He had been there a good quarter of an hour when he saw, facing him on the other side of the street, an open door. Far back in the deep shadow, something – a bodice or a shirt – stirred feebly. He crossed the street to ask for some water. It was a woman, sluggish and sweating, and breathing with great difficulty.

She said there was no water left; the pigeons had fouled the cisterns; she doubted if it was even worth trying to water the horse. But the animal snorted in the trough, rinsed its nostrils, and blew spray at the sun.

The woman had some melons. Angelo ate three. He gave the rind to the horse. The woman had some tomatoes too, but she said that these would cause fever; they could only be eaten cooked. Angelo bit into a raw tomato, so violently that the juice spurted over his fine coat. He hardly cared. His thirst was beginning to abate a little. He also gave two or three tomatoes to the horse, which ate them greedily. The woman said that it was this kind of recklessness that had made her husband ill, and that he had run a high fever since yesterday. Angelo noticed a bed in one corner of the room, piled with a thick flowered rug and an eiderdown that barely allowed the sick man's head to

15

protrude. The woman said that her man couldn't get warm. Which Angelo thought very odd and decidedly a bad sign. Also the man's face was purple. The woman said he had hardly any pain now, but that he had been convulsed with colic all morning and that this surely came from the tomatoes, for he had refused to listen to her and, like Angelo, had let himself go.

After resting nearly an hour in this room, into which in the end they had brought the horse too, Angelo set off again. The light and the heat were still waiting at the door. One could not imagine there would be an evening.

This was the moment when the navy medical inspector was saying: "Can't be helped!" and turning back to Toulon. It was also exactly the moment when, the Jewish doctor having rushed home, spoken to his wife, and made her pack a small bag for herself and their little twelve-year-old girl, that plump woman with her ox-eyes and eagle-nose was leaving Carpentras by the Vaison *diligence*, with instructions to push on without delay in a hired carriage as far as Dieulefit or even Bordeaux. She turned her back on the town where her husband was staying and, laying a finger on her lips, silenced the little girl, who sat opposite her, wide-eyed and sweating. At that moment Angelo was seeing the barbaric splendour of the terrible summer in the high hills: oaks turned russet, chestnuts baked white, pastures thin and verdigris-coloured, cypresses with the oil of funeral lamps gleaming in their foliage, mists of light whirling and evolving around him in a mirage, the tapestry, worn threadbare by the sun, in whose translucent web floated and quivered the ever-grey pattern of forests, villages, hills, mountain, horizon, fields, groves, and pastures, almost blotted out by air the colour of sackcloth.

At this instant, when he was asking himself for the hundredth time whether evening would come – having turned a hundred times to the east, still imperturbably pure ochre – time had stopped in La Valette, where the kitchenmaid was rotting with extraordinary rapidity in front of the few inhabitants of the village and her young mistress; they had stayed out of respect for the dead girl, who was melting visibly and soaking the bed on which she had been laid out fully dressed. And while they stood fascinated by the swift work of decomposition, Angelo could see opening around him the region of chestnut woods pitted with rocks and villages of which he had caught sight, early in the morning, from the top of the first hill. But whereas in the morning, and seen from afar, that landscape had had a shape and comfortable colours, now under this incredibly violent light it decomposed into syrupy and quivering air. The trees were like smears of grease spreading their shapes and colours among the threads of a coarse-woven atmosphere; the forests were melting like lumps of fat. At the hour when, in front of the corpse, the young mistress was thinking: "Only a few hours ago I sent this girl down to buy me melons," when Angelo was gazing eastward in the hope of seeing there at last the signs announcing this day's end, the navy medical inspector could stand it no longer. He went back up the rue Lamalgue, passed along the rue des Trois-Oliviers, crossed the Place Pavé-d'Amour, went down the rue Montauban, turned into the rue des Remparts, passed down the rue de la Miséricorde, where trickles of urine were ripening between white-hot cobblestones, descended the rue de l'Oratoire and the rue Larmedieu, across which, like a man blowing in his sleep, the harbour was exhaling the stench of its green stomach, mounted the rue Mûrier, where he was obliged to straddle the gutters from a public convenience, came out into the rue Lafayette with its plane trees, sat down at last at the terrace of the Duc d'Aumale, and ordered an absinthe. As soon as he had taken the first gulp, he told himself that he mustn't be more royalist than the king. It was time for a report: he had only to write it to be cleared of responsibility. Every year people said: "It's never been so hot." Perhaps it was only simple dysentery. A body worn out by excesses.

"A premonitory symptom, a premonitory symptom: how can you be sure of anything in a body ruined by alcohol, tobacco, women, knocking about the world, salt provisions; what would you say it was premonitory of? All I could say was that in my opinion it was a *prodromic* symptom. The Admiral would have looked very pretty, hauled out of his siesta to be confronted with a purely prodromic symptom! *Collapsus*. Even *collapsus*. Ruined bodies in which a simple attack of dysentery may take – Asiatic forms. Far from the Ganges. India, where the heat breeds elephants and clouds of flies. The Indus Delta. Mud, 120 degrees, no shade. Water rotting like an organism. Really this town doesn't smell as bad as they say; less bad than it did six months ago. Unless it's a question of habit. Though I still smell the absinthe well enough! Maybe the stink of this town has got so bad it couldn't be worse. In which case the dysentery might pass all bounds too. Raspail! The service of humanity! Very pretty indeed, but I'm a naval doctor, and a naval doctor has superior officers. Pass the buck to the Admiral in a report that will clear me of all responsibility. Otherwise . . . if I were a civilian doctor . . . but I'm only a cog. All the same, this evening I'll go and get an appointment with the Admiral. I'd better do so: between now and then, one of the civilian doctors might very well . . . He wouldn't take many pains over a case of *collapsus*. Whale-blue storm in the dead end of the Gulf of Bengal. Dangerous effluvia on board the *Melpomène*."

He ordered a second absinthe, asking if this time he couldn't have a little cold water with it. At the moment when the second absinthe was being brought to the medical inspector, at La Valette the young lady was saying to herself: "It seems a century ago!" The kitchen-maid's death had abolished time; the young lady was bemused by the blow that had abolished time for the kitchenmaid and destroyed all the roads of escape. At the same instant, more than forty leagues to the north, Angelo was penetrating ever more deeply into the high hills through grey forests of chestnut, grey heaths covered with grey centaury, under a grey sky. He felt like someone in boiling lead. The horse moved as if sound asleep. Meanwhile at Carpentras the Jewish doctor, having decided point blank on the immediate burial of the three corpses found on the threshold of the synagogue, was going home. He had put the fear of God into the syndic. He was sure that this man would not talk, at least not for a day or two. Afterwards? Well, afterwards nothing on earth could stop people talking; the thing itself would talk loudly enough. The main thing was to keep the rumours down until one was sure. The reason being that one should never put any mass of people in a panic. There were plenty of other reasons too. He wondered if Rachel would find a cabriolet for hire at Vaison. He trusted Rachel; she would manage to find a cabriolet. He congratulated himself on having thought of Bordeaux, which lies in an airy, windswept gorge, where the air keeps moving and does not linger. He was very proud of having had such presence of mind, almost instinctive.

"Intelligence that functions on concrete impulses and on planes altogether detached from the effective sphere. Would probably go on functioning even in my corpse. Problem of immortality of the soul – perhaps merely a question of an intelligence so automatically efficient that it continues to function even in the corpse. In that case, not universal, but the prerogative of certain individuals, perhaps of certain races, who would thus have immortality of the soul as their privilege." He was preparing little phials of laudanum, morphine in the form of opium extract, ammonium acetate, and ether, each with its own dropper; a hypodermic syringe for chlorohydrate of morphine, and a small bottle of oil of turpentine.

Just as he corked the bottle with a firm and accurate thumb, in the little village where Angelo had earlier eaten melon the man shaking under the eiderdown bolted out of bed like a steel spring and rolled to the feet of the woman who was gasping for air. He stayed sprawling on the brick floor; the black skin of his face, pulled violently back in a terrible grip, made his teeth and his eyes stick out. The woman bent over him. She told herself that it was probably a serious illness, catching. She hastily munched a clove of garlic. She ran to fetch the neighbours. The sun still filled up the street with pure plaster, with no shade at all.

Nor was there any movement in the east, towards which Angelo turned from time to time. He climbed knolls covered with grey chestnut trees, descended into grey ravines where the horse's feet raised flakes of ash, followed the twists in valleys whose walls were quicklime, scaled little hills to the slow pace of his sleeping horse, crossed over their white-hot crests, skirted woods of chestnut and oak where the air was like fire. Each time he reached the top of a hill, he looked to the east to see if there were not some sign of twilight. The sky in the east was the same grey as overhead. He could look anywhere in the sky without being dazzled by the sun; the sun was not a blinding ball; it was a blinding dust spread over everything. The whole sky was dazzling. The east was dazzling. He looked northward, trying to find, on the slope of the big mountain, signs of the little mountain village of Banon, towards which he had set out. The mountain remained a uniform grey, almost as blinding as the grey of the sky, and it was impossible to distinguish there the least detail. Angelo had resumed his military soul. He was marching on Banon through this oily summer, as if on some important objective under volleys of fire. He had slight indigestion. Heavy pains, sometimes stabbing like fire, flung handfuls of plaster whiter than the sky into his eyes. He thought the woman who breathed with such difficulty had been right in warning him to beware of the melons and tomatoes. But if he had seen any melons by the wayside, he would have got down from his horse and eaten more of them. He kept telling himself: "It's the air. This greasy air isn't natural. There's something in it besides the sun; perhaps a multitude of minuscule flies that you swallow as you breathe and that give you cramps." He was gradually coming to the top of a slope higher than all the hills he had so far scaled. It was, in its cloak of misty heat, one of the main spurs of the mountain, which was now visible from a great distance.

It was visible as well from Carpentras. It was visible to the Jewish doctor at his laboratory window, to which he had crossed drawn by the smell of rotting melon now beginning to fill the street. In the dazzle of the light and beyond the roofs of the town he could make out, ten or twelve leagues to the east, the spurs of the mountain and the somewhat higher eminence, looking from there like a grove of trees denting the long grey slope. He wondered if the infection could reach those heights; if he wouldn't have done better to send Rachel off by the Blovac *diligence*. Had it not been for the dazzling sky and the grey dust fogging the horizon, he could have seen from his laboratory window, above the stench of rotting melon peel filling street and town, the small height just to the right of the eminence Angelo had now reached, together with the village where the man shivering under the eiderdowns had finally shot out like a spring and plunged to his wife's feet, and was, at that precise moment, being contemplated by four or five neighbours, all munching garlic and chanting: "He is dead, he is dead," at a safe distance from his bared white teeth and protruding eyes. The Jewish doctor was telling himself that perhaps there was no ground for being so sure of his intelligence. Those heights seemed to him better than Bordeaux as a protection for Rachel and little Judith. He was now not at all sure of the privilege of immortality of the soul. He no longer took a simple pride in the thought that Rachel would manage to find a cabriolet at Vaison. She was certainly incapable of imagining that he might have been wrong in sending them to Bordeaux. But he could not warn them now; he had to stay here and do his duty. He cursed intelligence. He realized that what he ought to be cursing, in all logic, was false intelligence. He spat on false intelligence. He was in despair at not having true intelligence. He spat on himself. He spat on Rachel and Judith for being incapable of protecting Rachel and Judith for him. He spat on that race tormented by an inscrutable God.

While he was cursing, he noticed that the east was becoming troubled and that there was going to be an evening and a night. It surprised him, as if night were about to rise from the east for the first time. "All my thinking is fallacious," he told himself. "I even overlooked a simple thing like this. Let's not get ahead of ourselves. Rachel and Judith will be quite all right at Bordeaux, in any case no worse than anywhere else, and certainly better than here. For the rest, let's stick to the well-tried remedies. No more explorations of the intelligence." He went back to his phials, put some of them on the table in his room, and others into his bag. He whistled a little tune. He also listened for the sounds of footsteps in the street and on the stairs, at every moment expecting his doorbell to ring. Meanwhile, in the village that he could see from his window on the distant flank of the mountain spur, the women had gone to find the priest. The priest came as a good neighbour should, his cassock unbuttoned. "Night is coming," he said; "let's hope it will be less hot. Poor Alcide!" "He's already quite black," said a woman. "So he is," said the priest. "It's most extraordinary." He took a look at the corpse, which was a horrible sight, but found comfort in the approach of evening. "Just to have a little rest," he murmured, "to be able to breathe." The idea of being able to breathe enabled him to triumph over the appalling grimace of that mouth, unveiling to the gums its stumped and rotten teeth.

Evening was still only a hint of pale blue in the east. Enough, even so, to dull the pattern of tiny crescent moons that the foliage of the plane trees in the rue Lafayette cast upon the pavement by the navy medical inspector's wicker chair. He thought the cause must be a cloud. He let out a groan that drew the attention of the customers sitting near him at the terrace of the Duc d'Aumale. "And now rain," he said aloud, "God damn it!" But he had respect for his uniform.

He counted the saucers. "It'd take more," he thought, "than seven absinthes, even in quick succession, to stop me seeing that it's only the approach of evening." And he said, very calmly, out loud: "It's evening, but I've seen others." He meant that he had decided to approach the Admiral again. "All that I need," he told himself, "is to be able to pronounce 'Dangerous effluvia on board the *Melpomène*' correctly. The rest is up to him. I'm not going to get involved in 'premonitory' and 'prodromic'. I'll tell him what I think. If he balks, it's quite simple; I tell him: 'I say yes and you say no; we've got a way to find out who's right: an autopsy!'"

He called the waiter and asked the time. It was after half-past six. The medical inspector rose, squaring his shoulders against absinthe and Admiral, against all that had brought him to this terrace of the Duc d'Aumale. He set off down the narrower streets. He had on his side only the evening – a little bluer now – and that priceless idea of an autopsy, perhaps put into his head by the evening and all the hope it brought, just by the attenuation of the light. A magnificent proof – "undeniable" was the word he used – that hadn't occurred to him under the stunning heat of the full day, specially in that dazzling light that blinded, stifled, made one's temples throb and made one relive swift, tragic flashes of one's life, as when one dives deep into green water. It was as hot as ever; he still had to keep stepping over runnels from sinks and the yellowish seepings from public privies, but this relenting light allowed him to regain control of himself; "like an acrobat," he told himself.

"Quite so, Admiral," he said to himself, "but I know my trade. I've carved up Chinese, Hindu, Javanese, and Guatemalans." (This last was not true, he had only seen active service in Eastern waters. He had never been to Guatemala, but the word appealed to a small overdose of absinthe that he was working off by means of great resounding words.) "What makes me sick," he said to himself, "is being obliged to argue; having to explain matters when, in my fellow from the *Melpomène*, everything is explained clearly, positively, and beyond argument. What one needs to do, in cases like the present, is to take the wind out of their sails straight off, so that all they can say is: 'Hmm! Very well, do what has to be done.' Bring them the whole thing on a platter, all cut out and prepared ahead of time for the mathematical demonstration of the connections, highly disrespectful towards rank and society, between the distant exhalation of great rivers and the snuffing-out of, say, a hundred thousand human lives. Easier to explain with proofs at one's fingertips.

"Look: the viscous appearance of the pleura – see? And the contracted left ventricle; and the right ventricle full of a blackish coagulum; and the cyanosis of the oesophagus, and the detached epithelium, and the intestines swollen with matter that I might liken, sir, in order to facilitate your comprehension of science, to rice-water or whey. Let's open him up, Admiral whose siesta must not be disturbed, let's open up the six feet of the *Melpomène*'s quarter-master; dead at noon, Admiral, while you were sipping your coffee and your couch was being prepared: dead at noon, blown up by the Indus Delta and the air pump of the Upper Ganges Valley. Intestines the colour of pink hydrangeas; glands isolated, protruding as large as grains of millet or even hempseed; the *plaques de Ryer* gritty; tumefaction of the follicles, what we call psoriasis; vascular repletion of the spleen; greenish soup in the ileocæcal valvule; and the liver marbled: all this in the six feet of the *Melpomène*'s quartermaster, stuffed like a stinkball. I'm just a junior officer, Admiral, but I can assure you that we have here a bomb capable of blowing up this country in five seconds like a bloody grenade."

He heard a little bell; it was extreme unction being brought to some dying person. He saluted the cross like any good sailor.

At the Admiral's headquarters, the midshipman was more polite. This young officer was, in fact, plainly worried. His features were drawn and, when he laid his hand on the doorknob, the medical inspector noticed that his fingers were wrinkled and slightly bluish. "Aha!" he thought, "another one!" The midshipman opened the door and announced: "Medical Inspector Reynaut."

At exactly the moment when the medical inspector was entering the Admiral's office, in the hamlet of La Valette the priest touched the young lady's arm: "There's no use staying any longer, Madame la Marquise," he said; "these women will see to everything; I've notified Abdon about the coffin." The young lady sprinkled the corpse with holy water and went away with the priest. It was evening. But not noticeably so. There was still this sickening heat.

"I feel," she said, "that it's my fault; I sent that woman to buy melons for me in the worst of the heat. She must have had sunstroke on all those stone steps: the glare from them was deadly; I felt it when I ran down them. I am responsible for her death, Monsieur le Curé."

"I don't think so," said the priest. "I can reassure Madame la Marquise on that score," he added, "at the cost of frightening her on another; but I know how cruel the torments of conscience are. The other torments will certainly be easier to bear for an intrepid soul, such as I know Madame la Marquise possesses. Three other people died this afternoon, and in the same way," he said: "Barbe, Génestan's widow; Valli Joseph; and Honnorat Bruno. They were reported to me almost all at once, and I went to see them. To be quite frank, that is why I was so bold as to advise Madame la Marquise to return to the château." She shivered from head to foot.

"Let's run," said the priest, alarmed, "that will get your blood going again."

*   *

It was the moment when Angelo, having reached the summit of the slope, saw at last in the east the indications of evening. From where he stood he looked out over more than five hundred square leagues, from the Alps to the hills of the seacoast. Except for the peaks engraved high up in the sky and the far-distant blackish cliffs to the south, the whole country was still covered with the viscosities and mists of heat. But already the light was less violent, and in spite of the pains scourging his stomach every now and then, and an itch that inflamed his loins and waist, Angelo paused for an instant to make quite sure of the evening. It had come. It was grey and slightly yellowish, like stable straw.

Angelo spurred his horse into a trot. He was soon in a small valley, which after three bends set him on the threshold of a little plain, at the end of which, stuck on to the mountainside, he made out an ashen hill town half hidden among boulders and dwarf forests of grey oaks.

He reached Banon towards eight o'clock, ordered two litres of Burgundy, a pound of brown sugar, a fistful of pepper, and the punch bowl. It was a well-to-do mountain inn, used to the eccentricities of people who live in solitude. They watched Angelo tranquilly as, in his shirtsleeves, he made his mixture and soaked in it half a round loaf that he had cut into cubes. All the time he was mulling the wine, brown sugar, pepper, and bread in the punch bowl, Angelo held back a raging desire to drink, and his mouth was full of saliva. He gulped down his half loaf and the sugared and peppered wine in huge spoonfuls. His colic was abating. He ate and drank at the same time. It was excellent, in spite of the still excessive heat, which was cracking the high beams of the dining-room. Night had now come; it was grilling and clearly would bring no coolness. But it had at least brought deliverance from that obsessive light, so vivid that at times Angelo still felt its white dazzle in his eyes. He ordered two more bottles of Burgundy and drank them both, smoking a little cigar. He felt better. Still, he had to cling to the banister rail to get up to his room. But that was because of the four bottles of wine. He lay down across the bed, ostensibly to contemplate at his ease the handful of enormous stars filling the window frame. He fell asleep in this position without even removing his boots.

# 2

ANGELO AWOKE VERY LATE in the morning. He was astonished to find himself lying crosswise on the bed. His legs were stiff from wearing his boots all night long. His shoulders and loins ached, and at the least movement he felt as if he were putting his bones out of joint.

The horse was much worse off. Angelo had two bushels of oats poured into the manger. He sized up the hostler and entrusted the animal to him in a few words whose tenderness touched the simple man.

"You like horses," said this man with magnificent eyes; "so do I. Give me a couple of sous and I'll pour a litre of wine over these oats. I promise not to drink any myself. Our air here is acid because we're on a mountain. People don't notice they're on it because the rise is so gentle. But the animals get out of breath, and there's nothing better than wine for setting up the lungs. If I were to give you a bit of advice, I'd say to let this black horse of yours rest all day."

"That's what I meant to do," said Angelo. "Indeed, I'm very tired myself and I'm quite sure you're right about this acid air of yours. I know, too, that wine in the oats does wonders. Here are two sous; no, four. It's very hot, and I don't want you to have your tongue hanging out while you're giving my horse his drink. I'm going back to bed."

"Are you ill?" the man asked.

"No," said Angelo. "Why?" He had noticed the fear that the hostler didn't even think to conceal.

"Because," said the man, "this morning I heard something that was not very pretty. A man and a woman died last night, and our doctor sent a messenger to the *sous-préfet*. There may be danger."

"Not with me, in any case," said Angelo, "and here's proof. Go to your master and tell him to have a chicken roasted for me at once. I'll eat it in my room directly it's ready; let them bring me up at the same time two bottles of the wine I drank last night, and go and get me twenty cigars like this one, which I'm not going to give you because it's my last and I haven't yet had a smoke this morning."

Angelo went up to his room and drew the shutters. He took off all his clothes, and stretched out on the bed. There was a knock: "It's me," said the hostler, "I've brought your cigars."

"Come in," said Angelo.

"Well!" said the man, "this proves you're not feeling cold. The two last night kept shivering, they say. They had to be rubbed with turpentine. At the tobacconist's they say someone else has caught sick and is lying between life and death."

"Forget about it," said Angelo; "nobody ever dies except the sickest. Here, take this cigar and go drink your litre of wine. Don't forget to leave my horse his."

"Don't worry about that," said the man, "but take my advice and cover up your stomach. One should always keep one's stomach warm."

"He's right," thought Angelo. "I get on perfectly with mountain people. They have fine eyes and they know how to scare themselves."

He ate his chicken, drank a whole bottle of wine, smoked three cigars, and fell asleep. He awoke at four, and peered through the chinks of the shutters. Outside there was the same great, sad light. He went down to the stable. The horse had got back its wind.

"The man I told you about is dead," said the hostler.

"Don't worry about other people dying," said Angelo.

"Three in one day is a lot," said the man.

"It's nothing so long as it isn't you," said Angelo.

"At this rate it won't take long," said the man; "there's only six hundred of us here. You're leaving, aren't you?"

"Not tonight," said Angelo, "but tomorrow. Do you know the Château de Ser?"

"Yes," said the man, "it's on the other side of the mountain, beyond Noyers."

"Is it far?"

"That depends which road. The good one goes a long way round. The other – and I must say, with an animal like yours I wouldn't hesitate – is not so good but it's much shorter. It begins just ahead of us, there, and instead of going all the way round to the Megron Gap, it climbs very gently through the beech woods and follows a little pass straight down into Les Omergues, a little hamlet of twenty families, on the other side of the main road. From Les Omergues to the Château de Ser is five leagues; take the main road to your right."

"How far is it altogether?" said Angelo. "I don't want to start yesterday's fun all over again. It looks as if it's going to be hot again."

"And yet you don't realize it here," said the man. "It's hot enough to bake eggs. Take my advice; leave at four in the morning. Maybe you'll get a little air on the way up. You ought to reach the pass by ten; it's called the Redortiers Pass and overhangs Les Omergues, as I told you. From then on, at any rate from the moment you reach the main road, it's just a promenade. You can get to the château by midday."

Angelo left at four in the morning. The beech woods of which the hostler had spoken were very handsome. They were scattered in small groves over thin fox-red pastures, rolling fields that spread out as far as the eye could see under lavender and stones. The track, soft to the horse's hoofs, wound among clumps of trees in which the slanting light of early morning opened deep gilded avenues, and a vision of enormous rooms with green vaults borne aloft on multitudinous white pillars. Around these high golden recesses the horizon slumbered under black and purple mists.

The horse moved briskly. Angelo reached Redortiers Pass towards nine. From there he could look down into the valley that he was to enter. On this side the mountain fell away steeply. At the bottom he could see square infertile fields divided by a stream, white and obviously dried up, and a main road bordered by poplars. He was almost directly overhead, some fifteen to eighteen hundred feet above the hamlet that the hostler had called Les Omergues. One thing seemed odd: the roofs of the houses were covered with birds. There were even flocks of crows on the ground, around the door sills. As he watched, these birds all flew off together and came floating upward, level with the pass where Angelo stood. There were not only crows, but also a host of little birds with brilliant plumage: red, yellow, and even, in great abundance, deep blue birds, which Angelo recognized as tits. The cloud of birds circled above the little village, then slowly settled again upon the rooftops.

Leaving the pass, the way became rough. Finally Angelo reached the fields at the bottom. Though it was still morning, the ground was already covered by a thick layer of scorching, oily air. Angelo felt again the nausea and suffocation of the day before. He wondered whether the stale, sweetish smell that he found here did not come from some plant cultivated locally. But there was nothing but centaury and thistles in the little stony fields. The silence was unbroken save for the twittering of thousands of birds; but as he neared the houses Angelo began to hear a dense chorus of asses braying, horses neighing, and sheep bleating. "Something's going on here," thought Angelo. "This isn't natural. All these animals sound as if somebody were cutting their throats."There was also that throng of birds, which, viewed now from a man's height, was rather frightening, especially since they did not fly away; most of the fat crows darkening the threshold of the house Angelo was approaching simply turned their heads towards him and watched him come with expressions of astonishment. The sugary smell grew stronger and stronger.

Angelo had never, as it happened, been on a battlefield. Those "killed" in the divisional manoeuvres were simply fallen out and marked with a chalk cross on their coats. He had often asked himself: "What sort of figure would I cut in a war? I have courage enough to charge, but would I have courage enough to dig graves? You must be able not only to kill but to look coldly on the dead. Otherwise, you're ridiculous. And if you're ridiculous at your job, where else can you be elegant?"

Naturally he kept his seat when his horse suddenly shied as a huge clump of crows flew up to reveal a body lying across the track. But his eyes opened unnaturally wide, and his head was suddenly filled with the desolate landscape in the terrifying light; with this handful of empty houses gaping at the sun, through whose doors the birds went freely in and out. The horse was shivering between his knees. It was a woman's corpse, as could be seen from the long hair lying loose on the neck.

"Jump down!" Angelo told himself icily, but he gripped the horse between his legs with all his strength. At length the birds settled again on the back and in the hair of the woman. Angelo leapt down and ran at them, waving his arms. The crows watched him with an air of utter astonishment. They flew off heavily, and not until he was so close to them that they beat his legs, chest, and face with their wings. They stank like stale syrup. The horse, terrified by the beating wings, and even nailed by a drunken crow that blundered into its flank, turned and fled at a gallop across the fields, with stirrups flying. "That was clever of me," thought Angelo; at the same time he looked down at the horrible face of the woman flat in the dust beside the toes of his boots.

Naturally, they had pecked out the eyes. "The old sergeants were right," thought Angelo, "it's their favourite titbit." He clenched his teeth over a cold need to vomit. "So, trooper," he went on, "that's washed you up." He could hear his horse, which had reached the road and was galloping full tilt along it, but he would have despised himself had he run after his saddlebag. He remembered the sly winks of the old sergeants who had seen a fortnight's campaigning against Augereau. He leaned over the corpse. It was that of a young woman, to judge from the long black tresses of her bun, pulled loose by the crows. The rest of the face was horrible to see, with its pecked eye-sockets, its sunken flesh, its grimace of someone who has drunk vinegar. She smelled appallingly. Her skirts were soaked with a dark liquid that Angelo took for blood.

He ran towards the house; but on the threshold he was repulsed by a veritable torrent of birds that flew out and enveloped him in a rush of wings; their feathers struck him in the face. He was in a mad rage from understanding nothing and feeling afraid. He seized the handle of a spade leaning against the door and went in. He was immediately all but bowled over by a dog, which leaped at his stomach and would have bitten him badly had he not instinctively hurled it back with a blow from his knee. The animal was about to spring again when he hit it as hard as he could with the spade, seeing, as he did so, strange eyes coming towards him, at once tender and hypocritical, and a muzzle smeared with nameless gobbets. The dog fell, its head split open. Anger snarled in Angelo's ears, but at the same time it had lowered a troubled veil over his eyes, so that all he could see was the dog stretching out peacefully in its blood. Finally, he became aware that he was gripping the handle of his spade rather too tightly, and he could look around him at what was, happily, an almost incredible sight.

There were three corpses, in which the dog and the birds had created considerable damage. Especially in that of a few-months old child, lying squashed on the table like a large white cheese. The two others, probably those of an old woman and a fairly young man, were absurd, with their blue-painted clowns' heads, their disjointed limbs, their bellies bubbling over with guts, and with slashed and stiffened clothing. They were laid out on the ground amid a great confusion of pots and pans fallen from the dresser, of overturned chairs and scattered cinders. There was a sort of intolerable rhetoric in the way these two corpses grimaced and sought to embrace the earth with arms whose elbows and wrists bent the wrong way in their rotted joints.

Angelo was not so much moved as nauseated; his heart was pounding under his tongue, heavy as lead. At length he noticed a fat crow skulking in the old woman's black apron and proceeding with its meal. This so revolted him that he vomited and turned on his heels.

Outside, he tried to run, but he lurched and stumbled. The birds had once more covered the corpse of the young woman, and they did not bother to move. Angelo walked towards another house. He felt cold. His teeth were chattering. He struggled to hold himself very stiffly. He was walking on cotton wool, he could hear nothing but the buzzing in his ears, and the houses in the scorching sunshine looked to him quite unreal.

The sight of some mulberry trees, laden with leaves and still peacefully shading a little footpath, helped him back to his senses. He stopped in the shade, leaned against the trunk of one of these trees. He wiped his moustache on his sleeve. "I'm ready to fall flat on my back," he thought. Puffs of smoke, growing colder and colder, filled his head. He tried to unblock his ears with the end of his little finger. Whenever the deafening buzz in his ears let up, he could hear, very far off and like the twittering of fat in a frying pan, the concert of brays, neighs, and bleating. He felt ashamed, as though he had fainted on parade. Yet he was so used to talking severely to himself that he didn't lose consciousness, and it was of his full free will that he knelt, then lay down in the dust.

The blood returned to his head at once. and he could see clearly and hear with ears completely unblocked. He got to his feet: "Miserable wet hen!" he said to himself, "look what comes of your imagination and your habit of dreaming. When reality hits you, you take a quarter of an hour to get used to it. And all the while your blood treats you like a puppet. You go turning up your eyes because these people have elected to kill each other off like pigs! Unless, indeed, there's been some dirty work here, in which case you've got something to say about it! And try to say it on the right side!" He missed his saddlebag, which the horse had carried off. It had two pistols in its pockets, and he was anticipating a fight. But he went back bravely to fetch the spade, and carrying it on his shoulder, advanced towards the rest of the hamlet, whose few houses huddled together a hundred yards farther on.

"Aha!" he said to himself, "more birds!" At his approach, indeed, squalls of birds issued from the doors. "What the hell have people been up to in this stinking village? It looks as if they've all kicked the bucket. Is it a sort of vendetta, or what?" He talked in sergeant's language in order to put some fight into himself.

In the second house he came upon corpses that were not so fresh. They were not putrescent, however, but dry like mummies. The dogs' teeth and birds' beaks had ripped them into a bold fretwork, like bites and pecks in a side of bacon. Even so, they exhaled that syrupy smell which was the sign of recent corpses. They were blue, their eyes sunk deep in the sockets, and their faces, reduced to skin and bone, thrust out enormous noses, thin as knife blades. There were three women and two men collapsed like the others in a scatter of ashes, kitchen utensils, and overturned stools.

Many thoughts, red and black, whirled through Angelo's mind. He was quite terrified and frozen from head to foot, and he had, in addition, a perpetual and violent desire to vomit owing to the sugary smell and the grimaces of the dead. But these deaths were a mystery, and mystery is always resolutely Italian: that is why Angelo, in spite of his disgust and fear, leaned over the corpses and saw that their mouths were full of a matter resembling rice pudding.

"Could they all have been poisoned together?" he wondered. In this notion too there was something so familiar to Angelo, and capable of giving him so much courage, that he dared to step over the dead, to go and see what was happening in an alcove whose curtains were still drawn.

He found there a fourth body, naked, very thin, quite blue, curled up on the bed amid copious evacuations of milky curds. Some rats that were busy eating the shoulders and arms jumped aside when Angelo parted the curtains. He wanted to kill them with the spade, but he would have had to strike the corpse, too; besides, they were watching him with inflamed eyes, they were grinding their teeth, crouching on all fours as if to spring. Angelo was over-eager to enter into this tragedy, he was excessively angry with these animals; they were on the wrong side, like the birds and the dog. He couldn't think at all reasonably. He pulled off the sheets and with the spade killed the rats as they fell off the bed. But he was nearly bitten by two of the animals, which flung themselves at his boots. He put his foot on one and crushed it with his full weight; the other, terrified, ran across the room and raised a stench so horrible that Angelo had to get out of the house as fast as he could.

He was too wrought up to stay out of the other three houses that formed the centre of the hamlet along the road. At his approach they disgorged thick flocks of birds and darting animals that Angelo took to be foxes. But they were merely cats, and made off across the fields. In each house he found the same spectacle of corpses, grimaces, blue flesh, milky excreta, and that abominable odour, sugary and putrid, smelling like the calyx of the fly-eating terebinth plant.

There were five or six houses more, set apart from the little group. A few steps towards them were enough to raise clouds of birds, which infested their doorways, windows, and yards.

It must have been about noon. The sun was beating straight down. The heat, as on the day before, was heavy and oily, the sky white; mists like dust or smoke were rising from chalky fields. There was not a breath of air, and the silence was impressive despite the sounds from the cattle sheds: bleating, neighing, kicks against the doors, scarcely any louder than the sound of a pan of fat on the fire in the great mortuary chamber of the valley.

"I'm a fine one," thought Angelo. "I really ought to rush off somewhere as fast as I can with the news and get these dead buried before they start a first-rate plague. Especially if this air continues to cook them. And now I have no horse, and I don't know the country."

To return to Banon would mean recrossing the whole mountain. On foot it would take all day. Besides, in spite of his anger and Italian appetite for mystery, emotion had deprived Angelo of his legs. He could feel them giving beneath him at each step. Revolving these considerations, he walked along the little road bordered with still poplars.

It was straight, and he had hardly gone a hundred paces when he saw a horseman approaching at a trot. Furthermore, he was leading by the bridle something that must be the runaway horse. Angelo in fact recognized his horse. The man rode like a sack of spoons. "Watch your step," Angelo told himself: "don't lose face before a peasant who will certainly be dumbfounded at the story you've got to tell him, but afterwards will have everybody laughing at your drawn face." That steadied his legs and he stood waiting, stiff as a post, preparing a short, extremely nonchalant sentence.

The horseman was a bony young man whose long arms and legs bounced with the horse's trotting. He was hatless, though wearing a respectable coat, and tieless; moreover the coat was all covered with hay dust and even with cruder filth, as if he had emerged from a henhouse. "I should have kept my spade," thought Angelo. He stepped into the road and said sharply: "I see you're bringing me back my horse."

"I hardly hoped to find its rider still on his legs," said the young man. Pushing back the long hair that his ride had shaken down over his forehead, he revealed an intelligent face. His short curly beard failed to conceal a pair of fine lips, and his eyes were certainly not those of a peasant.

"He didn't throw me," said Angelo very proudly and fatuously. "I dismounted when I saw the first corpse." He had realized his fatuity, but counted on the word "corpse" to redress the balance. He had been disconcerted by the lips and by those eyes so clearly accustomed to irony.

"Then there are corpses here, too?" said the young man very calmly. Whereupon he made efforts to dismount, and finally succeeded, very clumsily, although his mount was a stout cart horse. "Did you touch them?" he said, staring fixedly at Angelo. "Are your legs cold? Have you been here long? You look queer." He undid a satchel tied with cords to the strap that held down the folded blanket he was using for a saddle.

"I've just arrived," said Angelo. "Perhaps I do look queer, but I shall be interested in how you look when you've seen what I've seen."

"Oh!" said the young man, "probably I shall vomit just as you did. The main thing is that you shouldn't have touched the corpses."

"I killed a dog and some rats that were eating them," said Angelo. "I did it with a spade. These houses are full of dead people."

"I thought you must have been throwing your weight about," said the young man. "You're just the type. Do your legs feel cold?"

"I don't think so," said Angelo. He was more and more disconcerted; his legs were not cold, but they once more seemed like cotton wool and very flimsy.

"Nobody ever thinks so," said the young man, "until the moment when they know. Drink some of this, take a good swig at it." He held out a flask that he had pulled out of his satchel. It was a rough liqueur, flavoured with herbs and very raw-tasting. At the first gulp – and he had gone to it eagerly – Angelo lost his head and would have laid into the young man with his fists if he had not been gasping for breath. He had to be content with glaring ferociously through eyes filled with tears. Still, after several violent sneezes, he felt restored, and his legs felt solid beneath him.

"To get to the point," he said, as soon as he could speak, "will you tell me what's going on?"

"What?" said the young man. "Don't you know? Where are you from? It's cholera, *morbus*, my friend. The finest shipment of Asiatic cholera we've ever had! Have another round," he said, holding out the flask. "Trust me, I'm a doctor." He waited till Angelo had sneezed and wept. "I'm going to have one myself, too, see?" He took a drink, but did not seem to be disturbed by it. "I'm used to it," he said. "It's kept me going for three days. The sight of the villages down there ahead of us isn't exactly a bedtime story either."

Angelo perceived that the young man was at the end of his tether and only kept on his feet by the force of things. It was his eyes that made him ironical. Angelo found this very likeable. He had already forgotten the chill breath of the corpses. "That's the way to be!" he told himself.

"You say these houses are full of dead?" asked the young man. Angelo described how he had gone into three or four of them and what he had seen in each. He added that the others were full of birds and that there was no chance of finding anyone alive there.

"That's the end of the story for Les Omergues," said the young man. "It was a decent little hamlet. I came here to treat some cases of inflammation of the lungs six months ago. I cured them too. I used to get some fine drinks right over there, believe me! I'll look the place over in a minute. You never know. Suppose there's still one who isn't completely mouldy in some corner or other. It's my job. But what the hell are we doing in the middle of the road?" he added. "Don't you think we'd be better off under those trees?"

They went into the shelter of some mulberry trees. The shade was not cool, but they felt freed of a cruel weight on their necks. The grass crackled as they sat down.

"You're in a bad spot," said the young man; "we may as well face facts. Leave your legs in the sun. What on earth were you doing in these parts?"

"I was heading towards the Château de Ser," said Angelo.

"The Château de Ser is done for," said the young man.

"Are they dead?" asked Angelo.

"Certainly," said the young man. "And the others, who weren't much better, piled into a post-chaise and decamped. They won't get far. I wonder what *you'll* do?"

"Me?" said Angelo. "Well, I don't mean to decamp." He was addressing the ironical eyes.

"Against this mess, my friend," said the young man, "there are only two remedies: fire or flight. A very old system, but a good one. I hope you know that?"

"You look as if you knew it yourself," said Angelo, "yet here you are."

"My job," said the young man. "Otherwise, take my word for it, I'd be off in an instant. Seems it hasn't started yet in the Drôme, and that's back yonder, five hours away by mountain trails; let's be sensible. How are those legs of yours?"

"All right," said Angelo, "they're damned good legs, but I can guarantee they only go where I want them to."

"That's up to you," said the young man. "You're a better colour now. Obviously, as soon as you're a better colour you're the sort it's difficult to make understand where his interest lies."

"Now it's you who look queer," said Angelo, smiling. The ironical eyes appeared to understand his smile perfectly.

"Oh, that! I admit I'm a bit washed out," said the young man. He leaned back against the trunk of the mulberry tree. "Would you mind passing me the drug, please?"

Thanks to the bitter-smelling alcohol in the little flask, and above all to the presence of the ironical eyes, Angelo's blood was back where it should be. He suddenly longed for a smoke. He must have a few cigars left, from those he had had the hostler buy him yesterday at Banon; there were just six when he opened his case.

"You want to smoke?" said the young man. "Well, that's a good sign. Here, give me one, just to see. I must say, for three days and nights I haven't given tobacco a thought; I can't guarantee it won't knock me out, you know." But he puffed away with great contentment. "Odd bodies we have," he said, when he was sure that the tobacco was doing him good. "I was a bit on edge just now when I ran into you."

Angelo, too, was greatly enjoying his cigar. "His eyes are looking better," he thought, "and they're now in harmony with those pretty little child's lips in that beard of his. Oh, I know all about that *last cartridge* irony! It must look lovely in the villages he's come from!"

The young doctor told him how the cholera had broken out at Sisteron, the town at the end of the little valley, where its stream joins the Durance. How the municipality and the *sous-préfet* had tried to organize things in the midst of the panic. How they had got the warning from a mounted gendarme who had come to tell them that there were jolly goings-on in the Jabron valley; how he himself had been given full powers; how he had arrived to find an unspeakable shambles. He had sent a shepherd-boy from Noyers with a note asking for ten soldiers from the garrison and some quicklime to bury the dead. "But who knows if the child will ever reach Sisteron? Maybe he's already passed out under a bush with my paper in his pocket." In any case, here the situation was clear. There were six left at Noyers. He had packed them off up the mountain tracks with their bundles and some drugs. "No way in particular; there are farms up there where if they're lucky they'll escape. The rest? Well, it's just a question of digging ditches big enough. There was one still between life and death – at the algid stage, though – in the little hamlet of Montfroc, a league down below those rocks; he slipped through my fingers this morning. It wasn't long after I had sat down outside his door – sat down! Well, sat like a sack because I'd had about enough – that I saw your nag strolling by, and he let me catch him by the bridle without any objection. If he'd raised any he could have done as he pleased! It was all I could do to stand upright."

He said that the worst problem was finding something to eat. Everything was so infected that one had to beware of swallowing anything, meat or scraps, loaves or cakes, to be found in the houses. It was safer to go hungry. Still one couldn't do this indefinitely.

"Tell me," he said, "is it just me, or do you hear those noises too." It was the noise from the cattle sheds. "That's one more thing," said the young man; "those animals haven't eaten for three days. I'll go and let them out; it's no joke, to die of hunger between four walls. But have you any pistols? Lend them to me; I'll have to finish off the pigs. They're voracious beasts and they eat the dead."

Angelo first took a good puff at his cigar. "I don't claim to be braver than another man," he said; "I've only the character nature gave me. I'm rather likely to be scared by something unexpected that upsets my nerves. But as soon as I've had a quarter of an hour to think it over, I become completely indifferent to danger. That said, and if you've no objection, I'll stay with you until those ten soldiers you mentioned just now get here. I'll lend you a hand. I don't want to hurt your feelings, but you're obviously all in."

"As soon as I saw you," said the young man, blinking, "I'd have bet forty to one that you were one of those who act the fool as naturally as they breathe; and I'd have won. In your place I'd give a couple of cigars to the imbecile with full powers in this valley of Jehoshaphat and I'd cut out for the Drôme, where you have some chance of escaping this mess, if what they say is true. At any rate, I'd have a try. One only lives once. That said – as you put it – I won't hide the fact that I'm in a cold sweat at the thought of spending one more night all alone in these blessed regions. You are obviously stronger than I am, and I can't send you on your way by force. You can't imagine," he added, "how nice it is to talk and hear someone talk; I could let it lull me to sleep …" It is a fact that Angelo, too, took pleasure in talking in very long sentences. The young man's eyes had lost all irony.

"Take a rest," said Angelo.

"Hell, no," he replied; "a dose of medicine, and let's get going. They creep off to die in the most unlikely corners sometimes; I'd so much like to save one or two. It's the sort of thing one remembers with pleasure in fifty years' time. Take care of the cigars. We'll reward ourselves with one after the dirty work."

Angelo checked his arsenal. He had two pistols and ten rounds for each. "Five for the big pigs," said the young man. "We'll club the small ones. Keep the other rounds, we may need them. Seriously," he went on, "thanks for staying with me. I feel quite fit. You're taking a huge risk – there, I've given you fair warning! Anyway, thank you; I know now that when there's cholera, especially the *morbus*, the only way to pry you loose would be to snip off your snout, like a tick. I'm a bit drunk, you know, but the thanks are sincere. And now to work!"

The animals had clearly not been fed for some days. As soon as the doors were opened the sheep galloped off across the fields towards the mountain. The horses' tethers had to be cut. They were so maddened by their empty racks that they shot out like rockets. Once free, they made for the stream, and from there, soon after, they could be seen setting off in groups in the same direction as the sheep. Angelo blew out the brains of three huge pigs; they were mad with rage and had already devoured half the door of their sty. From the top of a low wall the young man bashed in a sow's head with a billhook. This one was ferocious and charged the man like a bull. She had eaten her piglets.

"Well, now it's silent as a tomb," said the young man. It was true: there was now no longer any sound except the silky fluttering of the birds; they gave no cry.

"I'm going to take a look inside there," said the young man. "You wait here."

"What do you take me for?" said Angelo. "Besides, I've already been in; that's where I killed the rats."

"Excuse me, Your Highness," said the young man.

"You're laughing at my clean coat," thought Angelo, "but you'll find I can dirty it just as well as you."

"Unquestionably done for," said the young man before the spectacle of the corpses. "Did you look in the corners?" He opened the cupboards and the door of a low scullery, and began to rummage, striking a light from his tinderbox.

"What are you looking for?" said Angelo, who needed to talk.

"The last one," said the young man. "The last one must have dragged himself off to some unspeakable corner. As he's the one who has a chance, he's the one we have to find. I'm not here just to look around. When they've got the strength, they travel. I bet you there are some stretched out under the broom bushes. But in cases of sudden collapse, they go burrowing into places you'd never dream of. I wasn't born yesterday, you know. Let me talk, don't mind me. It keeps me occupied. Yesterday, I talked all day to myself. It's no joke finding blue people in rat-holes. At Montfroc, just now, I ran one to earth in the dovecote. A quarter of an hour sooner and I might have done something for him, but he had hidden himself too well. I wouldn't have saved him, but I could have done something for him. He'd have had a much more attractive death. Well! there's nothing here, old man, except something extremely precious for you and me, and anyone we come across who needs rubbing."

He emerged from the scullery with a bottle of a white liquid like water. "*Eau de vie*," he said, "the well-named. That's something we can let ourselves steal. It's a remedy. I ran out of my last drops of laudanum and ether long ago. I still have a little morphine left, but I'm saving it. To tell you the truth, I give 'em rather potluck treatment. Anyhow, with this we can do a first-rate massage. I'd have preferred to find something to get my teeth into, but that, of course, is taboo. Talk," he added, "talk without stopping, it relaxes the nerves."

They went over the house from top to bottom. The young man ferreted in the darkest recesses.

In one of those houses, apart from the main group, into which Angelo had not yet penetrated, they found a man who was not quite dead. He had hidden himself in a storeroom, behind some sacks of grain. He was doubled up in his death agony; his mouth was disgorging over his knees floods of that whitish matter like rice pudding, which Angelo had already noticed in the mouths of the corpses.

"Can't be helped," said the young man, "we're not here for fun. Grab him by the shoulders." They laid him on the storeroom floor. His legs were drawn up and had to be forced flat. "Cut me a twig

40

from that heather broom," said the young man. He made a little mop with some lint from his satchel and cleaned the man's mouth. Angelo had not yet touched the sick man except, and with great repugnance, to haul him out of his hiding place. Unbutton his trousers," said the young man, "and pull them off. Rub his legs and thighs with the alcohol," he went on, "and rub hard." He had poured some *eau de vie* into the sick man's mouth, which kept emitting a harsh rattle and a sharp hiccup. Angelo hastened to obey. He puffed out his cheeks to stem great retchings of wind that rose up from his stomach. At length, after a long struggle, rubbing those spindly legs and thighs with all his strength, though they remained blue and icy, Angelo heard the young man telling him to stop; there was nothing more to be done.

"Not one will let me have the pleasure of saving him," said the young man. "Hold on there, don't do more than you have to." Angelo hadn't realized that he had remained kneeling by the corpse, his hands spread flat on the thin thighs soiled with rice pudding. "Quite enough have got it, without your trying to catch it," said the young man. "Don't you think I have enough patients as it is? Pour some *eau de vie* over your hands and come here." He struck a light and set fire to the alcohol with which Angelo's hands were covered. "Better a few blisters than the squitters at a time like this, believe me. Anyhow, it only burns the hairs. Don't wipe them, let them alone, and come and smoke a cigar outside amid the beauties of nature. We've earned it!"

"The devil! I've hardly got the strength left to puff at your cheap stogey," he said when they were stretched on the dry grass, under the mulberry tree to which they had tied their horses.

"Go to sleep," said Angelo.

"D'you think it's as easy as that?" said the young man. "I may never be able to sleep again in my life without a nurse holding my hand." To his stupefaction Angelo saw that the young man's eyes were filled with tears. He did not, of course, dare give him his hand to hold or even go on looking at him. The afternoon was drawing to an end. Great layers of dusty mist covered the mountain and filled up the distances into which the road plunged. There was total silence.

"A fit of depression," said the young man. "It's my empty stomach, pay no attention."

41

When the night came, Angelo lit a small fire in case the soldiers should arrive.

Up till about midnight the young man did not speak another word, although he remained with his eyes wide open. From time to time Angelo put wood on the fire and cocked an ear in the direction of the road. All at once there was a queer sound, as though from an animal entangled in the bush five or six paces off. Angelo thought it might be an escaped pig, and loaded his pistol. But the thing gave a little moan, which was not that of a pig. For the length of a shiver Angelo felt the extremely disagreeable closeness of those houses full of dead lying in the shadows. He was clutching his pistol like a perfect fool when he saw a small boy advance into the firelight.

He might have been ten or eleven and seemed quite indifferent to everything. He even had his hands ostentatiously stuck into his pockets. The young man made him drink some of the drug and the little boy began to talk in patois. He stood sturdily planted on legs set well apart, and several times took his hands out of his pockets, to stuff them back again after hitching up his trousers. He seemed placid and sure of himself; even when he was looking at the thick night beyond the fire.

"Can you understand what he's saying?" asked the young man.

"Not altogether," said Angelo. "I think it's about his father and mother."

"He says they died yesterday evening. But I gather his sister was still more or less alive when he left. They're woodcutters who live in huts an hour from here. I think I'd better go up there. He claims one can get there on horseback. You'd better stay here, to keep up the fire and wait for the soldiers." Angelo muttered that the soldiers could perfectly well manage by themselves, if they were worthy of the name. And he swung into his saddle. "You're a damned conceited fellow," said the young man.

"Come here, you," he said to the child, "climb up on this horse, you can show us the way.

"Hi, you there!" he shouted suddenly to Angelo, who had started off ahead. "Get down and come back here. This little idiot's sick as a dog."

As he approached the horse, the child had begun to tremble from head to foot. "Shove some wood on the fire," said the young man, "and heat some big flat stones." He took off his coat and spread it on the ground.

"Will you keep that on your back, you fool!" said Angelo. He unbuckled his kit and threw his big raincloak and his bedding on to the grass.

"It'll be ruined," said the young man.

"You deserve one on the jaw for that," said Angelo. "Use these things and keep your thoughts to yourself."

The child had fallen on his side without removing his hands from his pockets. He had convulsions, and they could hear his teeth chattering. They made a bed with Angelo's things and laid the child on it.

"Damned fool of a kid with his hands in his pockets," said the young man. "Look at him! To show the world, eh? Where do they get it from? What a clever kid! Wouldn't you have said, when he arrived . . . ? What kept him on his feet? Pride, eh? You didn't want to be yellow, eh? Little bastard!" He undressed him. "Give me some hot stones. Take the bottle of *eau de vie*. Rub him. Harder! Don't be afraid of hurting him. His skin'll grow back."

Under Angelo's hands the body was ice-cold and hard. It was clouding over with purple marblings. The boy began to vomit and to let out a foaming diarrhoea that spurted from beneath him as if Angelo were squeezing a leather bottle. "Stop," said the young man, "he's now got eight grains of calomel in his tummy. We shall see."

They flanked him on both sides with about ten big stones, burning hot and wrapped in Angelo's shirts, and covered him over completely with the folds of the huge raincloak, which they had padded with the rest of the linen.

The child retched for a moment, then vomited a huge mouthful of rice pudding. "I'll give him another four grains and damn the risk," said the young man. "If you can, go on rubbing him, but don't uncover him; put your hands underneath."

"I don't know what it is," said Angelo after a while, "but it's all wet."

"Dysentery," said the young man. "I'll burn your hands. Get on with it. Now that we've begun."

"It's not that," said Angelo, "I'd give ten years of my life – "

"No sentimentality," said the young man.

The child's face, grown waxen and minute, was lost in the thick cloth folds of the cloak. They opened the cloak to renew the hot stones. They had to change the linen; it was copiously fouled. Angelo was amazed at the child's sudden thinness. The whole cage of his ribs was visible, sticking to the skin of his chest; his thighbones, shins, and kneecaps stood out starkly in his blue flesh. "Take the powder out of your pistol," said the young man, "soak it in the *eau de vie* and make me some poultices with handkerchiefs, or you can tear up this shirt; I'm going to try blistering on his back and over the heart. He isn't doing well. His breathing's too damned short. My impression is, he's sinking damned fast."

On account of his ceaseless massaging of that visibly thinning and bluing body, Angelo was covered with sweat. The blistering had no effect. The patches of cyanosis were growing darker and darker. "What do you expect?" said the young man. "I'm sent to hunt tigers with butterfly nets. Gunpowder isn't a therapeutic! They wouldn't give me remedies. They were too scared to part with anything. Thought the earth was going to vanish from under their feet. We haven't begun yet. He could be saved. If only I had some belladonna . . . I told them: 'What do you expect me to damn well do with your ether? It's not disinfecting I'm after, to hell with that! It's not to save my life, it's to help others in time.' They don't realize that anyone wants to save lives. Oh, to hell with the dirty cowards! They were in too much of a funk to kick me out, but if I'd laid a hand on their box of tricks they'd have bitten me. And now we're in for it, trying to get this blood going with our thumbs." He too was massaging all the time, back, arms, shoulders, hips, and chest. Every few minutes he renewed the wall of hot stones and the stomach wrapping – a flannel waistcoat that Angelo kept warming at the fire. The vomiting and diarrhoea had ceased, but the breathing was increasingly short and spasmodic. At length, the child's face, hitherto vacant and indifferent, was kneaded by convulsive grimaces.

"Hold on, old man, hold on," said the young doctor, "you shall have it, you shall have my morphine. Hold on." He rummaged in his

44

satchel. He was trembling so much with haste that Angelo came and held open the sides of the satchel, which kept shutting over his hands. But he fixed the needle firmly into its syringe. drew out with great care every drop in a little phial, down to the last one, and gave the child an injection in the thigh. "Don't rub him any more," he said, "cover him up." He slipped his arm under the child's head and supported it. Gradually the indifference returned to the face. Angelo remained lying over the child's body without daring to move. He felt instinctively that in covering him in this way he might impart to him that blessed warmth.

"There you are," said the young man, sitting up. "I shan't save one."

"It isn't your fault," said Angelo.

"Ah! flowers of that kind," said the young man . . .

*    *

Day had come. The heavy draperies of chalk were resuming their places in the silence.

"Disinfect yourself," said the young man, going to lie down in the yellow grass, in a place that the sun would soon reach. But Angelo came and lay down beside him.

The sun climbed over the crest of the mountains opposite. It was white and heavy, as on the previous days. Angelo let it warm him without moving, until his sweat-soaked shirt was dry.

He thought his companion was asleep. But when he sat up he saw that the young doctor's eyes were open.

"How do you feel?" he asked him.

"Get out of here," said the young man in a hoarse voice, unrecognizable. His neck and throat swelled, and he vomited so dense a flood of white and ricelike matter that it masked all the lower half of his face.

Angelo pulled off his boots and stockings. He stripped him of his breeches. He saw that they were stiff with diarrhoea, already old and dry. He stuffed these breeches under the young man's bare legs. They were icy, already mottled with purple. He sprinkled them with alcohol and began to massage them as hard as he could.

They seemed to be getting a little warmer. He took off his coat and wrapped it tightly around them. He cleaned out the young man's plastered mouth. He rummaged in the satchel looking for the drug flask. There was nothing in the satchel but five or six empty phials and a knife. He tried to make the young man drink some alcohol, but he turned away his head saying: "Stop it, stop it, get away, get away." Finally he managed to get the neck of the flask into his mouth.

He uncovered the legs. They were again icy, a thick cyanosis had passed the knee and was already spreading wide over the thighs. Still, under Angelo's ever more rapid rubbing, the flesh seemed to him to be softening, warming up, regaining a faint pearliness. He pressed on harder. He felt filled with a superhuman strength. But below the knee the legs were still icy, and now the colour of wine-lees. He dragged the body close to the fire. He heated some stones. Directly he stopped rubbing, the cyanosis stole out from the knee, ramified like some dark fern leaf, and mounted into the thigh. He managed each time to chase it back, driving it down hard with his hands and thumbs. The young man had closed his eyes. This made him terribly ironical, because the wrinkles at the corners of his eyes became strongly defined as the face went to pieces. He seemed indifferent to everything; but once, when Angelo, without noticing, heaved a sigh in which there was per-haps some small satisfaction (he had just driven the cyanosis once more out of the thigh), without losing his toneless expression the young man groped with his fingers round his shirt, pulled it up, and revealed his belly. It was completely blue, terrifying.

He began to grimace and to be shaken by spasms. Angelo no longer knew what to do. He kept on rubbing the icy legs and thighs, whose purple had joined with the blue of the belly. He was himself shaken with great nervous shudders every time he heard the bones crack in that writhing body. He saw the lips move. There was still a breath of voice. Angelo pressed his ear close to the mouth: "Disinfect yourself," the young man was saying.

He died towards evening.

"Poor little Frenchman!" said Angelo.

Angelo spent a terrible night beside the two corpses. He was not afraid of contagion. He didn't think about it. But he dared not look at the two faces, as the firelight flickered over them, their drawn-back lips baring jaws with dog's teeth ready to bite. He did not know that people dead of cholera are shaken with spasms and even wave their arms at the moment when their nerves relax, and when he saw the young man move his hair stood on end; but he rushed to massage his legs and continued to massage them for a long time.

# 3

THE SOLDIERS ARRIVED in the morning. There were a dozen of them. They had piled their equipment in a small field. Their captain was a fat ruddy man with a curling red moustache, so thick that it even hid his chin.

Angelo, having been afraid all night long and being in the habit of giving orders to captains, spoke very sharply to him about the soldiers who, before anything else, had set about brewing coffee some way off, joking in loud voices.

The captain turned red as a turkey-cock and wrinkled his little pug-dog's nose. "Gentlemen don't exist any more," he said, "and you're singing a little too loud. I'm not to blame if your mother produced a monkey. I'll teach you to watch your step. Take that pick and start digging if you don't want my foot up your arse. I don't like white hands, and you'll soon learn who I am."

"That's plain already," said Angelo; "you're an unmannerly lout and I'm delighted that you don't like my white hands because you're going to get them in your face."

The captain drew back and pulled out his sword. Angelo ran to the pile and took a soldier's short sabre. The weapon was not half the length of his adversary's, but Angelo disarmed the captain with ease. In spite of fatigue and hunger, he had immediately felt sure of himself and capable of magnificent cat-leaps. The captain's sword flew twenty paces in the direction of the soldiers, who hadn't ceased to stuff wood into their fire while they watched and sniggered over their shoulders.

Without a word Angelo went back to where he had lain, freed the poor doctor's horse, saddled his own, mounted, and made off, after casting a quick look at the two corpses, now snarling more fiercely than ever. He crossed the field obliquely at a jog trot. He had covered only a few hundred paces when he heard what sounded like large flies humming by and, immediately afterward, the faint patter of gunfire. He looked around and saw ten or so small white puffs of smoke beside the willows where the soldiers had piled their equipment. The captain had opened fire on him. He dug his heels into his horse and made off at a gallop.

Shortly afterwards he reached the road and continued to gallop. He now had neither cloak nor hat, his shirt was still soaked through with the night's sweat, his chest too was damp; he felt that it was not so hot as on the other days. Yet it was the same chalky weather, the same mists. He had now neither saddlebag nor linen; his two pistols were loaded with only one round each. "Anyhow," he told himself, thinking of his altercation with the captain, "I'd rather be hacked to pieces than kill a man with a pistol; even if he does insult my mother. I like settling accounts with weapons that allow me to humiliate rather than anything else. Death is no revenge. Death is odd," he said to himself, thinking of the "poor little Frenchman". "It seems very simple; and very practical."

He passed through a village where many people had tried this simple and practical device. The dead, fully dressed, in their shirts, naked, or worked over by the muzzles of the rats in their busy troops, lay piled in front of the houses on both sides of the road. They all had those fangs like mad dogs. Here there were already clouds of flies. The stench was so heavy that the horse was seized with panic and, probably terrified also by the carnival attitudes of some of the corpses, which were still standing and had their arms stretched out like crosses, took the bit between its teeth. Angelo let himself be carried on.

By the end of the morning, he had crossed a deserted stretch of country where nothing suggested the epidemic, except the fields in which the rye, although ripe, was uncut and beginning to flatten. He had slept a little in his saddle, although the horse had maintained a pretty lively pace; he was warm and did not miss his cloak; he had knotted a handkerchief round his head; and, apart from his empty stomach, he felt very fit.

He saw the Château de Ser among its trees, on a small knoll. He rode up as far as the terrace. It was a mountain manor house, crude and very dilapidated, the sort of place where one could imagine only a bachelor living. It was utterly deserted. His knocks on the door echoed through an empty house. In addition, under a large oak tree, he saw the earth freshly heaped over a rectangle of rather imposing size. All the same, he did not return to the road until he had circled the building two or three times and called repeatedly through a window on the first floor, which was still open, evidently because the shutters, rotted by rain and unhinged, wouldn't close. It was useless to call; the house was undoubtedly empty. None the less, he observed that here the dead and the fleeing had respected highly military rules. Nothing was left lying about, the grave had been filled in and, save for the open window under which he was standing, camp had been broken according to the laws of the quartermaster's science. Near the stables, even the hay had been forked over.

He took to the road again, at a walk. The day was ending. His hunger was now really fierce, and he thought of the coffee the soldiers had been heating while he stupidly quarrelled with the fat captain.

The valley was widening out, and he saw that ahead of him, perhaps a league away, it gave on to another, much wider valley at right angles, in which the setting sun revealed a whole vista of groves and long alleys of poplars.

He spurred his horse onward, hoping that he would find this region less devastated. He told himself that there wasn't really much risk in eating, for example, a roast chicken. His mouth at once filled with a flood of saliva, which he had to spit out. He remembered his cigars. He still had four. He lit one of them.

He was close to the wide valley when he saw that ahead of him the road was blocked by barrels piled into a sort of barricade. And someone shouted at him to stop. As the person persisted in shouting: "Halt!" yet remained concealed even when he had stopped dead in the middle of the road, he advanced again a little nearer the barrels. He saw a gun-barrel levelled at him, and at last there emerged the head and shoulders of a man in a sackcloth blouse. "Halt, I say," shouted this sentry, "and don't move, or I'll pump you full of lead."

The man had a startlingly coarse face, as though someone had amused himself by assembling upon it the basest and most loathsome features. He was sucking the stump of a cheap paper cigar and his chin was stained with nicotine juice. He had been thoroughly shaved: beard, moustache, and hair. He had been scraped in this way for so long that his scalp was as bronzed as his cheeks. "Come on, step forward," he said.

Angelo drew close enough to touch the barrels. The gun was still pointing at him. The man had little pig's eyes, very steady. "Got a note?" he said. As Angelo didn't understand he explained that he meant a sort of passport issued by the mayor of the village, without which he wouldn't be let through.

"And why?" asked Angelo.

"To make sure you aren't sick and bringing the cholera in your pocket."

"Hell," thought Angelo, "this isn't the moment to tell the truth."

"So far from bringing it," he said, "or wanting to bring it, I cleared out as soon as I heard there'd been a case. I went up the mountain and never went back to the village; that's why I haven't got a note or even a coat."

The man was studying the horse's head and its harness, which was very elegant: the frontal, cheekstrap, and noseband were encrusted with silver, the rosettes, curb chain and rings of the backstay were all solid silver. He darted a furtive look around him. "How much have you got?" he asked in a low voice. Angelo gaped. "Yes," said the man, "what it takes. Everything has to be explained to you, I see; you really are from the mountain," and he rubbed his thumb over his forefinger as if he were counting coins.

This naïveté saved Angelo from a much greater danger than that of missing his dinner. He was so glad, after days of heroism, to meet a man whose cunning spoke to him of the refreshing peace of self-interest, that he was literally fascinated. He was also extremely hungry, and in spite of his aloofness the cholera was beginning to weigh on his mind.

"Of course I have," said Angelo stupidly.

"Would you have at least a hundred francs?" said the man.

"Yes," said Angelo.

"I shall need two hundred," said the man, "but get off the road and go round by the little stream down there. Watch out if you see the other guards through the trees; they've gone on patrol as far as the barricade on the Saint-Vincent road; then come up here from that side. Don't try to bolt, I've got you covered, and remember, my boy, I'm not the least bit squeamish about shooting a man." He pulled back his sackcloth sleeve and showed on his arm – which was enormous and hairy – the official tattoo-mark of the convict

on heavy labour. He also tried to roll his little pig's eyes in a frightening manner, but Angelo, on the contrary, couldn't help drawing
great comfort from this performance, and even from his shaven
face, which displayed the signs of many vices.

Nevertheless, as he crossed the stream, after making sure that the
undergrowth was empty as far as he could see, he took advantage of
the moment when he was passing close to a thick clump of alders,
which hid him to the waist, to put his hand in his pocket and count
out ten louis into his handkerchief.

"The rest," he said to himself, "you can come and search for. You've
been most obliging, but I need it. I'll show you that we in the
mountains can handle a pistol too." It was pleasant, having to deal
only with two-footed riffraff.

"You're taking a long time," shouted the man. "This is no time for
counting daisies. I bet you stole that horse. Those who can't ride
should walk, my boy. I'm for sharing the wealth; you'll find that
out. Get a move on. All right, let's see the colour of it," he said when
Angelo got near him.

"Moron," thought Angelo, "can't you see that if I tighten the reins
and use my spurs you'll get both my horse's front hoofs in your chest?
And then, good-bye to your cash."

"Here's what I have," he said, "if it means anything to you," and he
pulled six twenty-franc pieces out of his handkerchief.

"That's what you say," said the man, "but I prefer chimes. Fork out
the rest. Who's to stop me giving you a barrelful and saying you tried
to rush the sentry?"

"Those men coming down the hill there would stop you for
sure," said Angelo coldly, and he took one of his feet out of the stirrup. The man turned his head to look towards the hill and instantly
received a booted toe on the chin. He fell backward, dropping his
gun. With a leap, Angelo was on him and pressing the pistol into the
small of his back.

"Hold on, citizen, stop this fooling," said the man. "Where did you
learn to vault? I've been obliging, haven't I? Don't play with fire-
arms. I could have made you cough up when you were the other
side. I don't mind telling you, I thought of it, only you seemed so
stupid. You're a good one at hiding your game, you know."

"Better than you think," said Angelo, "and I haven't yet shown you all I know. But I'm a decent fellow, and I'll let you keep what I gave you if you'll find me something to eat."

Angelo threw the gun twenty paces the other side of the barricade and ran his hand rapidly down the man's sides to make sure he had no knife in his belt; the sackcloth uniform he was wearing had, moreover, no pockets.

"Being a guest of the government makes a fellow rusty," said the man, getting up. "Five years ago that pirouette of yours would have misfired, young man!"

"The main thing is that it went off at the right moment," said Angelo, smiling. He had a considerable liking for this fat man who was as ugly as a louse.

"If you're a philosopher," said the man, "that's fine. I've some sausage and bread, will that do? They've been pampering us, ever since they made hospital orderlies out of us. You could have shown a bit more respect for my gun, though. This is what I get for being helpful."

In spite of his saliva, Angelo waited till he was mounted before biting into his hunk of bread. While the man was going round the barricade to fetch his gun he galloped towards a thick clump of willows, passed them, and galloped on for another half hour after having passed them.

Night was falling, but he trotted on for a good hour before it was dark. He saw that he was coming to the meeting of the valleys and that his path joined a main road running at right angles to it. "One must act here as one would in enemy territory," he thought, "and I'm learning fast. There may be more of those barricades; I'll cut across the fields." He had on his right the lower part of the stream that had enabled him to pass round the convict's barrier, and he could hear it, a little farther down, join a more important stream, which was rolling pebbles briskly along in the silence of the night. "Cross over," he told himself, "and keep at an equal distance from the road, whose poplars you'll always be able to make out, and this water, which is chattering too loudly to be overlooked." He was delighted at having to make use of his military sense. He had been dreading the return of night and the memory of that "poor little Frenchman", snarling in vain up there at the foxes or the captain's quicklime.

First he fell into some bramble bushes and only extricated himself with difficulty, leaving strips of his shirt behind; then he got on to a flat stubble field where he could walk in peace. The night was very thick, and there was not a star to be seen. He heard, close by him at various times, the silky sighs of the thickets he had made out at sunset.

The stubble continued indefinitely. From time to time the horse stumbled against the low banks of irrigation channels, but recovered at once with an adroit twist of the haunches. Soon Angelo thought: "All these fields must belong to a village, or at least to three or four big farms. It's amazing that they don't bring me to a house. It's not late, and there ought to be light in the windows." After looking hard, he saw in the depths of the darkness a few wan façades. Some of them seemed to have their doors and windows wide open.

"I must also," he thought, "be passing near some huge arbours or thickets of jasmine whose flowers have been slashed by some storm and are rotting," for he could smell a violent odour of sweetened dung. At length he realized that it was the smell of corpses left to rot and, despite the imprudence of doing so, he spurred his horse, which shuddered, but continued forward with extreme caution.

In these uplands the nightingales were nesting late. Angelo heard a great number of them calling to each other from thicket to thicket. In the hollow night their trills had an extraordinary lustre. He remembered that these birds were meat-eaters. He had some peculiar thoughts about them, about the rotting corpses they must be eating and about those golden raptures spilling back from the walls of darkness.

The smell, like that of crushed jasmine, soon became a much stronger one, so dense that, but for the night, one would doubtless have seen it swirling like smoke. Angelo, whose need to eat had been far from appeased by the convict's piece of sausage and hunk of bread, found it most appetizing, though most repugnant. It was as if someone were cooking, over charcoal, an enormous thrush; a fine blue woodcock; a pheasant fit for an old gourmand. "I don't much care for game," he thought, "but I gather it's a great standby for those who *have nothing left but the table*, and helps one get along without love. Anyway, just now, I wouldn't say no to a few slices of toast spread with gamey meat properly cooked." In the end, though, the smell was too strong not to become rapidly disagreeable, and made him feel sick: he was obliged to lean over and vomit up a flood of very salty saliva.

At one moment his path was barred by a dark bulk, which he recognized as a thicket, wider and deeper than the others. He didn't want to become entangled in undergrowth in the darkness; he had no desire to dismount; he made his way round the grove and then perceived, ahead of him, some lights glowing as red as blood. He realized that he was approaching a sort of hollow, at the bottom of which, no doubt, was the bonfire from which the smell came. This was now frankly unpleasant and even rather disturbing. Mingled in it one could distinguish the balm of resin and the special scent of beechwood smoke, but as a whole it suggested monstrous and unusual things. For all the disgust inspired by this monstrosity, it still appealed directly to the desire to eat.

As Angelo advanced, the lights grew more and more dazzling, although they retained that almost dark intensity of colour peculiar to blood. He noticed that they gave off a smoke blacker than the night, so heavy that it sank back to the ground and rolled along in greasy slabs. Soon he could see the white heart of the bonfire.

He heard someone who must be on sentry duty there hail him and call: "Monsieur Rigoard."

"I'm not Monsieur Rigoard," said Angelo.

"Monsieur Mazouillier?"

"Not him either," said Angelo.

"Who are you then?" said the man, coming out of the shadows and approaching.

"Someone profoundly astonished," said Angelo. "What's going on here?"

"Where are you from?" said the man. His features were barely visible, but he seemed quite ordinary, and his voice still had the gentleness usual when welcoming someone who has come to help you out of a ticklish situation.

"I'm trying to get down towards Marseille," said Angelo, eluding the question.

"You're going in the wrong direction," said the man; "you've got your back to it."

"Do you mean I must turn back?"

"Yes, and that's lucky," said the man; "they wouldn't let you through here."

"Why not?" said Angelo.

"Because of the cholera," said the man. "Nobody's being allowed into Sisteron, and you're at the gates of the town, don't you realize?" He pointed to the right, above the red glows. It was true; they lit, high up in the sky, a pale town and a citadel clinging to a rock.

"Nothing doing for me in that direction," said Angelo, as though talking to himself. "But what's that great fire down there?" he added.

"We're burning the dead," said the man. "We've run out of quicklime." Angelo suddenly wondered whether there was not, somewhere, mixed up with the universe an enormous joke being played.

"You've not seen Monsieur Rigoard?" the man asked naïvely.

"I don't know him," said Angelo, "and anyhow, nobody can see two yards ahead."

"I wonder what they're up to," said the man. "They should have been here an hour ago. I'm getting fed up with this." He wanted to talk. Angelo was as fascinated by the funeral pyre, the slow ceremony of the red flames and the greasy smoke, as he had been by that reassuring depravity imprinted on the convict's face.

The man said that an emergency committee had been set up of well-meaning men; but that he had always had doubts about M. Rigoard. "The rich always rush to get their names on some list: but when it's a question of getting to work, they leave everything to poor bastards like me. I knew he'd leave me by myself all night. I was sure, I was, that the first time it'd be necessary to come here in the middle of the night with a tumbrel full of dead, there'd be just me, just a few poor bastards. In point of fact, there's only me. The others are convicts. And yet it was M. Rigoard, M. Mazouillier, M. Terrasson, M. Barthélémy, all the bigwigs, who thought up this system of building a bonfire here and making the convicts cart the dead to it. In the middle of the night, so as not to 'alarm the populace'. To hell with the populace! The cart made more noise on the cobbles than all the drums of the regiment, and now there's this fire visible a league off and beckoning at their windows. Not to mention the smell. That must be lovely." Indeed the town, above the red flames, was silent and greenish.

"Are there many dead?" asked Angelo.

"Eighty-three this evening," said the man.

Angelo turned his horse suddenly, but the man leapt forward and seized the bridle. "Wait for me, sir," he said; "do you think I'm really any use here, now, at this fire? It could burn two or three hundred of them without being stoked. I've done my duty, believe me. I must say I don't want to stay here."

"All right, all right, come along," said Angelo, in a voice that he made as gentle as he could.

The man knew a trail leading to the road. It was the one by which he had come with the cart. At one moment the horse shied away from a form lying right in the middle of the trail, on which it had nearly stepped. The man struck a light, saying he was sure, all the same, that they hadn't lost any corpses. He leaned over, holding his light at arm's length. "It's a convict," he said. "A moment ago he was with me, and now he's dead. Let's get on, sir, please." He blew out his light and walked on, leading the horse by the bridle.

"Keep me company as far as the sentry post, if you don't mind, sir. It's not far," he said, when they had reached the road. They walked for a few more minutes in the darkness, then saw the light of a lantern that had been hung on the barricade.

"Would you like a cigar?" said Angelo.

"I won't say no," said the man. They each lit one of the little cigars. "That's quite set me up again," said the man. "Your way lies over there. Stick to the road. Don't cut across the fields again: there are bogs in which you might have some trouble."

"How about on the road?" said Angelo. "Don't you think there'll be a little lantern, like that one, where I'll have some trouble?"

"Not for two leagues," said the man; "not till you get to Château-Arnoux."

"And then what?" said Angelo.

"I don't know," said the man, "but in your place I'd rather kill four or five people, even by biting them, than stay here. Somewhere else it may be worse, but you never know."

\* \*

"And yet he stays," thought Angelo, watching him run towards the barricade. "I'd better go back and have another look at that convict lying across the track down there. He looked him over pretty hastily, I thought. Maybe he wasn't dead. Has one the right to abandon a human being? And even if he dies, shouldn't one do all one can to give him an easier death? Remember the poor little Frenchman, and how he looked for the *last ones* in every corner, 'those who still have a chance', as he put it."

He searched for the branching-off of the earth track along which they had come. He must have passed it; he retraced his steps. But the track must have emerged through a patch of grass; he tried in vain, groping along the banks, light in hand, to try to find the cart tracks. He remounted and set off towards the south. He was highly displeased with himself. He could see once more the ironic look of the "poor little Frenchman" and even the terrible irony imprinted on his face in its death agony.

# 4

IT WAS IMPOSSIBLE to tell if the night was ending. On all sides there were opaque shadows. The road led through woods.

Several times Angelo, advancing at a walk, had a feeling that he was passing close by hidden people. His nerves were on edge, and he felt more and more displeased with himself. He was sorry he hadn't stayed with the captain to dig the graves. If he could have found a way back, he would certainly have done something foolish. He had even reached the stage of thinking, not only that he was vulgar and base, but also that his face must have become vulgar and base; that his whole attitude, his way of riding, even his ease of manner, were vulgar and base.

"Without someone watching you, you're worthless," he told himself. "Since you couldn't find the path, you should have covered the fields until you came upon that convict, who must now be dying, and brought him back to the sentry post, where they'd have looked after him. Or at least have made certain he was indisputably dead. Afterwards, you'd have had the right to go on your way, but not before. Otherwise, you have no quality." And he even told himself: "You say it was difficult. Not at all. You had only to return towards the red flames, to the place where you met that frightened man, who was doing his duty in spite of his fright, and whom you've no right to judge anyway since you've never stayed in the middle of the night by a bonfire burning eighty corpses, and you don't know if, in his place, you wouldn't have done worse."

He was perfectly sincere. He entirely forgot the night and day during which he had ceaselessly tended the child and the "poor little Frenchman", as well as his vigil beside the two corpses, when he had behaved extremely well.

As soon as he heard anew some furtive sounds in the bushes, he halted and asked in a loud voice: "Is there anyone there?" There was no reply, but the springy carpet of pine needles crunched under footsteps. "Can I help somebody in there?" Angelo repeated, in a calm voice that must have sounded like music to the ears of people in trouble. The noise of footsteps ceased and, after a brief moment, a woman's voice answered: "Yes, sir." Angelo at once struck a light, and a woman emerged from the wood. She was holding two children by the hand. She screwed up her eyes to see who was behind the light of the flame that Angelo, without thinking, was holding close to his face, and drew nearer. She was young and dressed so elegantly for the place that she at first appeared unreal among these pine trunks, lit up by Angelo's tinder. The children too seemed out of a fairy tale: a little boy of eleven or twelve in an Eton jacket and a tasselled cap, and a little girl of about the same age, whose long white lawn pantaloons emerged below her dress and covered her lacquered shoes with thick ruffles of lace.

The young woman explained that she was the governess of the two children: they had all three come from Paris barely six days ago to the Château of Aubignosc, a week ahead of M. and Mme de Chambon, who were due to come by train and stop at Avignon; the latter must be at Avignon now, staying with their aunt, the Baroness de Montanari-Revest, without the slightest chance of reaching Aubignosc, since all the roads were blocked. She knew for a fact that the cholera was extremely violent around Venaissin, and that no one was allowed through. She had first thought she could keep the children safe at Aubignosc, which is a tiny village. But it had suddenly been swept by the epidemic, which, in a two days' fury, had not left ten persons alive. So she had set out with the children in the hope of getting to Avignon by way of Aix-en-Provence, where, it was said, things were not yet very bad. She had had the idea, since transport was lacking – "we came by the *diligence* and it isn't running any more" – to get to Château-Arnoux, only a league away through the woods, and there hire a cabriolet to take them down the valley of the Durance. But yesterday evening, around six, when they reached Château-Arnoux, they had been stopped at the barriers and turned back into the woods, along with about twenty other people from various places who were also trying to get to Aix. A gentleman from Lyon who happened to be there, fresh from Sisteron, where he had been supplying the hardware shops with tin saucepans, had been kind to her, and given her two slabs of chocolate and a small bottle of peppermint alcohol. He was a witty little man, very enterprising and with excellent judgment. With this gentleman and two other ladies they had tried to skirt round Château-Arnoux. On the hillside the saucepan dealer had fallen ill, the other two ladies had fled like lunatics, but she had had the luck, since the little boy was a good woodsman, to find the road once more. They had all three sat down by the roadside to wait for day. When they heard the horse coming, they had thought it must be a patrol of those Château-Arnoux people who had threatened to shut them up in quarantine, and when Angelo came abreast of them, they were withdrawing into the pine woods to hide.

Angelo asked a lot of questions, where the barriers were placed and what they were barring. He was indignant at the inhumanity of these people turning back women and children into the woods. The reference to quarantine had made him prick up his ears. "Here's another complication I don't like at all," he thought; "I'm in no hurry to be locked up in some stable full of dung. Fear can do anything; it makes people merciless killers: watch out! You won't get out of this as easily as you did with the convict and his barricade of barrels. What a pity I've only two rounds left, and that I have no sabre; I'd show them that generosity can be more redoubtable than cholera." He was deeply moved by the faces of these three lost people as seen by the light of his tinderbox.

He questioned the little boy, who seemed quite sure he knew the way to get round the barriers.

"Very well, then," said Angelo, "we'll go through the wood, which you say is not very deep. Once through it, we'll put the two young ladies on my horse; he's very gentle, and I'll lead him by the bridle. We'll go the way you say. I am heading for Aix myself, and I'll help you until you're out of trouble. Don't worry," he added, "I'm a colonel in the Hussars, and we'll do all right." He felt they needed to be given self-confidence and reassured about the vulgar and base appearance he believed he had: to which end he judiciously fancied the declaration of his rank might serve. He forgot that the night was covering him and that they could only hear his very kindly voice.

They left the road and cut through the wood. On emerging from the wood, Angelo set the young woman and the little girl on the horse and they began to pick their way over rocky hills where there was a little more light than at the bottom of the valley.

The little boy marched very pluckily at Angelo's side and was never in doubt about the direction to take. The young woman had a watch. It was three in the morning.

Daybreak began around four. It illuminated a vast, undulating wilderness. "All the better," said Angelo. "Here we can walk in peace. Besides, the main road must be on our left, in that sort of gully full of slumbering mists. Let's not worry, but push ahead. The most important thing now is to find a farm where the four of us can get something to eat." And he very solemnly congratulated the little boy; he knew that they are braver and bolder than men as soon as they are taken seriously. He wanted him to be able to go on marching gallantly. Besides, Angelo had taken a great fancy to him, and there was every reason to congratulate him; all night long he had proved an unerring guide.

Nevertheless, Angelo, with three days' growth of beard, his face all streaked with runnels of dried sweat and his shirt torn by brambles, did not seem to inspire great confidence in his companions. He noticed this when he met the green eyes of the young woman. Luckily, he had very handsome summer boots, of fine supple leather even though they were varnished, and so well-fitting that it was impossible to believe he had stolen them. "That's precisely why I paid Giuseppe a hundred francs for them," he thought; "I need a passport that I can use. Yet I can't push them into her face." He tried to talk about them, but all he managed to do was to convince the young woman that he was vexed at spoiling such fine boots on the cutting stones of the hills, and she proposed right away to give him back his horse.

"I'm an idiot," he said. "Sit quietly where you are. I was trying to give you good reasons for believing that I'm as decent a fellow as your saucepan dealer. I always overdo it. You'd have learned quickly enough, without my boots, that my one idea is to help you, and you'd have been the first to laugh at the anxiety I saw in your eyes just now when you observed my miserable get-up. What makes me so clumsy is that I always want to please people absolutely. Nine times out of ten, that makes them take me for what I'm not. I really am a colonel; that's not a joke. Only, like you, for three days I've been trying to get out of this infernal countryside, full of cowards and heroes, each more terrible than the other. And I've been through some very nasty moments."

The young woman, who happened to have fine green eyes, smiled and said that she wasn't afraid. It was evident that she did not believe the part about the colonel. Her smile, which was indeed charming, said that she had better things to do than dispute it's truth, and like a Madonna she clasped the sleeping body of the little girl to her.

The sun was completely up when they perceived, nestling in the folds of a small valley, a farm close by three terraces of olives and a big field of lucerne.

Angelo halted his party under an holm oak. The little girl was sleeping so deeply that she barely opened her eyes when she was lifted down from the horse and laid on the ground.

"Here's the first house with a smoking chimney," said Angelo; "we're in luck. You stay here; I'll go down and ask for something to eat at a good price. Don't worry about anything; I've got money."

The house was closed; even barricaded, it seemed; but for the smoke rising from the chimney one might have thought it deserted. Angelo called. A window opened and a man appeared, pointing a shotgun. "On your way," he said.

"I'm certainly not ill," said Angelo, "and I've got a woman and two children up there under that tree, you can see them from here. They haven't eaten for two days. Sell me a little bread and cheese; I'll pay whatever you want."

"I've nothing to sell," said the man; "you're not the only one with a wife and children. On your way, and make it fast . . ."

"He won't shoot," thought Angelo, and he advanced coolly. The man took aim. Angelo continued to advance. He was blissfully happy. At length he leaped forward and gained the cover of the porch. "Be sensible," he said, "you see how determined I am. I can easily smash your lock with one shot of my pistol. Afterwards we'd fight it out inside, where you'd have as good a chance as I, but no better. Throw me down a loaf and four goat cheeses. I'll pay you twenty francs; I'll slip it under the door. Gold never gets sick, but, if you're afraid, pick the coin up with some tongs and throw it into a glass of vinegar. You're in absolutely no danger. But be quick about it. I'll stop at nothing."

"Get out of there," said the man. Angelo clicked the hammer of his pistol. "Wait," said the man. After a few moments, he threw down on to the grass a loaf and four cheeses. "There's a crack near the lock," he said, "slip your coin through that and let's hear it fall inside." Angelo obeyed, and the coin rang on the flagstones. "I didn't hear anything," said the man.

"I'm not stingy," said Angelo, "I'll put another through: listen carefully." He slipped another coin through. "I didn't hear anything," said the man.

"Wait till you hear this," said Angelo, and he fired his pistol in the air, aiming at the window sill. The man slammed the shutters. Angelo picked up the bread and cheeses and climbed back to the ilex, forbidding himself to run.

*　*

After eating, they found a track that brought them fairly soon to the main road. "I fully realize," said the young woman, "that the wisest thing would be to walk on over the hills, but we must have covered at least five leagues and these children will die of fatigue. It would also be folly to suppose that we can go on like this as far as Avignon. We can't be far from Peyruis. There's a *gendarmerie* there. I shall explain my case, Monsieur de Chambon is well known; we are not ill, they'll certainly make out a paper for us and help me find a cabriolet. I can't continue to take chances with these children, who are in my charge." Angelo found the decision a reasonable one. "But don't let this prevent you from looking after yourself," the young woman went on. "The situation is quite different for a single man, resolute and on horseback. Leave us here, we can reach Peyruis by ourselves; it's only half a league, if it's that much." She was evidently very glad to be on the main road, and she wound up very clumsily: "You've pulled us through even better than I hoped. Monsieur de Chambon would certainly thank you very heartily if only he might know your name."

"I shan't leave you until I know you are in safe hands," said Angelo severely. "I have something to say to the gendarmes myself."

"So you think I'm afraid of them!" he said under his breath. "You really are a Parisian!"

They soon reached the barriers, which were guarded by gendarmes, who were very friendly and smelled of wine. The name of M. de Chambon worked wonders. They even promised to requisition a cabriolet. Angelo stated that he came from Banon. The gendarmes, who were experienced and observant, were impressed by his boots. They treated him diplomatically. He described a brush with some brigands to explain the loss of his saddlebag, coat, and hat.

"We can't be everywhere at once," said these guardians of order, who furthermore had their tunics unbuttoned, "and you've been lucky; some people lost much more. Some of the convicts they released at Sisteron to bury the dead have skipped, and not to Mass either. As for papers, you're sure to get them. You all look very fit. But you'll have to spend three days in quarantine here, it's the rule. We'll have you taken to a barn, over there, off the road; it's used just for that; it's not bad there, and you'll have company. There's about thirty waiting there now. Three days isn't a lifetime."

They were taken to the barn, which was full of people of every age and condition, seated sadly on trunks or up against baskets, bags, and bundles. The gendarmes led away the horse. They were friendly but cautious.

"I don't much like what is happening to us," said Angelo.

"What else can one do?" said the young woman. "They've promised me a cabriolet, I shall wait for it. But I'm concerned about you. You should already be well on your way."

"Perhaps it's better I should be near you," said Angelo. "In any case, come, let's find a corner to ourselves."

The sentry returned, accompanied by a fat man in a blue apron. He took a firm stand, and craned his neck so as to see everybody. "Those that want to eat," he said, "orders, now, please."

"What is there to eat?" said Angelo, coming over to him.

"Whatever you want, Baron," said the fat man.

"Two roast chickens?" said Angelo.

"Why not?" said the man.

"All right," said Angelo, "two roast chickens, some bread, and two bottles of wine; and buy me twenty cigars like this one."

"Give me the money," said the man.

"How much?" said Angelo.

"Thirty francs for you," said the man, "because you're so good-looking."

"You haven't lost your business sense," said Angelo.

"Nobody else has, either," said the man; "so I may as well keep mine. It'll be three francs more for the cigars. Have you got something for me to pack your stuff in?"

"No," said Angelo, "wrap it all in a cloth and put in a knife."

"One écu for the cloth and one for the knife."

Angelo was the only one who ordered something to eat. Everyone watched him with a mixture of curiosity and dread. An old gentleman, with a very pretty little white goatee and a severe expression, said to him: "You are causing everyone the gravest risk by your imprudence, young man. You are going to have a cloth brought in from the village, where there are doubtless cases of sickness. All one should allow oneself to eat in times like these is boiled eggs."

"I don't trust boiled water," said Angelo, "and where you go wrong, you and all the others who are staring at me so wide-eyed, is in not living as usual. For three days I've been dying of hunger. If I faint from malnutrition you'll think I've got cholera and, out of pure terror, you'll pop off like flies."

"I am not afraid, sir," said the goatee; "I've shown my mettle."

"Keep it up," said Angelo. "One can never show enough of it."

He ate his chicken, and was very glad to see the young woman and the children eat the other without apprehension. They drank some wine. To reassure everyone, Angelo threw the cloth out of a window. He went to give the sentry a cigar and remained on the doorstep smoking his own.

He had been there for a quarter of an hour, rather dazzled by the light of the great white sun, when he heard a commotion in the barn. People were precipitately drawing back from a woman stretched out on the straw. He went up to the poor creature; her teeth were chattering, and she had a great blue patch on her cheek.

"Has anyone any alcohol?" said Angelo; "any *eau de vie*?" he repeated, looking around at them all. At last a peasant woman produced a bottle from her basket. But she did not hand it to him. She placed it on the ground, moved some way off, and said: "Take it."

The sick woman was young, with very beautiful hair and a milky neck. "Is there a brave woman present," said Angelo, "to come and undo her linen, unhook her bodice and stays? I don't know how to."

"Cut the laces," said someone. A woman began laughing nervously. Angelo went back to the sentry.

"Get away from the door," he told him, "there's a woman taken ill. I've got to get her out and lay her in the sun to warm her and prevent this sorry lot from dying of fear. I'll undertake to look after her by myself. Anyway, I'll do what I can, unless there's a doctor in the village."

"You don't really think there'd be a doctor in the village?" said the sentry.

"Very well, I'll do all I can," said Angelo. "Stand over there, if you're afraid they'll escape. But you could catch the lot of them under a hat."

"Now look here," he said, going into the barn again, "I must have someone to help me carry this woman outside, a man or a woman. Or a child, if everybody else feels too grand," he added with a short, severe laugh.

"Don't involve the children in this sad business," said the little white goatee. "*Genus irritabile vatum* . . . I'll help you!"

They carried the young woman outside on a bed of straw. The old gentleman undressed her with great skill, and even managed to remove her stays without handling her too violently, a difficult feat, for she kept tossing her head and arms. During this operation she brought up a little of that familiar rice pudding, but Angelo cleaned her mouth and forced her to drink. The young woman's thighs, although icy and marbled with thick purple streaks, were plump and satiny. She kept fouling herself below, without stopping. The sentry had turned away and was gazing at the torrid hills where the heat was refracted in the steam off the grass as though on a prism. There was loud talk in the barn, with bursts of nervous laughter. At the end of two hours the young woman died. Angelo sat down beside her. So did the old gentleman. From the village came solitary cries and long, almost peaceful moans, which appeared black in the fierce sunlight.

"*If Paris had seen Helen's skin as it really was,*" said the old gentleman, "*he would have observed an irregular, rough, grey-yellow network, composed of disordered meshes each containing a bristle rather like a hare's: he would never have fallen in love with Helen. Nature is a grand opera whose scenery is an optical illusion."*

Angelo handed him a cigar. "I've never smoked in my life," said the old gentleman, "but I very much want to begin."

* *

Before evening, a man died in the barn. Rapidly. He slipped straight through their fingers and did not let them hope for a second. Then a woman. Then another man, who walked for a long time without stopping, halted, lay down in the straw, and slowly covered his face with his hands. The children began to cry.

"Make those children shut up and listen to me," said Angelo. "Come close. Don't be afraid. You can see, can't you, that I, though I look after the sick and touch them, am not ill? I who ate a whole chicken am not ill; and you who are afraid and suspicious of everything will die. Come close. I can't shout what I want to tell you over the housetops. There's only a single peasant guarding us. As soon as nightfall begins I'll disarm him and we'll go. It's better to risk one's life without a passport than to stay here waiting for a paper that isn't any good if one's dead."

The old gentleman was emphatically on Angelo's side. There were also two men with a solid peasant look and ten or so women with children who accepted this plan. The others said that luggage couldn't be left, and that they couldn't carry their trunks on their backs across the fields.

"The question is," said Angelo, "whether you prefer to remain shut up until these panic-stricken villagers and gendarmes give you a chance to live, or whether you prefer to make a break for it. What does a trunk have to do with this?"

But the trunks mattered a great deal, and they said that it was easy for him to talk.

"All right, stay," said Angelo; "everyone's free to do as he likes." But he tried to persuade the young governess.

"No," said she. "I'm staying here too."

She had unshakable confidence in the name of M. de Chambon. She was sure she would get a cabriolet and, above all, that famous paper, with which she saw herself flying across the country like an arrow.

"I cannot allow myself to run the risk," she said.

"You are running a much bigger one by staying here," said Angelo.

She then said, with greatly increased firmness, that she was quite determined to travel properly. There was no reason for her to take to the roads like a gypsy. The gendarmes, who knew perfectly well who M. de Chambon was, had promised her a cabriolet and a paper. She would not leave except in a cabriolet and with a paper, in the proper way. There was no reason for her to act otherwise. Yesterday evening she had been out in the woods, in the dark, by the roadside; that was one thing. Angelo had helped her. She was grateful to him, but now things were different. She had been given a definite promise. "You heard it as well as I did. They even said that, if there was no cabriolet willing to take Monsieur de Chambon's children to Avignon, they would requisition one. I haven't dared tell you who Monsieur de Chambon is: Monsieur de Chambon is chief justice of the High Court. Now do you see?"

Whereupon, evening having fallen, Angelo replied: "I'll show you what a gendarme is, genuine or false!"

He went up to the sentry and disarmed him with the greatest ease, for the man didn't realize why his gun was being taken away from him. He thought it was to look at it.

"Stand back and let us pass," said Angelo. "Some of us here want to make ourselves scarce."

"You don't need my gun for that," said the sentry, "and you might let me have it back. You're not the first to clear out, and the others didn't make such a fuss. And I'll tell you what: a hundred paces to the left of that cypress you can still see, there's a track that goes a short league around and then leads into the main road."

This placidity considerably disconcerted several of the women who had decided to leave; they now decided to stay.

The departure of Angelo and his followers was therefore rather sheepish, the more so as the sentry continued to shower them with the most detailed information on the way to skirt around the village. Angelo, however, persisted in thinking it better to leave. "And why complain when all goes well?" he said to himself. "Anyway, stop always imagining the worst and overdoing things. That little governess must be laughing at you."

They lost their way because of the excessive amount of information the sentry had given them, and because each interpreted it in his own fashion. The night, the open air, the need to act, and also the fear of having committed themselves to a plan that seemed less sensible directly it was available to everybody, upset the women with their train of sullen children. At last, at the end of an hour, they reached the main road, where they separated, the two peasants setting off across the hills and the women simply sitting down once more on the bank. Angelo went off with the man with the goatee.

They walked for more than two hours before they saw, in front of them by the roadside, a long, low house, from the main entrance of which there issued a bright light and a considerable din.

"Another fly-trap?" said Angelo.

"No," said the old gentleman, "this time it's a wagoners' inn; I know it."

# 5

As they drew near they could hear that the din was composed of raucous singing and the screeching of women, as harrowing as the wails of she-cats. Angelo could not help being excited by these cries of titillated women, so straightforward and unequivocal. He thought of love. He was quite put out at having been caught off guard so suddenly by an emotion that normally crept over him slowly after many detours and moments of melancholy. Furthermore, although he had had no trouble disarming the obliging peasant dressed up as a gendarme who guarded the quarantine at Peyruis, he was still in his heroic mood . . .

The main room of the inn, long and wide, contained about twenty men and women, drunk and past caring. They were seated round the big dining-table, where they had inflicted considerable damage upon the dishes, bowls, and bottles, some of which were upset. The scene was lit by two enormous stable buckets of flaring punch and a profusion of oil lamps and candlesticks, so arranged as to leave not one single corner of that vast vaulted chamber in shadow.

Angelo stopped a passing groom, his arms laden with bottles. He asked him sharply who these people were. He was furious on account of the postures and cluckings of some of the women, who were being openly mauled.

"They're people like you and me," replied the man, who was middle-aged and had a good smell of rum in his voice.

He went around distributing his bottles. He came back, dragging his feet. He wiped his hands on his leather apron. His look was vague and very benevolent.

"Anyway," he said, "what can I serve you to pass the time?"

As Angelo did not answer him and continued to frown angrily, the man, who was perhaps the innkeeper in person and mistook the reason for this anger, said to him: "There's no point in being annoyed. What good does it do? You're not the only one, as you can see. Wait a bit. Tomorrow morning, as soon as it's daylight, we'll find a way to get round the quarantine barriers. My son and I know the hills like our own pockets. But if you want to drink, be quick about it. Wine's going up. It's already three sous."

"Isn't wine harmful?" Angelo asked gravely.

"Mine never harmed anyone, at any rate," replied the man, nonplussed by this gravity.

Angelo did then order a bottle, but added: "I don't wish to drink with these people here. Haven't you a private room?"

"There's no lack of rooms, but you'd have to drink in the dark. They've collected all the lamps and candles in the house. They simply couldn't stand having a speck of shadow behind their backs. You must admit we're living in queer times. I don't advise you to drink Swiss fashion. The best thing just now is to be a good mixer. Who knows what's in store for us from one moment to the next? They all came in one by one. They didn't know each other this morning. Now look at them. In an hour, you'll be in there with them."

Angelo was too upset to be able to reply. He was scared to death of these women with their feet up on the bars of chairs, showing their legs up to the knees and an abundance of fine petticoats. He couldn't bear the sight of those bodices hanging open over slips and stay-ribbons. He thought of the valley where the poor little Frenchman had died, as of a paradise. He was convinced there was nothing ridiculous in feeling like this.

He took his bottle and glass to the end of the room, to a small isolated table.

The old gentleman with the elegant little white goatee had approached the company. Though still very decorous, he had raised his lorgnette and was fatuously, and with a dazzling smile, examining a dark, milky young woman displaying plenty of bosom. She was undergoing a spirited assault from two men with waxed moustaches, typical commercial travellers; her defence was a coquettish compromise with semi-defeat.

To calm his fidgety hands, Angelo fiddled with the latch of a small door behind his bench. Finally the door opened. It led into a stable. There were at least three or four horses at the feed boxes, and several of those light traps used by travelling salesmen.

"The hell with that rabble," thought Angelo. He called to the man who was bringing a fresh supply of bottles. "Like to earn three louis?" he said.

"We're counting by fives from now on," replied the other, who was used to commercial appeals and needed more than a familiar approach to turn his head. And as Angelo tried to take a lofty tone: "Your Highness," he said, "it's no use trying to diddle old Guillaume. I've seen enough in my life to know that you're not going to give me five louis, maybe even six, for a day's good deed. If I name my price, the rest is up to you. Come off it, and talk like the rest of us."

Ignoring the insolence with which this was said, Angelo explained at great length that his young wife and two children were being detained in the barn used for quarantine at the village. "Couldn't I borrow the horse and trap of one of these men or women?" he said, fiercely.

"It's purely and simply a question of money," said the man.

He added, after scratching his head, stroking his chin, and looking his interlocutor up and down: "Provided that … Where are you going afterwards?"

"To Avignon."

"Then come in here."

He pulled Angelo into the stable and shut the door behind them. The smell of the horses went to Angelo's head.

"This is the way I see it," said the man. "We can't leave the little lady and the children in that mess. People are dying like flies, you know. Fork out ten louis down and here's what I'll do. You saw the blonde who's losing her stockings back there? Well, she's well known. And when I say well known, I mean well known. She's fixing it up for sure with the fat old boy in the Souvaroff boots. He's a cattle merchant from around here, and he's got horses and carriages the way others have fleas. They're fixing it up between them right now. Myself, I'm a family man. I'll sell you the lady's trap outright; it's that one there. *And* the nice little chestnut. It'll get you to Avignon if that's your idea. I can't do better than that. Ten louis outright. I'll fix things up with the young lady's family, as they say."

Angelo ardently tried to beat him down to seven, not so much to save money as for the sort of victory he always wanted to gain.

73

But the man said gently, in a fatherly tone: "One doesn't haggle over the life of one's wife and children."

"The blonde can go hang," thought Angelo while the man was harnessing up. "But this'll teach that young lady, so proud and so confident in the gendarmes, once and for all, that clothes don't make the man." He was thinking also of the handsome little boy (he remembered that he had a nice well-starched English collar) and of the little girl whom, the day before, he had several times caught staring at him.

At the moment of leaving, and as Angelo was already shaking the reins, the man said to him: "I like you; you're a good-looking fellow. You'll surely get lost among the crossroads. I'll give you my son; he'll guide you. Afterwards you can just leave him on the road."

He came back with a boy of about fifteen, whom he was instructing in a low voice.

"And be polite to the gentleman," he added, with an odd expression.

After more than an hour's gallivanting along earth roads among plushy trees, which must have been willows and which kept brushing against the leather hood, they arrived at the famous barn that was used for quarantine. The creak of the springs over the hard ruts had roused all the owls, and they were calling desperately to each other through the echoes of an immense silence.

Angelo pulled up the trap in a thicket. He gave the reins to the boy.

"Wait for me here," he said. "And keep the horse quiet."

It was still hot, and there was a sort of smell, which, though faint, made the horse obstinately shake its head and clink its bit.

The silence was complete except for the mournful wailing of the owls.

"Everybody's asleep," thought Angelo. "I must be very quiet myself and take pains not to wake anyone except the little governess and the two children, to avoid any fuss. The sentry might be less amenable than the one this afternoon. I'll blow on my tinder-wick and I hope they'll have enough presence of mind to recognize me at once and not cry out at seeing my face lit up all of a sudden in the dark. First I'll wake the little boy; he seems very plucky."

At the same time he strove to make out in the extreme blackness of the night the place where the sentry must be standing. He had stopped some ten paces from the gloomy bulk of the walls, blacker than the night, and listened for the sounds, however light, that a man on watch never fails to make. After a moment, hearing nothing but the owls calling, he said to himself: "The sentry must be asleep too," and drew nearer, carefully muffling his steps on the grass.

He soon found himself at the barn door. It was wide open. There was no trace of any sentry. The silence of the barn was also somewhat surprising. He expected to hear the sounds of breathing and the crackle of straw under restless bodies, but the walls, having shut off the cry of the owls, held only a silence more compact than the night.

"Could we have made some mistake?" he wondered.

He groped his way forward. His foot met an obstacle. He bent over and touched skirts. He knelt down and struck a light. He blew upon the embers of his tinder-wick and, as it flared, he recognized, distorted in an appalling grimace, the face of the peasant woman who had refused to leave without her trunk. She was dead. He blew on the embers as hard as he could and looked around him, but the red glow gave him only a very small range of vision. He stepped over the peasant woman and advanced several paces to look some more. He found another body, a man's, and some abandoned luggage. At last he thought he recognized some frills of Irish lace over pretty little buckled shoes below linen pantaloons. It was the little girl. Her eyes were opened wide in terrible amazement. She must have died very rapidly, and without being cared for; her dress wasn't even disarranged. The little boy was a little further on, huddling into the young governess, who was all convulsed, her lips drawn back over cruel teeth like a mad dog about to bite.

Angelo kept blowing on his wick and thought of absolutely nothing. Later he walked at random in the dark and stumbled over two or three more bodies; or they may have been the same ones, for unexpectedly he found himself outside again with the owls.

He called. He searched for the thicket where he had left the trap. He fell into an irrigation ditch full of water. He shouted again. He felt the hard ruts of the track under his feet. He found the thicket and called at the top of his voice as he walked with his arms held out in front of him. The trap was no longer there. He heard, a long way off, the galloping of a horse and the rumbling of a vehicle on the highroad.

He was in such a fury that he kept hissing like a wood-fire and could not even manage to swear. He began to run straight ahead, and it was not until he had tumbled two or three times more into the irrigation ditch that he finally had the sense to sit down in the rushes.

He was staggered by the double-dealing of the boy who had deserted him, who had, no doubt, been carefully instructed. He was upset more by this than by the dead people.

The faint smell that had made the horse toss his head became somewhat more definite when a hot little wind began to blow fitfully from the direction of the village. Only fifty paces away, the barn had its own supply of corpses. Angelo pictured the livid and heavy sun that would be rising in a few hours' time.

His imperious need to be generous, especially at this moment when he was floundering in what seemed to be a hideous general misunderstanding, made him consider seriously the idea of staying where he was till daybreak and then going to the village to offer his help in burying the dead. But he remembered the indifference of the sentry and said to himself:

"Those peasants will hate you because you have your own ideas about courage; or simply because you know more about it than they do; especially if you talk to them of quicklime. It would take no time to pitch you into the trench with a knock over the head from a spade. That would be silly." This last word convinced him.

He got back on to the path. At all events, he would allow himself to pay the innkeeper back. He felt greatly consoled by the thought that that sturdy thickset man would probably be backed up by his son, who must have returned with the trap. "It'll be a fine party, and they won't forget me." He hated being made a dupe!

He reached the inn as day was about to break. The glow of the lamps was still visible in the threadbare night. But there, too, things had moved fast. The big room was cold and empty. A man lay stretched flat on his belly in the middle. It was one of the two with waxed moustaches. A woman sprawling over the table appeared to be asleep. Angelo called to her gently. He laid his hand on the woman's forehead. It was burning. He called to her again, saying: "Madame", with great gentleness. He lifted up her face. She was plainly dead. The two open eyes were white as marble. And it was only physical weight that caused the sudden drop of her lower jaw, opening the mouth and letting slowly flow from it a thick flood of that white matter resembling rice pudding, but extraordinarily evil-smelling.

Angelo went all around the room. There was another dead man, crouched behind some chairs in a corner. He passed him, then went back. He had just thought of the little Frenchman. He pushed the chairs aside, but when he laid his hand on the folded arms in which the face was buried, he felt such a stiffness in the clenched limbs that he realized there was no hope for this one either.

After visiting the kitchen, where the fire was still burning in the stove under pans smelling richly of beef stew, and the stable, where there were neither horses nor vehicles left, he went up the stairs to the bedrooms. There were about ten on each side of a long central passage. He opened them all, one after another, and was even scrupulous enough, in the case of some that were dark, to open the shutters. All the rooms were empty: beds untouched. Except for the last one, where he found an enormous granary rat, plump and shiny. It must have just come out of its hole, and it stared at him with its red eyes, one paw in the air. Angelo shut the door.

He went down, crossed the room, in which the three characters from *The Sleeping Beauty* had not stirred, and went out. It was as he went out that he realized that the dead woman was dark; she must be the one who had been laughing a few hours before!

He took the road leading south. Day was breaking. The sun was still well below the hills; the sky was half dark; there was only a pale fringe underlining the shadow in the east, and the heat was already stifling.

Angelo walked for over an hour before realizing that the silence was quite extraordinary. He was passing through woods of small pines and oaks. The trees were perfectly motionless, without the slightest tremor. There were no birds. The road overlooked the bed of the Durance, here about half a league wide. It was entirely filled with salt-white pebbles. There was no water. Here and there by the roadside he saw clearings in the woods around four or five olive trees, which stayed absolutely still. Daylight was spreading without colour. The sky was like the riverbed, entirely covered with pebbles of salt. Above the woods the crest of the hill bore a village the colour of bones. There was no smoke.

"She was quite right," he said to himself.

He was seeing again the dark woman laughing, with her foot up on the bar of a chair, showing her legs in a froth of white petticoats.

Gradually the sun rose above the eastern horizon. It had neither shape nor colour. It was made of dazzling chalk. For the space of a shudder, there occurred a faint rustling, like the rapid passage of invisible beings burrowing still deeper beneath the leaves and motionless grass.

At length Angelo heard a horse approaching at a trot. He put his hand in his pocket and drew one of his pistols.

Soon he could see the approaching horseman. He was a fat man, bumping up and down in his saddle. When he was three paces away, Angelo leaped at the bridle, stopped the horse, and levelled his pistol.

"Get down," he said.

The fat man showed every sign of the most abject terror. His lips quivered; he made the sound of an ill-bred man sucking up his soup. As he set foot on the ground he fell to his knees.

Angelo unbuckled the saddlebag.

"Only the horse," he said.

He took plenty of time tightening the girths and shortening the stirrups. He had put the pistol in his pocket. He felt a strong liking for the fat man, now brushing his knees and watching him with a furtive, frightened look.

"Get into the shade," said Angelo kindly as he jumped into the saddle.

He wheeled round and started off with a spell of galloping. The horse, which immediately recognized new knees, responded perfectly. In spite of the heat, which quietly burned the skin and fired the air, Angelo felt a sort of pleasure steal over him. It occurred to him that it was a long time since he had had a smoke. He lit one of his little cigars.

On both sides of the road the fields and orchards were abandoned. Several fields of unharvested corn had collapsed under the weight of the ears. The motionless olive groves had the glint of tin. There was no distance anywhere; the hills were drowned in almond syrup. Huge apricot trees smelled, as he passed, of rotten fruit.

At length Angelo saw ahead of him the opening to an avenue of plane trees; this signified a village. He moved up under the trees at a walk. He was expecting to find the usual barriers and had already noted a side road into which, if anybody tried to stop him, he could plunge at a gallop. But there were no barriers, and despite the already advanced hour, the village, its doors and shutters closed, appeared quite deserted. He continued to approach at a walk.

When he reached the street, Angelo was affected unpleasantly by being flanked by houses to right and left. The solitude had soothed him. It had not cost him any effort to face the terrible plaster sun, but these house-fronts, behind which he pictured dark rooms and heaven knows what explanation for this solitude and silence, worried him.

At the crossroads made by a small square containing the church, he saw a small black and white shape lying in a triangle of shade, at the corner of a house. It was a little choirboy in cassock and surplice. By his side lay the tall cross carried at funerals and the holy-water stoup and sprinkler.

Angelo dismounted and went up to him. The child was sleeping. He was perfectly well and fast asleep, as though in his bed.

Angelo put his hands under his arms and raised him, to wake him up. At first the child's head lolled from side to side, then he sneezed and opened his eyes. But on seeing Angelo's face bent over him, he gave a violent twist like a startled cat, seized the cross and stoup, and took to his heels. His little bare feet twinkled high under his cassock. He vanished up a side alley. He had thrown down on the pavement a small coin he had been clasping in his hand.

Angelo left the village without seeing another living soul.

The road ran fairly close to the dry bed of the Durance, winding along a range of hills. It entered little valleys, emerged again, passed through olive orchards and willow clumps, threaded avenues of Italian poplars, crossed streams. Everything was motionless in boiling plaster. On either side of the road the horse's trot set files of stiff trees with cardboard foliage turning like the rigid spokes of a wheel. Now and then small white farms, their eyes shut, their

79

noses in the dust, slobbering a little straw, would appear between two mulberry trees.

In the general immobility Angelo noticed, along the slope of the hills, a red blob moving. It was a petticoated peasant woman descending at a run. He saw her jumping wildly down the dry stone walls of the terraces on which the people of the region grow artichokes. She was making a beeline through hedges and bushes. She was heading for an area where there were large pine woods but no dwellings.

Much later, after the road had taken several turnings, Angelo again saw the red blob far away among the hills. It was still moving rapidly.

The horse began to show signs of fatigue. Angelo alighted and, leading the beast by the bridle, approached a clump of willows. He was entering the grey shade of the trees when he was halted by the appearance of a large dog, which had got up and was watching him with eyes like coals. Silently it opened a huge and bloody maw; its two long fangs were festooned with black gobbets.

Angelo retreated backwards, step by step. The horse danced behind him. A stench of carrion rose out of the bushes. The dog stood still, holding its ground. Angelo remounted and made off at a jog trot.

He was already far away when he thought of his pistols. "I'm not worthy of the little Frenchman," he told himself. And he fell asleep.

He was aroused by a swerve of his horse. After having walked on for a while, it too must have fallen asleep in the shade of a birch tree. It had been awakened by a scorching ray of sunlight breaking through the leaves to fall on its muzzle.

It must have been nearly midday. Angelo was hungry and, above all, thirsty. He had been foolish to smoke three of his little cigars. His mouth was plastered with thick, sour saliva. It was highly dangerous to eat fruit or indeed anything in the houses or inns. Besides, there was neither house nor inn in sight. Nor should one consider drinking from the fountains or springs. Angelo dismounted again, and leaned back against the birch tree, after tethering the horse in the shade of a thick bramble bush. And he lit a fourth cigar.

The heat plunged down in terrible, heavy, long, stifling torrents. Brushing his forehead as he pushed back his hair, Angelo noticed that his sweat was cold. His ears began to buzz, faintly yet so continuously that it made him drunk and giddy. Suddenly Angelo's stomach turned and he vomited. He looked closely at what he had just vomited. It was a mouthful of mucous. He went on smoking.

He straightened up without any previous decision to do so. He was strangely divided into two parts: one that kept watch in his sleep, and one that acted outside him, like a dog on a leash. He untethered the horse, led it to the road, mounted, and dug sharply with his knees. The horse began to trot.

He was just passing a small, shut house, when the door opened and he heard someone call: "Sir, sir, come quick!" It was a woman with a masculine face, but made beautiful by terror. She was reaching out her hands towards him. He jumped to the ground and followed her into the house.

In the unexpected darkness he could make out nothing but a sort of whitish form writhing with aggressive violence. He rushed towards it at the same time as the woman, before realizing that it was a man struggling on a bed whose sheets and counterpane had been sent flying across the room. He tried to hold the body down, but was hurled back as though by the irresistible release of a steel spring. Besides, his foot had also slipped in some sticky fluid at the foot of the bed. He steadied himself on a slightly drier part of the floor and began to wrestle in earnest, aided by the woman, who had slipped into the space on the other side and was clinging with all her strength to the sick man's shoulders and calling him Joseph. At last, under their combined efforts, the body fell back upon the bed with a crack like dry wood. Angelo, who was leaning with all his weight on the wretched man's arms, felt under his palms the disordered seething of the muscles and even of the bones, twisting in a mad fury. But the face, so excessively thin that it was no more than a skull with a covering of skin, began to pale, while the heavy lips, covered with hard bristles, drew back over blackened and decayed teeth which, against this blue, appeared almost white. At the back of their deep sockets the eyes, surrounded by wrinkled skin, wavered like the shimmering scales on the tiny heads of tortoises. Mechanically Angelo began to massage the thighs and hips of this body. Its skin was very harsh. A convulsion even more violent than the rest tore the sick man from the woman's hands and flung him against Angelo. He felt the teeth strike his cheek.

He had just noticed that the skin he was rubbing was encrusted with ancient filth. The man died; that is to say, the flickering in his eyes went out. His limbs continued to be swept in every direction by the tumult of the muscles and bones, which seemed to be in revolt and to want to break through the skin, like rats in a sack. Angelo wiped his cheek on a bit of dirty printed calico that served as a bed curtain.

The room, which gave flush on to the fields and was also used as a kitchen, contained a big table covered with vegetables with soil still clinging to them, and another, smaller, round one evidently used as a dining-table. In the corner behind the door Angelo saw an old man, all freshly shaved and suggesting an elderly actor. He was seated in an armchair and doubtless had some sort of paralysis of the legs, for there were two leather-handled sticks laid across his thighs. He was smiling. His lips, thin as wire, gleamed faintly with saliva. His gaze roved from Angelo to four or five pipes set before him on the edge of the round table, near a pigskin pouch filled with tobacco.

"Since Joseph fell ill he has taken his pipe and is quite happy," said the woman. She wiped her hands on her apron.

"It's this one," said the old man.

He stroked the pipe with obvious signs of the keenest joy. It was a clay pipe representing a Turk's head. It was mounted on a rather long reed stem, embellished with red woollen tassels.

"Wouldn't you like a little cigar?" said Angelo.

"No," said the old man, "I smoke this."

He began to fill the pipe with deft thumb-strokes and a great exercise of fingers. He laughed broadly, his toothless mouth wide open, and when he took the first puffs a thin thread of saliva fell on to his waistcoat.

Angelo sat down near the old man. He thought of nothing, not even of smoking. The smell of the clay pipe was revolting. Suddenly he remembered the horse.

"I expect he's skedaddled," he said to himself.

He went out. The horse was perfectly quiet. It was asleep on its feet, and from time to time, as it slept, it licked at the grass, so white that it seemed to be covered with flour.

Angelo spent more than two hours sitting on the ground, his back leaning against the trunk of a lilac. He felt at complete peace, and even in a way happy. He could see the woman coming and going in the garden. She must have felt an instinctive need to recommence immediately her habitual motions of housekeeping. Angelo's presence must also have helped her considerably, for she took her time pulling up carrots, fat turnips, and a few small plants of celery. She also gathered some sprigs of parsley, wiping the leaves on a corner of her apron, for they were covered with dust. Finally she fetched a pail and drew some water from an obviously unhealthy well.

These activities, this woman's movements, were in the true sense an enchantment to Angelo. A feeling ran through all his limbs as if he were being tickled with the tips of feathers and his brain were made of fresh down. Finally, he became aware that for some time his mouth had been spread in a fatuous grin; he stopped grinning and, seizing advantage of the woman's having gone in to poke her fire, mounted and took to the road.

Towards evening he passed by a lamenting village. The houses stood in a group four or five hundred yards from the road and a little below it. From his horse Angelo could see them cowering like so many foxes against the gravel of the Durance. There came from them a moaning, a dirge that must have been made up of a great many voices to be so sustained and to rise at the end to so high a pitch.

Angelo reached Manosque at nightfall.

# 6

Here there were serious barricades.

The road had been blocked with a dust cart, barrels, and a wagon with its wheels in the air.

A fat fellow with a shotgun-sling across his coat came out from the fortification.

"Halt!" he said. "No one's allowed through. We don't want anyone here, d'you hear? No one! All resistance is useless."

These last words cheered Angelo considerably, and he continued to advance. There was still enough daylight for him to be able to follow, on the pale face framed in cottony side whiskers, the spread of an ameless terror. The man retreated precipitately into his stronghold.

Four or five dumbfounded faces at once appeared over the top of the barricade.

"Where are you going?" – "Don't come any nearer!" cried uneasy voices. "What are you coming here for?"

"I heard reports about your beauty," said Angelo gravely, repressing a strong urge to laugh, "and I've come to see for myself."

This reply seemed to frighten them even more than the actual presence of the horseman.

"They're grocers, and the one in the coat is a footman," thought Angelo.

"Look here, you're a good fellow, I'm sure," said a fat grey face with quivering cheeks.

"I'm the wickedest fellow on earth," said Angelo, "as all who've had to do with me have soon found out. Roll back those barrels, and move out of the way, so I can get by. If not, I'll jump them, and you'd better look out."

At the same time he made his horse prance. It was tired and did not put much fire into it. But these pirouettes and a little whinny of pain – for Angelo, full of his game, was jerking hard at the bit – carried confusion into the fortress.

The heads vanished. A gun was levelled.

"Now they're wetting their pants," said Angelo to himself. "Let's give them some help."

He fired a pistol into the air. It made a great noise. Then he rode quietly off to one side, along a slope, and under some almond trees.

Ten minutes later he was in the gardens, under the town walls.

"Old man, you're free," said Angelo to the horse.

He took off its saddle and bridle, and sent the barebacked animal off with a friendly slap on the rump. He hid the harness in the bushes. Climbing over the reed fences he walked through cabbage patches. He crossed a small, evil-smelling stream. Ascending along the walls of a big tannery, he came out into a boulevard, under some lime trees. The street lamps were lit.

His skin was stiff as a board with sweat and sunburn. He went to wash at a fountain. Hardly had he plunged his hands into the water of the basin when he felt himself brutally gripped by the shoulders and pulled back, while mighty arms hugged him mercilessly.

"Here's another one," shouted a voice close to his ear. He fought, trying to kick, and received a hail of fists on his face and body. His legs were seized; he was pinned to the ground and held tight. He heard voices:

"He came from behind the tannery." – "Search him." – "He's got pistols." – "Take his packets of poison off him." – "He must have thrown them in the basin." – "Empty the basin." – "One of his pistols has been fired, it smells of powder."

Finally someone said: "Beat his head in," and he saw feet raised. But everyone began to talk at once and mill around him, while there came the sound of dull blows striking the plug of the basin to smash it open.

The nearest street lamp was still too far off for him to be able to make out what sort of people he was up against. It seemed to him that they were workmen. There were some leather aprons.

"Here, get up," someone told him, kicking him heavily in the ribs. At the same time he was lifted up and set on his feet with such violence that his head bounced against his shoulder.

At last he was able to see the faces surrounding him, indeed pressing up to him, and shouting insults. They were not so terrible, except that they bore the stamp of fear. A man of about thirty, well built, with curly hair and a large nose, was in the throes of a sort of hysterical trance. He was prancing round the group that imprisoned Angelo, punching at the empty air and shouting in a voice that suddenly took on a feminine shrillness.

"It's him. Hang him! It's him. Hang him! Put him to death! To death!"

His eyes were starting from his head. In the end his fury half choked him and he had a fit of coughing. Finally he spat in Angelo's face.

After contradictory proposals in which the decision was carried by a deep dark voice speaking very calmly, and after further jostling, begun by the large-nosed man who sought to get at Angelo with his fists, they set off. They went down the boulevard towards the heart of the town and turned into some little streets, where Angelo noticed some wide and very fine doorways, but also shutters hastily opening. There were now more than a hundred people behind Angelo. Luckily the streets were very narrow and kept this crowd away from the victim, for the hysterical man's falsetto cries could still be heard.

"You're certainly no coward, sir," said the big dark voice in Angelo's ear, "but let's be quick if you don't want to share the other's fate."

Since he had taken the liberty of noticing the beauty of the wide doorways, Angelo had gained a fair control of himself.

"I'm in no hurry," he said.

But he felt himself being dragged along, and it was in vain that he resisted; he was pushed into a guardroom practically at a run. Two gendarmes sprang to their feet, overturning their bench, and barred the door.

The man who had spoken in his ear had entered with him.

"Phew! This one's had a narrow escape," he said in his dark voice. "If I hadn't been there, he'd have gone the way of the other."

He was thin and dark-haired; he held himself erect and apparently unmoved, in a military posture.

There was also, on the other side of the table and illuminated by two three-branched candlesticks, a second person. He was quite military, notwithstanding a fine cravat of faille, for above the cravat his face was marked by a long scar extending from one cheek to the other and notching the nose.

"That's an old sabre-cut," thought Angelo.

86

He had never seen a finer sight than that scar. With the toe of his boot he righted the bench that the gendarmes had overturned.

"Give those rascals one on the snout for me," said the faille cravat.

The tumult was still going on outside. There were shouts of "Death to the poisoner!" The falsetto voice was nearing the door. They must have pushed the hysterical man to the front, or else he was elbowing his way there. He could be heard saying, in haranguing tones: "He's thrown poison into the Observantins' fountain. It's a plot to destroy the people. He's a foreigner. He's got aristocrat's boots."

The man with the faille cravat glanced at Angelo's boots.

"He's paid by the government."

The man with the faille cravat rose and went to the door. He pushed the gendarmes aside and planted himself on the threshold.

"How about you?" he said. "Who pays you for making a fool of yourself? You got three hundred gold francs by the last courier, and a letter from Paris. I've got a copy on my table. Tell us something about who pays you, Michu."

"The cholera's an excuse to poison the poor," shouted the hysteric.

"The man's mad," thought Angelo, "but I'll find him later and kill him."

"No need for an excuse," said the faille cravat; "for a long time now you've been acting like boys big enough to piss in wells. Shut the door," he told the gendarmes, "and shoot this scum in the belly if they dare to open it and come in."

"We'll see you later, Grandpa," shouted someone.

"Whenever you like," said the faille cravat.

He came back and sat down at the table. Angelo admired him greatly. He would have liked to be in his shoes. He was not used to being protected. If the man had spoken to him there and then, he would have admitted with pleasure who he was and even what he intended to do. He would have adopted a drawing-room manner and told him everything.

But it was a gendarme who slapped the bench with the flat of his hand and invited him to sit down.

"Where did they catch him?" said the faille cravat.

"At the Observantins' fountain," said the dark voice. "He had his hands in the water."

87

"The real joke," said the faille cravat, "is that Police Headquarters seem to want to make people think they believe it, or are they playing the fool to achieve their own ends?"

"If it's that kind of game," said the dark voice, "I should think things would be moving much faster."

"They're moving fast enough for me already," said the faille cravat. "Gendarmes," he added, "take your bench and go and sit outside. Put your guns between your legs and sit tight.

"Come over here," he said to Angelo, when the gendarmes had gone out. "Have you any papers?"

"No," said Angelo.

"You're not French?"

"No."

"Piedmontese?"

"Yes."

"Political refugee?"

Angelo did not reply.

"He's not scared," said the man with the dark voice. "He kicked like hell and didn't let a peep out of him."

"Oh! Then he's a priest," said the faille cravat.[1]

"Yes," said the dark voice, "but not, I think, the kind to put rat poison in the ciborium."

"You dispute that point?" asked the cravat.

"Of course."

The man with the faille cravat examined Angelo afresh from top to toe.

"Fact is," he said, "if you stuck this fellow in the last square at Waterloo, I bet he'd acquit himself with honour."

"You take the words out of my mouth," said the dark voice.

"Yes, but law and order," said the cravat, "what becomes of that? Now that everybody has the trots, as at Leipzig!"

"O Just Augustus! the reign of shit," said the dark voice.

"Take a look at yourself!" said the cravat.

"The telescope trick? If I try that, I see stars," said the dark voice.

"Tell us what colour," said the cravat.

"Bee-colour," said the dark voice.

"Not bad. You know there's a circular, signed 'Gisquet'?"

"What's in it?"

"Stories."

"What side are they on?"

"The fellows outside."

"That doesn't stop me thinking it's bee-colour. Quite the contrary."

"I grant you that would explain the 'Gisquet'."

"And Michu's gold," said the dark voice. "The louis were new, and new louis come straight from the Treasury. The way I see it."

"You're a deep thinker."

"Deep as a well in which Truth takes her hip baths."

"Then what's to be done with him?"

"Let him take off by the back door," said the dark voice.

During this conversation Angelo thought of the blows he had received. He was literally mad with rage at the thought that he had been beaten and dragged along the ground. He kept constantly repeating: "They spat in my face." He imagined appalling acts of revenge. He was so absorbed in this that he had an absent, wholly detached expression, not lacking in nobility.

"Follow this man," the character with the faille cravat told him.

And, as Angelo did not move, he spoke again: "Kindly follow this man, sir."

Angelo gave a slight nod of acknowledgment. He had not heard the first injunction.

"You've been splendid," the dark voice told him as they went down a long corridor.

The man climbed on to a stool and blew out the oil lamp standing in a niche in the wall. He opened the door. It gave on to some gardens. Still he went out cautiously and listened attentively, turning to right and left. They could hear the soothing chant of a great many tree frogs.

"One never knows with those cowards," he said. "They're so cunning! . . . But the coast's clear. Come with me. Just don't trip over the vine props."

"I don't understand any of this," said Angelo. "I don't understand why I've got to hide. I've done no harm to anyone."

"*Hush!*" said the man. "Never mention innocence. And if you need assassins, always choose cowards. They like their job because it calms them. While they're killing they forget their cowardices. Look out, step over the cabbages."

They were crossing a kitchen garden.

"I shall certainly never need assassins," said Angelo. "I felt the need once and I took care of the matter myself."

"Well," said the man, calmly, "don't mention that in the victim's house. And just now keep close to my heels: we're in my bean rows."

They reached a fence. Through it could be seen a deserted street under a red street lamp.

"I'll open the gate for you," said the man. But he touched Angelo's arm. "You've no idea," he pursued with a soldier's good nature, "what a weakness I have for the cockade. I'll bet you, at my age I could still make a revolution in a tasselled kepi. So there you are! If I say: 'Take it gently!' I mean take it gently. The cholera's a mess, but the rest of the story's worse. Don't show off."

"What's the rest of the story?" said Angelo.

"Some chaps have been paid to say that the government is having the fountains poisoned. What d'you make of that?"

"It's a coward's trick," said Angelo.

"But it's addressed to cowards so it works," said the man.

He opened the gate.

"The right goes into town; the left into the country," he said, pointing towards the street. "Good night, sir."

Angelo turned to the right. Beyond the lamppost the street wound between stables smelling richly of horse dung. Angelo took advantage of a shady corner to go through his pockets. He had stuffed everything into the three pockets of his breeches. One contained the pistol he had fired into the air in front of the barricade; another, a handkerchief and three small cigars. In the hip pocket he had the other pistol, loaded, and thirty louis, which he counted out. "If I hadn't acted so childishly a little while ago in front of those gentlemen hiding behind their casks, I'd still have two rounds left to fire; now I have only one," he told himself. "That soldier who's now in the police is quite right. One shouldn't show off. For the pleasure of spouting off a moment ago, I can now kill only one of those dogs. And if it isn't the one that spat in my face, I shan't be clean." He still had appalling thoughts of revenge.

The street emerged into a boulevard planted with giant elms in which resounded an incredible conversation of nightingales. They were also chasing each other, and their flapping wings made the foliage patter like hail. Angelo counted seven street lamps in a row under the dense vault of the elms. The boulevard was deserted. Yet it was not late. A belfry struck nine.

"I must go at once to Giuseppe's," thought Angelo. "I think I ought to go along here until I reach a sort of belfry with a wrought iron bulb on top and a gate underneath."

He was hugging the foot of the elm avenue very closely to keep in the shade, when he heard, coming from a side street, the rumbling and creaking of a heavily laden cart. He hid behind a tree trunk and saw two men appear, each holding up a torch. They were escorting a wagon drawn by two strong horses. Four or five other individuals, in white blouses and carrying picks, spades, and more torches, walked beside the wheels. It was a load of coffins, and even corpses simply wrapped in sheets. Arms, legs, heads wagging on long, thin, flabby necks, stuck out through the side racks. The procession passed close to the tree behind which Angelo was hiding, and he could observe the tranquil look of the gravediggers, some of whom were smoking pipes as they walked. A shutter opened in one of the houses along the boulevard, and a woman's voice, more like a screeching cat, screamed her appeal. One of the white-bloused men replied:

"Call the other cart; this one's full."

The nightingales went on singing and fluttering the leaves.

Angelo was going the same way as the cart. He let it get some distance ahead. It had left behind it a musky smell.

At length he reached the gateway he had remembered, with the wrought-iron bulb on top. It led into a dark, narrow street. All the houses were shut except one about fifty paces ahead, a shop with two glass doors, which emitted a little light. Angelo remembered a small café where Giuseppe had once taken him to drink some wine: it must be hereabouts. "If that's it," he thought, "I'll go in and ask for a bottle of wine." He had had nothing to eat since the chicken at Peyruis, but it was thirst that tormented him most and robbed him of any desire to smoke. "I'll also ask for Giuseppe's house; I don't think it's far from here."

It was just a small wine shop, with one lamp. Through the glass he could see four or five men standing up and drinking. Angelo pushed through the door. He was given some wine, but it took time. The shopkeeper watched him with eyes like those of a cat doing its business among warm cinders. The men who were drinking were probably bakers, to judge from their caps whitened with flour. They too opened their eyes wide when Angelo began to gulp down his wine straight from the bottle.

Angelo didn't realize that these men and the shopkeeper – who had all been drinking together without saying a word – were busy trying to calm their terror by customary behaviour, by a little gathering of the kind they used to have before the epidemic, and the taste of wine that was the usual prelude to forgetting their worries. This newcomer all of a sudden brought back the evil air. It must be admitted also that his way of drinking was suspicious.

They looked him up and down, and one of the bakers was collected enough to notice Angelo's fine boots. He immediately set down his glass and went out. He could be heard running down the street.

Angelo had reached that moment when thirst, long endured, has at last been satisfied, and when it is much more important to catch one's breath and lick one's lips than to study the surroundings. He had not seen the man leave. He noticed, however, that the others were full of engaging hypocrisy and faint smiles that never went beyond their lips. He frowned, curtly asked how much he owed, and paid with a half écu that he was clever enough to set spinning on the table. In two strides he was outside, while from instinct, the others were looking at the coin.

He had been put too closely on his guard by those hypocritical glances and smiles not to leap immediately into a shadowy alley. Even so, a hand clutched at him as he passed, sliding down the length of his arm and tearing his shirt, while a voice thick with hate said: "It's the poisoner."

Angelo started to run. "I mustn't allow myself to be taken for a fool by that fine police officer who obligingly took me through his kitchen garden," he thought; "and he'd have the right to do so, if I got caught again. If only I had two rounds to fire instead of one, I'd treat myself to the luxury of putting one of these dogs underground, where he'd be some use to the soil."

They were on his heels. Wearing light shoes and more at their ease despite the darkness on ground they knew well, they were running faster than he was. Several times, hands gripped Angelo's shirt and tore it still more. A kick he let fly in the dark landed fair and square in a belly.

The man whinnied like a horse and fell. Angelo managed to gain some ground, leap into a street to the right, then immediately into another that led down under an arch.

"Let's hope it's not a blind alley," he said to himself, running as hard as he could. "Now it's a question of life or death. Very well, I'll kill some." This thought soothed him and even gave him a certain gaiety. He stopped. Taking it by the middle he settled the discharged pistol into his right fist. "If I strike downward with the steel barrel as hard as I can, and have the luck to hit a face, I've got my man. Look here!" he went on. "Instead of running like a rabbit, I may even become the hunter. It all depends on my resolution. I can get enough cover from some doorway. If I bash in the heads of just one or two of them – and I owe them that – the others'll think again. And if they don't, at the last moment I'll burn my powder. After that, by God's grace ...They'll have paid dearly." He was as happy as a king.

He kept quiet. Soon he heard the sandals coming cautiously step by step down the street. His pursuers passed by him, within an arm's length. There were about ten of them. One of them said in a low voice: "Does the government pay for his boots?" – "Well, who do you think?" replied another.

"And that's the people," thought Angelo. This arrested his arm. "How ugly that voice was," he said to himself. "Low as it was, it couldn't conceal all the man's envy of my boots. Here are people ready to do anything for boots. Indeed, they think I am too. Does this make them sincere?" he added, after a moment.[2]

He was no longer thinking at all about the danger he was in. The men in sandals had reached the end of the street and, hearing no further noise, put their heads together for a moment; then they called out and received answers from the side of the adjoining street. They talked louder and louder, and Angelo realized that they had arranged to guard the issues of every street in the quarter.

"He certainly stopped somewhere in this street," said a voice in command. "You're not going to let yourselves be poisoned like dogs by a government that's out to kill the workers. Go back and make a closer search. That's what we must do."

"Oh well, that's how it goes! I shall have to do some killing," Angelo told himself. "Somewhere there is certainly somebody who is having a good laugh."

He took the loaded pistol in his right hand and gripped the empty one in his left fist.

He braced himself in his recess. He felt his back pressing against boards, which gave way. It was a door loose on its latch.

Keeping an ear cocked for the sound of sandals returning up the street, Angelo tucked the pistol under his arm and tried the wooden handle. The door opened. He went in, reclosed the door, and stood still, holding his breath in the dark.

He listened for a long time to the sounds from the street; then, after the men had looked everywhere (he even heard, upon the leaf of the door behind which he stood, hands going back and forth, trying to decide if the recess were empty) they settled down to watch under the archway at the top of the street and stayed there, talking in loud voices.

Angelo listened to the house's sounds. They were those of an empty house. He lit his tinder-wick and blew on it to make a faint glow. As far as he could see, he was in the entrance passage of quite a well-to-do house. At last he made out, not very far from the door, a small *étagère* on which stood a candlestick with a candle and several phosphorus tapers. He lit the candle.

What he had taken for an entrance passage was a hall. A broad staircase led to the floors above. There was no furniture, no pictures, but the banisters and especially the way they were finished in strapwork promised fine things.

Angelo deliberately made a slight noise and even coughed. He stood in the middle of the hall, his candlestick in his hand, looking up the staircase to where the handsome banisters widened into a gallery on the first floor.

"I can't look exactly pretty in my shirtsleeves and all ragged," he thought, "but in any case, the way I stand here holding my candle

and making no attempt to hide, it'd be hard to take me for a brigand."
He even made so bold as to say out loud, but without shouting and
in the most friendly possible tone: "Is anybody there?"

Rats were scampering here and there; and there was also the sighing
of the walls, the cracking of woodwork leading its woodwork life.

"Oh well, I'm going upstairs," he said to himself.

He did not dare open a door to his left, near the little console on
which he had found the candlestick. He was afraid of being seen to
do so: "Then," he thought, "they might really take me for a thief."

He went up, holding his candle high, seeing tall doors loom up
above the fine wrought-iron gallery. One of these doors was ajar. He
said: "Monsieur, or madame, have no fear, I am a gentleman." He got
to the landing: nothing had stirred or replied. The half-open door
stood neither more nor less open. He could now, however, see the
bottom of the door, and he observed that it was held ajar by a ball of
fur with very long hairs from which the flickering of his candle-flame
drew glints of gold.

His shudder of fear lasted only a moment when he realized that it
was a woman's hair. He heard the voice of the poor little Frenchman
saying in his ear: "It's the finest outbreak of Asiatic cholera ever seen!"

"Ah! yes, of course," said Angelo. "That's the story," he added. But
he went no nearer. He was upset by the beauty of the hair and by
seeing it spread on the ground; by the abundance of these loosened
tresses, which he now saw plainly with their lovely glints of gold; and
even, showing through them, the glimmer of a bluish profile.

She was a very young woman, or a girl. She was still beautiful,
snapping at the empty air with extremely white teeth. Emaciation
and cyanosis had given her a face carved from onyx. She lay on the
cushion of filth she had vomited. Her body had not rotted. She must
have died very quickly, of raw cholera. Under her long night dress,
although it was of linen, he could see her black belly, her blue thighs
and legs, drawn back like those of a grasshopper about to spring.

Angelo pushed open the door that the body held ajar. It led into a
bedroom. He stepped over the corpse and entered. The disorder was
that of death and hurry. The woman had just had time to leap out of
bed, then she had fouled sheets and floor with her spurting dysentery
in a straight line towards the door, where she had fallen. Everything

else was undisturbed: a fine marble-topped chest bore its clock under a glass globe, two copper candleholders, a box encrusted with sea shells, some very haughty daguerreotypes, especially one of an old man in uniform wearing a frogged dolman, hand on hip and moustaches like a bull's horns; and one of a woman at a piano, thrusting into it long, imperious fingers like lances; she was dark-haired. Next to the daguerreotypes a glass cupel held hairpins, a shell flower, stay-laces. Behind the clock-case were a bottle of Eau-de-Cologne, a small bottle of balm cordial, a box of smelling-salts. On each side of the chest, a tall window, with small panes and old repp curtains. Outside, a garden: the dark mass of foliage could be seen moving against the stars. Three easy chairs: over the back of one of them a pair of long black stockings and an elastic garter. A pedestal table, a vase containing paper flowers, then the curtains of the alcove, the bed, a cupboard; near the cupboard a little door covered by tapestry. By the door, a chair; on the chair, underclothes, pantaloons, and embroidered petticoats.

Angelo opened the little door. Another room. But here the disorder told of a more violent struggle. No smell: from the threshold one could just detect the faint violet fragrance of the underlinen piled on the chair. Once inside, there was another smell: that of dirty wool sprayed with water, or rather sprayed with alcohol. The bed was ripped apart, tossed and trampled, the sheets torn, soiled with excrement, and curdled with whitish matter. On the floor, basins full of water, swabs of wet linen. The mattress had been abundantly soaked. It had dried since, but the covering was stained with huge patches like rust with wide greenish halos. There was no body. "One must look for the last one," the poor little Frenchman used to say, "they go burrowing into places you'd never dream of." But nothing: not even behind the bed. Angelo pushed another small half-open door: another room, a strong smell of turpentine, again those struggles among dirty linen and torn sheets, but nobody. He went all round. He walked on tiptoe. He held the candle high. He touched nothing. He craned his neck. He felt taut and hard as wire.

He returned to the first room, stepped over the corpse and out on to the landing. He went downstairs, blew out the candle. He was about to open the door. He heard talking in the road. He went upstairs again in the dark, guiding himself by the banisters. He did not light the candle till he reached the first floor.

In addition to the door where the woman with the beautiful hair was lying, there were two other doors. Angelo opened one of them. It led to a drawing-room. The piano was there. A large winged armchair across which was laid a crutch. A couch, a screen, a centre table shaped like a four-leafed clover. Portraits, hard to make out, in heavy frames. One was that of a judge or something like a judge; another was of a man holding a sabre between his legs. There was nothing in here. But yes! While an icy chill shot down his back, Angelo saw something jump off an armchair; it was a cushion! And coming towards him! No, it was a cat, a large grey cat arching its back and lifting a long, quivering tail. It came and rubbed against the legs of Angelo's boots. It was fat, neither scared nor wild. What had it eaten? ... No, the window was half open. It evidently went out and foraged.

On the second floor, nothing: it took no time to see this. Three rooms, empty, or merely containing jars, bushels for measuring grain, a wicker tailor's dummy, baskets, sacks, an old violin-case open and unhinged, a trestle for picking olives, some pumpkins, some mattress springs, a music stand, a rat-trap, a demijohn of vinegar, some barrel hoops, an old straw hat, an old gun. But the staircase went on higher. Meanwhile it had become rustic: it smelled of grain and birds; it was even slightly strewn with straw. It ended against a true barn door, which, when pushed, opened with a horrible creaking on to a sparkle of stars.

It was what is called in these parts a "gallery", that is to say, a sort of covered terrace on the roof.

A warm and extremely supple wind had arisen, which fanned the stars and made the foliage of the trees sway and rustle. A clanging, which it had also set going in the sky, made Angelo look up; in the night, not very far from him, he discovered the iron cage of a belfry, then the jutting confusion of roofs, some of whose tiles were polished so smooth that the mere twinkling of the stars made them gleam.

Angelo was glad to breathe in this wind smelling of hot tiles and swallows' nests. He snuffed out the candle and sat down on the edge of the terrace. The night was so overloaded with stars, and they blazed so brightly, that he could see distinctly the different roofs fitted together like plates in a suit of armour. The light was of black steel, but from time to time a spark kindled on the crest of a gable, on the varnished edge of a dovecote, or a weathercock, or an iron bell-cage. Short motionless waves of an extraordinary rigidity covered the whole site of the town with an angular and frozen surf pattern. Pale pearl house-fronts, on whose surfaces the faintest of lights, like phosphorus, came to die, were inlaid with solid triangles of shadow, raised like pyramids or set horizontally like fields; slopes on which there danced a greenish light threw open, in every direction, rows of tiles like the ribs of a fan; rotundas filigreed with silver bulged with shadows where some large church emerged; towers and the black and grey interlocking of skewbacks and superimposed galleries rose up, bristling with the barbs of stars. Now and then the lamps in the squares and boulevards breathed up vapours of rust and ochre festooned with the frames and crowns of eaves; and the inky rents of the streets carved out each quarter.

The wind, which did not breathe but fell in one solid piece or rolled along slowly like a ball of cotton wool, set the whole expanse of roofs lapping, blew a sleepy booming through the hollows of the bells, brushed the muffled drums of the attics and convent roofs. The laden branches of the elms and sycamores groaned like masts in travail. On the distant hills one could hear rustle the fluttering and beating wings of the great woods. The swaying of the hanging street lamps cast red glows; and that heavy air, leaping like a cat across the heavy exhalation of the tiles, kneaded the colours under the night sky into a sort of bronzed tar.

"Men are indeed wretched," thought Angelo. "Everything beautiful happens without them. Cholera and catchwords are what they make. They foam with jealousy or die of boredom, which comes down to the same thing, if they're not allowed to interfere. And whenever they do interfere, there's a premium on hypocrisy and raving. One need only be up here or in the wilderness that I rode through the other day, to realize where the true battles lie, to become very particular about the victories one strives for. In short, to cease being *content with little*. As soon as you're alone, things lay hold of you by themselves and always force you to take the roads that are hardest to climb.

And even if you *don't get there*, what fine views you have, and how reassuring everything is."

Accustomed to obeying his youth without reserve, Angelo did not perceive that these thoughts lacked originality and were false besides. He was twenty-five, that is true, but at that age how many have already become calculating! He was one of those men who remain twenty-five for fifty years. His soul did not comprehend the full seriousness of society and how important it is to have one's place, or at any rate to belong to the party that distributes places. He always regarded liberty as believers regard the Virgin. The most sincere among the men he trusted saw it as a *relative thing*, which in any case should always be consigned to the philosophers if one does not want to be caught napping. He did not realize that, of those who always had the word "liberty" on their lips, some were beginning to sport crosses.

His mother had bought him his colonel's commission. He had never understood that his position as natural son to the Duchess Ezzia Pardi conferred on him the *right to scorn*, as on all those who have the *obligation of being*. Did he even think of all the rungs to be climbed that the word "natural" implies, after having been adored throughout his childhood? That is why he had surprised his acquaintances when they saw him take military service seriously and even regularly attend the drilling of recruits. People guffawed, though behind his back; but at the first review he appeared on his black horse like a golden ear of corn. They could not keep their eyes off the arabesques, the braided clover-leaves escalading his tunic, and the sparkling helmet with its pheasant plumes, below which they saw the purest and gravest of faces. One can see that henceforth he was entitled to the pinpricks of his peers and the love of the sergeants.

"Do I err," he continued, "in thinking that I'm bigger when I act alone?"

He was, at that moment, one of those *born leaders*, who are not rare, as people maintain, but on the contrary relatively common.

"But people will say to me, as they have said already: 'your actions are full of fancy gestures (they didn't dare say fancy steps) that attract attention. And we don't need attention, we need to succeed, which is entirely different.' Whenever it's a question of liberty, they are right."

The moment he thought of liberty, which he saw in the shape of a beautiful woman, young and pure, walking among lilies in a garden, he lost his critical sense. Liberty is the hobbyhorse of all beautiful children born to a country suffering alien rule, indeed tyranny.

"For those who accused me of irresponsibility when I killed Baron Swartz in a duel, while the orders were purely and simply to assassinate him, or to have him assassinated if doing it myself disgusted me (as they said later) – for those people, isn't the time I spent with the little Frenchman time wasted? Wouldn't they laugh at the sentimentality that made me keep watch over him after his death, and even want to be present at his burial, except for that lout of a captain? They certainly haven't the same reasons for pride as I have. Would they approve of the way I looked after that man yesterday afternoon? They'd say one should only have a single aim in view. Would they force me to *aim low*?"

The phrase delighted him. He repeated it several times. He found in it a justification. He was weak enough to seek one.

"Must I be insensitive like a stone or a submissive corpse?" he added. "If so, what good is liberty? Once I had it I'd be unable to enjoy it. It's quite essential, anyway, that once the goal is reached – in a word, liberty – obedience should cease; and how could it cease if liberty was then given only to obedient corpses? If, in the end, liberty has no one to turn to, shall we not have merely changed tyrants?"

But he believed in the sincerity of the men who were members of the same conspiracy as himself: of whom some were hiding in the foothills of the Abruzzi, and some had been shot (or even thumbscrewed, which he considered naïvely as an absolute proof of sincerity). He had several times gone to join them under the *green tent*, for important *vendite*,[3] always boldly, sometimes even carelessly, in full uniform. He had been much reproached for his audacity, his uniform, and that recklessness he so loved. That recklessness, always instinctively deliberate, so to say, had often affected the police, and even deterred them, by its mystifying inappropriateness (which made the cops suspect an official trick), from making arrests already decided upon and easy to carry out. Even men who were bombastic talkers and visibly cherished dreams of glory spoke to him then with every sign of the most Jesuitical diplomacy. He saw them turn yellow, as if prey to a sudden liver attack.

"Aren't they victims of the error of sincerity?" he asked himself, giving free rein to his naïveté at this moment when peace, the night, and above all the feminine velvet of the wind, lent eloquence to his heart.

He had nevertheless had some experiences that his pride would not let him forget. It was always in such moments of abandon that he had been duped. Now, as soon as he perceived his state, he said to himself: "You're flinching!" And to regain control of himself he began to use cavalry language, with as many f—s and b—s as possible. He had learned, in such cases, the high therapeutic value of these simple words.

"Those b—s," he said to himself, "would even try to back me into a corner about my flight just now through the streets. 'You acted like a rookie,' they'd tell me. 'You should have given them a taste of your pistol, but not like a paladin or Roland at Roncevaux; like a master, like someone who holds the right of life and death over them and regards them, what's more, as scum. The important thing was to get them to join the ranks. Ours, of course. The chief revolutionary virtue is the art of making others damned well respect you. Stunned by the sight of a corpse or two, they would have been in your pocket, and they'd have let you talk. You'd have told them how we are all brothers. We shall be needing a lot of beadles to say "Amen", even in France.'

"They're very good! For talk, one has to hand it to them! They have it down pat, as in a book. But you very rarely see them move from theory to practice themselves. How many of those little dark abortions, with priests' faces into the bargain, would be capable of being soldiers in the ranks they command?

"But it isn't given to everybody to command. That's their great phrase. If they aim low and see no farther than the end of their noses, they do really see the end of those noses. I'm sure they'd find this poison idea most appealing. The cholera is a windfall. It's a fine economy of means when one can take charge of ready-made terrors, drunken sprees to which God is treating the house. After all, aren't they right, if, in order to give liberty to the people, one must first become its master? Every little bit helps."

\* \*

By the middle of the night the wind had grown gentler. It had become very wily with its favours, despite some highly suspicious smells that it softly fanned up, or perhaps precisely because of these smells. The silence was so complete that Angelo could hear the ticking of the clock in the cage of the belfry a good twenty-five or thirty yards away. Alone, and at long intervals, there came the tired rustle of the great elms, in which the nightingales had fallen silent. Some latecoming stars had created on the angular, surf-like sweep of the roofs, a special glimmer. Several street lamps had gone out.

"Become their master to give them liberty," mused Angelo; "is that the only way? Is there no other goal for man except being king? As soon as passion has a free reign, everyone seeks to make himself king."

For some time, with the toe of his boot, he had been playing with something soft that lay at his feet. He struck a light and saw that it was a pile of empty sacks. Here was something to make a bed with.

"It'd be the very devil," he told himself, "if there were any danger of contagion from sacks that must have been exposed a long time to the sun. And anyhow, only the sickest will die."

He thought of the young woman who lay shrivelling in the door opening thirty feet or so below him. What a pity that she should have been one of the aforesaid "sickest". Death had carved a goddess in blue stone out of a beautiful young woman who had evidently been opulent and milky, judging by her extraordinary head of hair. He wondered what the most abandoned bigots of liberty would have done in his place, seeing that he himself had needed all his romanticism not to cry out when the glints from the candle began to gasp among these golden tresses.

"And is it really a question of liberty?" he asked himself.

* *

Angelo was awakened by a burning nausea. The white sun had just settled on his face, on his mouth. He stood up and vomited. It was merely bile. "At least I think so, it's green." He felt very hungry and very thirsty.

It was a stifling morning, like chalk or boiling white oil.

The town's skin of tiles was beginning already to exude a syrupy air. Waves of treacly heat, clinging to the ridges, drowned every shape in iridescent fleeces. The incessant squeaking of thousands of swallows lashed the torrid stillness with a hail of pepper. Thick columns of flies were smoking like coal dust from the streets' crevasses. Their continuous murmur created a kind of audible solitude.

Day did, however, place things with more precision than the night. The now visible details composed a different reality. The rotunda of the church was octagonal and resembled a huge tent pitched on red sand. It was surrounded by flying buttresses upon which past rains had painted long streaks of green. The wavy pattern of the roofs was flattened out under the uniform white light; at most, a faint network of shadows marked the differences in level between one roof and another. What, in the bosom of the night, had appeared to be towers, were simply houses higher than the rest, with five or six yards of slitless and windowless wall showing above the level of the other roofs. In addition to the belfry with the iron cage which, slightly to the left, reared its square bulk with three arcaded storeys, there was also, down below, another, smaller, flat-roofed belfry topped with a spike and, at the other end of the town, a lofty edifice crowned with an enormous wrought-iron bulb. For all that they were flattened beneath the light, the roofs kept up a play around the ridges, gutters, eaves, landmarks of streets, inner courtyards and gardens, which puffed up the grey foam of dust-laden foliage and threw out steps, landings, and projections to meet little stone walls of a dazzling whiteness, or to surround the rearing triangles of certain gables. But the swelling and thrumming of all this peeling marquetry, instead of being firmly indicated by shadows, showed only in infinite variations of blinding white and grey.

The gallery where Angelo stood faced north. He could see, in front of him, first the rows of rounded tiles, an intermingling of thousands of fans opening out in every direction; then the expanse of vague roofs diluted in the heat; finally, containing the town as though in a grey earthenware bowl, the ring of the hills grated by the sun.

There was an extraordinary smell of bird droppings, and some times a sort of explosion of a sickly-sweet stench.

Angelo, still half asleep, was trying instinctively to appease his hunger by swallowing thick saliva, when he was fully awakened by a cry so piercing that it seemed to leave a yellow streak before his eyes.

The cry was repeated. It clearly came from a place on his right, about ten yards away, where the edge of the roof broke off at the side of what must be a square.

Angelo jumped over the ledge of the gallery and advanced over the roofs. It was difficult and risky to walk up here in boots, but by clasping a chimney Angelo was able to lean over the void.

At first he could see nothing but a cluster of people. They seemed to be pecking at something, like chickens around a bowl of grain. As they trampled and jumped, the cry spurted out again, sharper and paler than ever, from under their feet. It was a man, whom they were killing by stamping his head in with their heels. Many of these executioners were women. They were emitting a sort of dull growl that came from the throat and was closely allied with lust. They paid no attention to their flying petticoats nor to their hair streaming down over their faces.

At last the thing seemed to be finished, and they drew away from the victim. It no longer moved, but lay stretched out, the arms forming a cross; from the angles that its thighs and arms made with the body, one could see that its limbs were broken. A young woman, rather well dressed (indeed she appeared to have come from Mass, for she was carrying a book in her hand) but dishevelled, went back to the corpse and planted her pointed heel in the poor wretch's head. The heel got caught between some bones; she lost her balance and fell, calling for help. They picked her up. She was weeping. They shouted insults at the corpse, with a great deal of laughter.

There were some twenty men and women there. They were moving towards the street, when the group they composed suddenly broke apart like a flock of birds when a stone is thrown. A man, from whom they had swerved away, was left alone. At first he looked dazed, then clutched his belly in both hands, then fell to the ground; he began to double up and pound the earth with his head and feet. The others were running, but, before disappearing into the street, one woman stopped, leaned against the wall, and started to vomit with amazing abundance; finally she collapsed, grinding her face into the stones.

"Die!" said Angelo, clenching histeeth. He was trembling from head to foot, his legs were giving beneath him, but he kept his eyes fixed on that man and woman who, a few steps from the mutilated corpse, were still racked with convulsions. He wanted to miss nothing of their lonely agony, which gave him a bitter pleasure.

But he was rudely forced to look to himself. His legs had ceased to support him, and even his arms, still clinging to the chimney, were beginning to loosen their grip. He felt a great chill on his neck, and the edge of the roof was only three feet away. He managed at last to lie down between two rows of tiles. Swiftly the blood returned to his head, and he recovered the use of his limbs.

He made his way back to the gallery.

"I'm a prisoner of these roofs," he told himself. "If I go down into the street, that is the fate that awaits me."

He remained for a long time in a kind of hypnotic trance. He could no longer think. The bell in the steeple struck. He counted the chimes. It was eleven o'clock.

"What about food?" he said to himself. And he began to suffer again from hunger. "And drink? Do they do things here as in Piedmont? There's always a storeroom just below the roof. That's what I have to find. And drink. Especially up here in this heat! I can, it's true, get down to the cellar of this house, but they're all dead of cholera down there. That's one indiscretion I won't commit. I've got to find a house where the people are still alive; but live ones will give me trouble. All the same, that's what I've got to do."

The grey cat he had disturbed in the drawing-room the night before put its head out of the cat-hole, slipped through, drawing its feet through the opening one after the other, and came to rub up against him, purring.

"How plump you are," he said to it, scratching it affectionately between the eyes. "What do you feed on, you? Birds? Pigeons? Rats?"

The light and heat were now intolerable. The white sky was grinding the roofs to dust. There were no longer any swallows. Only the flies, clouds of them. The sugary stench had thickened. Even this house was now exhaling a sour breath from its depths.

A hundred yards from where he was, towards the rotunda of the church, Angelo made out through the mists of the sun another, rather higher gallery, on which some linen was hung out on wires.

"Those who take the trouble to wash and dry things are alive," said Angelo to himself. "That's the place to go to. But watch out, you poor bastard; don't go getting your face bashed in."

He took off his boots. He still had to make up his mind whether to put them down and establish his headquarters here, where there were sacks to sleep on, or to set off by the grace of God across the roofs, in which case he must carry the boots with him. He found a piece of string, and that decided him. He passed the string through the straps, tied the boots together, and hung them round his neck. This left his hands free.

But the clay of the tiles, gorged with sunshine, burned like an oven-plate. It was impossible to walk on them barefoot or even in stockings. After a few steps Angelo had to beat a hasty retreat to the gallery. Finally he managed to make himself some slippers out of small, very thick sacks, into which he put his feet, tying them around his legs. He began to navigate over the rooftops. The cat followed him attentively like a dog.

It was relatively easy provided one could avoid being sickened by certain slopes that fell away towards inner courtyards, black and seductive, like well-mouths. These gulfs would appear abruptly, one could not avoid them. They lurked in funnels of shelving roofs, or concealed behind ridges. One only saw them on reaching the crest. Even from there they were, if not concealed, at least hypocritically covered over by sun vapours.

It was most unpleasant. On several occasions when Angelo, having reached the top of a gable (one of those black triangles he had seen in the night) found himself suddenly face to face with the dark pit that opened up behind it, he tottered, he even had to steady himself with his hands on the tiles and crawl off obliquely on all fours. Those depths were breathing.

But these fits of giddiness kept coming, and even when, having reached the other side of a ridge, Angelo saw nothing at the bottom of the slope but another roof rising in turn, he would let himself slide into this wave-hollow as instinctively as a sleepwalker. Yet his mind was alert, and he suffered cruelly from these lapses of physical strength. Fear gripped him by the stomach and each time he vomited a little bile.

As he neared a small tower, Angelo was abruptly enveloped in some thick black material that began to flutter, crackling and creaking. It was a pile of jackdaws that had just risen. The birds were unafraid. They spun slowly around him, keeping close and striking him with their wings. He could feel thousands of little gold eyes, if not malicious, at any rate extraordinarily cold, staring at him. He defended himself by flailing with his arms, but several beaks pecked him hard on the hands and even on the head. He succeeded in ridding himself of the birds only after a violent struggle, and he even struck down one or two of them as he swung around with his fists. As they fell they gave a moan that made the whole flock veer off behind the gable of a roof, and their claws rattled like hail on its tiles.

Other flocks of jackdaws and crows had by this time risen from the places where they were dozing, and they drifted up in ragged bands. But seeing Angelo on his feet and active, they slid away on stiffened wings, and settled once more on the roofs.

There were vast colonies of them. Grey with dust, their plumage blended with the dingy grey of the tiles and even with the pink of the sun-baked clay. They were invisible until they flew, but in all the time Angelo had been up here, this was the first occasion they had done so. Till now they had clung like black hoods to certain houses, through whose skylights, windows, and crevasses they need only pour to feed at their ease.

Angelo looked towards the gallery from which he had set out. It was very difficult to recognize places. The sun directly overhead, the reflections from the roofs, the uniform glitter of the chalk sky, filled his eyes with red moons. This expanse of roofs was not so flat as the light led one to believe. At length he recognized the place where he had slept. It was a sort of belvedere. He had not suspected this. Retreat was always possible in this direction. His sacking slippers were doing their job well. They prevented him from slipping, and he did not feel the heat of the tiles too keenly. He sat down in the shade of a chimney and recovered his breath. But he had to shut his eyes: the whole expanse had begun to turn and sway around him as though on a badly pinned axle. The cat rubbed against his arm and, raising itself up, pushed its head against his cheek. He felt its stiff little whiskers tickling the corner of his mouth.

"I'm not used to gutters, old man," he said.

He ached from hunger, but even more from thirst. It gave him no respite. He thought ceaselessly of cold water. He could not think of anything else save as a side issue and at the cost of enormous effort.

At last he reached his objective and, behind the linen hung out on wires, saw some cages containing yellow balls. They were hens.

He only realized that he had found an egg long after he had broken it and licked it up out of his hand. His mouth was full of shell, which he spat out. The white had eased his cardboard throat. He searched less feverishly in the straw of the chicken run. The hens, brooding in a corner in their midday sleep, did not cackle. He found two other eggs, and gulped them down in a more seemly fashion.

The door connecting this gallery with the rest of the house was shut, but on a simple latch that only needed raising to open it. It led on to a small landing, which was reached from below by a ladder. Below was the void of a staircase; silent.

"Have I dropped in again on the dead?" Angelo wondered. "In any case, eggs are safe." It was then that he noticed some maize freshly scattered in the hencoops. "There's someone alive here." Yet the house was completely silent.

He ventured down the ladder. He had hardly reached the bottom when a discreet mewing made him look up: it was the cat, which could not get down and was calling to him. He climbed up to fetch it.

His slippers made no sound, but they hampered him. He took them off, hid them under the ladder, and walked in his stockings.

"There may be people down here who stamp your head in with their heels," he told himself. "I must be nimble." He was not afraid. He even added: "It's the theory of the forager on active service. How often have you drummed it into thick heads on Coni? But, I'm damned if I ever thought that one day I'd go foraging with a cat!"

He was descending step by step, ears alert to the silence, when he suddenly froze. A door had just opened down below, on the first floor. Footsteps crossed the landing, then started to climb. The cat went down to meet them.

There was a startled exclamation.

"What is it?" asked a man's voice from below.

"A cat," said a boy's voice.

"What do you mean, a cat?"

"A cat."

"What's it like?"

"Grey."

"Chase it away."

"Don't touch it," said a woman's voice. "Come down. Come. Come. Come down. Don't touch it. Come."

All these voices were strained and fearful. The footsteps went down the stairs and hurried across the landing. The door was shut.

The cat came up again.

"Bravo!" said Angelo.

He breathed again. He climbed back to the foot of the ladder and sat down on the bottom rungs.

"Frightened people are the most terrible adversaries I know," he said to himself, "even if they don't dare touch me, and they won't, they'll go running outside and rouse the whole neighbourhood." He saw himself being pursued across the roofs, and it was not a pleasant prospect.

He waited for a long while. There was no further sound.

At last he said to himself: "I can't stay here forever. They're afraid of their own shadows; I'm thirsty. Let's get going. And if sparks fly, well! sparks will have to fly. I'm a big enough boy to take care of the whole damned town, if it's just a question of not losing face before that damned policeman who is so embarrassing with his kitchen garden."

Nevertheless, he began to descend with caution. Reaching the second floor he even paused prudently before going to listen at the three doors. Nothing. He looked through a keyhole. Nothing: blackness. Another keyhole: something light, but what? A white wall? Yes: he could make out a nail on the wall. What could there be in this room? Was it the storeroom? He went and listened over the stairwell. Below on the first floor, complete silence. Good. He boldly turned the handle. The door opened.

It was a box-room. Old junk, as in the other house. In the third room, more junk: barrel hoops, broom handles, baskets; a touching portrait of an old lady lying on the floor and ripped by shoe nails. Selfish people.

"Better go back to the dark room. That must be the one." No. Empty.

Selfish, and they must have raked everything in around them and piled it all up in the room they're in. There were some bare shelves, and by the light of his tinder Angelo saw that the wood still bore traces of pots that had been there at one time and were not there now.

There's nothing to do but go down there.

But first he took an esparto basket. If he found anything, he could put it in that.

On the first floor, two large doors. Not at all like those in the other house: less imposing. This was no house for pianos and bull's-horn moustaches; it denoted the well-to-do but unpretentious peasant: everything was shut. "Here they're in no danger of dying in doorways; they'll die in a heap, like dogs over poisoned soup. If they die."

Standing on the bottom step, one foot in the air, Angelo looked and listened. The people must be behind the farthest door. One could tell from the fingermarks on the door and the worn-down threshold. From their fear of the cat and the shoe nails on the old lady's portrait, it was a sure bet that this was the kitchen. People like that would only feel safe in a kitchen.

Better see. Angelo put his eye to the keyhole: black and a white strip forming a cornice above the black. A white strip of cloth, a white strip above which there are pots. It's the mantelpiece. The black is the fireplace.

Angelo suddenly started back: a face had just passed. No. It was simply the face of someone seated who had leaned forward and was staying in that position, the arms resting on the thighs, the hands clasped together. The person was rubbing them. It was a man. With a beard. He lowered his head.

"What about the cloud?" said a woman's voice.

"Which one?" said the man, not raising his head, but ceasing to rub his hands.

"The one shaped like a horse."

"I don't know," said the man.

He began to rub his hands again.

"It came over the rue Chacundier, and yesterday the carts loaded up there all afternoon."

The man was rubbing his hands.

"I saw it," said the woman's voice.

"What?" said the man.

He stopped rubbing his hands.

"The comet."

"When?" said the man. And he raised his head.

"Last night."

"Where?"

"There."

The man raised his head a little higher and looked towards the light. Something fell off a table.

"Do be careful!" said the woman. She had given a sort of low cry. A smell of leeks, garlic, tisane, came through the keyhole.

"Let's go farther down," thought Angelo. "If there's a larder, they've surely placed it as low as possible. Perhaps even underground."

It was down below but still above ground, in a shed where there were also stacks of faggots and split logs. A little daylight from the street penetrated underneath the door. Bottles. Angelo made straight for them. They were bottles of tomato ketchup. He took three of them. More bottles. A yellow liquid. A label he couldn't read. He put one of these bottles into the basket. "I'll see upstairs." Now for some wine: corks sealed with red wax. He took a pot of lard, two pots of what was probably jam. A ham? No, but two sausages and ten goat-cheeses, dry, hard, no bigger than écu pieces. No bread.

He hastily climbed back to the gallery. As he set foot on the ladder a little stifled mew called to him. He stuffed the sacks that had served him as slippers into the basket and took the cat under his arm.

On the roofs the heat was like a wall, into which one was immediately mortared with quicklime. He must get away from here as quickly as possible. People were bound to come to feed the chickens and collect the eggs. He would have to find some place to live up above. Out of the question to return to the old gallery. It was clearly contaminated. If one has to pick up embers with one's hands, well and good, but why play with the fire?

The simplest thing to do was to take shelter against the rotunda of the church. No risks there. The flying buttresses offered shade; they formed a sort of arbour over a small flat space.

It was in fact a real arbour, with a flat space covered with zinc. Despite his pressing thirst, Angelo waited to reach it before drinking. He was worried about trapdoors and giddiness. Hampered by his boots, his sacking slippers, his esparto basket, which kept one of his hands employed, he was extremely clumsy. He was sweating and icy. He had to open a sealed wine-bottle by hitting its neck with the barrel of his pistol. But the wine was good, with a strong flavour of grape. When he had made a meal out of two cheeses and a good slab of lard, and finished the wine, Angelo began to view things with greater confidence. The sun was playing its terrible mid-afternoon game. The cat was washing itself, slowly passing its paw behind its ears. Where the buttresses leaned against the wall, there were swallows' nests containing black, homely birds that kept charmingly twisting their heads with their yellow eyes. Near Angelo, as he sat on the sacks, a white church window yielded a scent of incense through its lead joints.

Angelo now looked down upon the side of the town that he had been unable to see from his old gallery. It covered less ground than the other side. The dovetailing of the roofs came to an end against the battlements of a gate and the reddish masses of some great elms. In the other direction Angelo had an excellent view, below him, of the whole square in front of the church and, in enfilade, two streets that ran into it. The square was deserted except for four or five blackish heaps that he took at first for large slumbering dogs, since he saw them through the sparse foliage of some small plane trees. One of these dogs unrolled as if to stretch, and Angelo realized that it was a man convulsed in his death agony. Soon indeed the dying man stretched out, his face in the dust, and moved no more. Angelo could not find the least sign of life in the others. As his eyes became used to the dappled brightness under the trees, he made out other corpses. Some were stretched out on the pavement, others crouched in the recesses of doorways; still others, who had collapsed against the edge of the fountain, seemed to be bathing their hands in the water of the basin, and they were resting on its rim black faces that bit the stone. There were a good twenty of them. All around the square the houses were bolted, from their doors and ground-floor shutters to their roofs. One could hear distinctly, in the silence, the deep rumble of flies and the fountain spurting into its basin.

A funeral drum began to roll slowly but violently at the far end of one of those streets running into the square. It was the tumbrel rolling over the cobbles. A man dressed in a long white shirt was leading the horse by the bridle. Two more men in white walked by the wheels. They stopped in front of a house. The men in white came out again almost at once carrying a corpse, which they hoisted over the rails. They returned three times into this house. The third time they brought out the corpse of a huge woman, which gave them considerable trouble; finally she too went over the rails, revealing enormous white thighs.

In the square, the men picked up the dead. Then the tumbrel rolled its drum through the side streets for a long while, with halts and then more drum-rolls and halts. Suddenly Angelo realized that he no longer heard it. There remained only the exasperated buzzing of the flies and the sound of the fountain.

Long after the noise of flies had settled to a protracted lullabye, some footsteps passed below. It was a group of people arriving by one of the streets that Angelo could see in enfilade. There were about ten women in groups, preceded by one of those men in white shirts. The women were carrying pails, but they huddled so close together that the metal clanked as they moved, like a knight's armour. Angelo decided that they were the women from some part of town being taken to the water of a fountain thought to be safe. In any case, they ignored the fountain in the square, but as they were about to enter the street from which the tumbrel had come, they began to shriek and crowd together so frantically that they resembled a bunch of rats. They raised their arms in the air, pointing and yelling, and Angelo heard them shout: "The cloud! The cloud!" Others screamed: "The comet! The comet!" or "The horse! The horse!" Angelo looked in the direction they were pointing. There was nothing but the white sky and the infinite scattering of the monstrous chalk of the sun. Finally they scattered in all directions, still screaming, and the man ran after them calling: "Rose! Rose! Rose!"

Again Angelo heard from below the fountain and the flies, then the creak of a shutter. In the façade of a house on the square a shutter half opened, a head appeared and looked all around the sky. Then it withdrew with the rapidity of a tortoise's head, and the shutter again closed.

The fountain. The flies. The tinkling bell of a sporting dog. It made a tour of the square and spent a long time bounding in and out of the surrounding alleys.

Angelo was listening so intently for the slightest sound that he heard a tiny footstep. It was a little girl. She emerged from one of the streets. She walked slowly, peacefully, swinging her arms like an idle grown-up. She disturbed neither the fountain nor the flies. She went by, sauntering in her little collared frock.

Some dogs passed. They raised their muzzles towards the houses, their noses twitching. Suddenly they cowered, as under the threat of a blow, and galloped off yelping. One of them sat down at the corner of the square and, after stretching out its neck four or five times as if to sniff the sky, began a long-drawn-out howling.

The heat spluttered on the tiles. The sun had no longer any body; it was rubbed like blinding clay over the whole sky; the hills were so white that there was now no horizon.

Blows rang out both in the square and just below Angelo. They resounded even in the window by his side. Someone was beating steadily on the door of the church. At length it stopped, and a voice cried three times: "Holy Virgin! Holy Virgin! Holy Virgin!" It was impossible to tell whether it was a man's voice or a woman's.

Angelo uncorked another bottle of wine. He told himself it would be wiser to eat that raw tomato ketchup, it would refresh him more, but he had an idea that wisdom was no longer of much use. It was pointless to make oneself miserable for the sake of wisdom. A little vacuum in the soul remains the best thing in critical moments, whatever they may say. Reason and logic are all right for normal times. In normal times, without question, they do wonders. When the horse runs away, it's quite another thing. What disgusted him most was that little girl in her collared frock and long embroidered pantaloons. She had swaggered along like a lady. And that, really, was enough to make one sick. If she had run, or cried out, or wept with her fists pressed into her eyes, there would have been nothing to prevent one taking that in along with everything else; but it was impossible to stomach those tranquil little steps and the slight haughtiness with which she strolled. She could have only just touched the pavement with the tips of her toes. And coming back to reason (for old tools fit quite naturally and easily into the callused hand accustomed to using them), isn't it absolutely reasonable to put one's trust in a vacuum in the soul? In which all is serene; especially the impossible, since in really critical moments, the impossible is exactly what one needs. Naturally, I don't call a duel with Baron Swartz a critical moment, really critical. That certainly demands reason, logic, and all kinds of prudence and self-control. But I'm as cold as ice by nature; no need to cool me down. It's absurd for anyone to doubt that. I don't even call the death of the little Frenchman a critical moment. I call these moments difficult moments. Difficult: like over-hot soup. No use appealing to the vacuum in the soul if one's merely burning one's gizzard. But if you hear someone pounding and kicking at a closed church door and crying: "Holy Virgin! Holy Virgin! Holy Virgin!" what'll you do with reason and logic when the first "Holy Virgin!" already fills your stomach beyond its capacity, and the second picks up your stomach the way a hand picks up a sack by the bottom and tips it over, and the third comes on top of the others with aloes, bitterness not to be borne, reasons for chucking everything?

Here on the rooftops I'm like a Battista Cannesqui (though it was in fact a grain-pit he was hiding in before they dragged him through the streets), or like a Nicola Piccinino on the roofs of Florence; a Simonetta Malatesti; a Neri de Gino Capponi.[4] There have been many adventures on the roofs of southern cities. Not to mention the Romeos, the Paolos of Rimini, and the garret windows through which they slipped in full armour, and they landed on the roofs in their iron shoes like kitchen pots falling off the hooks. Where is my beloved's bedroom? I am not the lark! Scraping the narrow corridors with their bulky battle-plate; busy preparing revolutions in cities or in women. All I do is filch some wine and goat's cheese.

And lucky at that. For I'm not in a difficult moment, oh! not at all; there's nothing difficult about it. I'm in a critical moment; that's not the same thing. There's absolutely no connection. All that can happen on the roofs of a town – the Gino Capponis, Malatestas, Bentivoglios, passing halberds or sabres through garret windows, with legs clad in steel, breasts of steel, arms of steel; or, for that matter, velvets and scents, depending on whether the aim is to incite revolt in the heart of the city or the heart of a bed – all this is a matter of law. But a little girl who takes a walk through everything down there like a reasonable person, or those blows struck at four o'clock in the afternoon on the door of a church and that "Holy Virgin! Holy Virgin! Holy Virgin!" (as if she were expected to lean out of the window and say: "Yes, what is it? I'm here"). What can you make of it? It's nothing you can settle in an ordinary way; it has no law, it does what it likes. And that's where there are really many more resources in a vacuum in the soul than in reason. What good is reason at these times? Except, in just such cases, to lose the little life that's left to us? Much good it does corpses if, before dying, they've reasoned well. That's a fine diploma to pin on their bellies right now. "He reasoned well." "And that got him a long way," cries the corpse in reply, rotting on the cobbles till it is hoisted over the rails on to the cart. They really seem to be saying, as they are tossed into the cart: "We made out well with our reasoning, didn't we?"

At this moment how many human beings are there, by the *force of things*, halfway between life and death? I mean beings, all of whose affections, all of whose love, have gone over to the other side. Human beings who have been left alone, while all that they loved, all that they hated has been carried off by the stream. They have nothing but their lonely selves on this side; if they love or hate at all, it's the dead. (For the time being, but that's the time that counts.) If they love or hate at this moment, they have to love or hate people who are dead. They've nothing left to love or hate on this side. They are forced to look in both directions. But mostly to the other side, to try to see again those who have borne off with them their love or their hate. Maybe that's what they call a comet. Perhaps they see them, rolled into balls and hurtling by, leaving behind them a glittering trail of love or hate that tends to suck them in behind it. Or else it's a horse: love's gallop through the gorges. And when I say "love" I mean also and especially hate, for it's a much stronger feeling because of its unquestionable sincerity. Thus there is some for everybody. Anybody can be sucked up in the hissing of a storm or carried off at a gallop. So they cling to tussocks; a little prancing walk to set the collared frock nicely ballooning (it was a Sunday frock, but who can still count on Sunday, even on one more Sunday? And one has to hurry to play the lady, for can anyone tell what tomorrow will bring?). He felt an irresistible desire to vomit, because of this unaccustomed bitterness. In normal times, a child of six is usually at her A B C's. She was still too young to knock at church doors as though at the door of a mill. This desire to vomit was also provoked, one may suppose, by the burning, syrupy air, which smelled of clay, sourness, and sugar. Angelo made a little cushion of the sacks; he lay down on the burning zinc and closed his eyes.

His eyes had been shut for an uncertain length of time when he felt himself being slapped by downy little paws, struck painfully around the temples, and claws raking through his hair as if someone were trying to plough it up.

He was covered with swallows, which were pecking at him.

He sprang up so violently that he nearly rolled off beyond the buttresses on to the steeply sloping roofs. Badly shaken, he slapped himself and ran his hands through his hair.

"They thought I was dead," he said to himself. "Those cosy little creatures that were watching me with their lovely yellow eyes were trying to eat me."

He recovered his spirits but suddenly wanted very much to smoke. He rummaged in his pockets and was very put out to find that he had not a single cigar left. "And I haven't smoked at all since I fired that ridiculous pistol shot in the air before the barricade. I really must be in a critical moment. I'd be sure to think of smoking at the moment of a charge, although the chance to test that kind of cool-headedness hasn't yet presented itself. But didn't I smoke a cigar while I was killing the Baron with all the etiquette I've been so blamed for? So, if I want to smoke, it's a good sign. My kingdom for a cigar!"

He continued to make fun of himself, but the attack of the swallows, so instinctively cruel, continued to prey on his mind.

He spent a very bad night. There were only faint puffs of wind, a torrid and stinking wind. He dreamed that he was sleeping beside one of his sergeants, who kept breathing into his face from a foul stomachful of leeks. He kept trying to push him away, but the other naturally grew to such an extent that his breath bent enormous Piedmontese chestnut trees.

He had another dream, in which there appeared a cockerel: it was clearly no ordinary cockerel. It had chalk-white plumage; although, looking at it closely, one could see glints of sulphur on its comb and crop. In any case, it was gigantic, and left only a tiny thumbnail strip of sky visible behind it. This creature rolled about in the atmosphere, spreading a foul stench. It spread its rump feathers, and its intention was plainly to brood on Angelo's face. Fortunately, the huge seed dish, in the zinc lining of which Angelo lay, overturned, and the enormous rump with its white feathers spread in the sun was unable to sit down right on his face. Unfortunately, Angelo was stifled all the same, with his nostrils full of down. Fortunately, by pressing his face sideways close to the ground, he could still breathe, level with the soil, a little air, which, unfortunately, smelled of dung. Then Angelo began scratching the ground to dig himself a little hollow under his nose. But his fingers sank into excrement moulded into the shape of a little girl's face.

He woke up.

An appalling smell of cooking was drifting by in the night, under pink, flickering lights. Angelo went all around the rotunda. Three pyres had been lit in the hills to the north, and waves of greasy smoke were being flung back on to the town by the twitching of the wind.

Angelo rubbed his eyes with his fists for a long time. He returned to his place and sat down. He must have fought violently in his sleep; the basket was upset, and he couldn't find his boots. He rummaged once more for a cigar. The smell of the smoke filled his mouth with a nauseating clamminess.

He had many other dreams, though kept half awake by a constant desire to vomit. He saw, in particular, a comet; it was breathing out poison in glittering jets, like a pin wheel. He could hear the velvet drumming of the deadly rain it threw off; it streamed across the roofs, through the garret windows, flooding the lofts, flowing down the stairs, slipping under doors, invading the rooms where people, seated on chairs as adhesive as sticks of glue, began to scream and then to rot.

The first gleams of daylight brought him great relief. There, once more, was the white and already heavy dawn, but for all its hopeless colour it put things back in place, in a familiar order.

Long before the sun rose, a little bell began to ring in the hills. In that direction, on a pine-crowned eminence, there was a hermitage that looked like a little bone. The light, still relatively clear, permitted a view of a track winding up to it through a forest of grey almond trees.

The small church window began to transmit, by the shaking of its panes in their round lead frames, the agitation going on in the depths of the church. The tall doors, pounded at in vain the day before, opened. Angelo saw some children in white, bearing banners, line up in the square. The doors of the houses began to pour out women in black like ants. Others came filing down the streets that he could see. In a short while, there must have been, all told, about fifty, including three waiting priests in golden carapaces. The procession moved off in silence. The bell tolled slowly for a long time. At length the white banners appeared under the grey almond trees, then the carapaces, still golden despite the distance, then the black ants. But while all these tiny insects were slowly climbing the knoll, the sun leapt up. It seized the sky and turned the world into a crumbling avalanche of plaster, chalk, and flour, which it began to knead with its long colourless rays. Everything disappeared in this dazzling storm of whiteness. There remained only the bell, which continued to toll in great hiccups; then it fell silent.

This day was marked by a terrible recrudescence of dying.

Towards the end of the morning, in that part of the town which Angelo overlooked, there were murmurs, then piercing cries, which first broke out in separate places, and then burst forth on all sides. The shutters of one of the houses in the square flew open with a clatter, and there appeared the head and gesticulating arms of a man. This man uttered no cry; he seemed merely to be trying to cram both fists one after the other into his mouth as if he had a fishbone in his throat. All the while he kept jigging from side to side of his open window like a puppet in a Punch and Judy show. Finally, he toppled back and disappeared. His window remained open. The innumerable swallows, which had resumed their twittering merry-go-round, began to approach. The cries were at first those of women, then there were some from men. These last were extremely tragic. It was as if they were blown on buffalo horns. Contrary to what one might have thought, it wasn't the dying who cried out so on every side, but the living. Several of these panic-stricken creatures crossed the square.

They appeared to be seeking help, for some ran towards one another and even embraced, then pushed one another away and began to run again. One man fell and died quite quickly. The clatter of tumbrels became audible on all sides. It was ceaseless, and the clock struck noon, then one, two, three o'clock; it continued without stopping, rolling its drum over the cobbles of all the streets. A reddish smoke coming from the hills to the north soiled the sky.

A strange event took place under Angelo's very eyes. Some of the tumbrels passed through the square. Emerging from a street alongside the church they were just reaching the corner under Angelo's perch and so clearly in view that their whole load of corpses was visible. It was there that one of the tumbrels stopped; the man in white leading the horse had suddenly crumpled up. This man was writhing about on the ground, getting entangled in the sort of white blouse he wore, and his two companions were watching him from a distance, when one of these two companions himself crumpled up, uttering a single, but very piercing cry. The third was preparing to run away and was already tucking up his blouse, when he seemed to stumble over an obstacle that mowed his legs from under him, and spread flat, face to the ground, beside the other two. The horse flicked away the flies with its tail.

This planned attack of death, the lightning victory, the proximity of the field of battle right below his eyes, impressed Angelo deeply. He could not take his eyes off the three men in white. He still hoped that they would rise again, after a moment's rest, and go about their task. But they remained quietly stretched out, and apart from one who twitched his legs convulsively as if he were kicking, they did not stir.

The traffic of the other tumbrels continued in the streets and alleys round about. The cries of women, strident or moaning, the men's piercing calls for help, kept breaking out from one direction or another. They received no answer but the rolling of the tumbrels on the cobbles.

Finally, one of these, which had been jolting along the neighbouring streets, arrived in the square. The men in white came up to their prone comrades and turned them over with their feet. They loaded them into the tumbrel and, taking the horse by the bridle, led it away.

A dense swarm of flies was buzzing over the place where the load of corpses had been standing full in the sun. Some juices had dripped from it that they didn't wish to lose.

"I mustn't stay here," Angelo told himself. "It's a hotbed of the plague. The exhalations are rising. This square is a crossroads. And anyhow, wasn't it already strewn with dead? I must get out. There must be, in this town, some quarters less hard hit, or else it's a matter of three or four days and there'll be no one left. Except me up here. And is even that likely?"

He started to wander over the roofs. He no longer paid the least attention to the gulfs that the inner courtyards suddenly opened up before him. He was busy with a different giddiness. He even went off calmly to recover his boots from the rather steep slope of a roof where he had rolled them in the night during his struggles in his dreams.

It didn't take long to go round the roofs over which he could walk. To the west, the square prevented him from going any farther. To the east, a fairly wide street barred his way; to the south, another street, not only wide but bordered with very steep roofs; to the north, a narrow street. He wondered if he wouldn't do better to go down firmly to the streets by some inside staircase. "And what then?" he asked himself. "Even admitting that the lunatics who chased me have now other fish to fry, which isn't certain, I shall be completely in the soup." He had the impression that, below him, the town was one great putrescence. "The thing is simply to get out of this quarter somehow."

He was sauntering over the roofs exactly as though on terra firma. He would have been greatly astonished had he been told he had exactly the same heedless, indifferent gait as the little girl in the collared frock. The belfry, the rotunda, the little walls, the undulation of the roofs around him were no more than the trees, groves, hedges, and hillocks of a new country; the gloomy openings of the inner courtyards were mere puddles to be skirted; the streets, streams at whose brink one had to stop.

It was not a farcical dream, it was a most bitter mystery with no way of escape. There was no getting around that, nothing to do but make the best of it and put off cunning for a later time when this new world should have started up a fresh set of instincts. When the boundaries between the real and the unreal disappear and one can pass freely from the one to the other, one's first feeling, unexpectedly, is that the prison has contracted.

He was gazing at a massed network of roofs and walls when he saw, framed in a garret window, a human face with the broad black smear of a wide-open mouth. Before grasping its reality, he heard a piercing cry. He quickly threw himself behind a big chimney.

He was two or three yards from the window and well concealed. He heard several anguished voices saying:"She's seen the plague, she's seen the plague!" The same voice that had cried out continued to moan: "He's there, he's coming, he's on us." Feet stamped across a floor, then a man's voice asked rather more firmly: "Where? Where is he? Where did you see him?"

Through a chink between two bricks, Angelo could see the window. There emerged from it an outstretched arm and a finger pointing up into the sky. "Up there! Lord! A man with a great beard." Then the cries began again, and Angelo heard the sound of galloping on stairs.

He waited a long while before emerging from behind his chimney. He slipped off behind some high roof ridges and gained the shelter of his flying buttresses.

Evening fell. He was more determined than ever to reach another block of roofs.

The alley to the north was really very narrow: three yards wide at the most; and at one place where the eaves jutted the gap seemed even narrower. With a plank, or better with a ladder slid across it, it would be easy to pass over. He remembered the ladder joining the gallery to the top floor in the house where he had taken the food. He took advantage of the remaining daylight to go and see if he could remove it without making any noise. It was not fixed, and when he tried to pull it towards him to see if it were not too heavy, it was so far from being so that he was able to drag it up to the floor of the gallery without a sound. There remained the question of whether it was long enough. It seemed to be. He carried it to the rotunda.

He slept very well, dreamlessly, after eating some tomato ketchup and a little lard. He awoke at the precise moment when the night, still very dark, was slowly tearing itself apart in the east. He felt hale and hearty. He assembled his equipment.

Sliding the ladder across the void proved easier than he had expected, on account of the narrowness of the place he had picked and the lightness of the ladder. He realized, too, that this very first break of dawn was the ideal moment for crossing. The alley below him was still so dark that he couldn't see its abyss. The only difficulty was to cross it with the esparto basket, which still contained two bottles of ketchup, the pot of lard, two pots of jam, the bottle of yellow liquid whose label he had been unable to read, the sausages, and two bottles of wine. As for the boots, he had again strung them round his neck, and that worked well; but the rest was more tricky, and he was determined to have both hands free. Finally, there was no way and time was passing. "I'll leave the basket on this side," he told himself. "If I can't find anything to eat on the other side, which seems to me very unlikely, the worst that can happen is having to return to this side to eat. But I don't believe it. The most important thing is not to fall."

He got down on all fours and went across without flinching. He drew the ladder after him and hid it behind the roof ridge. He lay down beside it and waited for sunrise. He noticed with astonishment that he was very glad of the heat of the tiles warming his back. He had gone through all the motions dictated by his resolution, but was ice-cold from head to foot.

"What's happened to the cat?" he wondered. He realized he hadn't seen it since yesterday morning. He thought as well that he might have put a sausage in his pocket before crossing. The truth was, food wasn't the main thing. On the other hand, he missed the cat badly until the sun was up.

In the moment of calm that he spent lying there on the warm tiles, he realized that since yesterday the noise of the tumbrels had been continuous. He had been too preoccupied by his plan to hear them. Now he heard their drumming anew.

His rooftop domain turned out to be much larger than the previous one. The streets bounding it were far removed from one another. It was a mass of houses so compact that it had had to be ventilated by various courtyards and even by inner gardens; some of these gardens even had trees. These courts and gardens were shut in on all sides: he could therefore go round them. They all belonged to well-to-do

123

houses. Angelo kept a close lookout for signs of life inside these houses through the big windows giving on the gardens, but despite the clear glass panes through which he could see chairs and carpets, nothing was stirring behind them. At one moment he was close enough to a kitchen window to get a distinct view of the mantelpiece, cleared of all its pots. Those people were not dead; they had gone.

"There's the excuse for all revolutions," he thought, "and even for the way I was manhandled the other evening. You're a fat-head," he added, "these people haven't died here, but who's to say they haven't died somewhere else? There's the whole difference. This is the thought of a leader of men." He was very proud of it. "If I wanted, I could go and loll in their chairs, but I'll leave that to others! I don't believe the plague's a bearded man, but I'm quite sure it's a little animal, much smaller than a fly and perfectly capable of inhabiting a chair cover or the web of a tapestry. The rooftops haven't done me badly up to now, let's stay there. In any case, this looks poor in victuals to me."

The houses of this quarter had no galleries, and Angelo searched further in vain in all directions for flat places where he could sleep. No places even where he could get into the shade, as he had under the rotunda's buttresses. The sun was even whiter than usual, the reflection from the polished tiles was as burning as its direct rays.

He nevertheless had the pleasure of seeing the cat appear. He never knew how the animal had managed to rejoin him. Perhaps it had jumped? In any case, from then on it remained at Angelo's heels like a dog, and took advantage of each time he stopped to rub against his legs. It went all around the domain with him, and when Angelo sat down at the foot of a low wall in a bit of shade, the cat jumped on to his knees and made a great show of affection in its fashion.

From the direction of the church square the traffic of the tumbrels continued. From time to time cries, appeals that echoed long in vain, and groans, rose up from the depths of the streets.

In the low wall against which Angelo was leaning his back there opened a rectangular garret window, through which, after a time, the cat jumped. As it did not return, Angelo called it, then inserted his head and shoulders into the window. It gave on to a spacious attic full of miscellaneous objects, the sight of which brought his soul a deep feeling of peace. Angelo immediately tried to climb in, but the opening was too narrow. After another look at the raw glare of the rooftops, at the pale hills on which the pyres had just been fed and were beginning to send up enormous, twisting columns of greasy smoke, Angelo felt an irresistible desire for another sight of that yellow, translucent attic, guardian of old bits of stuff, polished wooden clubs, fleur-de-lis fire irons, parasols, skirts on wicker dummies, old hoods of shot taffeta, bookbindings, odd drawers, mother-of-pearl garlands, bouquets of orange blossom, fruits of an elegant and easy life laid to rest in honey. The bodices, dresses, tuckers, bonnets, gloves, jackets, box coats, top hats, stocks, of three generations, hanging from pegs, festooned the walls. Tiny high-heeled shoes of satin, leather, velvet, slippers with silk tassels, hunting-boots, stood upon low pieces of furniture, not in the absurd rows of tidy footwear, but as if the feet had just left them; better still, as though shadowy feet still wore them; almost as though shadowy bodies were still weighing upon them. Lastly, laid flat on the marble top of a chest, a sword in its scabbard. A cavalry sword with its gold sword-knot: all this brought caresses as soothing to the heart as the caresses of the cat. Indeed, the cat was there, lying on an old quilt, and it called to Angelo, cooing like a dove, smooth and melancholy, like the very voice of the vanished world.

Angelo was clinging to the window like a prisoner to the window of his cell.

A scent of long slumbers, of bodies grown old in peace, of tender hearts, of incorruptible youth, of blue passion and of violet-water came from the fair loft.

The bonfires were rolling down upon the town a heavy smoke that tasted of wool fat and cheap candle grease, but made him hungry. Angelo thought of the esparto basket he had left on the other side of the street. With some *victuals* (as they say), if he could squeeze through the narrow window, he could live in there indefinitely.

He wandered over the roofs till noon without being able to take his mind off a need for gentleness.

"Here's a strange and very ill-timed need," he said to himself. "Things are clear and it's no good beating about the bush. Far from believing the danger comes from a bearded man or from clouds – even clouds shaped like horses – or from the comet even if you too dreamed about it, you know it's simply a question of little creatures smaller than flies, which give people cholera. Not to speak of lunatics who smash in the heads of those who touch the fountains. That's your concern. I can't see why that should have anything to do with the old bodices and satin slippers. Only the sabre, if you reason coolly, might be of some use to you, but a few rounds for your pistol would settle things much better. And if you did think of the sabre, it was only from a taste for flourishes and panache, because you can handle one marvellously, because your old trade comes back into your wrists – in a word, because you'll never be able to cure yourself of those swashbuckling habits that have already made you look a fool often enough. Not to mention the famous duel, which you could easily have avoided by slipping a louis to a professional assassin. Nothing's sillier than generosity, when generosity goes to the length of lodging in politeness and a feeling for the fitness of things. It's lucky you've no taste for love, as that poor Anna Cleves said; otherwise, heaven help you! But revolutions and cholera can also take you in, like women, if you're not clever! Everything belongs to the clever; they're the masters of the world. Could you be timid, by any chance? I must admit I adore those clothes hanging on the walls, over there. They're all exquisitely made. They've belonged to sensitive beings. Yes, I could live indefinitely in this attic."

But the smoke from the pyres enfolded him with its taste of tallow, and as he pronounced to himself the word "live" he thought of the esparto basket.

He moved on to the roofs of a long house suggesting a barrack. The buildings were disposed in squares round an extremely well kept garden. On the other side of the garden Angelo saw part of a façade pierced by large, regular, barred windows, towards which rose the foliage of laurel and fig trees. The terraces below were alive with what looked like mice. By sliding forward on to the point of a dormer, Angelo could see that they were nuns, bustling slowly about cases, bundles, and trunks, which they were tying up, setting a whole chessboard of black robes and white coifs rustling. The work was supervised by a figure as white as marble and smaller than life-size, who stood motionless beneath a bower of oleanders. For a moment Angelo was afraid he would be seen by this commander, whose immobility and composure were impressive. Then he perceived that it was the statue of a saint.

He had only to climb back to the top of the roofs to hear the ceaseless traffic of the tumbrels, a muffled clamour full of groans, and the sound, like fine rain, made by the smoke from the pyres brushing the tiles.

Angelo went back to sit by the window of the attic. For several hours he breathed it in every now and then, the way one smells a flower. He put his head through the opening, he gazed at the bodices, the dresses, the little shoes, the boots, the sabre; he savoured the perfume of souls he imagined to be sublime.

"I'm not generally considered frivolous," he said to himself. "How many times haven't they reproached me for my lack of taste for pleasure? And I certainly made that poor Anna Cleves unhappy with my coldness, although really she asked very little of me, to judge from the way the young officers who went to the same fencing-school as I in Aix-en-Provence carried on with the ladies. She'd never believe me capable of creating a being who puts on these shoes, wears these dresses, carries this parasol in her hand, draws this mauve faille hood over her head and walks in this attic (which is moreover a park, a château, an estate, a country complete with parliament), and who is bringing me at this present moment the greatest pleasure I could have (indeed the only one), merely at seeing her walk."

He went back to sit by the little wall. Again he saw the black smoke riding in the chalky sky. He heard the tumbrels rolling over the cobbles, stopping, starting again, stopping, starting again, indefatigably going their rounds through the streets. He listened to the great silence relentlessly pressing down around the noise of the tumbrels, around groans and cries for help.

At length he tried to squeeze through the window. He only managed to wedge his shoulders and scrape his arms. But suddenly he thought of the attitude one adopts when giving a thrust according to the rules, the right arm stretched out, head flat against the right shoulder, left arm straight down the thigh, left shoulder drawn back.

"It's a regulation thrust that's needed here," he told himself. "If I can hold myself that way, I bet I can get through."

127

He tried, and would have succeeded but for the pistols bulging his pockets. He stuffed the pistols into his boots and lowered the boots into the attic. The window, inside, stood about four and a half feet from the floor. He reached down as far as possible, but had to let his boots fall all the same, with no hope of being able to recover them if he failed to get through.

"You've burned your bridges," he thought; "now you must go ahead. If you stay here without boots and pistols, you're just a yokel."

In spite of his thinness and the perfection of his duelling position, he remained stuck, luckily at the hips. By wriggling like a worm and pushing with his right hand, he managed to wrench himself free and roll down inside, where he made a considerable noise falling on the wooden floor.

"Madonna!" he said, picking himself up, "grant that the people here are dead!"

He remained a long while on the alert, but nothing stirred.

The attic was even more enchanting than it had appeared. The far end, invisible from the window and lit by a few glass tiles scattered about the roof, now struck by the setting sun, was bathed in an almost opaque syrup of light. Objects emerged only in fragmentary shapes that no longer bore any connection with their true meaning. That gracefully curved chest of drawers was now just a belly covered with a plum-coloured silk waistcoat; a tiny headless Dresden figure that must have started life as an angelic musician, had become, through the enlargement of the sweeping shadows, through the keen sparkle the light gave to the break at its neck, a sort of South Sea island bird: a Creole girl's or a pirate's cockatoo. The dresses and coats were really at a party. The shoes showed beneath fringes of light as though peeping from under a curtain, and the shadowy people whose presence they thus betrayed were standing not on a floor but on the tiered perches of a vast bird cage. The rays of the sun, darting in glittering linear constellations of dust, brought these strange beings to life in triangular worlds, and the perceptible descent of the setting sun, slowly shifting the circles of light, filled them with movement stretching indefinitely as though in the tepid water of an aquarium. The cat came to greet Angelo, stretched itself too, opened its mouth wide, and gave an inaudible mew.

"A grand camping-ground," thought Angelo. "Only the victual-ling's a bit shaky; but when it's dark I'll go and explore the depths. Anyhow, here I'm in clover."

And he lay down on an old divan.

He woke up. It was night.

"*En route!*" he said to himself. "Now I really must have something to get my teeth into."

The depths, seen from the little landing outside the attic door, were terribly dark. Angelo lit his tinder. He blew on the wick, saw the top of the banister in the pink glow, and began to descend slowly, accustoming his feet gradually to the rhythm of the steps.

He came to another landing. This seemed to be the third floor, judging from the echo down the stairwell, in which the least slither had its shadow. He blew on the wick. As he had supposed, the space around him was extensive. Here, three doors, but all three shut. Too late to force the locks. He would see tomorrow. He must go down further. His feet recognized the feel of marble steps.

Second floor: three doors, also shut; but these were unquestionably bedroom doors: their panels were adorned with round bosses and quiver-and-ribbon motifs. These people had surely gone. The quivers and ribbons were not the attributes of people who allow their corpses to be piled into tumbrels. Indeed, the chances were they had swept the kitchen clean, or rather had it swept clean, to the smallest recesses of its cupboards. He must look lower down. Perhaps even as far as the cellar.

From this point the stairs were carpeted. Something slid between Angelo's legs. It must be the cat. There were twenty-three steps between the attic and the third floor; twenty-three between the third and second. Angelo was on the twenty-first step between the second and the first when, opposite him, a sudden streak of gold framed a door, which opened. It was a very young woman. She was holding a three-branched candlestick, level with a spearhead face framed in heavy dark hair.

"I am a gentleman," said Angelo stupidly.

There was a brief moment of silence, and she said:

"I think that was just what needed saying."

She was so far from trembling that the three flames of her candlestick were stiff as the prongs of a fork.

"It's true," said Angelo.

"The oddest thing is that it rings true," she said.

"Thieves don't have cats," said Angelo, who had seen the cat slip in front of him.

"But who does have cats?" said she.

"This one is not mine," said Angelo, "but it follows me because it has recognized a peaceable man."

"What is a peaceable man doing at this hour and in the place where you are?"

"I arrived in this town three or four days ago," said Angelo. "I was nearly hacked to pieces as a fountain-poisoner. Some people with one-track minds chased me through the streets. When I took refuge in a doorway the door opened and I hid in the house. But there were corpses, or, to be exact, one corpse. So I went up on the roof. I've lived up above ever since."

She had listened without moving a muscle. This time the silence was just a little longer. Then she said:

"So I expect you're hungry?"

"That's why I came down to look," said Angelo. "I thought the house was empty."

"Be thankful that it isn't," said the young woman with a smile. "My aunts leave deserts behind them."

She drew back, though still lighting the landing.

"Come in," she said.

"I don't want to intrude," said Angelo. "I shall be disturbing your company."

"You're not intruding," she said, "I am inviting you. And you aren't disturbing any company: I am alone. Those ladies left five days ago. I myself have found it very hard to get enough to eat since they left. Even so, I'm better off than you."

"Aren't you afraid?" said Angelo, moving towards her.

"Not the least bit."

"If not of me – and a thousand thanks for that – " said Angelo, "what about the plague?"

"Don't thank me, monsieur," she said. "Come in. Our doorway compliments are absurd."

Angelo entered a fine drawing-room. He immediately saw his own reflection in a tall mirror. He had eight days' growth of beard and long streaks of black sweat all over his face. His shirt hanging in ribbons over his bare arms and chest covered with black hair, his dusty breeches still bearing traces of the plaster from his entry through the garret window, his torn stockings from which two rather savage feet emerged, conferred on him a highly regrettable appearance. All he had in his favour was his eyes, which still, in spite of everything, had an attractive warmth.

"I'm terribly sorry," he said.

"What are you terribly sorry about?" said the young woman, who was lighting the wick of a small spirit lamp.

"I realize," said Angelo, "that you have every reason to mistrust me."

"What makes you think I mistrust you? I'm making you some tea."

She moved without a sound over the carpets.

"I suppose you haven't had anything hot to drink for a long time?"

"I can't remember how long!"

"Unfortunately I have no coffee. Anyhow, I wouldn't know where to find the coffeepot. Outside one's own home one can never find anything. I arrived here eight days ago. My aunts left nothing behind them; I'd be surprised if they had done anything else. This is some tea, which luckily I thought of bringing with me."

"Please excuse me," said Angelo in a stifled voice.

"This is no time for apologies," she said. "What are you doing, standing there? If you really want to reassure me, behave in a reassuring way. Sit down."

Docilely, Angelo placed the tip of his backside on the edge of an exquisite chair.

"Some cheese that smells of goats (indeed, that's why they left it), the bottom of a pot of honey, and, of course, some bread. Will that do?"

"I've quite forgotten the taste of bread."

"This bread is hard. You need good teeth. How old are you?"

"Twenty-five," said Angelo.

"As old as that?" she said.

She had cleared the corner of a table and laid on it a huge soup bowl on a plate.

"You are too kind," said Angelo. "I thank you with all my heart for anything you care to give me, for I'm dying of hunger. But I'll take it away; I couldn't sit down and eat in front of you."

"Why not?" she said. "Am I repulsive? And what would you take your tea away in? I couldn't possibly lend you any bowl or dish, put that out of your head. Take plenty of sugar, and break your bread as you would to dip it in soup. I've made the tea very strong, and it's boiling. Nothing could be better for you. If I embarrass you, I can go out."

"It's my dirtiness that embarrasses me," said Angelo. He had spoken abruptly, but he added: "I feel shy." And he smiled.

She had green eyes and could open them so wide that they filled the whole of her face.

"I don't dare give you anything to wash in," she said softly. "All the water in this town is contaminated. Just now it is much wiser to be dirty but well. Eat quietly. The only advice I can give you," she added, smiling in turn, "is to wear shoes if you can, from now on."

"Oh!" said Angelo, "I've got some boots up there, indeed very handsome ones. But I had to pull them off to be able to walk on the tiles, which are slippery, and also to come down into the houses without making any noise."

"I'm a perfect idiot," he said to himself, but a sort of critical sense added: "At least you are naturally so."

The tea was excellent. At the third spoonful of soaked bread, he no longer thought of anything but eating voraciously and drinking the boiling liquid. For the first time in a long while he was quenching his thirst. He actually did not think any more about the young woman. She was walking across the carpet. As a matter of fact, she was busy preparing a second pot of tea. As he was finishing, she refilled his bowl to the brim.

He would have liked to say something, but his throat had begun to work madly. He couldn't stop swallowing saliva. He felt as if he were making a terrible noise. The young woman was watching him wide-eyed, but she did not appear to be astonished.

"Now I shan't give in to you any more," he said firmly when he had finished his second bowl of tea. ("I've managed to speak firmly but politely," he told himself.)

"You haven't been giving in to me," said she. "You've been giving in to a hunger even greater than I'd supposed, and above all to thirst. This tea is a real blessing."

"I've made you go short?"

"No one's making me go short," she said; "don't worry."

"I'll accept one of your cheeses and a piece of bread to take away, if you'll let me, and ask your leave to withdraw."

"Where to?" she said.

"Just now I was up in your attic," said Angelo. "Needless to say, I shall leave it at once."

"Why needless to say?"

"I suppose I don't really know."

"If you don't know, you might just as well stay there tonight. You can decide tomorrow when day comes."

Angelo bowed.

"May I make a suggestion?" he said.

"Please do."

"I have two pistols, one of them empty. Will you accept the loaded one? These exceptional times have let loose a lot of exceptional passions."

"I'm pretty well provided for," she said; "see for yourself."

She lifted a shawl that had been lying all this time beside the spirit lamp. It covered two powerful horse pistols.

"You are better equipped than I," said Angelo coldly, "but those are heavy weapons."

"I'm used to them," she said.

"I should have liked to thank you."

"You've done so."

"Good night, madame. Tomorrow, first thing, I shall have left the attic."

"Then it is for me to thank you," said she.

He was at the door. She stopped him.

"Would a candle be of help to you?"

"The greatest help, madame, but I've only tinder in my box; I can't strike a flame."

"Would you like a few matches?"

Returning to the attic, Angelo was astonished to find the cat still at his heels. He had forgotten this creature whose company had given him so much pleasure.

"I'm going to have to squeeze through that narrow window

133

once more," he told himself, "but in all decency a gentleman can't remain alone with so young and pretty a woman; even cholera is no excuse in such cases. She kept perfect control over herself, but there's no denying my presence in the attic could easily be an embarrassment to her. Ah well! I'll squeeze through that narrow window once more."

The tea had given him strength and, above all, a great feeling of well-being. He was full of admiration for everything the young woman down below had done. "Had I been in her place," he said to himself, "would I have carried off as well as she that air of cold scorn for danger? Could I have played as well as she did, a hand where I had everything to lose? One must admit I'm pretty terrifying to look at; even, what's worse, repellent." He was forgetting the light in his eyes.

"She didn't once give a trick away, and yet she is hardly twenty; let us say twenty-one or two at the most. I always find women old, but I can see that this one is young."

Her reply on the subject of the horse pistols also intrigued him greatly. Angelo had plenty of wits, above all in the matter of weapons. But even in these cases he only had an *ésprit d'escalier*. A solitary man acquires, once and for all, the habit of brooding over his own dreams; he can no longer react immediately to the assault of suggestions from outside. He is like a monk at his breviary in the middle of a ball game, or a skater who takes too much trouble with his form and can only answer calls for help by describing a long curve.

"I was angular and all of a piece," said Angelo to himself. "I ought to have behaved like a brother. That would have been a splendid way of playing my own cards. The horse pistols were a good opening. I should have told her that a small weapon well handled is more dangerous, inspires more respect than a big and heavy weapon, which is a great nuisance, especially when there is such a difference in size as there is between her hand and the thick butt, fat barrels, and heavy metalwork of those pistols. It's true she's facing dangers of a quite different kind, and one can't fire pistols at the tiny flies that carry the cholera."

At this point he was overcome by a thought so appalling that he started up from the divan where he was lying.

"What if I have given her the plague myself?"This "myself" froze him with terror. He always responded to the most trivial acts of generosity by a debauch of generosity. The idea of having probably brought death to that brave and lovely young woman, and after she had made tea for him, was intolerable. "I've been with, I've not only been with, I've touched, I've tended cholera victims. No doubt I am covered with vapours that don't attack me, or perhaps haven't attacked me yet, but may well attack and kill that woman. She was very sensibly keeping out of it, shut up in her house; and I forced my way in, she received me nobly, and she will perhaps die for that nobility, for that unselfishness, from which I've been the one to benefit."

He was overwhelmed.

"I went all through the house from cellar to attic where the dry cholera had struck down that woman with the lovely golden hair before she could reach the door. This one is darker than the night, but dry cholera strikes like terrible lightning and people haven't even time to call for help. And ... have I gone mad, or what does the colour of a woman's hair count in a case of dry cholera?"

He listened with ferocious attention. The whole house was silent.

"In any case," he tried to reassure himself, "this famous dry cholera has not bothered me up to now. To give it, one must have it. No: to give it, one need only carry it, and you've done all a man could to carry more than enough of it. Still, you didn't touch anything in the house. You just about did your duty, like the poor little Frenchman who'd have done much more and would certainly have been conscientious enough to look under the beds. Come, what are you imagining? Vapours aren't bristling with hooked feelers like burdock seeds, and the fact that you stepped over that corpse doesn't mean that they necessarily stuck to you."

He was half asleep. He again saw himself striding over the woman's corpse, and his half-sleep was likewise filled with comets and horse-shaped clouds. He tossed about on his divan so much that he disturbed the cat as it lay close by him.

All at once he was frozen with terror. "The cat spent a long time in that house, and not only the fair woman but at least two other persons died there. It may be carrying cholera in its fur."

He could no longer remember if the cat had gone into the drawing-room down below or had stayed out on the landing. He tortured himself with this thought during a great part of the night.

1 The conversation that follows is deliberately cryptic. The two police officers are groping and do not particularly wish to enlighten Angelo. They are ex-officers from Napoleon's armies, hence the references to Leipzig and Waterloo. At this moment (1838) Louis-Philippe was reigning and this explains what they say about the coins and the bees (which are, of course, the imperial emblem). [Translator's note.]

2 The speaker is an aristocrat, although a *Carbonaro*, and very young besides.

3 Secret meetings of the *Carbonari*. [Translator's note.]

4 Conspirators of the fifteenth century, who figure in Machiavelli's history of Florence. [Translator's note.]

# 7

IT WAS STILL DARK when Angelo went out through the window.

Facing east, it nevertheless framed a small rectangle of pale grey in the direction of the extinguished stars. Angelo waited for sunrise, crouching against the little wall.

Still the same white dawn.

Beyond the convent's long rooftops there rose a square tower, surmounted by a spike that must be a sort of lightning-conductor or a former flagstaff. Angelo had not yet gone as far as there. He did so with the first rays of the sun.

It was a small belfry. The wooden louvre boards had been gnawed by wind and rain, and it was easy to slide through into the dwelling-place of the bells. From there, a ladder went down to a spiral staircase that led finally to a door – which opened. It gave on to the aisle of a church.

The rising sun, striking in through the windows high in the vault, disclosed all the signs of a hasty exodus. The high altar had been stripped of its candlesticks and all its linen; even the door of the tabernacle had been left open. In the nave, the benches were stacked against a pillar. Straw, rags evidently used for packing, planks bristling with nails, and even a hammer and a roll of wire were lying on the floor.

The sacristy was empty. From it, a low door led into a cloister. This enclosed the garden of box and laurel in which, the day before, Angelo had seen the nuns bustling about. All was peaceful. The height of the walls maintained there a coolness favourable to the scent of green things.

Reaching the corner of the arcade that ran round the garden, Angelo perceived at the other end a body lying on the flagstones. He was so accustomed to corpses that he was nonchalantly approaching when the body stirred, sat up, then rose to its feet. It was an old nun. She was round as a barrel. Two claws of little black moustache clipped her mouth together at each side.

"What do you want?" she said.

137

"Nothing," said Angelo.

"What are you doing here?"

"Nothing."

"Are you afraid?"

"That depends."

"Ah! So you're one of those who make their fear depend on something! And hell – are you afraid of that?"

"Yes, Mother."

"Well, isn't that enough? Will you help me, my child?"

"Yes, Mother."

"Blessed be the glory of the Lord in His Heaven! He couldn't desert me. Are you strong?"

"Less so than usual, because I haven't had enough to eat for several days, but I'm willing."

"Don't boast. Why haven't you had enough to eat?"

"I'm lost in this town."

"Everyone is lost in this town. Everyone is lost everywhere. So you think that eating will make you strong?"

"It seems likely."

"It seems likely. That's fair enough. All right, come and eat."

She gave him some goat's cheese. "These people live on nothing but goat's cheese," said Angelo to himself.

She looked very tired. Weighty reflection made wrinkles at the top of her nose.

"Are you the messenger?" she asked.

"No."

"How do you know?"

"I'm nothing, Mother. Don't ask."

"Nothing? What pride!" she said.

Although sitting on a chair in that little white cell, made whiter still from the shelves laden with goats' cheeses and lit by a shaft of sunlight, she was panting as if she had been climbing a hill, and her lips blew small bubbles like the lips of certain old men when asleep.

"I shall mortify you," she said. "Take that and put it on."

It was a long white shirt like those worn by the corpse-carters.

"Wait till I get into my boots," said Angelo.

"Hurry up, and take that bell."

She was standing. She was waiting. She was leaning on a strong oak stick.

"Let's go. Come!"

She led the way down the length of the cloister. She opened a door.

"Go through," she said.

They were in the street.

"Swing your bell and get a move on," she said.

She added, almost tenderly: "My child!"

"I'm in the street," thought Angelo. "I've left the roofs. That's over with!"

The reverberations of the bell raised torrents of flies. The heat was strongly sugared. The air greased the lips and nostrils like oil.

They passed from street to street. All was deserted. At certain places in the walls, gaping passages sent back echoes; at others the clang of the bell was muffled as though deep under water.

"Get a move on!" the nun kept saying. "Some elbow grease there! Ring! Ring!"

She moved rapidly, all together, like a boulder. Her jowls quivered in her wimple.

A window opened. A woman's voice called: "Madame!"

"Let me go first," the nun told Angelo. "Stop your ringing." On the threshold she asked: "Have you a handkerchief?"

"Yes," said Angelo.

"Stuff it in the bell. One sound from it and I'll shake your teeth out." And tenderly she added: "My child!"

She darted like a bird towards the staircase, and Angelo saw an enormous foot place itself on the first step.

Upstairs there was a kitchen and an alcove. Near the open window from which the call had come stood a woman and two children. From the alcove came a noise like a coffee mill. The woman pointed to the alcove. The nun drew the curtains. A man stretched out on the bed was grinding his teeth in a ceaseless chewing that drew back his lips. He was also shivering so that his maize mattress crackled.

"There, there," said the nun. And she took the man in her arms. "There, there," she said, "a little patience. Everybody gets there; it's on its way. We're here, we're here. Don't force yourself, it's coming by itself. Gently, gently. Everything in its own time."

She stroked his hair with her hand.

"You *are* in a hurry, you *are* in a hurry," she said, and she pressed her huge hand down on his knees to stop him from thrashing about in the wooden bed. "Just look what a hurry he's in! You'll get your chance. Don't worry. Keep calm. Everyone has his turn. It's coming. There, there, that's it. It's your turn. Pass, pass, pass."

The man gave a twist and lay still.

"We ought to have massaged him," said Angelo in a voice he didn't recognize.

The nun sat up and turned to him.

"What's this about massaging?" she said. "So you're a free-thinker, eh? You'd like to forget the Gospel, eh? Ask that lady for a bit of soap, and a basin, and towels."

She was rolling up her sleeves over her fat pink arms.

"Ask her," she said, "speak to her, make her move, stop her from standing by that window. Make her light a fire and boil some water. Come on, let's get moving if you please."

She was round and heavy and homely. She went over to the hearth and broke some wood across her knee. She had left the alcove open. The man was stiff on his bed.

The woman never stirred.

"Come on," said the nun.

The woman took a step towards the hearth, near which the nun was kneeling. The woman pushed the children slowly away from her apron. She stroked their cheeks furtively with a gesture that seemed to come from outside time. She came and knelt by the hearth. The nun handed her the wisp of paper and the tinder.

"Light it," she said, and stood up.

This nun was astonishing; she had an extraordinary way with her. Where she was, all became orderly. She came in and the walls held no more tragedies. The corpses were natural and, down to the tiniest detail, everything immediately fell into its proper place. She did not need to speak; it was enough for her to be present.

Innumerable times Angelo was thunderstruck by this. He never got used to it. He entered behind her (she always insisted on going first) into charnel houses where an almost ludicrous domesticity was mingled with the terrifying appearances of the curse that preceded time. The last grimaces of people dying in cotton nightcaps and long underpants were widening over lips distended by false teeth, and prophetic mouths; the wails of weeping women and men had recaptured the breathless cadences of Moses. The corpses continued to relieve themselves into shrouds now made out of any odds and ends, old window curtains, sofa covers, tablecloths and even, in wealthy houses, bath covers. Chamber pots full to the brim had been placed on the dining-room table, and people had gone on to fill dishes, washbasins, and even flowerpots, hastily emptied of their green plants – fern or dwarf palm tree – with that mossy, green and purple fluid that smelled terribly of the wrath of God. The survivors clung to their own lives with puppet gestures. The inward neighing that some could not even restrain, as they turned away from the one who to them had been dearest in the world to gaze towards the open sky of the window (though it was chalk, torrid, nauseating), was of a magnificent grandeur, uttered as it was in these bedrooms or on the thresholds of alcoves where they had always been, up to now, the good father, good husband, virtuous wife, obedient son and child of Mary. The eye of Cain in the peaceful face of a haberdasher, whose jowls bore whiskers down to the collar; the royal-blue breasts of some lovely young woman still warm, still kicking and shuddering more than an hour after her death, who had to be wrapped up like an eel; the muscles that broke, making the thighs resound like violin-bodies; the spurts of dysentery on the flowered wallpaper or among the cinders of the hearth, or into kitchen utensils, on quilts, on the polished floors, or even streaming full into the face of the loved one; the nakedness whose last details it was impossible to hide, what with the kicking, shuddering, tremors, convulsions, moans, cries, hands clenched on the sheets, settled permanently in the homes of the bourgeois and the peasants, who are still more prudish, under the eyes of the children (the children were very interested in all these phenomena and took their silence, their great astounded eyes, their iron rigidity with them everywhere): a new order (called for the moment disorder) was abruptly organizing life within new horizons. Very few were still able to believe in the virtues of the old cardinal points. They no longer kissed the children. Not to protect them; to protect themselves. Moreover the children all had a rigid bearing, monolithic, with wide eyes, and when they died, it was without a word or a groan and always far from their homes, burrowing into a dog kennel, or into a rabbit warren, or hutches, or curled up in the big baskets used for brooding turkeys.

Often the nun went hunting them. She would open the chicken runs and search. She would kick the sides of the kennels. The dog would put out a snarling head. She would seize it coolly by the collar. The child was generally at the back. She dragged it out without undue ceremony, but carried it off exactly as a mother should carry a child. The little corpses were like the corpses of the grown-ups, that is to say, absurdly indecent, *crying out the truth*, with their nails tearing at their bellies, their capital of filth. But in the nun's arms they became once more poor little children dead of a terrible colic.

At the moment when people were asking whether one should still believe in anything, if she arrived the walls became walls again, the rooms rooms, with all their stalactites of memories intact, their power to shelter intact. Death – oh! well, yes, but it instantly lost its diabolical side. It was no longer growing, threatening to break totally free; it no longer crossed any but reasonable frontiers; one could no longer permit oneself those spasms of selfishness in which, most of the time, the living reproduced, by a sort of Satanic mimicry, the agonized spasms of which they had been the spectators.

A few very simple gestures sufficed. The nun would have been much surprised had she been told that two thirds of her worth came from her physical appearance, her large pot belly, the pout of her large lips, her large head, her large hands, her large-woman's placidity, her large feet under which the floors always shook a bit. It was this bulk that authorized miracles. Had she been more agile she would have been able to make twenty gestures, among which the good one might have passed unnoticed; fat, clumsiness, weight allowed her to make only one. It was the good one. And there it was, as indisputable as the nose in one's face. People were obliged to believe in its virtue, for it was an old and ordinary gesture that they themselves had made a hundred thousand times, and of which the consequences were certain.

She would arrive and there would be sometimes one, sometimes two corpses stretched out in those appalling comic attitudes, the thighs wide apart, the hands dug into the belly, the head thrown back in that great white and purple laugh of the cholera-stricken. Sometimes, even, these corpses seemed to have bounded across the room and collapsed over the unlikeliest pieces of furniture. Hidden in corners or, preferably, in window recesses (the desire to flee), there would be a man or a woman transformed into a dog, groaning, coughing, barking, ready to fawn on the firstcomer; one or two children, inflexible as justice, with eyes like eggs; and she would come in. Often, when the sight was so horrible that it rasped the skin, this is what she would do; she would sit down, put the coffee mill between her thighs, and begin to grind coffee. Instantly, the man or woman stopped being a dog. With the children, it was at once more tricky and more easy: they would be immediately attracted by the nun's enormous bosom; then with a very simple gesture she would push her pectoral cross aside.

At other times (but always with exact and unerring science) there would be other solutions than coffee mills. She would enter one of those bourgeois houses where the kitchen is out of sight, where all the furniture is under dust sheets. These were always places where the corpses were extraordinarily pungent. Here, most of the time, the sick people had not had much care lavished on them. Generally no one had had the courage to keep them in bed; they had been left to get up and wander about; the tendency had been to flee from them. The chairs were overturned as if after a fight, the tables no longer stood directly under the chandelier, the music stand was smashed; people seemed to have been bombarding each other with waltz music; the dead man had streamed in all directions before collapsing over the piano.

The moment Angelo came through the door, he would say to himself: "And here, what is there to do?" Over the nun's shoulder he saw this bourgeois interior ploughed up for a terrible sowing and the survivors huddled into a corner of the drawing-room, like little monkeys in the grip of the cold.

Immediately, the nun would pull the table back to its place, pick up the chairs, straighten the armchairs, collect the sheets of music. She would open the door into the bedroom. She would ask: "Where are the clean sheets?" These words were magical. They gave her the most lightning victories. No sooner spoken than the rattle of a key-ring would be heard from among the huddling monkeys. That sound itself had a virtue so powerful that a woman would emerge from the huddle and become immediately a woman and immediately mistress of the house. Some of these women whose faces were more particularly smothered in bedraggled hair would still totter a bit, and even, in their giddiness, hand her the keys. But the nun never took them. "Come and open the cupboard yourself," she said. After that, they would tidy up the bed. It was only once the bed was made that they would deal with the corpse, and then thoroughly. But already the wheels of the house were turning once again, and already death could strike another diabolical blow in this family without destroying anything essential.

She was uneducated. She had been married young. Widowed young, she had entered the Presentines' convent, to do the heavy work. She scraped carrots, peeled potatoes, followed the lines with her finger when she read. She was not one of the leading spirits of the sisterhood. Indeed, she was only admitted to it as an exception and thanks to the protection of a benefactress. When the convent had moved to escape the contagion, her only instruction had been to look after some provisions that could not be taken away immediately.

She told Angelo how delightful the empty cloister had seemed to her. The two of them always returned to it at nightfall. They would make their rounds again towards two or three in the morning, the bad hours. Before setting out on this they had a good rest. They ate goat's cheese, gooseberry jam, and honey. They drank white wine. They sat on the stone seats of the cloister. They went to sleep there, sometimes all of a sudden without having time to lie down, especially the nun, who had a great faculty for sleep. She would fall asleep in the middle of a smile. She often smiled: first at the angels, then at the lonely passages of the cloister, lastly at Angelo. When she had time she used to say: "Lord, bless me." But more often the phrase was rudely cut in two as if by the stroke of some scythe, and she would begin at once to snore. After a time she adopted the practice of asking for the Lord's blessing as soon as she sat down on the stone bench, while Angelo was bringing the bread, cheese, and wine. "And now, Lord, bless me," she would say.

Angelo would smoke one of his little cigars. In the course of these patrols he made with his little bell, just ahead of the nun, he had passed that famous police station into which he had been pushed on the day of his arrival. It was now deserted, its doors stood open. He could see inside, at the back, the desk behind which the faille cravat had stood. Now no one stood behind the desk. "Here's a lamppost I was nearly hanged from," he said to himself. In another street he saw a tobacco shop. The desire to smoke emboldened him to stop ringing his bell and say to the nun: "Wait for me." He offered an écu and asked for some of his usual small cigars. The box was held out to him. "Help yourself," he was told. His écu was refused. He realized it was because of his corpse carter's shirt. He had missed smoking so badly and wanted it so much that he helped himself lavishly and filled his pockets. "This job has its perquisites," he said to himself. He was also astonished at the calmness with which the nun waited for him in the street. She always insisted on going at a gallop and feverishly ringing the bell. All she said was: "What did you take?" He showed her the cigars. They continued with their round.

When he saw that the nun could smile, he considered the thing in its miraculous aspect. He was a little like the man who sees the first day succeed the first night. When he perceived that she often smiled for herself alone, then for him, he settled down in the sweetness of that smile, which was extremely childlike.

The nun never nursed the sick. "I take them over," she said. "They are my clients, I am responsible for them. On the day of the Resurrection they will be clean."

"And the Lord will say to you: 'Well done, sergeant!'" replied Angelo.

She retorted: "If God says: 'Well done!' poor idiot, what have you to say, you creature?"

"But some of them can be saved," said Angelo; "at least, I think so."

"And what is it I'm doing?" said she. "Of course they're being saved."

"I mean," he said, "brought back to life."

"They've been dead a long time," she said; "all this is only a formality."

"But, Mother," said Angelo, "I too am stuffed full of sins."

"Hide yourself, hide yourself," she said.

She covered her face with her huge hands. At length she looked at him between her fingers and, lowering her hands, said: "Give me a cigar."

She had rapidly acquired a taste for smoking. She seemed ready-made for the pleasures of smoking. The very first time, she held her cigar not like a clumsy and rather scared woman, but like a man who knows what to expect and needs it. She even seemed to enjoy the first puff. Angelo had gladly given her the little cigar, but he knew they were very strong and watched in case she felt sick. She didn't bat an eyelid; her huge lips opened slowly to emit an already skilful jet of smoke. As the peak of her coif kept the smoke before her face, she screwed up her eyes; with her lion's nose and greedy mouth, she appeared through the blue mist like the embodiment of some very ancient wisdom.

She knew more than she said. She had not a very wide vocabulary. She had only that of the book she had read, following the lines with her finger. Nor did she talk much. She was so tired that she couldn't even bring herself to wash her hands. "Washing the dead is enough," she said. In fact, her hands, which were not only enormous but very plump, had the washed-out and whitish skin of washerwomen's hands. A sort of faint white dirt remained in halos around her nails and in the hollows of her finger joints. The same fatigue made Angelo fidgety and talkative. He was always scratching at some spot on his breeches. Once he even washed his shirt in the well bucket. The nun never touched the filth that caked her robe. Her ample sleeves, which had trailed through countless messes, were stiff as leather. She would lay her hands flat on her knees. She would then settle like an enormous, squat, rectangular rock, like one of those enormous stones earmarked by the architect to serve as foundation stones. She smoked without touching the cigar, leaving it planted in her mouth for as long as it lasted. She would say peacefully to herself: "Alleluia, glory to Thee, Oh God! Praise to the heavenly host! Holy Trinity! God, Creator of the whole world, help me! Ever-lasting and true God!" Then immediately afterwards there would be a long silence, during which she often fell asleep. Angelo, watching her, would come over and take from her mouth what was left of the cigar.

Once she also said: "Immaculate Virgin!" then, immediately afterwards, "Let's go!"

She always went out on a sudden inspiration. He had to obey promptly. She never waited. She became furious and choked in her rage like a peacock. At those moments she used a sort of language made up of unrelated words, any old words strung one after the other, almost shouted; she would end up with wild cries that had in them something of a dirge and of a beast's roaring. Angelo was literally fascinated. He thought only of her.

A few days after he had come down from his rooftops, and when the first fierce impulse had passed, Angelo had asked the nun if she knew a certain Giuseppe. She might have. On her rounds? She went no rounds. Her order went no rounds. It was a convent for rich girls. Her job was in the kitchen. There was no more question of Giuseppe than of Peter or Paul. Who was this Giuseppe? An Italian refugee. More precisely, a Piedmontese. What did he do in the town? Oh! Nothing: he probably passed unnoticed. He was a shoemaker. He lived very simply, alone, speaking to nobody. He had quite enough to say to himself. The last time Angelo had seen him was more than a year ago, and at night. All Angelo could say was that he lived in a room in a very big house where there also lived, as in a barrack, some tanners and their families. A shoemaker, did he say? All the nun could tell him was that the sisterhood had its shoes resoled by a man called Jean, who was also an Italian. No, it wasn't he. And what was he doing, looking for Giuseppe? It was too long a story: among other things, this Giuseppe was in touch with Angelo's mother. What sort of touch? Oh! she came from Piedmont and ... no relation to a shoemaker. My mother is young and very beautiful. She's a duchess? Ah! good. She corresponds with this Giuseppe because I am always *par orte*, on the road, in the hills and valleys. She writes to Giuseppe and sends him money for me; he acts as a sort of treasurer for me. Ah! yes. No, she didn't know who Giuseppe was. It was the first time she had heard of such a thing.

Angelo told himself that perhaps in going about the streets he would run into Giuseppe. But now the streets were deserted. Only from time to time he would meet a white-shirted man as he preceded the nun with his little bell.

He now thought only very seldom of Giuseppe. He hardly had any need of what Giuseppe could give him. "It's all right," he told himself. Along the streets, in the bedrooms, in the charnel houses, he told himself: "It's all right." He could no longer reflect about very much, or develop his ideas. He helped to wash the dead: he plunged his grass brush into the pails of hot water. For a long time now the sound of the grass rubbing over parchment skins had ceased to astonish him; he didn't even worry about saving lives; he knew that, all in all, one can get to be perfect at washing a corpse. He felt a self-satisfaction he had always sought and never attained. Even the Baron had not given him this spiritual contentment. As he delivered his thrust and felt it strike home, he had had a brief feeling of intense joy, but happiness had been far away.

He was on the right side of the cholera. "What pride!" he exclaimed suddenly one evening.

"Ah! son of a Pope," said the nun softly, "you've found that out!" She covered her face with her huge hands, then asked for a cigar.

Those nocturnal patrols, at three in the morning, through a town desolated by the epidemic, were as gloomy as could be. Most of the street lamps were out; only a few were still kept going. Angelo carried a lantern. He rang his bell only at jerky intervals, between which there stretched a silence rendered still more silent by the twittering of the nightingales and the nun's heavy tread as she dragged her huge shoes over the cobbles. Night encouraged selfishness. People brought their dead down into the street and threw them on to the pavement. They were in a hurry to get rid of them. They even went so far as to leave them on other people's doorsteps. They parted from them in every possible way. For them the main thing was to drive them away as quickly and as completely as possible from their own homes, to which they quickly returned and hid. Sometimes, beyond the halo of the lantern, in the half-darkness, Angelo saw pale shapes fleeing, agile as the beasts that leap into the thickets of the woods. Doors shut slowly, creaking. Bolts were rammed home. Nobody called. The bell, which Angelo swung every now and then, rang in a pure void. Nobody wanted help. Night permitted everyone to look out for himself. They all did so in the same way. Nobody found a better one.

"Did they love one another?" said Angelo.

"Lord, no," said the nun.

"In a town like this, though, there are surely people who loved one another?"

"No, no," said the nun.

Often indeed, when Angelo clanged his bell, the bands of light framing certain shutters went out. The groaning and wailing ceased abruptly. He imagined hands clapped suddenly over mouths.

They washed abandoned corpses. They could not wash all that they found in the night: they lay in every corner. Some were sitting up: they had been deliberately arranged to look like persons resting. The others, thrown down anyhow, would be hidden under filth, even under dung. Some were curled up in the recesses of doorways, others stretched flat on their bellies in the middle of the street, or on their backs with their arms forming a cross. It was useless to knock on the doors outside which they found them. Nobody knew them. Neighbourhoods were surreptitiously exchanging their corpses. Making their rounds, Angelo and the nun could hear the faint sounds of this furtive traffic. It might be a body borne by two men, one at the head, one grasping the legs like the handles of a wheelbarrow; a wife dragging her husband over the pavements; a man carrying his wife like a sack of wheat on his shoulder. They all crept through the dark. Children were sent to smash the street lamps with stones.

Angelo would swing his bell. "Come on," he would mutter, "come on, come on, get the hell out of here, get the job done!" He would walk slowly, without haste, before the nun, who followed heavily as if on two church pillars. He had the right to be scornful.

They washed only the foulest. They carried them one by one to the side of a fountain. They undressed them. They scrubbed them with plenty of water. They laid them out neatly to be picked up when day came.

It was utterly useless. Massaging the dying was also utterly useless. The poor little Frenchman had saved no one. There was no remedy. At the beginning of the epidemic he had seen sick people die like flies though surrounded by every care; others who had hidden themselves to smother their colic sometimes emerged fresh as daisies. The choice was being made elsewhere.

"If I'm going to die," said Angelo to himself, "I shall have time enough to be frightened when my moment comes. Just now, fear is out of place."

When he was in some deserted square, in the dead of night, in this town so completely terrorized that the most ignoble cowardice appeared quite natural, alone with the nun, when four or five naked corpses were spread out within the circle of their lantern and they were washing these corpses, as he fetched water from the fountain, he would say to himself: "I can't be accused of affectation. No one sees me, and what I'm doing is quite useless. They'd rot just the same, foul or clean. I can't be accused of running after a medal. But what I'm doing classifies me. I know I'm worth more than all these people who had social rank, who were addressed as 'sir' and now throw their loved ones on the dung-heap. The main thing isn't that others should know and even acknowledge that I'm worth more: the main thing is that I should know it. But I'm more exacting than they. I demand from myself unquestionable proof. And here at least is one."

He had a taste for superiority and a terror of affectation. He was happy.

It is true that the sound of the hemp swab as it rubbed over these skins, stiff and resonant from the cholera, stretched over bodies with the flesh calcined inside, was rather hard for anyone with imagination to bear. It must also be admitted that the gasping flame of the lantern never ceased to drape the shadows. A romantic soul might find a certain exaltation in a struggle with these things, simple though they were.

There was very little ugliness in his pride. At any rate, barely what was necessary to make it human. "I left that loutish captain to look after the body of the poor little Frenchman," he thought. "He certainly had it thrown into quicklime like a dog. The soldiers must have dragged it by the legs without ceremony. I see it as if I were there. And yet I had more than love for that man: I had admiration. It's true I was quite ready, body and soul, to bury him with my own hands, decently. And even to embrace him. No, that would have cost me nothing; on the contrary, I'd have done it gladly. I was chased away by gunfire."

But he added: "Well, you should have stood up to the guns." He went so far as to say: "You should have been humble enough for them not to want to fire guns at you. You preferred to be arrogant with the captain. Wouldn't the sign of a really superior spirit have been not to reply to his insults? Not to give in? You don't give in to other people. But is that enough? It's to yourself that you mustn't give in. You gave in to the immediate pleasure of giving an insolent man an insolent retort. That's not strength. That's a weakness, because look at you now, filled with remorse at having failed to perform a duty that was dear to you or, to be frank, a deed which would give you self-esteem. In reality the poor little Frenchman doesn't give a damn for you and your clean hands. Quicklime for quicklime, the soldier's hand did the job perfectly. What would have interested the Frenchman would have been to cure at least one. How conscientiously he looked for the last ones! But am I using the right word? For him, now dead, and for me, still alive, is it really a matter of conscience? Was conscience the motive when he rode his nag up that valley of Jehoshaphat? He was certainly the very image of conscience, alive all alone amid the corpses and seeking to save. But was he there to do his duty, or to satisfy himself? Did he have to force himself or did he enjoy it? Wasn't his way of seeking out those whom he called *the last ones* even behind the beds, the way of hunting-dogs? And if he had managed to save one, would his satisfaction have come simply from seeing life restored, or from feeling himself capable of restoring life? Wasn't he quite simply trying to earn a medal from himself on grounds of nobility? We're all bastards in the same boat. Isn't that why I admired him – I mean, envied him? Wasn't I looking for a medal myself when I stayed with him? First-class men always want to put their backsides on two chairs at the same time. Could there be such a thing as devotion without a desire to please oneself? An irresistible desire? That's what makes a saint. A cowardly hero is an angel. But what merit does a brave hero have? He acts to please himself. He satisfies himself. It's human beings, male and female, of whom the priests (and they know) say: they find satisfaction in themselves. Is there ever a disinterested devotion? And even," he added, "if it exists, isn't the total absence of self-interest then the sign of the purest pride?

"Let's be thoroughly frank," he told himself. "This fight for liberty, and even for the liberty of the people, which I have undertaken, for whose sake I've killed (with my usual attitudinizing, it's true), for whose sake I've sacrificed an elevated position (bought with good money by my mother, it's true), did I undertake it really because I think it is just? Yes and no. Yes, because it is very difficult to be frank with oneself. No, because one must make an effort to be frank and it is useless to lie to oneself (useless but convenient and usual). Good. Let's grant that I believe my cause is just. All the daily pleasure of the fight, all the advantages of pride and position that this fight brings me, let's forget them, let's push all that aside. This fight is just and it's for its justice that I took it on. Its justice – its justice pure and simple, or else the esteem I feel for myself at the moment of taking up the fight for justice? There's no denying that a just cause, if I devote myself to it, serves my pride. But I serve others. In addition only. So you see, the word 'people' can be removed from the discussion without loss. I could even put anything I liked in place of the word 'liberty', on the one condition that I replace the word 'liberty' by an equivalent. I mean, by a word that has the same general value, equally noble and *equally vague*. What about 'the fight', then? Yes, that word can stay. The fight. That is to say, a trial of strength. In which I hope to be the stronger. At bottom, it all comes back to: 'Long live me!'"

He would wash the dead and say to himself: "Haven't we, the nun and I, the merit of extreme honesty in performing this completely useless act, which none the less demands so much courage? Useless, let's get it clear, useless to everyone but very useful to our pride. Here we are, alone in the night with this disgusting work, which does, however, give us a high opinion of ourselves. We're deceiving nobody. We need to do something that will class us. We couldn't do anything more clear-cut. It's impossible to work for one's self-esteem with less affectation."

They were really very lonely beside their fountain. The town stirred only as a dying man stirs. It was struggling in the peculiar selfishness of its death agony. Under the walls there were dull murmurs as of muscles relaxing, lungs emptying, bellies opening, jaws chattering. One could no longer ask anything of this social body. It was dying. It had enough to do, enough to think about, just dying.

The lantern only lit a small space, just the four or five spread-out and stripped bodies around which Angelo and the nun were busy for their own sakes. Beyond them, the muffled murmurs, the sound – like the rubbing of hands – of the elms and sycamores in which the wind and the birds were stirring.

The nun's chief care was to prepare the bodies for the Resurrection. She wanted them clean and decent for that occasion. "When they stand up with their thighs plastered with shit," she said, "what will the Lord think of me? He'll say to me:'You were there and you knew; why didn't you clean them?' I'm a housekeeper; I'm doing my job."

She was very taken aback one night when, after throwing some buckets of water over a corpse, it opened its eyes, then sat up and asked why it was being treated in this way.

It was a man still in the prime of life. He had fainted in a fit of cholera and been taken for dead. His relatives had put him out in the street. The cold water had brought him round. He asked why he was naked, why he was there. He would have died of fright before the huge nun, who didn't know what to do, if Angelo hadn't immediately started to talk to him with great affection, and even to wipe him and then wrap him in a sheet.

"Where is your house?" Angelo asked him.

"I don't know," he said. "What is this place? And you? Who are you?"

"I'm here to help you. You're in the Place des Observantins. Do you live near here?"

"No, indeed. I wonder how I got here. Who brought me here? I live in the rue d'Aubette."

"We must take him home," said Angelo.

"He's tricked us," said the nun.

"It's not his fault, don't talk so loud. They thought he was dead and got rid of him. But he's alive and, I think, even saved."

"He's a swine," she said. "He's alive and I washed his backside."

"No, no," said Angelo, "he's alive and it's wonderful. You take one arm and I'll take the other. I'm sure he can walk. Let's take him home."

He lived at the far end of the rue d'Aubette, and it was quite a task to get him there. He was beginning to realize that he had been taken for dead, that he had been mixed up with the dead. He was trembling like a leaf and his teeth chattered in spite of the stifling heat. He kept tripping over his shroud at every step. All the time he kept leaping like a goat, and Angelo and the nun had to pinion him with both arms. All his nerves in revolt were trying to rid themselves of fear. He kept throwing back his head and neighing like a horse.

"So you pulled a fine trick on me," the nun kept saying, and she kept shaking him as roughly as a policeman.

At last he sighted his house and tried to run for it; but Angelo held him back.

"Wait," he said. "Stay here. I'll go in and let them know. You can't turn up suddenly like this; you know how bad shocks can be. Who is in there? Your wife?"

"My wife is dead. It's my daughter."

Angelo went up and knocked at the door, under which light could be seen. There was no answer. He opened it and went in. It was a kitchen. In spite of the stifling heat, a fire was lit in the stove. A woman of about thirty, wrapped in shawls, was huddling close to the fire. She was shuddering all over; only her enormous eyes were motionless.

"Your father," said Angelo.

"No," she said.

"You took him down into the street?"

"No," she said.

"We found him."

"No," she said.

"He's down below. We've brought him back. He is alive."

"No," she said.

"What a fuss about nothing," said the nun from the doorway. "It's as simple as day. Just you watch!"

She had dropped the man's arm. He followed her in, let fall his shroud, and sat down quite naked on a chair. The daughter huddled into her shawls, pulled them up over her face, just leaving her eyes visible. The nun removed, one by one, the pins holding her coif. She held them between her lips while she took it off. Her head was round and shaved. Then she shut the door and strode over to the coffee-grinder, rolling up her sleeves.

On leaving the house they returned to their labours. There were still three other corpses by the fountain. These were impeccable. They washed them and prepared them very nicely.

One morning Angelo and the nun were as usual in an arcade of the cloister, lying on the flagstones, more dazed with fatigue than asleep, when a sharp little step, tapped out clearly with the heels, set the vaults ringing. It was another nun, this one thin and young. She was dressed cleanly and very elegantly. Her coif was brilliantly starched, and her huge pectoral cross was of gold. All that could be seen of her face was a sharp nose and a pointed chin.

Immediately the huge nun became subdued. She clasped her hands and, with lowered head, listened to a long, low-voiced homily. Then she followed the thin nun, who had turned quickly on her little heels and was making for the door.

Angelo had followed the performance with eyes half closed in the stupor of his fatigue. Immediately after, he fell asleep. When the burning of the white sun on his face woke him up, it was late. He half thought he had been dreaming, but the fat nun was not there. He looked for her. He gave up and went out.

He did not have his bell, and he no longer knew what to do. His head and heart were perfectly empty. Finally, after some time, he was struck by the silence of the streets. All the shops were shut, all the houses barricaded. Certain doors, certain shutters were even nailed fast with crossed planks. He passed through a good part of the town without meeting even a cat or hearing any sound but that of a slight breeze which caused echoes in the passages.

In a little street near the centre, however, Angelo did find a draper's shop open. Through the window he even saw a well-dressed man sitting on a bench, measuring cloth. He went in. The shop smelled of good-quality velvet and had other comforting odours.

"What do you want?" said the man.

He was tiny. He was playing with the trinkets on his watch chain.

"What has happened?" asked Angelo.

The little man was amazed at the question, but kept his poise and said: "Well, well, a visitor from the moon!"

At the same time he studied Angelo from head to foot.

# 8

ANGELO MURMURED some sort of story. Of course he knew there was cholera, devil take it!

"If I want him to show me some consideration," he told himself, "and, damn it, that's just what I do want, I simply must not tell this man, trim as a gamecock, that I've been washing dead bodies."

He noticed also that the little man, otherwise dry in manner and even leaning slightly backward in his anxiety not to lose anything of his stature, twitched every time he heard the word "cholera".

"Why do you keep talking of cholera?" the little man said at last. "It's just a simple contagion. Why not call it what it is, instead of looking for nonexistent trouble? This country would be healthy, only we are all more or less obliged to reckon with the land. A cartload of manure costs eight sous. You can't get away from it. No one's willing to pay those eight sous. During the night people dam up the streams, pile straw there, hold back filth of every kind, and so get manure cheap. There are even some who pay two sous for the right to set open crates over the outlets from the privies.

"This is a well-aired town. It's watered by eighty fountains. It's exposed to the northwest wind. But the price of manure's too high, and without manure, nothing doing! Talk about contagion, and I'm with you," continued the little man, squinting at Angelo's still-magnificent boots. "But cholera, that requires thought. And I'd even," he added, rising on his toes, then dropping back gently on to his heels, "I'd even say: beware! The point is, there'll always be need of manure. Note the fact. And the contagion will pass. Cholera, that's a big word, and words cause fear. Once let fear in, and you won't be able to move a step."

Angelo stammered something about the dead.

"Seventeen hundred," said the man, "out of a population of seven thousand, but you yourself look like a horseman in difficulties. Can I be of any help?"

Angelo was literally enchanted by the little man. "He waves his arms, he squeaks his boots, but he *never gets outside his skin*," he said to himself. "He's still got a clean collar, a well-brushed waistcoat, and

156

in his shop he's put everything tidy, even the shadows on his shelves. He's right: lying is a virtue. The man's an obstinate microbe, too. His hypocrisy is much more useful than my extravagance. It takes many more like him than like me to make a world in which, as he says, there'll always be need of manure. This is the very proof of his simplicity, of his all-of-a-piece solidity, which nothing can demolish, neither cholera nor war, perhaps not even our revolution. He may die but he won't despair. Still less will he despair *in advance*. And that, on the whole, is the way of a man of quality. To know everything or to know nothing amounts to the same thing."

Meanwhile many other things were being explained to him; for example, that drastic measures had at last been taken.

"You've surely noticed that there's no one left in the town. Except me. All the rest have gone to camp in the fields, in the open air, on the hills round about. There's only me. There had to be someone to keep an eye on the provisions. I have, under my roof," (and this expression assumed, in his mouth, an impressive air) "storerooms for my cloth. They'd been stuffed full of camphor for a long time. Against moths. It's perfect against the fly that brings the contagion. It's a little fly, not even green."

"Touch my hand," said Angelo.

"Gladly," said the little man, smiling, "but kindly dip it first in this jar of vinegar."

In the end Angelo felt ridiculous.

It was without haste, and swinging his arms as though going for a walk, that Angelo left the town. The nun was forgotten. He was even chewing a sprig of mint.

The hills formed an amphitheatre. On their tiers, the whole population of the town was assembled, as though to watch some great game. The people were encamped under the olive groves, the clumps of oaks, and in the undergrowth of the terebinths. Fires were smoking on all sides.

Angelo was naturally used to soldiers' encampments. They would stack arms, get out their canteens, and after that life was fine. They sang, stirred their soup; they had no need of a drawing-room. They were poor bastards, but they knew that a splendid refuge can be made by thinking about nothing.

The first thing Angelo saw by the roadside was a screen planted under the olive trees of an orchard. It was painted in bright colours, perhaps on silk. It had been designed, no doubt, to cheer up some dim corner by a fireside. Here it stood full in the sun (the threadbare foliage of the olive trees gave hardly any shade), full in the furious sun. The screen spluttered with gold, bright purples, and hard blues. It bore a design of the plumed warriors and swelling breastplates of a canto of Ariosto that Angelo at once remembered. It was set out in the open beside an easy chair covered in tapestry, likewise telling a tale, on which were piled a box encrusted with shells, a parasol, a silver-knobbed cane, and some shawls that the wind had disarrayed so that they trailed on the grass. Right at the foot of the nearest olive tree had been placed (dead level, with the aid of sticks wedged under the legs) a small escritoire, nicely polished and coquettishly bearing its glass-domed clock, its candlesticks, its best coffeepot under a faille cosy braided with ribbons. All around, over a space of seven or eight square yards, were disposed with the utmost harmony an umbrella stand, a tall lamp stand, a pouffe, a foot-muff and a green plant in a pot – a rubber plant, supported by a bamboo cane. Not far off, upturned and pointing at the sky its two shafts, from which dangled chains, was the small cart that had transported the whole paraphernalia; and the mule, its straw and its droppings.

The sight was so incongruous that Angelo stopped. Someone beat on the footwarmer with the cane. A large girl who must have been sitting in the grass got up and approached the screen.

"Who is it?" asked an old woman's voice.

"A man, madame."

"What's he doing?"

"Looking."

"What at?"

"Us."

"Good-day, madame," said Angelo, "is everything all right?"

"Perfectly all right, monsieur," said the voice. "What concern is that of yours?" And to the girl: "Go and sit down."

Then the cane began to thump on the ground like the tail of an exasperated lion.

There were also, at every turn, families of work people sitting in the shade of a wall or bank or bush, or under a small oak, with children, bundles of linen, boxes of tools. The women were rather at a loss, but they had already set up a few utensils, lines stretched between two branches, a tripod supporting a stew pot, and even, here and there, a row of boxes arranged in descending order of size: flour, salt, pepper, spices. The men had been much more disoriented. Their hands would not as yet unclasp from around their knees. They were glad to call good-day to passers-by.

The children weren't playing. There was very little noise, except that of a light wind rattling the sun-roasted leaves, and, from time to time, the noise of the sun itself like a rapid crackle of flame. Only the horses and mules shook their bridles, kicked at the flies, and sometimes neighed, not to each other but in complaint and furtively. Some donkeys tried to start a concert, but there was a sound of sticks thwacking on bellies, and they choked back their braying. Vast flocks of crows kept wheeling, also in silence, above the trees. The sun was so violent that it turned their feathers white.

The peasants had installed themselves more comfortably. They seemed to unstiffen more quickly. They had all, moreover, chosen extremely favourable sites: oak trees, hollows in which the grass was dry but long, pine clumps. Most of them had already cleared their sites of stones. They were even busy all at the same time, but each for himself, cutting branches of broom that they then transported in bundles into their bit of shade. The women stripped the larger sticks and plaited them into hurdles. Children, looking grave and frowning, sharpened stakes.

Several old women, who were not plaiting the broom and seemed to be invested with diplomatic powers, went off with a smile on their lips to prowl round the other encampments, under cover of gathering plants for a rustic salad. They were getting organized. They had even begun very carefully to make little piles of manure with the litter of their beasts.

The only slight dislocation was in their coops full of chickens, not yet let loose; and the pigs tied by the feet to stumps, torturing themselves by straining at the thongs knotted round their hocks but not squealing, scarcely even grunting, and mostly sniffing with extremely mobile snouts towards the smells stirred up by all these strange movements. They had already learned to crouch down under the bushes whenever there passed overhead the rustle of the great flocks of crows.

Locksmith tits, whose song is like grating iron, called ceaselessly, establishing a void where their cries rang, and a distance by the answers they received from remote trees. One could also hear some rather triumphant children's voices, women calling out names, men speaking to their beasts and the bells of hunting-dogs setting out on some scent.

They had transported sideboards, sofas, stoves complete with pipes – which they were struggling to fit together and then attach to branches – cases filled with pots and pans, baskets of crockery and linen, mantelpiece ornaments, firedogs, tripods, trolleys. The furniture was set in the orchards, under isolated trees, even out in the wind. It had quite clearly been arranged here just as it used to be in the rooms from which it was taken. Sometimes it even stood around a table, covered with its oilcloth or carpet, with five or six chairs set around it, or armchairs, in their covers. There would then be an idle woman sitting on one of these chairs instead of on the grass, with her hands on her knees, and always by her side or in the immediate vicinity her man, standing and vacant, like a hero caught unawares. They never stirred. They were like characters in a *tableau vivant*, their eyes fixed on some private horizon, looking at once very knowing and very vulnerable.

Others had heaped merchandise, piles of pieces of cloth, full sacks, cases; and, with their backs against the heap, or even lying on top of it, men, women, and children kept watch.

"Shall I ever find my Giuseppe among all this, or is he dead?" Angelo wondered.

He admitted that, if Giuseppe were dead, well! the situation was grave.

Instead of staying with the nun, he should have looked for Giuseppe. But where in town should he have looked? Whom should he have asked? (Once more he saw the square piled with dead bodies, people dying in heaps on the ground, and the panic of those whom he had seen racing like dogs through the streets; he heard the carters pounding their drums to the echo in every quarter.) One saw things differently here in the groves, in the open air, in spite of the flocks of crows and the rabid sun. Anyhow it was true, he'd wasted his time with the nun. He thought so. One doesn't always do the sensible thing.

He found, by the roadside, one of those small pairs of scales with horn pans in which tobacco is weighed. It lay overturned in the grass. He looked up on to the bank. An old woman was arranging some boxes against an olive stump.

"Madame," asked Angelo, "do you sell tobacco?"

"I did," she said.

"You haven't got a little scrap left?"

"Why mess around with scraps?" she said. "I've got fresh tobacco." Angelo jumped over the bank.

She was a shrewd old crone. She had little magpie eyes and she chewed her gums like a powerful quid.

"Do you have any cigars?" said Angelo.

"Ah, you're a cigar smoker! I've cigars for all ages, sweetheart. If they pay!"

"We'll manage to pay you for them."

"Well, what do you smoke?" She looked him over. "Marshmallow?"

"Give me some *crapulos*," said Angelo drily.

"I'm low on them," she said; "can you make out with half of one, sweetheart?"

"Don't talk so much, Grandma," said Angelo. "Give me a boxful."

Actually, a box was a pretty tall order. He had exactly four louis left. It was truly essential for Giuseppe to be alive, otherwise times were going to get hard. But it was truly essential to put that woman and her quid in their place.

She rummaged in the sacks she had been unpacking and found a box of cigars, for which Angelo paid with a markedly casual air.

"I suppose *you* know everybody around here?" he said.

"Well, I know quite a few."

"Do you know somebody named Giuseppe?"

"Sweetheart, that's not the way I know people. What does your Giuseppe look like? What do his friends call him? Does he have a nickname?"

"I don't know; what nickname would he go by? The Piedmontese, perhaps? He's a tall fellow, thin and dark, with curly hair."

"Piedmontese? No, I don't know any Piedmontese. Dark, did you say? No. You're sure he's not dead?"

"I'd very much like him to be alive."

"You're not the only one who'd like somebody to be alive. The chances are, your Giuseppe's pushing up daisies. Everybody's dying these days, haven't you noticed?"

"Not quite everybody," said Angelo; "there's still some of us left."

"Oh! yes, a fine lot we are!" she said.

While they were busy talking a woman came to buy snuff. She was a housewife. She looked completely out of place in this orchard.

"Hold on," said the old woman, "here's someone who may give you some news about your Giuseppe."

"Madame Marie," said the woman, "give me a little of the best, please. Not too dry, if you can manage."

"I can always manage, beautiful; pass me the sack there on the left by your feet. And what are you doing with yourself these days?"

"I try to keep going. It isn't easy."

"Where are you bunking nowadays?"

"I'm with the Magnans, down there, under the oaks."

"You share grub?"

"It isn't just grub," said the woman, gazing at Angelo with bold eyes. "Living outdoors scares me. I need company. Theirs is as good as the next, isn't it?"

"Well, perhaps you may hit it off with this fellow. He's looking for something. He'd like to find somebody named Giuseppe."

Hands on hips, the woman settled her body in her corset.

"Who's Giuseppe?" she said.

"A man, beautiful," said the old woman.

"He's a friend I'm looking for," said Angelo.

"Everyone's looking for a friend," said the woman.

She hesitated between pushing back the hair that was falling down upon her forehead and taking a pinch of snuff. She looked Angelo up and down and decided on the snuff.

The next visitor was a man; he lifted the low branches of the olive tree.

"What do you want?" said the woman.

"Well, can't you see? Madame Marie," he said, "it's time you found me my tobacco. You're getting things straightened out, aren't you?"

"Cléristin," said the old woman. "You've found a corner for your mule, haven't you? I still can't lay my hands on your tobacco. You got everything mixed up, tossing it around like that. Your tobacco is down at the bottom, under those boxes. Do you want to move them for me, or will you try another brand? Why not take a chance, my boy?"

There was nothing boyish about him. He was a thick, heavy fellow with bow legs and the arms of an ape. But he had sharp eyes ...

"This young fellow is looking for somebody named Giuseppe," said the woman.

"Giuseppe who?" he asked.

"Just Giuseppe," said Angelo.

"What's he do?"

"Shoemaker."

"Don't know him," said the man. "You'd better go see Féraud."

"That's right," said the woman.

"Féraud's a shoemaker too; they all know one another."

"Where is Féraud?"

"Go up there through the pines. He's a bit higher up, among the junipers."

There was a track that climbed from terrace to terrace. On these levellings supported by small stone walls stood the olive groves with their black twisted trunks. They wore a fleece lighter than foam and retained, on the undersides of their leaves, a residue of opalescent colour that the sun had almost completely effaced. Under this shelter, as transparent as a silk veil, the people were camping in small groups. At the moment they were eating. It was nearly noon.

The pines pointed out to him were a long way up the hill, well above the orchards. Angelo asked where he could buy bread. He was told to go a bit to the left, towards some cypresses. It seemed there was a baker there who had tried setting up a field oven.

Long before reaching the cypresses one could smell a fine scent of baking. A slowly mounting blue smoke, to which the sun's dazzling whiteness gave a shimmer, also indicated the spot.

The baker, naked to the waist, was sitting at the foot of the cypresses, in the axis of the shade. He let two powdery hands hang down over his knees. He was a man of about fifty, very thin. On his chest the ribs stuck out, furrowed with grey hairs.

"You're just in time," he said; "we're about to open the oven. What it'll be like, I don't know; maybe bread, maybe a flat pancake; perhaps just a dirty mess. It's the first time in my life I've worked under these conditions."

He had built a sort of kiln, like those in which they make charcoal. Covered with lumps of turf, it allowed the smoke to seep out, pure blue and so thick that it slowly rose straight up, joined and intertwined a dozen feet or so above the leaves of the olives, and went on ascending slowly, a pillar reflecting the sunlight, to a great height in the sky, where, before dissolving in the shimmering white heat, it spread out a whole chain of mirrors for the larks.

"It will be what it will be," said Angelo.

"You've said it," the man replied.

Angelo watched a squadron of crows, high above the hilltop, playing with light puffs of wind. On motionless wings, the birds danced and dipped, approached, joined, and separated from each other like grains of oats in the currents of a stream.

"They're the lucky ones," said the baker.

"True enough," said Angelo. "But pretty soon we'll get things straightened out."

"That's not the way it looks."

"How does it look?"

"As bad as ever."

"There are still cases?"

"If you can believe your own eyes. And there's no reason not to."

"People look worn out, but they're still living."

"They were just as worn out in town and they were still living, but you didn't see them. All you saw was the dead. Out here it seems the other way round, I know, and that's all to the good. But take a good look down there, in that direction. The little valley running off into the hills, the plane trees and the little field. See those yellow tents? That's an infirmary. And down there towards the Saint-Pierre quarter, in the cherry orchards, more tents. Another infirmary. And down there, on the north slope, more tents; another. If you'd been resting like me at the foot of a cypress ever since the oven was lit, you'd have seen them carting off more than enough. I've counted at least fifty since this morning! Don't you think fifty's quite a number?"

"The thing can't stop all at once."

"I don't know what it can't do, but I know what it does. How about that up there?" (He pointed to the thick clouds of hawks and crows, which had begun to circle in the wind above the hill. There came from them a resonance like the beating of a fan.) "Those fellows are more intelligent than people think. They know what they're doing. Don't worry, they aren't there for nothing. You can blaze away into the thick of them with a blunderbuss. They stay where there's something to eat."

"There's certainly something in what he says," Angelo reflected, but he was hungry, and the smell from the oven was exquisite.

"I did the kneading in a pig trough," said the baker. "Clean, of course. I found it in the small hut down there. I said to my wife: 'That's Antonin's hut. I bet you anything you like he's got a pig trough.' My God, I was getting bored. I said to myself: 'I'm going to make some bread.' Anyhow, it turned out well; people come after it. 'And to start with, they're going to give it a thorough washing out for me,' I said. That's right, water! You been yet to the water?"

"No."

"I suppose it is a problem," thought Angelo. "Where can there be any water in these hills?"

"If you haven't been there, I'll show you. You'll see what a job it is. See that oak down there? Good. Well, in a straight line above it, aim at that willow copse. It's there. It's a clay-pit. The water's all right, though you couldn't call it clear or very cool. There's quite a lot. But it's all the way down. Going and returning with buckets takes more than half an hour. The wife, the daughter and I have made at least twenty trips. And we're not the only ones. Look."

It was true. In the shade of the willows could be seen the red, blue, green, and white of jackets, petticoats, aprons. Their colours disappeared as soon as they emerged from the shade into the full sunshine, and all that remained was the sparkle of buckets of water by the sides of small dazzling silhouettes.

The loaves that the baker finally drew out of the kiln were flat as pancakes, and very unevenly cooked.

"You're never sure of your bakings with this system," he said. "The one before was passable; this one's not worth a rabbit's fart. Give me a good brick oven. The scurvy had to get into our houses. A fine mess we're in! What shall I charge you for this? Give me what you like. Let's say two sous, and take three or four of them." His indifference did not stop him from carefully placing the burning-hot loaves on a bed of thyme, from which their heat drew an exquisite fragrance; and he looked round to see if it was reaching the other campers.

Angelo took a flat cake and walked on for a while, letting it cool.

A little higher up, on the edge of the pine woods, he found a fine little family silently lunching, gazing at the wide landscape and chewing each mouthful very slowly. There were a red-haired fleshy man and a woman, sturdily built but maternal from top to toe, as women of such breadth of shoulder generally are. The woman was holding on her lap a delicate, pale little girl with dreamy eyes. The freckles sprinkled around her nose widened her cheeks like a Venetian mask and gave them the *morbidezza* of the Primavera.

"Careful!" said Angelo to himself. "She's the apple of their eyes. If they knew that I'm going to sit down in their neighbourhood just to be able to look at that exquisite face while I eat my dry bread, they'd think I was sucking the marrow from their bones."

And he went and sat down casually under a pine tree. He leaned his back against the trunk. He began, like them, to chew his mouthfuls slowly in front of the vast landscape. He only glanced sideways at the little girl's face, and at careful intervals. Despite these precautions, he several times met the eyes of the mother, and even of the father. They had instinctively seen through his manoeuvre and, without knowing exactly why, far from finding it inoffensive they were suspicious. The woman was holding the little girl like a church candle and kept shifting her from knee to knee.

At the bottom of the hill lay the town: a tortoise shell in the grass; the sunlight, now slightly slanting, checkered the scaly roofs with lines of shadow; the wind went in by one street and out by another, trailing columns of straw dust. Shutters were grinding on their hinges and banging, doubling the sadness of the houses.

Beyond the town rose a plain of yellow grass, stained with great patches of rust. These were grain fields from which the harvest had not been gathered in, and would not be, because the owners were dead. Further on, winding and flat, a rocky, whitened Durance, without one drop of water. The horizon was cluttered with mountains. The roads were empty.

Empty also the roads of hope. The sky was plaster, the heat like glue. The dry wind bestowed no breath but only blows; it smelt of goats and other, terrible, things.

Angelo crossed the pine woods. A few families had established themselves in the shelter of the trees. Each group kept to itself, withdrawn and quiet. Among them also he noticed one or two fine pairs of eyes, one or two fine-looking people whose presence was mysteriously reassuring. Their families were jealous of these and huddled around them like hungry dogs. Neighbours and passers-by were lucky to get half-smiles, mainly showing the teeth.

People were huddled like this without speaking, sometimes around a man, who was not even handsome but gave them, by his sturdy demeanour, an impression of solidity, almost a pledge of permanence. Sometimes it was a woman. Some of these were old, with peace in their faces. One could never tire of looking at these mouths and eyes that nothing disturbed, over which flickered the grey-green shadows of the pine branches. Others were young women whose hair, eyes, complexion, gestures were of precious material, therefore incorruptible; or children who, because they no longer laughed, seemed suddenly profound, bowed down with knowing.

Higher above the pine woods, Angelo heard groans and sobbing. There was such silence round about that the wails sounded like a lonely fountain. It was two men tending a third laid out under an ilex. All were weeping.

Angelo offered help but was not welcomed. It was beyond question an attack of cholera in its first stages, and the two men were managing very efficiently. Angelo realized that they were mainly afraid of being reported and of having the sick man taken off to the infirmaries.

"Learn a little selfishness," he told himself; "it's very useful, and keeps you from looking like a fool. Those two have sent you packing, and they're right. They're intent on their own business and doing it the way they want to. They haven't the slightest wish for you to come and meddle in it. Whether this sick man gets better or worse, in a quarter of an hour they won't be weeping any more: they'll only be thinking of what to do next. Do you imagine generosity is always good? Nine times out of ten it's offensive. And it's never manly."

These reflections brought him considerable peace, and he continued to climb the hill, towards the clump of pines where the man should be who perhaps knew where Giuseppe was to be found.

Cries broke out. This time they were not lamentation but shouts of pursuit. Two or three men had risen and were peering into a ravine. Angelo approached. Through the bushes he could see people running.

"I bet it's a hare," said Angelo.

"You'd lose," came the answer. "Besides, in this heat the hares aren't such fools. They don't budge."

The men looked at Angelo with slight contempt. Though the contempt was faint and only on the surface Angelo was deeply mortified. He maintained that in his country the hares ran in spite of the heat.

"Then you're lucky and have special hares," he was told ironically. "Here we only have ordinary ones. Down there it's just an old bastard who's escaped from his daughter. The joke is that he was paralysed and was carted out here in his armchair; and now he's leading them the devil of a dance."

In fact, one could see, down below, an old man hobbling through the grass. The pursuers caught him. There was a confused mêlée from which spurted up the yelping of a woman. An argument began, with much gesticulating. At length, two men linked their arms to make a chair, the old man was installed in it, and they started back up the hill.

He passed close to Angelo. He was an old eagle-headed peasant. He kept turning his alert eyes in the direction of the town. Someone had rolled him a cigarette to calm him. He was smoking it.

His daughter ran to meet him. She thanked everyone. She went on and on thanking them and saying: "But why, Father? What's the matter with you?" She noticed the cigarette:

"Did you say thank-you, Father?" she asked him.

"I said f— you," said he.

He choked over his dribbling and his cigarette, which he began to chew furiously like a stalk of hay.

The clump of trees where the man called Féraud had set up camp was, to begin with, well placed near the summit of the hill and just in the path of the wind that curled over the crest. Furthermore, it contained the only real encampment in all that area. The space between the trees had been carefully cleared of undergrowth, and wattles of interwoven branches a span high had been stretched from trunk to trunk. In the shelter thus formed, pine needles had been heaped, and when Angelo arrived three women were busy spreading a fine white sheet over this mattress. Two other trimly folded sheets showed that they were determined to make a proper bed here. Of the three women, two were hardly more than twenty and were doubtless the daughters, the other being their mother; and all three were working energetically.

As for Féraud, he had set up his bench at the edge of the trees, half in the shade, half in the sun, and was simply busy fashioning a sole with his paring-knife. He was humming.

The man looked quite young in spite of his white beard.

He knew where Giuseppe was.

"See that hill planted with almond trees?"

"You mean the other hill, over there?"

"Yes. He's there. Probably a little higher up, towards the ilexes."

"Are you sure?"

"Absolutely sure. Go there and you'll find him. As soon as you're on the hill with the almonds, ask anyone. They'll take you straight to him."

"D'you know him well?"

"I know him very well."

"And how can I get over there?"

"That's easy. Go straight down as far as the cypresses."

"Where the baker is?"

"That's it. Go sharp right for a hundred yards and you'll strike a road. Take it and keep straight on. You're not afraid of the infirmaries?"

"No."

"You'll pass close by. And your road leads on. Look, you can see it down there. It rises. You come out right among the almond trees. Ask the first person you meet for Giuseppe and you'll find him."

Finally he laid the shoe down in the grass and asked: "What do you want with Giuseppe?"

"I'm a relative," said Angelo.

"What relation? It's not to do with Italy?"

"Yes," said Angelo. "It's just a little to do with Italy."

Féraud called his wife.

"It's the gentleman Giuseppe's been expecting so impatiently," he said.

"Have you had anything to drink?" the woman immediately asked Angelo, resting her hands on her hips with relief.

"Not a drop for two days," replied Angelo. "My mouth's like tin."

"I'm glad to hear it," said the woman. "These days a tin mouth means a tin belly. That's what worried Giuseppe. All day long he kept repeating: 'You'll see, he'll drink. He won't be able to stop himself. He'll die on me from drinking!'"

"I haven't died from drinking," said Angelo, "I drank wine when I could. When I couldn't, I went without."

"I shan't give you wine: we haven't any. But water, boiled twice over. And just half a cup. D'you know what we must do? I keep telling them all the time," she said, pointing at her husband and daughters, "but they laugh at me: we must get used to making saliva and only drinking that. These days a person who drinks his saliva doesn't die."

"He doesn't die, but he cracks apart with thirst," said Féraud.

"I tell you what, I'm going to give him half a cup. Now that Giuseppe is going to see his gentleman, it's no time to kill him off under his nose, that's for sure!"

This family was very united, and soon the daughters, who had finished making the bed on the pine needles, approached their father and stroked his beard. Between the two of them hanging on his shoulders, he purred. The mother appeared to run things with a firm hand, but in reality she was easily discomposed by caresses, in which she visibly delighted.

She managed none the less to give Angelo his promised half-cupful of boiled water.

Finally, they asked him to stay and share the evening meal. It wasn't much, but at least there was a potato stew and some mutton cutlets. There was, it seemed, under the oaks a hundred yards or so to the left, a butcher who was slaughtering. Angelo learned many other things besides.

They seemed to hold Giuseppe in great esteem. Esteem was indeed rather too weak a word. Giuseppe, it seemed, was a boy of the same age as Angelo, within a few months. He was his foster brother. And Féraud was a steady man with a white beard, and dreamy eyes, it is true. Angelo wondered several times if it were really his Giuseppe whom they meant.

"A thin fellow, like a dry stick."

"That's him."

"One lip thin."

"The upper one. Like a razor."

"The other thick."

"The lower one. A girl's lip."

"Well, thick, anyhow."

Angelo found it hard to imagine how they could say Giuseppe's lower lip was girlish. Giuseppe had been his orderly. The King of Sardinia's army may have been only the King of Sardinia's army, but it was still thousands of men living together. It only needed a fortnight for a lip to be no longer judged by appearances.

The daughters laid great emphasis on his black curly hair.

"It's like parsley," they said.

The day the general had had those parsley locks sheared off, Giuseppe had served the soup holding his galley-slave's head high.

"He's turned you into an egg," Angelo said to him.

"Your mother's too fancy," retorted Giuseppe. "But I'm the one who suffers; you're a colonel."

Angelo had kicked the soup tureen out of his hands. The two of them had hacked the mess room to pieces with their swords as they fought. But as soon as they saw each other's blood they had fallen into each other's arms. At the next day's parade, Giuseppe gravely sported a head with all his colonel's hair glued on to it. Angelo, without a helmet and shaved like a convict, pranced before the ranks smiling with happiness.

It had been a good game. Giuseppe's speciality was games of every sort, including bloody ones. Wasn't the esteem – or more – in which

Féraud with his white beard (and dreamy eyes, it is true) held him, perhaps the result of some game? And not just *any* game, since Féraud had asked so precisely *if it hadn't something to do with Italy?*

Angelo was treated like a fighting cock. The daughters even seemed embarrassed at not giving him his share of the family caresses. As they took the dish round, two or three times they laid a hand on his shoulder.

"It'll soon be dark," said Féraud; "are you set on finding Giuseppe this evening?"

"As soon as possible," said Angelo.

"I understand. Well, you must go a slightly longer way round than the one I showed you just now, but it's safer. I know you're not afraid of passing the infirmaries; all the same it's best to be careful at night, and I'd rather keep you away from them. It's not ghosts I'm thinking of. It's because people go and leave their sick all around there on the sly, owing to the quarantine that's imposed on the relatives who've looked after them. Suppose, as you were passing, you fell in with a patrol and they suddenly flashed their lanterns on you (they get a bonus every time they catch someone), you'd be inside for forty days. And just now a lot can happen in forty days. Do you know what I'd do? Just spend the night under that oak, ten yards off. You won't bother us. I'll lend you a blanket that you can spread on the dry leaves. Tomorrow you'll have daylight."

"That may be what I ought to do," replied Angelo, "but I shan't do it. I'll go now. I'll manage. They can flash their lanterns, they won't get me.

"Anyway," he added, to see what had been the basis of Giuseppe's game (if there had been one), "I'm homesick," and he talked about Italy for a full ten minutes.

But Féraud's eyes remained dreamy. His white beard seemed to clothe him entirely with innocence.

Although night had fallen, Angelo found the cypresses easily. The baker who had chosen to make his home at the foot of the tree was preparing another ovenful. From there, following Féraud's fresh instructions, he was to take the road at right angles (which he did) and cross the flank of the hill, along terraces placed like avenues one above the other. The directions were clear: never to go down, but to

172

keep straight on around the hillside until he reached a deep ravine, which he would have to climb through in order to reach the other side, and to keep skirting the bottomlands where the infirmaries lay. In this way (Féraud had traced the whole route for Angelo with his fingertip in the expiring twilight) one could reach the almond-tree hill beside a rocky cliff, which one circled around until one met a fairly wide track, almost a cart track, cutting across it and leading on to the tableland where Giuseppe was.

Fires were being lit everywhere. Close by stood tall braziers whose flames writhed and twisted. They chattered like peasant women dancing clogs on a wooden floor. Further on, through the foliage of the olives, pines, and oaks, red lights were dancing violently. A medley of voices and shouting rose up all around along with the crackling of the braziers. Even on the most distant crests, which just now in the daylight had seemed deserted, fires were being lit, against which the silhouette of a tree, of a rock, stood out. In the groves where the infirmaries had been set up, people were attaching lanterns to the branches of trees to make the work of the patrols easier. In every thicket, under every bush, behind every mass of foliage, shone red grids, plates of incandescence, phosphorescent birds like huge purple hens, vermillion cockerels. In the swaying and palpitation – the furious fanning of these flames, the leaping of all those golden calves, the assaults of all the sharp flakes of fire – the night crumbled away on every side. An inaudible avalanche of boulders, violet, purple, or red like embers, pitched in the sky, covering it with rosy dust, splitting it with indigo crevasses. The reflections struck the empty town below, revealing the top of a belfry, the opening of a street, the porch and battlements of a main gate, the chessboard of a roof, the silk of a wall, the socket of a window, the brow of a convent, the frill of eaves, chimneys rising from outspread roofs like stumps in a field. Two leagues beyond the town, the fires hidden under the forests of the Durance glowed on the ground between the tree trunks like embers in a grille, all down the river. In the shadows of the valley, on the crisscross of roads and footpaths, small points of light were moving: they were the lanterns of the patrols, the stretcher-bearers' lamps, the torches of the corpse-carters at work. The thyme, savory, sage, and hyssop of the moors, the very earth and stones on which all these fires were kindled, the sap of the trees heated by the flames, the sweat of the smoked leaves, gave off a thick scent of balm and resin. It seemed as if the whole earth were an oven for baking bread.

The ravine that Féraud had mentioned was steep and appeared very deep. As Angelo paused on the brink a small black shape brushed against him and an old woman's voice: "It's this way. There's the path; follow me."

"Ho!" thought Angelo, "have they already enlisted ghosts?"

He heard a patter of feet on the pebbles; he plunged down behind it.

"Be careful," the voice went on.

A bony hand seized his hand.

"Thank you, madame," he said.

But he was icy cold from head to foot.

As step by step he followed the hand guiding him down an extremely slippery slope, he reassured himself with memories of the *Carbonari*. It was by such rugged paths that one reached their camps in the Apennines.

"You're at the bottom," said the voice.

And the hand let him go.

He was indeed on level ground but in thick darkness. He did not dare move. He heard someone walking; the bushes scratched against cloth; there was whispering. He was incapable of a rational thought. He gripped his pistol and asked, very stiffly:

"Who goes there? Who are you?" (He just barely kept from shouting.) "Advance and be recognized."

He was on his guard and felt behind him with his hand for something to put his back against, in order to make an honourable stand.

"We're the women from up above, going to the *ora pro nobis*," came the reply.

"What have I been seeing in these flames and smoke?" he asked himself. "An episode from Ariosto; and it's just some people going to pray not to die."

He found a path without any trouble, and followed the ghosts, some of whom now were bending pipes, mouths, and red beards over the sparks of their tinderboxes.

"My eyes always look at things through a magnifying glass," Angelo told himself. "Everything I see is magnified at least ten times, and naturally I do ten times too much. Just because the night is painted in all the colours of the inferno, there's no reason to imagine I'm going to see the swift mountain leopard arrive, and the she-wolf and Virgil and 'Abandon hope all ye who enter here.' It's nothing but the reflections from the fires these people have lit because they're afraid of the night. It's quite plain to a simple man. But I'm not simple: I'm double, triple, even centuple.

"This isn't the first time I've wanted to kill flies with a cannon. It's the hundred-thousandth. It happens to me every day and all day. I always expect the worst and carry on as if it were the worst. Well! Get into the habit of realizing that ordinary things happen too. Don't be all the time throwing in the reserves. As soon as you have to do with anything or anyone, you go wild. You invent giants and monsters at every turn in the road. The first wretch that comes along, as soon as he crosses your path, becomes an Atlas. This is pride. Those who objected to your duel with the Baron were right. A simple little stab would have done the job and, admit it now, done the job much better. He was only a small police spy. It was purely and simply a matter of getting rid of him. A question of disposal of some rubbish. To rid the world of him. Why add fancy steps to a clean-up operation?

"You're incurable: your eye glued to the magnifying glass, your mouth to the megaphone. Why say now that we had to 'rid the world of him'? The world! What a big world! It was Turin we had to rid of him. Turin isn't the world. And the Baron was no trouble to the Chinese. He didn't even trouble Turin. He merely troubled our little group of patriots.

"You'll never manage, let alone to behave, even to speak like everyone else," he pursued, with genuine sorrow. "There they are again, the big words, the big ideas, the majestic enterprises. Won't you ever use down-to-earth, carpet-slipper words? Off you go with your word 'patriot'! So we're patriots! Are you more of a patriot here in this gully than the master mason stirring his mortar in a suburb of Turin or Genoa, even if he's only building a hunting-lodge or a barber shop? More of a patriot than the Lombard shepherd who passes his time planting acorns with the end of his crook while he guards his sheep on the lonely heights? The saddlers in the Via del Perseo may be stitching leather that will do more for the glory of their country, something surer and more permanent, than all your flag-waving . . . And by what right do you speak of your country if you don't know that any farm labourer and all the *basso continuo* of humble lives are building it more solidly, furrow by furrow and task by task, than all your *Carbonari* in their fever bushes and forests?

"You never put yourself where you belong. You're always putting yourself in some place that you invent. And God knows you invent lofty ones! Men aren't worth much. Agreed? Well, you're a man. Still agreed? The whole thing's there.

"Granted, you're not a coward. You're even the opposite. For what you are, one would need to invent a word that would outshine 'brave' the way 'cowardly' does 'nervous'. When you took out your pistol just now, it wasn't from fear of the night or even because of that dry hand which was guiding you down the slope (you had goose flesh and it was plainly some old granny's hand); it was because you will never admit that you may just be dealing with a simple ravine and extremely simple people who don't give a damn about you and are just going to pray not to die."

Having spoken to himself in this way, Angelo felt sharp, clear, and ready for any folly. For some time now he had been hearing grunts that suggested some pigsty or a huge troop of crows. But he realized that this time he had bid too low and that they were the sounds of a harmonium. Indeed, the music was very beautiful and had an extraordinarily chivalrous quality. Soon he heard also the rhythmic murmur of a multitude of voices all pronouncing the same words together.

The track was now lit by the red and wavering light of a few braziers still hidden by a shoulder of rock. Flames now and then leapt over the crest like purple grasshoppers.

After a detour, Angelo found himself at the approach to a sort of amphitheatre surrounded by tall oaks, where a religious meeting was in progress. About a hundred men and women kneeling in the grass were giving the responses to a litany. The priest chanting it was standing a few paces in front of the farther trees and between two big fires so stoutly fed that the flames stood up straight like scarlet columns.

176

A woman, who at first sight seemed old though she was dressed in white, was playing the portable organ. She was not playing a concert piece; she was just accompanying the priest's words and the responses in an uninterrupted flow, or, to be more precise, with music like the endless unrolling of a chain connecting earth and heaven.

Angelo thought at once of the angels ascending and descending Jacob's ladder.

The glare of the fires, which lit the vaults, flying buttresses, and ribs of the branches, the green frescoes of foliage, built a natural temple over the worshippers.

"And here's what simple folk come to," said Angelo. "The nun and I may have washed with our own hands and prepared for Judgment Day the father, mother, brother, sister, husband, or wife of one of these men or women here, simply begging all the saints to pray for them. They are right. This way is much easier. It can't help being the solution. We ought to have something like this in politics. If it doesn't exist already, we must invent one."

After a benediction and a sign of the cross the priest withdrew from between his two braziers and went to sit under an oak at the edge of the shadow, while the faithful too sat down on the grass. The organist raised her arms and arranged her bun. She continued to make the pedals hum.

She was a young woman. She seemed nearsighted. She gazed at the assembly, plainly without seeing it. She seemed affected only by the silence, in which nothing but the crackle of the braziers could be heard. She wiped her forehead and resumed playing.

Freed from religious trappings, the music affected Angelo violently. Even the priest, back there in the shadow and the flickering firelight, was now only a sort of gilded insect. Every face was turned towards the organist. Angelo noticed some handsome profiles. They belonged to various grave men whose sunburn was reddened still more by the light, and to certain women who looked like Junos and Minervas. What with these faces, the great fires, and the depth of the woods, the music created a world without politics, where the cholera was no more than an exercise in style. Finally, with nothing by way of warning that the end of this world was drawing near, the young woman raised her hands and, after letting the instrument sigh away, closed the lid over the keyboard.

Angelo perceived that he had not followed Féraud's directions. At the spot where he had descended into the ravine, he should have gone up the slope on the other side, straight ahead. He had followed the shades, he had kept along the ravine, descending. It was no good counting on finding the place again in the dark. The simplest thing was now to follow straight down the path. Patrols, quarantines, lanterns would be seen approaching. These famous patrols were unlikely to rake the plain with too fine a comb. There should be ways of passing between the teeth.

He had not walked half an hour when he found himself facing an orchard whose every tree carried at least one lantern. Sometimes they bore two or three, especially along the roadside. It was an orchard where an infirmary had been set up. Indeed, one could see, far back under the trees, the white patch of the tents, some of them lit up inside and looking like huge phosphorescent caterpillars. He heard continuous groans, conversations, and all at once some sharp cries, while the tent from which these came began to rock its lantern like a boat caught by a squall in the night.

He had noticed a very rough, thick hedge that ran between some willows. He went towards it. Fortunately he was walking in a field where his steps made no sound, and he took the precaution of concealing himself behind a willow trunk before taking refuge in the hedge. He heard someone at the foot of the hedge calling in a whisper a name that he couldn't catch. A voice replied from up in the willow, which stood in the hedge itself.

"Not yet," it said, "it's a bit early, but I can see some of them up there; there's no doubt they're getting ready."

Angelo looked in the direction of the hill. The fires were no longer throwing up any flames, but the embers were very bright; against their redness could be seen in certain places the silhouettes of people all very busy and sometimes stooping towards the ground.

"Are we in a good place?" resumed the voice from the hedge.

"They're certainly going to try to dump them down here this evening," replied the man in the willow.

The speakers were middle-class townsmen. Even so, two or three gun-barrels could be seen gleaming along the hedge.

For quite a long while there was no further sound.

"It's extraordinary," thought Angelo. "Can these bourgeois really be capable of mounting guard properly? If so, they might give us a good beating before they're through."

He kept his ears pricked, but there was not another word to be heard, not even the sound of someone clearing his throat. They had so much as put the guns out of sight.

"If I didn't know they were there, I'd fall into the trap myself," he thought.

He was full of admiration for their efficiency.

"Here's something I must tell Giuseppe about."

Suddenly on the left there was a noise of rustling leaves, as if an animal were trying to break through the hedge. Several shadows were moving at the edge of the light from the lanterns.

Angelo had to admit that these bourgeois knew how to crawl and spring out as well as anyone. All he heard was a slight clink of weapons, then he saw black shapes pass swiftly in front of the lantern. The patrol had just caught two men in the act of swinging a corpse over the hedge.

They had not won the day yet, all the same. The two men caught in the act seemed very excited and were gesticulating violently.

"Keep quiet or we shoot," shouted someone. "We know who you are, and if you run away we'll come and get you up there in your grove. The law applies to everybody."

"Let them go, messieurs," begged a heart-rending girl's voice. "They're my brothers. It's our father we've brought. We couldn't bury him up there."

They continued to harangue and bully.

"This is the last straw! Poisoning everybody! You have to declare your dead and be quarantined. We don't want to die like flies."

"It's in your quarantines that people die like flies."

"Shut up and come here. I'll shoot you just as soon as the men."

A few low cries came from the girl.

"Doesn't she know that these bourgeois are always caught short by the unforeseen?" said Angelo to himself. "If she suddenly takes a good jump backwards, she'll escape them. Or simply if I shout 'Halt!' rather loudly, from here.

"Hold on," he added. "Are you going to get yourself knocked off by a pack of bourgeois? Keep quiet."

He had just remembered the sentinel in the willow. Had he stayed at his post, or had he run off with the others?

"Who'd have thought these shopkeepers could stump me in my own trade?"

He had the sense to lie low and keep quiet.

Two men of the patrol led away the prisoners, who were now subdued.

The others returned to mount guard.

"Who was it?" asked the voice in the willow.

"The sons and daughter of Thomé."

"Was it old Thomé they dumped?"

"Yes. He seems quite dry. They must have kept him at least two days. They're stubborn as mules. There's no stopping them."

"A firm hand's the only thing."

"That Marguerite tried to soft-soap me, but you heard me tell her I'd shoot her just as soon as a man."

"Did they catch anybody down on the right?" asked another voice.

"They haven't budged."

"Thanks for the information," thought Angelo. "So there are others, down on the right, and perhaps down ahead, and down on the left. This is good to know. So you want to play at war, do you? Well, war isn't like hunting, my boys. When you score a hit, you have to be as careful afterward as before. These fellows will always be amateurs. If we can't beat them in open battle, we can win in a skirmish."

He took advantage of the fact that the conversation was quietly receding. He soon found, with the tip of his boot, one of those streams that divide fields in two. It was dry as tinder and deep enough to hide a man crawling on all fours. It also ran under a little bank, and the lanterns cast no light there.

Angelo passed close to another patrol huddled against an enormous willow trunk, and he met a third party walking along with their weapons slung. This time he had only to lie flat in the stream and it concealed him completely. One member of the patrol stepped over him totally unawares. Angelo wouldn't have traded his place for anything.

He was so delighted with his own skill that he stood up to his full height as soon as the patrol had passed. He was just a few yards away from a thick shadow, into which he leapt. He tripped over a kneeling figure and fell full-length on top of a man who said: "Don't say a word; let me go; I'll give you a sugar loaf."

"What are you doing with a sugar loaf?" said Angelo.

"Ah! You're not one of those fellows?"

"What fellows do you mean?"

"Keep still. They're coming."

Angelo heard the patrol returning. He remained lying, motionless, on top of the man – who was only a little boy.

The patrol beat the bushes with their rifle-butts at the edge of the shadow, but they did not come closer.

"If you moved a little I'd be able to get up," said the boy, when the patrol had moved off.

"I'll let you up when you've told me all about your sugar loaf," said Angelo, still in the full tide of happiness. He had even spoken out loud, very pleasantly.

"I was helping a friend," said the boy. "His sister died this afternoon, and we came to leave her down here, because the infirmary people bury all the bodies they find. But if they catch you, they take you off to quarantine. That's why I hid when they went by; then just afterwards you fell on top of me."

"How about your sugar loaf – what's it got to do with all this?"

"Sometimes they let you go if you grease their palms."

"A sugar loaf isn't very much. You can get one for a dozen sous."

"That's what you think. Since the plague started, not many people have sugar with their coffee. My family own a grocery. And there's some people who've come with louis to spend and gone away empty-handed. If you really let me up, I'll give *you* the sugar loaf. Don't you believe me?"

"Of course," said Angelo, "but I don't want your sugar loaf."

They both stood up and instinctively stepped back several paces deeper into the shadow.

"You scared me so much I can hardly stand up," said the boy.

"What's happened to your friend?"

"Oh, don't worry about him, he's a fast runner!"

"He left you here?"

"Of course. What was the use of us both getting caught?"

"You're a decent lad, I must say."

"And who are you? Did you bring a body down too?"

"No. I'm just passing by. I'm looking for a road."

"It's dangerous to look for it over there."

"I'm tough," said Angelo. "Besides, what am I risking?"

"They're tougher than you. Don't you trust them. If they catch you, they'll put you in quarantine."

"And what then? One fine day they'll have to let me go."

"They won't ever let you go. Everyone dies in quarantine. Of all those who've gone in, not one's come out."

"Because their quarantine hasn't finished."

"Something else has finished for a lot of them. We've got eyes in our heads: we've seen them building a big trench. They tried to do it on the sly, at the bottom of the ravine, but we saw their spades shining."

"That was to bury the other dead."

"Then why did they dig it right in front of the quarantine area? And why did they wait till three in the morning, when everyone was asleep, to put the bodies in? And why was there all that coming and going of lanterns between the quarantine and the trench? Don't think we were asleep! . . . We wanted to see. Well! we saw. And why, since yesterday, is there no sentinel any more at the quarantine?"

"Doubtless because you're right," said Angelo.

"Where are you going?" asked the boy.

"I'm trying to get to that hill planted with almond trees, which must be over there, I think. I'm no longer exactly sure which way it is."

"Just about where you said, but it's hard to get up there from where you are now. You'd have to go right through the part where the infirmaries are. If you escaped some, you'd fall into the others."

"I've got my pistol," said Angelo.

"They've got guns and they don't mind using them. They are either bird shot or rock salt. Just enough to shoot you."

"That's a real bourgeois idea," thought Angelo. Not for all the gold in the world did he want to make a fool of himself by getting wounded with rock salt or bird shot.

"I'll take you, if you like," said the boy.

"You know the way?"

"I know a way nobody else knows. It leads straight there."

"All right, let's go," said Angelo. "At any rate, if they catch us I'll kick up a row; while that's going on, you get away."

"Right," said the boy. "Don't worry."

They walked more than an hour through a maze of very dark sunken lanes. After gradually becoming convinced that there was no danger, Angelo stopped playing the game that had so delighted him, and started to chat with the boy. The boy told him that here they might think themselves lucky: in Marseille, in certain streets, the dead were piled higher than the doors of the shops. Aix, too, was devastated. An appalling variety of the epidemic was raging there. The sick were first attacked by what seemed drunkenness, which set them running in every direction, staggering and uttering horrible cries. They had blazing eyes, hoarse voices, and appeared to have rabies. Friends fled from friends. A mother had been seen with her son running after her, a daughter pursued by her mother, newlyweds hunting one another; the town was now no better than a hunting-ground. They had recently decided, it seemed, to beat the sick senseless: instead of stretcher-bearers the roads were patrolled by a sort of dog-catcher armed with cudgels and lassos. Avignon was also in delirium; the sick threw themselves into the Rhone, or hanged themselves, hacked their throats with razors, tore open the veins of their wrists with their teeth. In certain places the sick were so burned up with fever that their corpses turned into tinder and would catch fire suddenly of their own accord, whenever a breath of wind passed over them, or just from their own excessive dryness, and they had set fire to the town of Die. The stretcher men had to wear leather gauntlets, like blacksmiths.

"There are places in the Drôme where the birds have gone mad. At any rate, not very far from here, on the other side of the hills, the horses have refused everything. They've refused oats, water, stabling, the care of the man who usually looks after them, even when he seems perfectly well. It's been noticed, too, that when a horse refuses, it's always a very bad sign for the person or house it refuses. The sickness may not be apparent, but it's sure to turn up immediately afterward. The dogs: naturally there's the dogs belonging to all those who have died, and they wander all over the place, feeding on corpses. But they don't die; on the contrary, they grow fat and give themselves airs; they no longer want to be dogs; they change their appearance, you ought to see them; some of them have grown moustaches; they look so funny. But when you go by, they hold the middle of the pavement; you threaten them: they get angry; they insist on respect; they have swelled heads; it's no joke! Anyway, one thing's sure: they don't die, far from it.

"There's a little place not so far from here, in the hills, first the people sweated blood, then they sweated everything: green phlegm, yellow water, and a sort of blue cream. Of course they died. Later, it seems, the corpses began to weep. There's a woman from here who went to visit her sister-in-law. She says there was a lot going on all at the same time. She distinctly saw stars in broad daylight, next to the sun, not standing still like they do at night but toddling off to right and left, like the lanterns of people looking for something. Where it seems to be really bad is in the valleys, down behind there; and it's quick. They're eating in a farm, seven of them. All of a sudden all seven fall with their noses in their soup plates. Pass the nutmeg. Or else a man's talking to his wife and doesn't finish what he's saying. You can't be sure of anything. You're sitting down, will you ever get up? They don't even bother now to say: 'I'm going to do this' or 'I'm going to do that.' Does anyone know what he's going to do? They've stopped giving orders to servants. Orders to whom, to do what, and why? How long will the servants be there? People just sit and look at each other. They wait. But that's nothing to what's happening over Grenoble way. The people rot on their feet. Sometimes it's the belly; all of a sudden it's so thoroughly rotted that it won't hold any longer and bursts in two. But they don't die at once: that's where the pain comes in. Or else it's the leg: you're walking and it falls in front of you, or you leave it behind. You can't shake hands with anyone. To lift a spoon to your mouth is quite a business. You'd need to be sure of still having fingers and an arm. Naturally you get a little warning in advance from the smell. The trouble is, there's already a fine old smell of rotting with all the dead bodies and the heat. So you never know if what you smell is your own smell or the others!

184

"They say that if you went into Grenoble you wouldn't hear a sound. There's nothing to be done, is there? Haven't you heard about that shepherd who's made a remedy out of mountain herbs? Not just any old herbs. They say it's a job getting them. They grow in impossible places. But he got them. They cure completely. When they found him, he was the only one left alive. 'You've been lucky!' they said. 'I know the cure,' he said. He let some people drink from his bottle: they all recovered. It seems that a fat gentleman wanted to buy the whole bottle for a hundred thousand francs, but he said to him: 'Since you're so rich, send your servants to fetch you some.' It was a good answer. Apparently it had a great effect on him. The gentleman said: 'You're right. I *will* send my servants, but it'll be for everyone; show me the place and I'll pay you.' That was good, too. The shepherd has a cart and two horses now. He's got a regular set-up. I think they're going to have some here – the medicine, I mean. Some people are attending to it.

"Then, there's another thing you can do. This happened at Pertuis. There's a priest who says Masses, but not the usual ones. It seems he's got something that's a little more complicated but has better results. He's cured a lot of people, and what's so specially good is that he protects you in advance. No danger any more. You've no more need to worry. You give your name and, well, I don't know if you pay; I don't think so; he's an old priest with a beard. And that's that. Maybe you also repeat some words. Anyhow, it works. At Pertuis they've perhaps had less than a hundred dead in all. To my mind that proves it. Seems that all around that priest's house it's full of people camping, sleeping, cooking meals, waiting. As soon as he comes out, you ought to see it! The people climb on each other's backs to say: 'Me, me, me!' And they shout out their names. Well, in the end, he writes them down on bits of paper and says: 'Don't worry, it will be all right. I'll just go into the church.' Then the whole lot follows him. That seems very fine. A hundred dead all told since the start, that's nothing. And now that he's got things properly going, he has pictures that he can send in a letter, and they stop you from catching the plague, and even cure you."

185

In this way they arrived at the foot of a cliff. The almond-tree hill was up above. Gazing upward, one could see foliage black against the stars. A path climbed up through the rocks.

"All you have to do now is to take this path," said the boy. "You don't need me any more. I turn off here. You see? I knew the way all right."

The sentinel posted under the big oak let Angelo go past, then said to him: "Hey there, artist, where are you off to?"

Once more he began to explain that he was looking for a man called Giuseppe, but this time he received the answer: "If that's it, it's easy; come over here. I'll take you."

As they passed a brazier, Angelo saw his guide. He was a young labourer who had strapped a belt over his blouse. The trigger-guard of his rifle glittered.

"The weapon's well kept," thought Angelo.

Giuseppe lived in a handsome reed hut with a fire burning before its door. He was evidently not asleep, for as soon as Angelo moved into the light of the flames he shouted from inside: "Ah! Here's his mother's son, at last!"

They chewed each other's muzzles like two puppies. Giuseppe had half risen from a low bed on which a young woman was asleep, with all her extremely opulent bosom uncovered. Giuseppe rubbed her belly, which was broad and supple, calling out: "Lavinia! Here's My Lord!" And he burst out laughing because she swiftly crossed herself before opening her eyes, still pouting adorably with lips darkened by a faint down.

"You see," said Giuseppe, "he isn't dead and he's found me."

The young woman had a round head and huge, startled eyes; however, she narrowed them knowingly when she was thoroughly awake.

"No," said Giuseppe to Angelo, "first you're going to sleep. I shan't tell you a thing tonight. Only this: you're lucky. If I'm not dead, it's because I've nine lives like a cat: but it's sheer good sense that keeps me going. I lead a regular life and I'm going to make you lead one. Come over here. There's room for three in this bed. It'll be a bit of a squash but that's the right thing when you're fond of each other."

Angelo pulled off his boots and, especially, his breeches, which he had been wearing for more than a month.

"Have you been sensible?" Giuseppe asked at last, in a solemn voice.

"What d'you mean by sensible?" said Angelo.

"Have you taken the precautions you should against falling ill?"

"Yes," said Angelo. "At any rate, I don't drink the first thing I see."

"That's at least something," said Giuseppe. "But," he added, "*I* could make you drink anything, if I wanted."

"How?" said Angelo.

"I'd say you were afraid; then you'd drink! . . ."

"Of course," said Angelo.

# 9

ALL WAS WELL on the almond-tree hill. Everyone seemed to feel at home there. The women were strong women, the men decidedly hale and hearty. The women were massive, built for hard work: thick arms, throats, full, often heavy, and baked to a tan by the sun; broad hips, solid legs, slow of gait, dragging crowds of children with each hand.

"Come to think of it," said Angelo to himself, "who was that sentinel who greeted me? And what was he guarding?"

It did no good to search: there was no infirmary on the top of the cliff. It wasn't a place for harmoniums either. But there was a markedly heroic atmosphere. Numerous workmen, with belts round their blouses and rifles slung over their shoulders, were moving about on every side. There were just as many old men as young; some with sharp girlish faces under peaked caps; others sporting long, wide, curling beards, red or black or even snow-white, and wearing felt hats or broad, swaggering berets. They were walking about with the air of gamekeepers on a private estate, or even like the owner, quietly dropping a word to right or left, here to have the rubbish collected and taken to a trench, there to organize fatigues whose job it was to fetch water or wood for everyone.

They even had a guardroom, a meeting-place in a grove of oaks, where one of them with no gun, only a naked sabre hanging from his belt, issued orders. Angelo was much affected by the sabre, which was a handsome and noble weapon.

One day, this sort of militia made some of the encampments move. These were set up in a rather deep gully congested with rocks and undergrowth, forming the dry bed of a stream. A storm was threatening. Already thunder was rolling at the back of the hills. The sky had not changed colour. It had remained chalk-white; it had barely lost that satin brilliance lent to it by the crushed sun. It wasn't growing black merely where the thunder came from, under the approaching clouds; it was darkening uniformly all over and, had it not been for the hour and the sudden flashes of lightning, one might have supposed it was the onset of night. The guards in blouses made everybody decamp from the stream-bed. They were extremely obliging; they lent a hand; they carried pots and pans, kettles, infants, without letting go of their guns.

Giuseppe had handed over to Angelo, with much ceremony, a letter from Italy. "I've had it in my coat pocket for at least two months," he said. "It's from your mother. Look at the envelope well and get ready to swear on your life that I've kept it with the utmost care. It's not *your* mother I'm afraid of: it's mine. I'm sure she'll ask me, with her eyes of fire, if I didn't stuff it in with the handkerchief I spit my tobacco into. Swear you'll tell her. I am scared to death of my mother when she digs her nails into my arms. And when it has anything to do with the Duchess or you, she always digs her nails into my arm."

The letter was dated in June and ran: "My dearest child, have you found any chimeras? The sailor you sent to me told me you were foolhardy. That reassured me. Always be very foolhardy, my dear, it's the only way of getting a little pleasure out of life in this factory age of ours. I had a long discussion about foolhardiness with your sailor. I like him very much. He watched for our Teresa at the side door as you told him to, but, as he mistrusted a tall lad of fifteen who has been playing hopscotch every day in the square from seven in the morning till eight in the evening ever since you've been in France, he smeared a poor dog's muzzle with shaving-soap, and the hopscotch-player took to his heels shouting: "Mad dog!" The same evening General Bonetto suggested a dog hunt to me because of this dragon. So now I know exactly where the hopscotch-player comes from, and I gave the right sort of look to let the General know I know. Nothing is more fun than seeing the enemy shift his batteries. There's a lot of rabies in Turin. All the young people who have unprepossessing faces and stand less than four and a half feet high are rabid. The same epidemic is ravaging the envious and those who have never known how to be generous to their tailor. The rest are well and full of plans. There are even some who are so deranged they want to adopt that English fashion, bad for organdy and tight breeches, of going picnicking in the country. They even say: as far as the Roman tombs. Which I find excessive, at any rate, as an ambition. But the roads are open to all. Let them go where they please. Good hikers wander away at every detour to see the landscape around the next bend, and that's how they sometimes turn a simple walk into a military march. It would be all right if there were not fewer and fewer people able to rely on their hearts. It is a muscle people no longer make use of, except for your sailor, who in this respect seems to me a pretty remarkable gymnast. A negligible kindness of mine towards his mother quite overwhelmed him, and he went off and got into uncomfortably close quarters with the two over-decorated men responsible for your sudden journey. As a result, they became grievously ill the same day. A pity. I thought your sailor was a bit quick on the trigger. I gave him some very involved reasons for making another voyage. I was so mysterious that he was beside himself with joy. I like taking a long time to aim.

"And now let's talk of serious matters. I'm afraid you may not be doing enough crazy things. This doesn't interfere with either gravity, or melancholy, or solitude – those three passions of your character. You can be grave and wild, what's to stop you? You can be anything you like and wild into the bargain, but it's essential to be crazy, my child. Look around you at the ever-increasing number of people who take themselves seriously. Apart from making themselves hopelessly absurd to minds like mine, they condemn themselves to a dangerously constipated life. It's exactly as if, at one and the same time, they stuffed themselves with tripe, which is a laxative, and with Japanese medlars, which are binding. They swell, swell, then they burst, and that makes a bad smell for everybody. I couldn't find a better image than that. Besides, I like it very much. One should even add three or four dialect words so as to make it even more foul than it is in Piedmontese. You who know my natural distaste for everything coarse will see from this search for the right image how great is the danger run by people who take themselves seriously before the judgment of original minds. Never become a bad smell for a whole kingdom, my child. Walk like a jasmine in the midst of them all.

"And, incidentally, is God your friend? Are you making love? I ask for this every evening in my prayers. In any case there is here, besides me, a woman who's mad about you. I mean our Teresa. To seduce one's nurse is not so common as they claim. Anyhow I am paying her back in her own coin. I really have a sort of passion for her son. Tell him so when he hands you this letter. I love that shepherd-of-lions act he has such a taste for. I never could make out whether he was a tamer of wild beasts strutting in a cageful of sheep, or a pastor leading flocks of lions through the countryside. Whichever it is, in either case, he has eyes like Christopher Columbus. I am enchanted to see you two together. I was, the very first time I saw you both in Teresa's arms. You were no bigger than puppies then. Everyone kept telling me that with her thin breasts she wouldn't have enough. You were gluttons and kept butting her in the breasts, the way kids do nanny-goats. No one knew that Teresa is a she-wolf. I knew. When she had the two of you hanging from her neck and I drew near, she'd growl. I trusted her. I was sure that if her milk ran out she'd give you blood rather than wean you. Ah! you were a perfect Romulus and Remus.

"Teresa is beginning to get used to the idea that Lavinia sleeps with her son. 'As husband and wife should,' I told her, and nearly had her nails in my eyes for it. She'd like to be everything. One can only hint at these things. I believe that, in this, Giuseppe takes after his mother: that that's where he gets his Christopher Columbus eyes from. Do you still fight like dogs, you and he? If you do it with sabres, be careful with him. You know you're more skilful than he is. The police commissioner told me so, apropos of Swartz, as soon as he had seen that thrust, as clean as a sword-cut (I was very proud), running straight through the swine's heart. The annoying thing is that you sign your blows, he said: each of them has in it ten years of practice and three hundred years of hereditary nonchalance. If a man can sign his sabre-blows like that, he has no excuse for killing his foster-brother. If you always keep your guard *en huit*, the one I used to call your 'calabash', the most you risk, even allowing Giuseppe all the luck, is a hole in your right shoulder. You owe him that, after all, because (never forget) he is the she-wolf's son and it's just as necessary for him to keep his anger fed as for you to have your breakfast. I laugh to myself at the thought of what would happen if Giuseppe pierced your shoulder. I can hear his wails from here. It would hurt him much more than you.

"I am off to La Brenta. Tell Lavinia I miss her. She's the only one who ever knew how to arrange my petticoat under my riding-skirt. All the others, now, rummage around under my ribs for hours on end till they emerge half suffocated, and I have to sit in my saddle as though on a handful of nails. If the three of you had stayed here I shouldn't have my behind in vinegar like this. Political assassinations and love affairs have, as you can see, unforeseeable consequences. Remember it is the same with revolutions. Everything in the end comes down to a petticoat rucking up under somebody's buttocks.

"Besides, if you hadn't killed Baron Swartz, I wouldn't have to go to La Brenta. I am going because a dog is never so strong as in its kennel. I'm taking the little priest. He's getting more and more like a wedge for splitting wood. He now has a passion for perfumes. I find this most useful. No one suspects him. They all believe he is my *cicisbeo*, and you can imagine the care I take to give those who believe it satisfaction. So now I'm armed from head to foot. The Bonetto will arrive on Sunday, upon a formal invitation. He imagines you are behind every bush. Each time a branch cracks he jumps and puts his hand to his belt. It would make you die laughing.

"I'm going to enjoy myself. Monsignor Grollo arrives on Monday. The minister who has such dirty hair will be there on Tuesday. I must tell you a *mot* of Carlotta's: she calls him the *minestrone*. When one knows that he lived on soup all his life until he became His Excellency, the joke is quite a good one. Biondo and Fracassetti will come on Wednesday. I feel well able to tie those two in knots on the same day, even in my sleep. And on Thursday we shall all be on the steps to welcome Messer Giovanni-Maria Stratigopolo: *il cavalier greco*! It's a plot, as you see. And aimed at your dear head. Admire my strategy. I begin with the most chicken-hearted. You know how depressing those long empty Sundays are among the chestnut forests. Bonetto will have to spend one in the company of the little priest and myself between these old, moaning, melancholy walls. I shall have a headache from two in the afternoon onward. There he is, stuck with the little priest. They will take coffee in the famous round room in the North Tower. Let us hope there'll be a slight *tramontana* blowing. Our forebears wisely placed there a good number of squeaking shutters and rusty weathercocks (who will ever assess the part played by exasperation of the ear in Sardinian politics?). I put my trust in my little priest. There's no one like him for distilling hell drop by drop, should he have any help from the surroundings. I shall join them again at nightfall, and, by the Madonna, if the General isn't trembling when he goes to bed, I'm willing to lose my reputation. The next day there'll be Grollo, but Bonetto will be in such a state that he'll leave us a clear field. I know very well how to deal with Grollo when he's alone. He'll fall for it. The *minestrone* will arrive when the others have been fully besieged and indeed a breach opened. I can see you laughing at the thought of his being obliged to sustain the fire of my batteries all alone. Not a worthy adversary for me, in fact. No more than the next day's couple, barely the *dispatch of current business*, as they say. That leaves only *il Cavalier*! But he will arrive on a battlefield already laid waste, and God will inspire me. Besides, I was forgetting: there will be Carlotta. She will be there two hours before him.

"Do you think of Carlotta sometimes? She often throws herself furiously into my arms. Do you know, she is very handsome? Even I, a woman and your mother, am not altogether indifferent to pressing to me that firm throat, that full yet supple waist. She's an impetuous creature, the kind I like. It was the devil's own work to make her accept my way of fighting. She wanted simply to give them bad coffee. I told her: 'Then all that would be left for us would be to roam the roads of France.' 'Why not?' was her reply. If we don't win the battle of La Brenta that might indeed be a solution. For the fun of the thing.

"Your sailor will be leaving this evening for Genoa. He and this letter will be there the day after tomorrow; in twelve days they will both of them reach Marseille. All three, rather; he's also taking the little bag. I first thought of sending you two drafts of a thousand francs drawn by Regacci brothers of Naples on the house of Charbonnel at Marseille, which is more solid than the Colossus of Rhodes. After thinking it over I prefer sending you liquid cash. I am sending you also a hundred Roman crowns, for the pleasure of feeling them. The minting is infinitely more beautiful than that of the French crowns. Change them gradually; they will give you a great deal of pleasure. You will also find fifty bajoccos folded in wine-filter paper. They're a present from your Teresa. She has saved them up one by one out of heaven knows what. Had I refused them, I saw by the look in her eyes that she would have stabbed me in the night. And besides, she is right. One must pay for those one loves. The more one loves, the dearer one must pay. But there are some who would like to give the treasures of Golconda but only have at their disposal fifty bajoccos. As you are my son, I know you will never laugh at them.

"The sailor is not staying at Marseille: he is going on to Venice; you know why. He will hand over the letter and bag to the rabbit-skin merchant. That means that, in twenty days at the most, the whole will be in Giuseppe's hands. And if you are there you will be able to receive, on the spot, the little kiss I am placing here, on this cross. It is addressed to the left dimple of your upper lip. Before you had even opened your eyes you used to laugh when I kissed you there."

Angelo did not laugh as he pressed the cross on the paper to the left corner of his mouth.

Angelo described his adventures with the little Frenchman.

"You deserve to have your face bashed in," Giuseppe told him. "What would the Duchess and my mother say if I let you die, and above all if you die in some absurd way? They would hold me responsible. That little Frenchman had a passion. He died for it. You had no business to get mixed up in it, or to keep gaping over it now. The bodies of those with cholera are full of dusts that fly in all directions. And nothing's commoner than dying from some dust one has breathed in.

"You're too stupid. Your mother knew what she was doing when she bought you a colonel's commission. There's somebody who sees clearly! In normal times, you'd have made yourself a career. If you want to end up at sixty like Bonetto who's afraid of everything, you must, in fact, begin by being afraid of nothing. For there's a God of imbeciles; they end by believing in him; and then, beware of those last moments; there's never a scapulary big enough. One trembles at them twenty years ahead. In the work we've begun you'll have a thousand opportunities to show courage. But to do it for nothing is just being a freak. If you'd done that at Turin, even *before a commissioner for oaths*, I might understand. It could be useful. A sonnet could be written on it, or a pulpit sermon; it was merely a question of organization. And you had the benefit or, more precisely, what we are doing had the benefit. Believe me, faith justifies everything, and good works are ineffectual."

Angelo told him how, on reaching Manosque, he had nearly been hanged. Giuseppe began to laugh.

"Well, well! they didn't do things by halves!"

Angelo turned scarlet with anger. He remembered the demented voice of Michu, the hatred flaming in his eyes and the ardour with

194

which he had communicated it to all those men who, cowards though they were and very frightened, would have ended by disembowelling him as they had disembowelled the poor devil whose torture he had seen from the rooftops.

"Yes," said Giuseppe, "Michu's a fine fellow and he earns his wages. Certainly, if he'd got you hanged, he'd have done something that wasn't in his instructions, but how could anybody imagine that you were going to turn up and that he'd happen just on you? If we had to weigh all the pros and cons, we would never get anywhere. There are always some chances we have to take: I confess this one sends cold shivers down my spine. But it would have been impossible for me to repudiate Michu. I could have ripped his belly open behind the first bush, but I wouldn't have been able to alter the principle of the thing. Besides nothing could have brought you back and my knifing him would, in all fairness, have been morally questionable. I recognize, though, that it would have been impossible for me not to do it. And in a rage too. That's love, but it's not revolution. Bah! you'd have been well worth a little exception, and Michu's no more than a soldier who can be replaced."

Giuseppe's cold way of speaking of the incident threw oil on the fire. Angelo lost his temper and even allowed himself to wax quite lyrical. He could still see the nails of the shoes that had tried to crush his face in. Above all, he shuddered at the thought that he had nearly fallen a victim to panic-stricken cowards, any of whom, alone and face to face with him, would have run like a rabbit.

"There's no reason why we should be alone. On the contrary," said Giuseppe. "That's where you make your error. You were wrong in the way you killed Baron Swartz because you let him defend himself. Duels are not for us. We can't afford the luxury of allowing slavery a chance of any kind. Our duty is to win; we must keep all the chances for ourselves, and even the false cards too."

"I don't know how to assassinate," said Angelo.

"That'll hamper you," said Giuseppe. "And, what's much more serious, it'll hamper us."

"I was sure of my sword," said Angelo, "and I proved it. He had to die and he did die. I gave him a sabre and he defended himself. I needed him to defend himself."

"What matters is not what you need, but what the cause of liberty needs," said Giuseppe. "There's more revolutionary virtue in assassination. We must take even their rights from them."

He lay down in the grass and put his hands behind his neck.

"Don't talk of cowardice," he said, "or if you do, admit that it's useful to us. In my opinion it even has it over courage. Where it passes it leaves the field more open. You make out that the man who put it into their heads that the enemies of the people were poisoning the fountains was a coward addressing cowards? That's a police opinion. Like to know a secret? It was I who spread that rumour. And take it from me, I laid it on thick. May I shrivel up on the spot if I didn't multiply the charnel houses by ten. I was speaking to cowards? All right. Where I began to be pleased with myself was when I saw how well it was working. As for saying I'm a coward myself, I'm ready to ram that back down your throat this instant, if you're the least bit set on maintaining it. You can take your famous sabre, if you wish: we have them too. I'm not afraid. I can even settle your hash with my fists, if such a weapon fits the nobility of your character. You were nearly hanged. If you had been, I'd have cut Michu's throat, and perhaps my own too. But those who really got hanged, as the result of my little conversation with the cowards, were the most determined enemies of our ideas of liberty. I had things well in hand and the names were carefully marked on a list that Michu returned to me with a cross against each name. I don't trust to chance. And I consider that Michu's idea of hanging an extra one wasn't bad. A stranger, in particular! That made it fair. He has his head screwed on."

"I shall have to teach him a lesson," thought Angelo. "And with my fists, what's more, since that's where he thinks he's strongest. He's very proud of those velvety eyes of his. I'll give them a colour he can't be proud of."

He was irritated by Giuseppe's common-sense tone, which seemed to form a part of a lecture on how to live.

"An exile isn't given the middle of the pavement anywhere," continued Giuseppe. "What's more, I'm a shoemaker. That's not one of your trumpery professions. And don't forget I've been here barely six months. With my talent for choosing the right moment to say the things that impress cowards, I've had six or seven swells, who had the *préfet* in their pockets, strung up on lampposts. With the duelling system you'd hardly have managed to kill one of them! And even that's not certain! It would have brought the police to the spot. And that would have been that, and my colonel would have been taken with his legs in irons to the Alps. We're in a country where the bourgeois use their elbows if you tread on their toes. Now there's six or seven less of them. They've been taken care of without danger because I understood that for the moment people had other fish to fry without sticking their noses into the hysterical goings-on of twenty-odd blackguards. And, a great advantage, the swells didn't die with the honours of war. They can't be made much of. Even their families are seeing to it that nothing more should be said of them. As for the poison, does anyone know whether it isn't true after all?"

Angelo uncrossed his legs.

"The stitches I put into your boots haven't held," said Giuseppe, unclasping his hands from behind his neck and even sitting up. "Take them off and give them to me. I had glazed the end to be able to polish it, and the hot wax must have eaten into the thread. I don't like seeing you with unstitched boots. Besides, I made them and I'm proud of them. You've a nice leg, but nobody else could have fitted you so closely and so well."

He talked of the boots with passion. He gave details about the leather, the thread, the wax, the polish. Inexhaustibly. He had stood up. He even rolled his eyes and smiled, the better to describe a polishing-cream.

Angelo's costume was indeed very important to Giuseppe. He seemed, on this subject, to have some idea at the back of his head.

"I want you to look nice," he told him, from the very first days. "You know that's my hobbyhorse, and I shall never regret anything so much as that splendid hussar's uniform you wore so well, especially the one the Duchess ordered for you in Milan. Your face is never so attractive as when it's under the helmet and supported by the gorget. Spurs suit you, too. As soon as you've gold on you, you freeze the blood. And that's what's wanted. One feels you're a lion."

And he made several affectionate remarks.

"You ought to be thrashed," he added, "for having wrapped that mountain boy in your fine riding-coat. Your mother and I spent more than a week thinking about that cloth. And the number of times my mother dug her nails into my arm while we were choosing it at that famous Gonzageschi's, who's such an expert on colours. It was a fat lot of good taking so much trouble to find you a cloth as blue-black as the night and of such fine quality that it draped like a curtain in the right places. D'you suppose your little cholera patient wouldn't have died just as well in his own togs? But Monsieur must always exceed orders. Above all, when it serves no purpose. You've reached me in a queer condition! And that beard, which you haven't shaved since I don't know when, makes you look ten years older. Worst of all, it gives you such a look that no one would dream of trusting you."

He gave one of the stern but obliging guards in blouses a message, and a few days later he took Angelo to the other side of the almond-tree hill, on to a slope that looked down on a golden village like a boat lifted by a wave of rocks.

Here there had been a landslide long ago, and the soil, moistened by various small, deep springs that the collapse of the hill had brought to the surface, stretched out in fields that the burning white sun had failed to turn yellow. There were also some very thick, very tall groves of birches.

It was among these groves, as Angelo observed, that the guards had a sort of barrack or general encampment. One constantly came upon sentinels, and even guards, without weapons, their belts undone. They were peacefully smoking pipes. They all seemed to have great respect for Giuseppe: they saluted him, and one young workman guarding a sort of tent even presented arms to him, very clumsily but completely serious about it.

Giuseppe led Angelo into a copse of green oak trees where numerous bales were stacked under tarpaulins.

"Many tradesmen," said he, "have died without heirs; or else the heirs too have gone west. There are a good many families the cholera has scraped to the bone. All these goods would be lost. We've collected them together. And look what good sorts the people are. They've most conscientiously stood guard over the lot, but they haven't touched a thing. You don't find prodigals among *them*."

Helped by a workman with his belt properly buckled and his gun slung across his back like a dragoon's bandolier, they found several pieces of cloth, in particular a roll of drugget and a roll of velvet.

"I've an idea," said Giuseppe. "I'm sure it's a good one and you'd never have thought of it. I can lay my hand on just the man we need. He's worked in Paris and can cut you a coat with almond tails better than Gonzageschi, whose word, after all, is only law in Turin. Have you any real idea what's in store for you? We don't know what the cholera's going to do. Perhaps, a month from now, we shall all be lying flat among the mallows. But here we mustn't envisage the worst. If only you're still alive and me too, or even if you're alive all by yourself, you'll soon have to edge your way into the Alps and get to where – you know what has to be done. Especially if your mother has won the battle of La Brenta. Which is almost certain, as she said in her letter. I told you that this workman I know would cut you a coat better than Gonzageschi, and it's true. He could also make you a riding-coat of the proper marble cut, better than anyone. But there are only bourgeois stuffs here, and for a tail coat or riding-coat we must have the very best. This is my idea."

Giuseppe's eyes, which were very fine and velvety with long black lashes, were alight with a fire of passion.

"The peasants round here sometimes have very pretty velvet jackets," he continued. "And they're ornamented with big brass buttons showing hunting-scenes, stags' heads, boars' heads, and even little love-scenes. If they're carefully polished with chamois leather, those buttons glitter like gold. That's the jacket you need. I'd better tell you right away that the people who wear these jackets are considered to have feathered their nests, and feathers are their chief attraction. Peasants don't have intelligent faces, except in our country. Here their faces are as flat as on coins. You, no matter what you wear, will have your lion look. What they with their slyness have devised to cover wool stockings will now form the clothing of valour: imagine the effect. Republicans have an unfortunate love for princes. Don't think they kill them for any better reason. They need them and they look for them everywhere. If they find one who's of their own skin, they're happy at last to die for him."

"Don't forget that I fidget," Angelo replied, "and that I will never sit for my portrait. Besides, I believe in principles."

"A mere hint and you understand me," said Giuseppe. "That's how I like you. And how well you said your little piece about principles! Keep up that tone. It's inimitable. You've just made me shiver with pleasure. It's not, anyhow, among people with flat-money faces that you should stand for valour, but among people whose smallest bootblack has the features of Caesar himself. If you can talk to them of principles in the tone you used just now, anything is in the bag. Only it must be that exact tone and that conviction you put into it. Naïveté sometimes takes the place of genius in our line of country, but will you remain naïve? That's why you must have drugget breeches as well, rather close-fitting, because you're well-made. And a cloak; for who knows if you won't be obliged to cross the Alps in winter?"

This riding-cloak – it was a marvel, but even the sight of it was not to be borne in that heat – was carefully folded and scented with thyme and lavender by Lavinia. She even wrapped it in one of her petticoats and placed it at the bottom of a chest in the north corner of the hut, which the sun never reached. The velvet jacket and breeches were also put in the chest.

In spite of the advanced season, one could scarcely bear even linen next to the skin. Lavinia was naked under her *caraco* and skirt. She was a very beautiful girl already famous in Turin for her loveliness. At every *corso* someone would come and ask the Duchess for the loan of her to personify Diana, or Wisdom, or even the Archangel Michael. She had grown into the way of these allegories and never forgot them. Not even when crouching to blow on the fire under the soup.

The other women who lived on the hill kept their cotton stockings on for a long time, but the heat became so unbearable that they finally overlooked a great many conventions. They never reached the stage of a mere *caraco* and skirt, however. Some of them even persisted in retaining their whalebone collars. They were workmen's wives. They were all dressed like decent, humble, bourgeois women. Their hair was drawn back in an atrocious fashion and firmly knotted in tight buns. Sometimes they were to be found behind bushes, combing their long hair, then twisting it, braiding it, filling their mouths with pins, and then sticking the pins one by one into their buns. After this, they would get up, dust themselves, clean their combs, fold them in paper, stuff them into their bosoms; they would pat their hips, smooth their basques, and jerk their rumps two or three times like hen-pheasants to set their bustles in place before getting back to their work, which was never simple and easy, but here consisted in going a long way to fetch water, with a bucket in each hand, or chopping wood, or even massaging their husband or brother, son or daughter, down with an attack. They too had attacks themselves in this paraphernalia and sometimes died before anyone could cut the laces of their stays, which they defended still with both hands at the height of the pain.

Often Lavinia very softly sang tiny, lively songs, which she mimed with little movements of the head, smiles, and a fluttering of the eyelids. The song barely passed her teeth, but the miming and the broad wrinkle shaped like a tripod that then marked the top of her nose and gave her by its movements a braggadocio or saucy air, her great eyes that she would widen afterwards in a most pathetic manner, her pouts, and in fact all these antics, some of which were very artful and even, now and then, highly depraved, created a sort of miniature Italy.

"Let's save this people," Angelo would think, watching her and drawing close to listen. "It has all the virtues. This girl is the child of woodcutters and their wives born in woods belonging to my family, and she was brought to my mother when she was quite small, to serve as a plaything. She was lady's maid for more than ten years, for by the time she was eight my mother was making her burrow under her heavy riding-skirts to smooth out her petticoat; and she would willingly die for me. More even than for Giuseppe, although he carried her off with him when he left, taught her love, and, I hope, has married her. What loyalty! How beautiful she is, and how pure her heart!" (He didn't see certain positions of her lips, extremely voluptuous and even sometimes rather vulgar.) "She deserves the Republic. Nothing's too good for her. This is the task of my life. This shall be my happiness. And how it carries me away!"

At these moments, in this miniature Italy, Giuseppe enjoyed himself greatly. He was wholly absorbed in putting his mouth close to Lavinia's and accompanying her song in thirds or an octave lower (just a murmur, of course, for not far away people were dying or, at the very least, in trouble; this was a personal matter). At these times his features were unstrained and peaceful, composing a pattern different from that of his normal face. Angelo even found in it a great nobility, despite its striking resemblance to Teresa.

The weather changed. The white sky lowered until it touched the tops of the trees. It even engulfed the tops of the cypresses, which seemed to be cut off by scissors. During the summer this white sky had, in spite of everything, kept its veils pretty high in the air. One could still see a few grey winds circling beneath the plaster dome. Now it descended and established a sort of flat ceiling twelve or fifteen feet above the ground. The birds disappeared for most of the time, even the crows, which from now on led a mysterious life above the ceiling, sometimes seeping down from it like huge black raindrops.

Immediately the heat rose, as in an oven when its door has been shut. There was no longer the march of the sun, nor the revolving of the shadows. Day was simply a throbbing whose intensity rose steadily up to the blinding noon, then fell little by little to a static extinction during the night.

One phenomenon greatly disturbed everybody: voices no longer carried. However hard you tried to talk to someone, you were still talking confidentially to yourself. Your interlocutor stared at you in silence, and if he began to speak too, you only saw his mouth moving and there was still the silence, a rather chiding silence. If you shouted, the shout rang in your ears, but you were the only one who heard it. And this went on for several days.

The air was of course made of plaster, and the view very limited. To see a long distance, one was obliged to stoop, as though to look under a door.

Without any wind, two or three smells arrived, all of them extraordinary. The first was a violent smell of fish, as when one is near a net that has just been emptied on to the grass. Next it turned into the marsh smell of rotted rushes and hot mud. That smell, like the others, moreover, gave people hallucinations. The plaster air seemed to turn green. Next (or perhaps at the same time) there came a smell resembling (but on a vaster scale) emanations from an ill-kept dovecote, pigeon droppings whose acridity is so sharp. That smell too (given that one could see nothing around one except a blinding whiteness) caused the most disagreeable hallucinations, among them notably the idea of monstrous pigeons brooding and fouling the earth under stifling thicknesses of down. Finally, there must also be noted a smell of sweat, very salty and violent, which stung the eyes like the vapour of sheep's urine in enclosed sheep pens.

In spite of all the imagining that these smells prompted, they were not frightening; or at least it was not of them that people were afraid. The plaster ceiling began rapidly to grow old; fragments of the plaster fell away, revealing above it a sort of gloomy loft. The day gradually darkened. At length, flashes began to flit across it, but they were abortive. This was no frank, clear lightning; it was a series of candle-flickers: a yellowish, bilious flame ricocheting indefinitely with a weak rattling noise, before going out without a thunderclap. It spread a strong smell of phosphorus.

In contrast, one day, and without anyone noticing the slightest flash, a sudden clap of thunder was heard, sharp as a hammer-blow. From then on, these hammer-blows, which seemed to be bashing something in, were heard unceasingly. The rain began as a mere fine warm muslin, lasting for several days. Then its streaks became visible. For two or three days more, without a break, it drew its streaks closer and closer together until it took all the colour out of the trees. Finally it fell in slabs, in endless slabs so thick and heavy that the earth echoed dully to their thudding.

The camps were all thrown into confusion and ploughed up by torrents. The huts fell in. At every moment families had to be helped as they waded about, trying to save their belongings. There was no shelter anywhere. The highest rocks of the hill were streaming with black water. The workmen of the militia in blouses and leather belts threw themselves into the general rescue work. They were to be seen everywhere. They busied themselves on every side with futile generosity. These men, always weighed down with guns, wet babies, and righteousness, began to get on Angelo's nerves.

"And yet," he said to himself, "what have you to reproach them with? On the other hill over there, where there's no militia organized, who is troubling about rescue work? And how does one man alone in some wild corner save his family?"

The rain tumbled down in heavier and heavier slabs for about forty hours; without fury; with a sort of quiet peace. Finally there was a magnificent clap of thunder, that is to say, it made a fine red rent and was so resounding that it unblocked every ear. The sky opened. On every side of the rent, giddy, many-storeyed castles of cloud rose up and the sky appeared, as azure as one could wish. As the cloud castles drew apart and revealed more and more sky, the azure changed to gentian blue and a whole monstrance of sunbeams began to wheel at the farthest edges of the clouds.

The women took off their bustles. Being of cotton, instead of horsehair like those of ladies, they had become swollen with water. They also had to let fall their skirts, too ample, heavy and muddy. In their underskirts they looked very republican, except for their faces, which remained very ladylike under their hair, not a lock of which hung loose. They were ashamed of moving their legs with ease.

Four of five old men whom the rain had pierced to the bone died almost at once. They could not be got warm again in spite of great fires, which yielded more smoke than flame.

The valley below was unrecognizable. The fields had vanished under many feet of flowing water and foam. Nothing was left of the places where the infirmary tents had stood. On the flank of the other hill, right at the edge of the great torrent that had flooded the valley, a small group of black men was busy like a pinch of ants around some whitish debris. Above them, the olive orchards were deserted. A few little black men were also swarming higher up, at the edge of the pine woods.

All the water from the valley was gathering at the outskirts of the town and rushing through one of its gates. The clouds remained grey for some days, then turned blue.

Two children died. It was from a throat disease. The women began murmuring that there was going to be an epidemic of croup. It worried them badly. Their faces grew beautiful with their fierce eyes, and they kept their children hugged to their bosoms. But there were only a few mild and smothered complaints. The militiamen had managed to dry some wood. They had taken no rest, never taking off their wet blouses and trousers, and all their equipment. A few fires were got going, and those who were shivering were brought to them.

The men in blouses also crouched near the fires. They took their guns to pieces, dried the parts, greased them, assembled them again, tightening the screws with the points of their knives. There was a sort of arms inspection.

"Are you mixed up with this too?" Angelo asked Giuseppe.

"I'm mixed up with everything," replied Giuseppe, with some pride.

The clouds became dark blue. They were piled along the edge of the horizon. At length they took on a violet, then a wine-red hue that attracted every eye. There was a slow movement going on among them: it caused the crumbling-away of the cloud banks beyond the hills, freeing more and more of the sky, in which there spread an azure of unimaginable purity. Finally, without any question of a sunset glow, there arrived, due south, a red cloud, exactly the red of a poppy.

The sun was dazzling. The least puddle of dirty water began to smoke. The days were torrid, the nights cold.

There was a case of lightning cholera. The victim was carried off in less than two hours. He was a militiaman. He was on guard duty. He first had what seemed to be a sudden lack of confidence in his gun. He put it down against a tree. Immediately afterwards the stages followed each other in quick and terrible succession. His convulsions, then his agony, preceded by cyanosis and an appalling coldness of the flesh, cleared a space all around him. Even those trying to help him recoiled.

His face was a masterpiece of cholera symptoms. It was a *tableau vivant* depicting death and its sinuous approach. The attack had been so swift that for a moment the signs of a stupefied astonishment still lingered there, childlike, but death evidently faced him at once with so horrifying a display that his cheeks lost their flesh while one watched, his lips drew back over his teeth for an eternal laugh; finally he gave a cry that put everyone to flight.

Up until that moment the victims had never cried out. They had been worn threadbare before death; it came upon bodies ready for anything. From now on, it struck them like a bullet. Their blood decomposed in their arteries as quickly as the light decomposes in the sky when the sun has fallen below the horizon. They saw night coming and began to cry out.

From then on, the cry rang out day and night. All activity was extinguished. Nobody did anything any more: except wait. For the bullet struck to right, to left, as though fired by a sniper with his rifle propped. At one moment it was that man walking along the path, who bowled over like a hare; at another that woman blowing on her fire, who would fall with her face in the embers. There would be three, four, at the foot of a tree, a family; the father would cry out; the others would have to get up and run away. They would abandon him, for he was already dying, past anything anyone could do. The wife, the children, would run like partridges, would stop panting behind a bush. And sometimes the sniper would make a dead set against this covey. Almost before they recovered breath, the mother or one of the children would cry out, and again the skirts would flap in flight, leaving the new victim on the ground, who would thrash anew as his nerves distended.

One saw more and more gunless militiamen, their guns left lying on the grass or against a tree.

The faces of these dead had their eyes half closed under heavy, weighted lids; a faint colour, but fixed like a stone, shone from between the lashes. The sickness, which devoured the flesh like lightning, left the colour of the eye intact, visible through the opening. With some young women, of whom nothing remained but a pallid skin mottled underneath by patches of corrupted blood, there was little identifiable but long, curved eyelashes leaning over a blue pool, an emerald, a topaz of the purest water. The cheeks were violet and the lips black, tight-shut but always letting through the tip of a tongue, poppy-red, startling, nauseatingly obscene, clashing violently with the eye half open over its colour; to which, when one was obliged to look at one of these faces, one returned, in spite of the contemptuous, proud, haughty quality of this still gaze, seemingly fixed on distant horizons, in a body lying in the mud and sometimes already verminous and rotted. For it was again very hot during the day.

Angelo tried to tend some of these stricken people. The workmen talked of the Raspail method and had great faith in camphor. But they regarded it more as a prophylactic and carried little bags of it hung round their necks like scapularies. Four or five brave and steady men joined Angelo. In the short time they had between the moment of attack and that of death, they tried to make the sick person drink infusions of sage. But as soon as the bullet had struck them, the dying passed into such a delirium that they twisted with convulsions like osiers. Strait jackets of a kind had to be made, into which they were laced. Each time, Angelo took the victim's head in his arms, to raise it while someone tried to force the neck of the bottle of infusion between the clenched teeth. Bleeding was also prescribed. But these bleedings, carried out with clumsily handled pocket knives on tranced bodies, were appalling butcheries. And besides, neither sage, knives, nor camphor were any help.

Yet Angelo continued to jump to his feet as soon as he heard a cry. (One day he ran in this way, only to find four or five children trying to launch a kite.) He had also got into the habit of watching those who suddenly raised a hand to their eyes, for the attack often began with a dazzling light; or those who stumbled as they walked, for sometimes it was a dizziness, a sort of drunkenness, that heralded death.

"I don't like this at all," said Giuseppe. "With their mania for not staying where they are, people may come and die next to us. Really, they've no shame. Since it takes them all of a sudden, why don't they stay in their own places? They might easily fall on top of Lavinia or you or me. Or anyhow, soil our patch of grass. They've no business playing about with this disease."

Giuseppe folded his arms over his chest. From time to time he also crossed the first and second fingers of his left hand and, with his interlaced fingers, touched his own, Lavinia's, and Angelo's temples.

"I don't like what you're doing, either," he went on. "Let them die quietly, don't get mixed up with them. What are they to you? I'm your foster-brother and Lavinia's my wife, not to mention that she played with us as a child. And by meddling with people who mean nothing to you, you risk bringing us the plague and killing us all."

In the end he could hardly contain his fear. Indeed he made no effort to conceal it, and said that it was natural.

He even spoke threateningly and so close that Angelo, tired of having his face breathed into, pushed him away rather violently.

They fought. Lavinia watched them with great interest. Some of Giuseppe's blows, had they not been promptly parried, would have been almost mortal. But Angelo made his nose bleed, and Giuseppe lay down, clawed at the grass and earth, foamed at the mouth, and wept with little childish sobs. Lavinia was very pleased, but she cajoled him; he kissed her hands. She made him sit up. Angelo was looking with horror at his bloody fists. They hastily embraced, all three of them.

So many were dying that people wondered whether it would not be better to return to the town. Several workmen from the tanneries argued that the oak bark macerating in their vats would be a better protection than the country air, and went off with their families. But the day after their departure a small boy came back and said that the others had all died as soon as they arrived. One woman also survived and got back to the hill that afternoon. She described how all the streets were covered with gravel and mud, following the recent heavy rains, which had driven torrents through the town, and how, at the very moment the men had begun to shovel this silt, they had fallen like flies, then the women and children after them, all in the space of a few hours and without leaving them even the time to go into their houses. She had lost her two sons, her husband, and her sister, and the little boy who had arrived before her was now also alone.

Things were no better on the hill opposite. All that could be seen there now was a few small groups, widely separated from one another and not stirring. In the valley between, the torrent had carried away the tents of the infirmaries and literally flayed the fields till the bones showed. It was filled with that dread poisoned silt, to judge from the mists steaming up from below. But an appalling thing was also happening in it. Ever since the start of the epidemic, a large number of the dead from the town had been buried there in enormous trenches. The dead had been covered and the trenches filled in with quicklime. These trenches were naturally bound to be simmering with the juices of the corpses, but now, soaked by the rain, they were boiling with great bubbles like filthy soup. One could hear them sizzling, see their steam, smell their stench.

"Let's go," said Giuseppe; "we must get away from here. Let's move farther on, into the woods."

But several militiamen came to see him and had a long conversation with him. They were old men of sixty to seventy; they had kept their guns. Almost every one had lost his entire family, and they were in the habit, quite recently acquired, of looking unblinkingly at people for a long time. A young man of about twenty accompanied them, likewise utterly cleaned out, having lost a young wife whom he had only married three months before.

Giuseppe made every possible and imaginable gesture of entreaty and talked most of the time with his left hand before his mouth. He went particularly for the young man, who seemed to have considerable influence over the others. This man kept looking at Lavinia and speaking in acid tones. Several times he used the word "duty". Each time the elderly orphans approved.

"They're mad," said Giuseppe, "they're forcing me to stay. But you wait. I told them a thing or two they won't forget."

In fact, only one night went by. They came back the next day. The young man avoided looking at Lavinia. He said that they had had second thoughts, that in fact it was perhaps better to go a bit deeper into the woods. He added that he and the five or six with him were volunteering to stay and do what they could, maintain order, look after people a bit. Giuseppe congratulated them with great warmth and spoke of the people, of their qualities, of the example he was setting, of its unparalleled value "in the service of the idea". He made a few gestures beyond the gestures of entreaty.

There were about two hundred who left, with Giuseppe at their head, taking charge of everything, very animated, giving fatherly advice and urging all speed. Lavinia went along. She had asked Angelo what he proposed to do.

"You go with him," said Angelo. "I shall follow too."

After having tended some hundreds of sick he was obliged to recognize that he was of no use. The four or five fellows who had joined him at the outset had long since given up. Not only had he failed to save a single life, but now, when he approached, the victims associated his presence so closely with certain death that they passed at once into a final convulsion. He was nicknamed "the crow", the name given to those dirty, drunken men who buried the dead with indecent, repellent brutality. He had to admit that he was not popular.

He found Giuseppe and his troop established in a delightful spot. It was a deep ravine carpeted with thick grass under gigantic oak trees. A fresh spring flowed into an old kneading-trough sunk in the ground. The place, though well sheltered by the leaves, was none the less aired by the north winds. At one time it had held a sheepfold, of which a few stumps of walls still remained. The murmur of the leaves was very soothing. The architecture of the enormous oaks, the interlacing branches, suggested sturdiness and strength.

When Angelo arrived, Giuseppe had just posted an armed sentry near the fountain. He had also allotted everyone a camping-place, grouping several families together. There was much talk of laws. Proud talk. The militiamen were armed. Angelo wondered where they came from, all these healthy, ruddy, and sturdy men. He hadn't seen any down below. One of these robust men died suddenly with all the usual symptoms. He tumbled over while he was eating a hunk of bread beside some stacked rifles.

"Down below," said Giuseppe, "these men were in charge of the supplies. That's why you never saw them. Did you imagine that the potatoes, rice, and maize flour that Lavinia cooked were gifts of God? How did you suppose everyone was able to have something to eat? We had stores; everybody was rationed. These healthy men guarded the supplies: doesn't that make sense? What would you have proposed, after all? Tell me once and for all. D'you know what cutting one's losses means?"

The dying man did not stay on the grass a minute more than was necessary. He was carried off at once. Four men, with their shirts outside their trousers and thus wearing the regular uniform of crows, arrived with a stretcher. Angelo noted that the stretcher was made of newly peeled branches. The four crows, for their part, had a special camping-place, more than a hundred yards from the camps of the community. Giuseppe had summoned them by whistling.

For two or three days everyone was absorbed in definite, organized jobs. Fatigue parties of strong young men, escorted by armed militiamen, carried out the moving of the supplies from the lower depot. Other fatigues constructed latrines, rubbish-pits. The orders regulating this work were anonymous. Some militiaman or other would arrive with his rifle slung over his shoulder and say: "I must have . . ." – "I must have so many men to do so-and-so." Giuseppe only spoke directly to give a piece of advice: this was to dig the latrines a long way downwind. He spoke so amusingly about bad smells that he managed to make the women laugh, and even the men. Almost every evening ten very burly and red militiamen held a meeting at the eastern edge of the ravine, the side from which night was coming. After they had been met for some time and everybody was gazing westward where the glow of twilight still remained, Giuseppe would join them.

Three or four people died but were carried off even before they were dead. They began to call the four men who had put their shirts outside their trousers crows in earnest. Angelo noticed their faces: he was stupefied.

There were again, in quick succession, about ten deaths, six of them in one day. A woman, who had just lost at one and the same time her husband and her son, shrieked and fought with the crows. They carried her off too while she was still shrieking, violently kicking, and waving her arms like a swimmer. They set her down on her feet, far beyond the trees, on a wild slope overlooking shadowy valleys. The militiamen could be seen making signs to her to leave, to go straight ahead. She went. The wind fluttered her undone hair.

The scene had caused great agitation. There was a sound of conversation almost as loud as the rustling of the leaves. Giuseppe climbed on to a stump of the ruined sheepfold. He spoke to them all familiarly about this woman who was departing into the wild valleys; and he said some very touching things about her. Misfortune must be respected, and comforted. Beyond the woods, as everyone knew, there was a village, which she would undoubtedly reach. Its hospitality was well known; it had even become proverbial. He had not the slightest doubt that, after she passed through the woods, the woman would be made welcome there, fed, looked after. He wished to draw attention to something very important. He would say once more: misfortune was to be respected. There was no need to dwell longer on that point. One thing was certain: the dead were a great danger to the living. It was therefore pure and simple common sense to get rid of them as quickly as possible. Two or three minutes more made no difference in the matter of sentiment; on the other hand, they made a great difference as regards the contagion. When a dear one dies, you rush to him, you kiss him, you clasp him in your arms, you try to hold him back by every means. It was absolutely certain that none of these means were of any help, alas! in keeping anyone on this side when death had decided to summon them to the other. But these embraces helped greatly to spread the plague. In his opinion, it was these embraces that were to blame for the duplication of disaster that often struck the same family. It was again a question of common sense, pure and simple. Well! there it was: that was all he had to say to them.

Lavinia glanced covertly at Angelo.

During the night there were four, five, six, seven, eight, nine deaths. The crows and the militiamen went round with lanterns. Giuseppe sighed on his bed, spoke to Lavinia in Piedmontese. He called to Angelo, who was sleeping six feet away from them. "Talk to me," he said.

In the morning the ravine was clear: there was no trace of agitation nor of death. Only, a few circles of trodden grass, marking where hearths had been, were deserted.

One man more died that morning. He was carried away before the final cry. His wife and son did up their bundles and without a word followed the militiamen, who led them out of the ravine.

That was the only death of the day. Towards evening, Angelo was smoking a little cigar when he heard a sound similar to that of a light wind among the leaves. It was the sound of conversation from group to group, starting up again.

The night was peaceful. Several times, however, Giuseppe spoke to Lavinia in Piedmontese. She did not reply. He called to Angelo and said: "Talk to me." Angelo talked to him for a long while about Piedmont, about the chestnut woods, and finally set himself to imagine all the *beffas* with which one could make a fool of Messer Giovanni-Maria Stratigopolo. Every time he stopped to recover his breath, Giuseppe would say: "And then, what else could one do to him?"

The next day there was no death. A light breeze blew from the north, gay and lively. It was wonderful to hear the stout branches gently creaking. The militiamen who were keeping order around the fountain were obeyed at a gesture or a glance. Their ruddy, sensual faces now reflected a grave, almost spiritual confidence. This phenomenon astonished Angelo. Giuseppe took a walk around the encampment. He was greeted with considerable respect. Even Lavinia was greeted, although she was becoming more and more allegoric.

"I greet thee, Goddess of Reason," Angelo said to her.

She gave a sibylline smile.

Angelo led Giuseppe towards the edge of the wood, on the westward side.

"It's good," he said, "that people should realize that you're protecting me."

And he showed his teeth under his moustache.

"Don't laugh," replied Giuseppe, "I'm quite aware that last night you talked about Stratigopolo simply to distract me. I won't hide it; this disease disgusts me. You want me to tell you I'm frightened? Well, I will! My hide peels back like the hide of a skinned rabbit. D'you want to know what I really think? One isn't required to be brave in cases like this. The danger's too great. Seeming to be brave is enough; it gets you to the same place and at least it gets you there alive; this, in spite of that little laugh of yours which I don't like, is the most important thing. Look at it any way you wish: death is total defeat. People must be able to use others. That's natural and everybody understands it, even those you use as mattresses to block up your windows. Men stop bullets better than wool. Everyone has that much common sense in his blood. That's why I'm closer to the people than you are. You appear mad. You don't inspire their confidence. They can't believe in virtues they can't imagine. Just make an experiment. Tell them you had to hold my hand all night like a child, or show them you don't take me seriously, and you see if they don't smash your face in."

Below them opened the wild valley down which, two days before, the first exile had been driven. It was filled with enormous blue beeches. There was no village to be seen, but everywhere blue woods.

Angelo said nothing.

"Let's go back to Italy," he said at last, "and get killed."

"All right," said Giuseppe. "How?"

"I'll put on my colonel's uniform, you your hussar's, and we'll go back arm in arm to the barracks."

"And suppose they don't kill us? All the quartermasters are *Carbonari*. There are twenty NCO's who are heads of *vendite*. Half an hour later, the officers are dead, and work has to be begun in the streets of Turin with a thousand conscripts shouting: 'Long live

Colonel Pardi!' But they'll shout it a good deal less the next day when there's only five hundred of them left. And how could we enlist the factory workers? Nothing's possible without them, and they won't like your gold braid and the Castle of La Brenta. Not to mention the explanations to be given to all those who've already set out the laws of Italian liberty on paper or in their heads. Don't forget there are lawyers and teachers."

"I'll get arrested without uniform."

"But Bonetto, who wants to become Minister of War, or perhaps even of Justice, will shout your arrest from the housetops. That, I must admit, will cool off my quartermasters and noncoms, who think you're an eagle; they will imagine that you've been made a fool of, or even that you've betrayed the cause and that the whole thing's a transparent trick. But that doesn't prevent you from becoming a colour-bearer. There are none better than the *agents provocateurs*. Even if all our people believe you've betrayed us, the people whose job it is to look after public opinion will concoct a whole romance out of your imprisonment. That represents at least two hundred scuffles, if they take eight days to sentence you. At two deaths per clash, and we must reckon on that, there you'll be with four hundred deaths on your conscience and perhaps our slavery prolonged by ten years. If they shoot you, there'll be a pretty little firework display besides. Not to mention the intrigues of your mother, myself who'll go around stabbing people in the streets, and our Carlotta who'll test her claws right and left. Which represents a further two or three hundred dead, and that's being moderate. If they lock you up for the rest of your days, then the blame's on us, because we'll have to leave you to die in prison, even (what am I saying? above all!) when Italy is free. Are you depressed? I admit our present situation isn't calculated to raise the spirits."

"The cholera doesn't worry me," said Angelo. "That's a way of dying that settles everything. I can't be happy neglecting my duty."

"I forbid you to die," said Giuseppe, "especially in that way. As for duty, why worry about everybody's duty? I thought you had more pride. Make yourself a personal duty!"

# 10

THE CHOLERA WAS NOW stalking like a lion over towns and woods. After a few days' respite, the people in the ravine were again attacked by the contagion. The dead were pitilessly taken away, even shortly before they were really dead. The survivors of each family affected, those who had tended the victims, were driven away.

"Where are you sending them?" asked Angelo.

"Down where we came from: under the almond trees."

Angelo went back down. He returned sickened. He said that it was a charnel house where there were still a few living people, reduced to skeletons, reeling over the corpses left unburied among flocks of carrion birds. He spoke of it stiffly.

Giuseppe's first retort was that they were not downwind and that those corpses were not dangerous. But immediately after he corrected himself and said:

"You must get away from here."

"So must you," said Angelo.

Unexpectedly, Giuseppe raised few objections.

"You are too important in the fight for liberty," Angelo told him. "You must be saved. Your death would serve no purpose. I've made myself a personal duty, as you advised me. It is, in the first place, to preserve the troops intact before the fight."

He even gave him other reasons, still more specious and very neatly put.

"Here, you are frightened," he said, "and yet I know your courage. In fact, sometimes I've experienced it. So there must be peremptory reasons for your fear, and these peremptory reasons are simply that you're afraid of a pointless death."

He talked at great length about this.

"It's the honest truth," said Giuseppe when he had done: "that is my nature exactly. But these workmen whom I've armed are used to have me command them; they now might force me to."

"Anyway," said Angelo, "I don't matter to them; they've made that quite clear: they consider me a crow. Without your protection, I'd

215

have been sent back down there long ago *by your command*. If I disappear, they'll hardly notice it, or they'll think I've gone off to die in some corner. I'll go ahead and buy some horses. Does that village of yours on the other side of the valley really exist?"

"I think so, but I'll find out."

"Better still," said Angelo, "I'll go first. I'll leave you twenty louis so that you yourself can buy Lavinia's horse and your own. We mustn't attract attention, and if I bought three horses the birds would be singing my name and description."

"We ought," said Giuseppe, "to have an extra horse too; then we could take provisions."

"And I'll go and wait for you a bit farther on."

"We'll start three or four days after you," said Giuseppe, "long enough for me to answer any questions about you, if there are any, and to put some rice, beans, flour, and bacon in a sack. But where shall we go?"

"Let's get nearer to Italy," said Angelo. "Is the plague there too? We have no idea. Anyhow, let's get up into the mountains."

"Listen," Giuseppe now said; "I've been turning all this over in my mind for a long time. The shortest route goes up the Durance Valley, but it's certainly patrolled and blocked at every village by barriers where one has to show a pass. What you've told me about your adventures in getting here proves it, if proof were needed. Naturally I'll make out all the passes you and I could want. I took the rubber stamp from the mayor's office. But even with the best of luck we'll get bundled into prison fifty times – if we survive the first forty-nine. And when I say prison I mean quarantine. You've already made my teeth chatter with them. But there's another route that has tremendous advantages. We go deep into Vaucluse if we start westward from here. And from there we go on to the Drôme. That's as wild a country as one could wish. And in it there's a valley that's even wilder, which goes up into the mountains. I'll show you."

He made a map on a piece of paper. He knew the main roads and even the small tracks.

"Put that in your pocket," he said. "And wait for us at this spot where I'm putting a cross. I know the way you ride! Even if they sell you an old nag, it's only three days from here. It's neither a town, nor a village, nor even a crossroads. It's a roadside chapel in a spot that gives you the creeps. It's called Lower Sainte-Colombe. Upper Sainte-Colombe is a mountain all made of green rocks, over-hanging, enough to make your teeth chatter."

Angelo found a horse at a farm a league away. The people had no business sense. There was only an old granny left and a woman of about fifty, presumably her daughter-in-law. But the well-polished gold pieces produced by Angelo delighted them.

"You're not counting it," said Giuseppe when Angelo gave him some money. "Do you even know how much there is in the little bag your mother sent?"

"No."

"Don't be so casual about it. There's enough to keep a family for three years. Minus ten very pretty gold pieces. They're the ones I pinched for the cause; the ones ostentatiously delivered by post to the good Michu, who made you so welcome when you arrived here. You had paid to get yourself hanged."

"Now I understand why the police had seen the louis."

"You won't understand altogether till you realize that they had been most opportunely advised of this delivery by an anonymous letter, beautifully written, without a single spelling mistake and including two or three of those adverbs that come automatically to the pen of an old town-councillor, even when his boss makes him work under cover."

"You've learned traitors' ways?"

"There's a bourgeois expression for you," said Giuseppe. "I love liberty. I love the idea. I'll throw myself in the fire for it, and even get myself killed. In love, who considers a friend? And anyway, they're Frenchmen."

Angelo went to spend the night at the farm, to be near his horse. He distrusted the farmer's wife and her taste for pretty gold pieces. Giuseppe carried the bundle in which the velvet jacket and the winter cloak were rolled up.

"We're at the end of September," he said; "you'll soon be needing it. As for me, I'll take some cloth, and Lavinia will sew me something in her spare time. I don't need a well-cut coat like you, but take a peep at what I've put in the bundle."

It was a fine little Garde Nationale sabre, so placed that by sliding a hand under the cloak's facings you found its hilt; one pull, and you had a naked weapon ready.

"Of course, I've loaded your pistols, but I know you prefer cold steel, especially the kind you can flourish. Well, there you are. You never know what to expect on the roads, especially in these times."

Angelo was very grateful to him for the sabre. More so than for the good half-hour he spent on his knees examining his boots by the light of his tinder.

"They're all correct and would pass a royal inspection, but two looks are better than one. Anyhow, in ten days at the outside we shall see each other and be together again."

Once more they brought out the map on which was drawn the route and their meeting-place. Giuseppe explained everything afresh, gave supplementary details, exacted promises, and wept.

"Above all don't go near these two little towns I've marked here. Cut across the fields. If I lose you now I shall blow my brains out."

"I promise nothing," said Angelo: "I even think I shall make straight for the first one and go right in if there's anyone left there. I've a terrible longing for some of these little cigars, and I've only three left. But directly I've bought a hundred, then, I swear to you, I'll take to the fields."

They kissed each other, shivering. Angelo trembled with joy as he hugged his friend, his brother, in his arms, and he felt that he too was going to cry.

"There, run along," he said, "you've still a few days to spend in your kingdom, and as you say, they're French; tell them they must love one another; what can that cost you?"

For a half-louis Angelo procured a peasant saddle worth a good three francs, to which he strapped his baggage. The pistols were in his pockets. The sabre fitted nicely inside the cloak.

It was a fine morning with a north wind. He entered the blue forest. For a good half-league he wandered in the most angelic rapture, listening to the wind in the beeches and rejoicing in the incomparable conflict of golden lances with which the sun pierced the wood. His horse was not too cloddish, and it too took great pleasure in the smells and the play of light.

They reached an old track all covered with centaury and enormous burdocks. Before them the valley descended beneath the darkness of the trees. They had been walking down it for half an hour, stiffened a little by the shade and the silence, when Angelo saw, lying across the path, a red-striped petticoat which he at once recognized as that of the woman who had been the first to be driven out of the high ravine. There indeed she was, already devoured by animals and covered with huge slugs finishing off what was left.

At the end of the woods, the farmlands spread hawk's wings on either side of a stream that had flooded the fields after the recent rains. Here, as elsewhere, neither hay nor grain had been scythed. The crops, left standing, flattened by storms, choked with cornflowers, thistles, and brambles, were ravaged by clouds of birds. The entire horizon was shut in by hills, above which appeared the violet or even purple spurs of mountains, no doubt covered with box.

In spite of the sun the wind was cold. Angelo decided to put on the famous velvet jacket and make himself respectable: to shave, for one thing. In spite of the keen air he would gladly have bathed in the stream whose overflowing sent clear water with silver reflections trundling over a thick bed of grass. But he had to be careful. Who could tell what it might be infested with upstream? The villages thought nothing of throwing bandages, excrement, carrion, and even corpses into the watercourses. At a fair distance from the stream he found a large pool of rainwater that seemed healthy.

Lavinia had thought of everything, even of a little box of violet-scented brilliantine with which Angelo now smoothed his moustache. The bundle also contained a clean shirt and three very neatly darned handkerchiefs. Giuseppe, for his part, had thought of thirty rounds for the pistols. The sabre, though homely in style and rather snub-nosed, had good balance and weight. It was a householder's sabre, but could be highly dangerous if used in anger.

The jacket was damned well made. Angelo gradually used more refined language to himself as the velvet brought warmth into his arms. He recalled the workman who had taken his measurements. This man had certainly been a perfect representative of the barricades, with his sickle moustaches and his impersonal stare, standing at ease and guarding something or other of ineffable importance on the hillside. At Giuseppe's request he had immediately leaned his gun against the trunk of an almond tree, hitched up his blouse, and taken a tape-measure out of his breast pocket: "With pleasure! If Monsieur would kindly write down his measurements himself in pencil. Monsieur has a handsome pair of shoulders. Forty-eight. If Monsieur would be so good as to bend his arm. Thank you very much. At your service." He had then picked up his gun, corrected the sights, and resumed his impersonal military stare.

"People, I love you!" said Angelo out loud. But immediately he felt a twinge of conscience and wondered if in reality he did not love the people as one loves chicken.

The day was bent on gaiety. The wind kept the clouds scudding. Angelo was like the sky: sun chasing shadows, shadows chasing sun.

He had no trouble buying cigars in the village, which was a good way further on. They had not suffered many deaths.

"So far as I know," said the tobacconist, who was very old, had piled her bedding in the shop, and was doing her cooking on a small charcoal stove set on the marble counter.

The street, however, was deserted. No cackling of hens or stable noises to be heard: on the other hand, clearly audible, the creaking of the weather vane on the belfry and the trampling of the wind on the tiles.

Angelo bought five boxes of cigars, three yards of tinder-wick, a bag of flints. The old woman wanted to sell him the whole shop.

"People aren't smoking much nowadays in these parts," she said.

There was really nothing but the sound of the wind. And in a half-open door, a shoe and half a man's leg that seemed to belong to a sleeper.

Angelo stuck a cigar in the corner of his mouth and allowed himself a stretch of galloping.

He covered more than two leagues without thinking of anything but the tobacco, the delicious coldness of the wind, and this personal liberty of his.

He was coming out of a narrow valley that had been caressing him with pungent-smelling mint, when he saw ahead of him a main road full of all sorts of halted vehicles. There were also other vehicles, carts, saddled horses tethered to trees in the fields off the road. Farther on, a considerable group of people on foot was piling up against a barricade and some kepis, whose red tassels were distinctly visible.

"Now the fun begins," he said to himself.

He cut across through a pine wood to the left. He reached a knoll from which he could take in a fairly wide stretch of country. It looked as if a frontier had been set up. On every road and even each tiny path a knot of kepis and barricades was holding back a small dark clot of carts, vehicles, and people.

"The game is to saunter along," he told himself. "Let's go down there like an amateur. I only need a gap a yard and a half wide to get by. It's really the devil if I can't find a yard and a half."

But as he approached at a trot a way that seemed to him to be clear, a soldier – a regular – sitting in the long grass stood up and shouted:

"Down you get, peasant! You've been told again and again not to come up mounted. If you want to argue, go along to the road and you'll find an officer. *I* shoot."

And he worked the breech of his musket. Ten yards away from him another soldier got up and also worked the breech of his musket.

Angelo saluted them and quietly turned his horse's head.

"If the panic is armed and determined," he said to himself, "the tune is going to change. These aren't those little guards I saw at Peyruis. He called me a peasant. The next trick is to make him believe I really am one. What would a peasant do in my place? He'd go and talk things over with the others. Let's do that."

And he approached the group clustered together on the road.

It consisted of about twenty people, including some haughty and highly disconcerted ladies and gentlemen. They all had papers in their hands.

"I don't give a damn for your passes," the officer was saying. "I know all about stunts like that. You don't have to teach an old monkey how to pull faces. My orders are: 'Halt them and keep them out!' and I'll halt you and keep you out till doomsday. Baron or no baron. I'm like cholera, no respecter of persons. All in the same boat. If it's really so wonderful where you come from, go back there. Unless there's a fly in the ointment. Well, it's just that fly we don't want. About turn."

He was a thin, colourless fellow like a parsnip, but with boot-polish eyes. He gave Angelo a sharp look.

The peasants, men and women, took the rebuke very well. Brief, knowing looks passed between them. But the barons and baronesses were really vexed. All they could think of was to hold their passes in their hands.

"Things must be getting hot where they came from!" thought Angelo. "Here they are, swallowing insults right in front of everybody, and they're not shocked by this at all. Conclusion: 'Long live the cholera!'"

Among these smartly dressed ladies who had not put on any powder for twenty-four hours and were beginning to study the toes of their shoes, Angelo noticed a green skirt, short and even, above boots against which a whip was tapping. The hand holding the whip was certainly not subdued. All this belonged to a small, Louis XI-style, sulphur-yellow felt hat and a very white neck. It was a young woman, who turned her back resolutely on the discussion and walked towards a horse tethered to a tree. Angelo saw a small pointed face, framed in heavy dark hair.

"I know her," he thought at once. "But where from?"

He had surely never met and forgotten a woman of that kind. She busied herself with the girths of a man's saddle with very short stirrups and in doing so raised a flap from which the mother-of-pearl of some large horse pistols shone out.

"I'll be damned," he told himself, "if it isn't the young woman who so bravely made me tea in that house with the remarkable attic."

He went up and said: "Can I help you, madame?"

She looked at him sternly.

"Payment for services rendered," he added drily.

"What services?"

"Two bowls of tea."

"Bowls?" she said.

"Yes," he said, "very big bowls, *café au lait* bowls. And I think if you'd had a soup tureen handy, you'd have served me the tea in a soup tureen."

At that moment, Angelo was cursing his peasant's jacket, but he was quite pleased with his cold manner, which he imagined to be very English. For an inexplicable reason Angelo had boundless confidence in the English manner. The young woman seemed more to be thinking of something funny.

"Ah!" said she. "I know! The gentleman!"

The word astounded Angelo. He had quite forgotten his state of mind on the stairs in the dark, and how then his chief fear had been that he would cause fear.

In spite of the little Louis XI hat set dashingly over one ear, the young woman unquestionably needed to talk. She congratulated him on having escaped the sickness during the paroxysm that immediately preceded the evacuation of the town. He described, in colourless words without any adjective, his adventures with the nun and how he had reached the almond-tree hill, then what had happened there. He did not mention Giuseppe but only the species of lightning cholera that had strewn the ground with abandoned corpses.

"We were no better accommodated on the hill where I was," she said.

And she too described a series of horrors.

"But what are we doing here?" said Angelo.

"For three days they've been preventing us from passing into the next *département*. I'm tired of being insulted by a monster who imagines that death gives him control over me. There he's wrong. I prefer your lightning cholera and I'm going back to it."

"It's easy to put up barricades in the little valley where we are," said Angelo, "but there must be a way of passing through the hills over there. They just count on our being bad riders and never daring to venture over rough ground."

"I've tried," she said, "but they've foreseen that. They're so frightened that they tend rather to overestimate everybody."

"Everybody, perhaps," said Angelo, "except those they should. A moment ago there was a peasant in a big black hat here. Where is he now? He's disappeared, and with him the horse that was harnessed to that trap left standing under the willows – look. And there's no one to be seen on the roads leading back. Just now, while the monster was showing off, I caught these country people winking at each other. They must know a place where it's difficult to post sentinels; they'll slip through there one by one. And if you ask me, the big fellow over there with the pale beard, who's just drifting off with the two women in red petticoats, is another of them. Watch. The two women are looking innocent. Too innocent. There:

isn't that one going to pick a sprig of mint? I never saw a peasant woman pick a sprig of mint merely to pass the time. Believe me, that's innocence invented for the occasion. There's a lot underneath the surface."

"You have terribly sharp eyes," said the young woman. "You're right, there is something there."

"Do you still want to get to the other side?" said Angelo. "Here's what we must do. Oh no, not follow them! Play safe. Leave the risks to them. Let's see which way they're going. We're old enough to go by ourselves if they aren't kicked back in a short while. It's quite easy. Let's draw aside a bit and not lose sight of them. I could see those women's petticoats two leagues away, with a red like that. Even if it were in the woods, over there on the crest."

Angelo and the young woman went and sat down on the grass near the abandoned buggy.

"People don't leave an almost new buggy like that by the roadside without good reason," he said. "And they've taken off everything they could, down to the cords of the side racks."

"Meanwhile our people have vanished," said she, "I can't see the red petticoats any more."

"There must be a low path over there," he said.

In fact, ten minutes later, they saw a red blob under the chestnuts that covered the lower slopes of the hills.

The sun was sinking. Its slanting rays penetrated deep into the forests rising like an amphitheatre around the little plain. They could easily follow the progress of the three who had escaped. They had first described a wide arc starting from the point where the road was barred; they were making for some high escarpments that appeared impassable.

"That looks to me like a passage that is just possible for people on foot," said the young woman. "I value my life, but I certainly won't abandon my horse to save it."

Never had Angelo been so happy. That feeling, which he understood perfectly, expressed by a voice with such charming inflections and by eyes that looked so sincere, seemed to him the most beautiful in the world. There was no question now of English coldness. He put a certain passion into saying:

224

"I would get myself killed for my horse. And I've only had him since yesterday evening. But," he continued, "I noticed your shortened stirrups and I deduced from that that you're an excellent horsewoman. Besides, look carefully at that little bald patch just above the forest, below the escarpment: it must be a small grazing-ground. I can see a dark blue spot moving over it. I believe it's the bay horse and the tall peasant in the blouse who were still here, no more than half an hour ago, at the foot of that birch. The monster talks a lot; he has dark eyes that make an impression and must terrify his company, but I wouldn't want him even guarding the kitchens; he doesn't realize that there are now five carts unharnessed and abandoned around us."

Without gestures, so as not to attract the soldier's attention, and in the terse language of a military report, he drew the young woman's attention to four or five other brown spots moving slowly over the grazing-ground in the direction of the left-hand ridge of the escarpment, round which they disappeared.

"Nothing would rejoice me more than to give that foul-mouthed officer a fine farewell," said the young woman.

"Let's give it to him at once," said Angelo. "We're no stupider than country people."

He was in his element. He helped her into her saddle without even realizing that she was wearing skirts and that she rode astride.

They made a wide detour across the fields and did not take the right direction until they were concealed by a coppice of oaks.

"Your horse has a lot of spirit, but my old plug has good sense," said he, when they had reached the chestnut forest. "Let me go first, he'll pick the best path. The secret is to head for the light reflected from the rocks, and I can sight through the leaves."

At every step they found obvious signs of others having passed there recently. They were already well up the mountain when they overtook the man with the red beard and the two women in scarlet petticoats. They were resting at the edge of a vermillion clearing.

"You're very good at this game," said the young woman when they had passed the others.

Angelo was intoxicated by the smell of the autumn woods. He naïvely showed that he didn't know what she meant.

"I mean," she said, "that there are two ways of escaping from the charnel houses you described to me earlier on, and which I am running away from too. One of these is to ask everyone the way. I don't like doing it."

"There was nothing to ask," replied Angelo, even more naïvely. "I've two eyes, just like the man with the beard. So I don't need his to reach that escarpment: it's now in front of us, as plain as the sky above the sea."

"What I said," remarked the young woman drily, "was only to vindicate myself in my own eyes."

At the foot of the rocks there was, in fact, a narrow defile, but in it Angelo discovered fresh horse-dung. He could not contain his delight, and he spoke of this dung as though it were nuggets of gold. He was in earnest and his exaltation was sincere, but there was a certain charm in disporting oneself at this height, over the tops of the chestnut trees, and it began to be clear that he was disporting himself like a madman. He even used some very Italian words and gestures to describe the extraordinary landscape that one saw from this spot. The sun, now even lower on the horizon, made the vivid enamel of all the crests glitter to its light, stabbed the black forests with flaming arrows, and on the little plain below, already in shadow, sparkled from the bevelled blades of all its grasses.

The young woman advanced boldly across two or three rugged places where there was danger of slipping on the loose scree. Finally they turned the corner of the escarpment, and beyond rolling spurs covered with thick forests they saw in the distance a broad valley, riverless but verdant and with a small round town in the middle of its fields.

"The promised land," said Angelo.

From the height where they stood, however, the way was still a very long one. For more than a league they exhausted themselves holding their horses to a steep, twisting path under enormous beeches. The light was now sinking fast. They reached a defile full of grey twilight.

"During the two days I was held up by the soldiers' barricade," said the young woman, "I heard many things, but especially that the dragoons from Valence are patrolling this whole region and arresting without mercy all who are not resident in the *département*."

"That applies to me wherever I go," said Angelo. "I'm not resident anywhere."

"Be careful," she said.

"You don't live in this region either?"

"No."

"I know the places they put you in in such circumstances," said Angelo. "They call it quarantine. I consented to that once. I have every respect for the welfare of mankind and the common weal, but no desire to fall into a booby trap again."

They went down the defile, which gradually broadened and finally opened out into a lake of grass half a league wide. In the centre, beneath tall sycamores, could be seen the white walls and belfries of what appeared to be an abbey. Amid the pearl-grey twilight and the muffled music of two or three huge fountains, the place was so peaceful that they left the shelter of the trees and took to the meadows. They were too far from the edge of the woods when they heard lusty voices challenging them and saw three horsemen in red uniforms emerge from a clump of willows and gallop towards them in a very pretty enveloping movement.

"Leave this to me," said Angelo.

"Here's two more of these f—g swine," said the horseman bearing a corporal's stripes.

Angelo replied with an insult that was too long and, before he had finished, the other shouted scornfully:

"Give him one in the snout!"

Angelo plunged his hand into his saddlebag, was lucky enough to find the little sabre's hilt at once, and drew it.

"Throw that away, you poor fool, it pricks," said one of the soldiers with a snigger.

Angelo was busy with his horse and was thinking: "The hardest thing's going to be to put some fight into this damned old nag."

Indeed, he was holding his sabre like a broomstick. The horsemen had unsheathed their long dragoons' blades and were preparing to strike at him with the flat side, when Angelo sensed that his horse was more intelligent than he had thought and was even ready to do some rather pretty work on its own account. He launched it so violently against the corporal's mare that this man, in blank astonishment, lost his stirrups, fell like a bag of spoons, and remained stretched out on the ground. The soldiers slashed at him, jabbering like rats, but Angelo briskly turned their blades and in a few adroit passes put them both on the defensive. While giving a brilliant display of swordsmanship, he voluptuously took the time to say, in a drawing-room voice:

"Do me the kindness, madame, of galloping straight on. I propose to give a little lesson in manners to these blackguards."

He saw that his adversaries' faces were red as boiled pigs.

"Bad soldiers," he thought; "they're dying of rage."

In a second he contrived a magnificent backstroke that sent the weapon of one of them flying out of his hand in such lightning fashion that the rider heard his own blade whistle past his ears and lost his seat from astonishment. Angelo, standing in his stirrups, brought his sabre down flat on the other's helmet as hard as he could. The two men turned tail. The disarmed one dug with both spurs; the other, stunned but in his saddle, went off with his legs flapping, like a man who has had his fill. The corporal was still lying in the grass.

"Good old Giuseppe," thought Angelo.

He was quite surprised to find the young woman still there. She had not moved. She was blithely holding one of her horse pistols pointed at the prone man.

"Is he dead?" she enquired.

"That would surprise me," said Angelo.

He dismounted and went to see.

"He won't die of this," said he. "He's just a conscript who's had his first shock! But you may be sure, when he comes to, he'll tell a terrible tale. Let's make off under the trees and get away."

They rode very rapidly for a long time under the trees, taking several cross tracks, and even wading in a stream for more than half a league.

"I think we're doubling back," said the young woman.

"I'm sure we're not," said Angelo. "In the first place, I've been taking care always to have the sun behind us, and in all our windings I've never stopped aiming for that big star. It rose while I was settling their hash, and it occurred to me that it was just what we needed to get us safely away from those buildings we saw among the trees, where there was certainly a platoon in reserve. If we keep straight ahead, we should come out of the wood at the side opposite where we went in."

Half an hour later, they emerged into fields. Night had fallen. Here too the grain had not been cut. The flattened crops covered the ground with a phosphorescent glow.

They passed by farms, silent and dark.

"I don't much like these houses without lights," said Angelo. "And still less this smell that comes from them. What are we to do now?"

"You used your little sabre very ably."

"It's far too little to get us into the town we caught sight of earlier on. That must lie somewhere ahead of us, in the darkness. There's bound to be a barrack for these soldiers who are patrolling and barricading the roads. They must be talking there already about a woman who carries big horse pistols."

"Let's stay at the edge of the woods," said the young woman. "At least until daylight. And let's push as far ahead as we can, if you're still sure of the direction given by your star."

"Now that we're no longer under the trees, I've a better one," said Angelo. "There's the Great Bear. Before I met you I saw, from the top of the hill, the whole line of troopers barring the roads. It ran from east to west. Let's ride on the Bear, which is due north: then we're bound to be getting farther from the soldiers. Unless the whole region has been filled with them, but I don't believe that. Have you any food?"

"Of course. Am I destined to be your commissary?"

"Far from it. I don't set out without biscuits myself if I can help it. Besides, the hardest thing is getting something to drink."

"Have you forgotten that one of my virtues is to have tea about me?"

"But we can't light a fire before dawn. This country's black as a pot, and before midnight there'll be a good fifty foragers straining their eyes every which way with the simple hope of nabbing us beside our teapot. I can teach people lessons they don't forget, but they'll never forgive you for not having collapsed in a faint and for having stood up to them with a pistol bigger than your head. Cavalrymen like women to scream. If on horseback you can't even scare a woman, what chance have you got on foot? Believe me,

229

they're busy thinking it all out in their minds; they're thinking of everything, even that one is obliged to drink boiled water in a country full of carrion. They're counting on that to trip us up."

"You know some strange horsemen?" said the young woman.

"Horsemen," said Angelo, "generally ride on horses. They never like it to be a waste of time."

And he told a story of barrack life.

They had reached a hillock.

"Can you manage to get through the night without drink or food?" said Angelo.

"Perfectly well, if necessary."

"That would let us get away without giving the impression that we're running like poor idiots who've had a little luck and taken to their heels."

"Who do you think is getting that impression? The night's like ink. We're a hundred leagues from all that."

"One's never a hundred leagues away, and we know nothing about anything. This is what I suggest. It smells good here. We're clearly in a pine wood. Let's stay in it till daybreak. I want to see what I'm doing when the soldiers begin their games."

"Do you think they've the time and the desire to play one? They have other fish to fry; mounting guard in particular."

"I know how they mount guard," said Angelo. "I know also how the tiny brain of a corporal who's been unhorsed by a civilian works. I could repeat, word for word, the story he's telling at this moment. The two dragoons have taken the measure of my sword play; it's not every day that someone sends their blades flying out of their hands with a cabbage-chopper. They're mad to find us, and have the last laugh. We surely interest them much more than cholera."

"Then we haven't been very clever," she said.

"I'm never clever when I'm insulted. And all in all, we're better off here than in quarantine, which is where they'd have put us, after a lot of bad jokes, what's more."

The scent of the pines was exquisite. They must have sweated copiously all the summer, and now in the coolness of this autumn night their sap was yielding its most delicate perfume. Even the horses rejoiced in it; they instinctively followed a soft path under the trees, and from time to time gave little sighs of pleasure.

"I'm like you," she said, "I don't much like last laughs."

"They're peasants who've been given sabres and are stupid from being insulted twenty-four hours a day. The day they find themselves on top, they don't show much mercy."

"Let's stop here, then."

They dismounted. Angelo recognized an ilex from the sound made by the night brushing against hard foliage. They entered the shelter of its branches. It was warm in there. The ground was dry, springy, and crackling.

"Let's not unload the horses," said he. "Are you sure of yours?"

"He stayed with me three days in front of the barricades. No doubt I lacked initiative, but I fed him well. I knew I should end by doing something rash."

"That's not the name I'd apply to what we've done."

"Perhaps it's the name for what we shall do tomorrow."

"We shall do what has to be done."

"Anything rather than wait about stupidly for that unclean death. You can't imagine how welcome those soldiers were. The sight of their sabres was a joy. Naked steel is comforting. I'm not afraid."

"So I saw."

"But I have a horror of vomiting."

"There's no need to do that here," said Angelo. "Don't think about it. The soldiers were welcome for me too, and we were welcome for the soldiers. We're all in the same boat. Everyone has a horror of something."

There were hardly any stars, no wind, and a great silence. Now that for once Angelo was playing at war with really hostile cavalry, he was throwing himself into it heart and soul. He thought of the young woman as of baggage wagons in the rear, to be protected at all costs.

"You're still not quite at ease?" she said.

"I'm afraid of grocers when they have guns," said he. "Panic has given a taste for adventure to people who were used to dozing by their hearths. They're cats who've suddenly had their tails trodden on; they lash out with their claws at random."

"They won't come this far."

"I'd feel easier if I knew what's at the bottom of the hill. If it's a town or a big village, the local worthies will certainly be out on patrol."

"Don't you rather see them with every chink stopped up and their noses under the sheets?"

"Death's been tormenting them for three months, they've exhausted every resource of that kind. Now they need action, it doesn't matter what sort."

"I see their point. To tell you the truth, I myself took to the roads with pistols for scapularies."

"But you have somewhere to go."

"In theory, yes. I'm going to my sister-in-law's: she lives in the mountains, above Gap. But that's just an idea like any other."

"That's the way I'm going," said Angelo. "I'm going back to Italy."

"Are you Italian?"

"Isn't it obvious?"

"You speak French without an accent," said she. "I admit, though, that when I surprised you in my house, and you surprised me too, you had rather a foreign way of speaking."

"I don't think so. I used to talk French with my mother, even in Italy. I think in French, and I believe that's the language I used, the moment I saw you with the candlestick."

"You must have been taken aback?"

"I was anxious for your sake."

"That's what I call a foreign way of speaking. You had the knack of reassuring me straightaway."

"Who could have wished anything else?"

"Let's not draw up a list of them, if it's all the same to you. I'd already had to deal, two or three times, with thin, badly shaved, crazy-looking men, who talked what is known as French."

"I know them: they're the better sort of people in those famous patrols. They don't like to imagine that death is independent. They have an absolute need to find somebody responsible and to treat him accordingly."

"Let's say, then, that your solicitude and your skill with the sabre come from a country that I call foreign and you call Italy."

Angelo had never been so Italian. He was passionately pursuing his dearest whim. He was making an inventory of the noises, the echoes, and even the most innocent sighs of the night. Nothing now had savour or sense for him except to discover thereby under the compact darkness the shape of the surrounding country. He saw in his imagination a valley with murmuring poplars. He had made out the course of a little stream along which clumps of reeds were rustling; fixed, about a hundred yards to his left, the limits of a small, probably narrow valley, filled with tall trees and perhaps containing houses; identified a sort of solemn rumbling, rather high up in the sky, as being that of a chain of mountains that must rise up some leagues away. He kept posting sentinels everywhere. He was on his guard against every approach.

He heard a curious noise. It was like the flapping of sheets on a clothesline. It was moving through the air, sinking and rising; it came up from the valley, approached and passed overhead, not very high, faded, returned, then slid off into the distance. Something had dropped as it passed into the branches of the ilex, from which, after a moment, there came a cooing, a tender summons, sad as a pigeon's, but somehow imperative.

"They were birds," said Angelo. "At all events, this is a bird."

"It has a funny voice: almost like a cat in springtime."

"It settled on our tree when the whole flock brushed by us. There are more coming."

It was true: a heavy and calm beating of wings was approaching.

Angelo remembered all his encounters with the birds, particularly in the village where he had seen the cholera for the first time, and later on the roofs at Manosque.

"They're no longer scared of man, now that they can eat as much of him as they like," he said.

And he described how he had had to defend himself against swallows, swifts, and clouds of nightingales.

"These seem to be going still farther," said the young woman. "Listen to them: wouldn't you say they were wooing us?"

There was, in those voices descending from the ilex and the pines, a sort of persuasive tenderness, an amorous force that sought to compel, gently but resolutely.

"It's an urgent courtship," she said. "And they're full of hope, it seems."

233

Angelo threw stones at them, but was not able to silence them or drive them away. They had the patience of angels. They said what they had to say diligently and soulfully. Apparently it had for them the sense of indisputable logic. After having expressed themselves directly and with some authority, they paused and waited for a surrender to their prayers. Then they began again, requesting the same thing and giving the excellent reasons they had for doing so, lingering over their velvety trills, very gentle, very enchanting, very sad. Finally, after perhaps an hour of this, they began to put a certain sharpness into their demands. The two horses were frightened and began to pant and shake their bridles.

Angelo went to calm the animals.

"They're trembling like leaves," he said.

"So am I," said the young woman. "You know what they want?"

"Of course. I can't understand why the soldiers have set up so many barricades. This part of the country is no better than the one we've left. Here comes something else as well."

At the bottom of the hill there were rustlings in the undergrowth, then a sound like wheels on stones and stifled whispering.

"People," said Angelo.

"I can't hear anything."

"It isn't soldiers. There are women and children, and they're carting their furniture. They're fugitives like us. They've been attracted by the smell of the resin."

"I can hear nothing but the wind in the pines."

"There isn't any wind. It's the creaking of axles and a voice speaking, probably to a horse."

"If there were horses, ours would have already scented them. I can hear something creaking, but it's a branch."

"Don't think I've been upset by the birds," said Angelo. "I assure you, there are people who've come this very instant to huddle at the foot of the hill."

"The birds have certainly upset me," said the young woman.

"Would you like us to move on?"

"That wouldn't be any help. It's an idea we're carrying about with us. No, I've got goose flesh, but that's for me to deal with."

They spent a most unpleasant night. In the morning Angelo

hastened to verify the existence of the camp of fugitives. He searched in vain; he found no trace of it.

It was now light enough to kindle a fire without undue risk. The first thing was to find a spring from which to fill the teakettle. The landscape bore no relation to the one Angelo had pictured. It was a small, austere valley made beautiful by autumn. Two or three poor farms stood at the centre of a diminutive circle of fields between oak woods and wastes of grey stones.

The wind rose. The dawn was red and presaged rain.

"I'm going to look for water," said Angelo. "Wait for me."

"I'll come with you."

"No, take a rest, now that we can see a little. And guard the horses. I'm going up to those farms. There must be a well there, but those thickets may have eyes and we don't know what's hidden under all those oaks. We'd better continue to take precautions. I'll keep low and I shan't be seen."

"I've been lacking in initiative," thought Angelo. "Alas, Giuseppe, you have too much confidence in me. I think you're betting on the wrong card. When it comes to fighting for liberty, I'm not even worthy to pull your boots off. What'll become of the least little revolution if I can't stop always following in someone else's footsteps? The old sergeants know more about it than I do. Under fire, one should be as coarse as barley bread; otherwise nobody can stand up to it. I haven't the gift. With a couple of well-timed oaths, that woman would stop being frightened. And so would I."

He reproached himself for the night spent listening for sounds and attaching importance to them.

"If you want to be someone," he told himself, "try not to understand anything. Then courage comes easy and it is impressive. *You* speak your thoughts out loud, and people always know what you're at. Nobody can have confidence in you. Stupidity always works wonders. Here, anyway, nothing could be more help. Peasants, in our place, would have slept."

In addition, he was very dissatisfied with this *esprit d'escalier* coming to him now as he crept along the hedges.

As he drew near the houses, he perceived that they were humming like beehives. From the open doors and windows he saw clouds of flies coming out. He knew what that meant.

There was no smell, however. He went to take a look: it was the expected sight, but the corpses were a month old. Of a woman, all that was left was the enormous legbones protruding from a trampled skirt, a torn bodice over bones, and hair without a head. The skull had broken loose and rolled under the table. The man was in a heap in the corner. They must have been eaten by the chickens that had huddled together on Angelo's arrival, silent, one foot raised, but very arrogant. Swarms of bees and huge wasps had deserted their hives and built combs and nests between the stovepipe and the fireplace.

Angelo heard a shot. It had been loud and not far away. He looked first towards the road, then realized that the noise had come from their little hill. He returned there at the double.

The young woman was standing, pale as death, with a pistol in her hand.

"What did you fire at?"

Her face contorted with horrible laughter, while the tears poured down her cheeks. Her teeth were chattering and she could only stare shudderingly at Angelo. He had already seen horses in this state. He stroked her skilfully with his hand. At length the eyes, swollen with tears and flooded now with tenderness, turned away, and the young woman sighed.

"I'm quite absurd," she said, withdrawing rather nervously from Angelo's hands, "but this won't happen to me again. I was taken by surprise, and by something nobody can get used to. I fired at the bird. When you had gone, he became extremely pressing and, I must say, extremely charming. I've never heard anything more horrible than that lullaby he kept endlessly singing to me. I felt syrupy from head to foot, and had a longing to close my eyes. I must have yielded to it for two seconds and he was on me. He stank. He struck me with his beak here."

She had a small scratch close to her eye.

"That carrion bird certainly had its beak full of cholera," thought Angelo. "Can the disease be transmitted this way?" He was aghast.

He made the young woman drink some alcohol. He himself took a good gulp of it. He carefully disinfected the little red spot; it was really nothing much, the merest graze.

"Let's get the hell out of here," he said. "Pardon my language, but what does it matter? There's nothing but dead bodies in the farms over there. This place is unhealthy. I didn't even look for water when I saw how things were. Let's go." They set off along the ridge, through the pine woods.

"Do you know what sort of bird it was, really?" said the young woman.

"No."

"A crow. They were crows that wooed us last night; and it was a crow that passed from words to deeds this morning and at which I so stupidly fired."

"It wasn't stupid," said Angelo. "Let's remember to reload your pistol directly we've calmed down a bit. But I've never heard crows with voices like that."

"No more have I. When you left me just now, I was tired out by our sleepless night, and perhaps I was dreaming with my eyes open, but I've never heard a creature address me in that way. It was repulsive, but seductive to a degree you can't imagine. It was horrible. I could understand perfectly and realized that I was giving in, that I was consenting. It was only at the first peck that I screamed and leapt for my pistols. Even the stink of it didn't disgust me, to tell the truth."

"Forget it," said Angelo, rather roughly.

The forest was warm and very light, in spite of the cloudy sky, which seemed bent on rain. A few puffs of wind were already moist. The pines, very tall and widely spaced, left free a wide expanse of undergrowth.

They reached a ledge overlooking a valley covered with red earth and the straight lines of a fairly large vineyard. A prosperous farm, with a green-shuttered house, sheds, sheepfolds, and stables, sprawled there between wide ponds, under tall plane trees already turned to copper. Two threads of smoke rose from the chimney of the house and that of the farm buildings respectively. Here the people were alive.

They descended by a rugged track, but the young woman was an excellent rider and above all she wanted to atone for the pistol shot. At the bottom they found a lane, which ran straight through the vines towards the tall plane trees. Everything was well kept and gave evidence of hard work and constant care.

They were trotting towards the fountain when someone sitting by its basin stood up, fifty yards ahead of them, and shouted to them to stop. At the same time he raised a gun to his shoulder.

The morning's events had brought Angelo before the bar of his Italy, and in spite of the weapon pointed at him he slowed his horse to a walk but continued to advance.

"Don't move or I'll fill you with lead," shouted the man.

He was young, and, in spite of several weeks' growth of beard and hands black with filth, he wore with ease a well-cut hunting jacket and a fine pair of boots.

Angelo advanced upon him without replying; on the contrary, clenching his teeth. He never took his eye off the black circle of the barrel facing him and the extremely dirty finger resting on the trigger.

He was on top of the young man, who hastily fell back, continuing to shout the order to stop.

"Don't be unpleasant," he said. "We haven't come to harm you. All we want is water."

"We don't want anyone coming near our water," said the young man. "We leave others alone; let them leave us alone."

"I suppose this is too complicated for you," said Angelo, "but I have no wish to cause any extra fright, either in you or in your family. Are there any other fountains besides this one where we can fill our kettle?"

"Go to the village."

"Excuse me," said Angelo coldly; "I never go to the devil when people suggest it."

He dismounted without looking at the gun. He went to the young woman's stirrup.

"Pass me the kettle, please; it's tied to your saddlebag."

While she was untying it she whispered: "I've still got one loaded pistol."

"It's not needed," he answered in a low voice.

"Here's my kettle," he said, placing it on the ground six paces from the young man. "I'm not interested in going near your water, but this lady wishes to drink and so do I. If you have a grain of common sense, this is what you'll do. Go and fill a jug at your fountain – at the spout, please, not from the basin – and come and pour it yourself into our kettle."

238

From the hunting-jacket and boots Angelo judged that he must be the owner of the estate; on the other hand, there was the beard, the filth, and the gun. "I was even dirtier than he on the roofs of Manosque," he thought, "but I had nothing. Besides, he could have fired just now. I wasn't stingy about giving him a target."

He added, aloud, with the utmost insolence: "Since you prefer to act as my servant."

"We've had our fill of fine manners, you know," said the young man.

"Who's 'we'?" replied Angelo, more insolently than ever.

The other growled, but did what he was asked.

"Now put your gun down and draw back ten paces while we turn."

"I shan't shoot," said the other, "be off with you."

Angelo assumed his most English air, and accepted condescendingly. He transferred the water from the kettle to his goatskin bottle, then remounted and, making the young woman ride ahead, went off protecting the rear.

In the middle of the vineyard they found a public road leading towards thickly wooded and narrow gullies. They proceeded along it until they considered they were off the estate. They were at the entrance to a defile into which the road descended. They lit a fire against a bank. At last they could eat and drink.

They had been there about an hour, and were half asleep after their meal of bread and tea, when they heard the trotting of a horse. A mounted man was approaching, undoubtedly a dragoon. He had the red dolman.

"Don't let's move," said Angelo. "He's alone and I'm his match."

It was indeed a captain. He was riding in the open country as though on parade, with great arrogance and affectation. He was careful to make his little Sunday cloak flutter as it should. He passed without saluting.

It was still very dark under the cloudy sky. As often at the approach of rain, absolute quiet had laid hold of the countryside. Everything was motionless, down to the smallest blade of grass, and the topmost leaves of the trees did not stir.

Angelo asked permission to smoke a small cigar.

"They're very pretty," said the young woman.

"They're very good," he said, "but you're right, I like them besides because they're long and thin. If you feel sleepy, go to sleep, and I'll mount guard. If not, we ought perhaps to hold a little council of war. Are we going the right way?"

"Where are we, first of all?"

"I don't know. We'll see at the next village. Did you have a plan?"

"First of all, to get away, but I've done that. Next, as I told you, the idea of going to take refuge with my sister-in-law, at Théus near Gap. I realized it was no good taking the main road, because of all the barricades. Once I crossed over the mountains from this side with my husband. I've come back here instinctively."

"If you know the country, that will make things easy."

"I don't know it at all. We travelled partly by night in hired carriages. I only saw the scenery, not the route. I know one goes through Roussieux, and later through Chauvac, because we slept in both those villages, but that doesn't get us much further. I know the country is poor and deserted (that's what decided me). There's also a fairly important town called, I think, Sallerans, or something of the sort. And that's all I know."

"It's better than nothing," said Angelo. "Now we've got some landmarks. I can accompany you as far as Théus, because that's on my way. And I think it's just as well I should. But we must find a spot called Sainte-Colombe."

He pulled from his pocket the piece of paper on which Giuseppe had drawn the famous map.

"With the name and this little plan," he continued, "I believe we can get there, if we ask peasants the way. Apparently it's a hermitage in a gorge, precisely one of those deserts you mentioned. I have a rendezvous there with my foster-brother and his wife, who stayed behind at Manosque and are to join me after settling some business. We shall be four, and from then on our troubles will be over."

"You misjudge me because of that pistol shot," said the young woman, "but I don't consider we've had many troubles up to now. Without claiming that I exactly foresaw the crow, I did expect quite a bit of trouble and I was relying on myself alone. We'll go to Sainte-Colombe, since that's where your business is, and very gladly."

"I'm so far from misjudging you," said Angelo, "that I now ask you to let me reload your pistol."

"I shall do it myself," she said. "I like to be sure of my rounds."

She took her tools from a satchel, and did the job very dexterously. She put in a full charge with a little extra, and backed up the bullet with small shot.

"We must take care not to goad her to heroism," thought Angelo, who could be penetrating about other people. "There's enough there to kill three."

He was also very intrigued by her way of tearing the wad with her teeth like a trooper and without braggadocio.

"A full charge like that will give a remarkable recoil," said Angelo.

"A remarkable splash, too," said she. "By the time my wrist hurts, the bullet will have already left for its address."

They struck camp and entered the defile. The road descended gently and wound between wooded slopes. They emerged on to a little heath covered with pale junipers.

They had gone half a league over this wide empty space overwhelmed by clouds, when they saw a riderless horse trotting briskly towards them. They placed themselves so as to bar its way, but the animal suddenly swerved, almost under their noses, and set off at a gallop across the heath. There could be no question of catching it.

"It's the horse of that dragoon who passed us not long ago," said Angelo. "The stirrups are hitting him in the belly. He'll bolt. So an officer lets his horse give him the slip. Not in the manual!"

He laughed at that arrogant man who had the good fortune to be in uniform. But a quarter of an hour later they found the captain lying in the middle of the road, his face already black, his cheek buried in his vomitings. There was obviously no need to help him.

They spurred their horses to a canter, and kept to it for a long time.

The heath must have stretched for three or four leagues in the direction they were travelling. From horseback they commanded a view over the low vegetation; as far as they could see there was nothing but this grey desolation and, ahead of them, a mass of lowering clouds, through which they could sometimes distinguish the black bulk of a mountain. They passed by a ruined house, long uninhabited. The roof and floors had caved in. In what remained of a small cellar, however, there were traces of a fire recently made between two stones. They heard a fox bark. Finally they perceived some thin fields, shocks of carefully scythed barley, almond orchards, and a crossroads with a small watering-trough and three houses. All three empty.

"I don't understand," said Angelo; "here they had shelter."

Then he thought of the captain.

The horses, which had covered a lot of ground the day before and had not been unsaddled all night, were beginning to snort. Angelo took great pleasure in watering them, washing them, grooming them. The leather of the saddles and saddlebags, the hides salty with sweat, had a comforting smell of barracks, of male fraternity, in this desert, in this sinister light. He was very pleased with his stout farm horse. He remembered the little skirmish in the meadow and the fine spirit he had suddenly felt in the animal. The young woman's horse was likewise very sturdy, though better bred. Also he was more subtle. He preened a little under the curry-comb and responded prettily to the grooming hand. He tended to take an interest in distant objects. He pricked his ears and rolled his eyes when Angelo tethered him in a little field, beside the big farm horse.

"What's his name?"

"I don't know," said the young woman. "I stole him. I wanted to buy him at first, but they held a knife at my throat."

"Did you really steal him at pistol-point, as I did this summer on the high road?"

"No, I broke a padlock. I went groping for him in the dark in the stable where they'd showed him to me."

"You made a good choice. He's certainly a half-blood. One can see at once that he's got sturdy legs. If he were trained over fences he'd make an excellent hunter."

"I saw that too, at the first glance. Later the desire to have him became irresistible. I didn't wave my pistols under anyone's nose because there wasn't anybody guarding him; but I'd have done so. I was mad to get away. Not, as the phrase goes, to save my skin, but to leap, to fly over the obstacles, the barricades, the disgusting corpses, to bound off into the Alps. The cholera frightens me. I shouldn't like to die in that way."

"Nor should I: it's too stupid."

"What's the good of being a captain," he was thinking, "if one has to die vomiting something that looks like boiled rice?" He was drawing a contrast with the corpses left behind on the field by a charge.

"When I see the reason for something, I don't care," he said; "but in this case I'm like you. Something you don't even know picks you up by the ears like a rabbit from a hutch, gives you a sharp blow on the neck, and you're done for. There's no way of gilding that pill."

"Add that it's the common lot," said she, "and then we're ready for most things."

In spite of the grey light that flattened out colours and shapes, they were enjoying their delicious insecurity near those emaciated houses.

"The only unpleasant thing," thought Angelo, "is that corpse lying across the road, a couple of leagues from here."

They heard the sound of nailed shoes attacking the road, and they saw come out from the crossroads a man carrying a largish bundle on his back. The stranger waved, obviously in friendship, and approached them. He was a figure so moustached and bearded that he no longer looked human. He greeted them from a long way off by raising his hat. He took care, nevertheless, to keep his distance: he stopped twelve or fifteen feet away from them, put his bundle down, and greeted them again. Only his smiling eyes were visible in his hairy face.

"Good day, m'sieu-dame," he said. "May I have your leave to rest my legs by the side of two living Christians?"

He was a sturdy peasant with enormous hands.

"Things seem to have been shaken up here too," said Angelo.

"We must cling to straws, monsieur," said the other. "It's the only way."

"What's this place called?"

"This is Villette, madame."

"What happened to make them leave?"

"They went two different ways, monsieur. The green shutters over there was Jules's. He kicked the bucket more than a month ago. The others wouldn't stay. It's understandable. If they'd listened to me, I'd have given them the formula."

"The formula for what?"

"The formula for keeping alive, by God!"

"If you know that, you'll make your fortune."

"I don't exactly make a fortune, but I make a living."

"You sell it?"

"Well, you don't think I'd give it away? It isn't dear, that's a fact. One little écu, three francs, what's that when you've got your arse in a fire? Sometimes I give it away. In certain cases. But it's a queer thing; I'll have to admit that in those cases it doesn't work very well. People have to pay. Then it works. And properly. I've already saved hundreds and thousands."

"What with?"

"With what's in this bundle of mine, madame. Herbs. I go a long distance to get them, and it's hard on my shoes. They're not very plentiful, and you need a sharp eye. If *you* wanted to get some, you could search till you dropped. But I know a lot of things. I give my fellow men the benefit. You've got fine-looking animals. You wouldn't like to sell me one? I've got money in my pocket."

"No, my friend," said Angelo. "These are our herbs."

"I'll bet they help," said the man. "And where are you going?"

"Do you come from here? Do you know the country well?"

"Like my pocket, madame. There's not a bush I haven't looked at all the way round. I live up there, and I'm making my rounds for about the twentieth time."

"Where does this road go?"

"That way, monsieur, takes you to Sainte-Cyrice. But it's not very nice there."

"And the other way?"

"There you might have a little less trouble. You go through Sorbiers, Flachères, and then Montferrant before you hit the highway."

"The highway to where?"

"The highway to everywhere. Wherever you want."

"Doesn't it pass through Chauvac, or Roussieux? Do you know a place called Sallerans?"

"Sallerans, no. But Chauvac — that's a long way off. If it was clear, you'd see a mountain over there. It's called Charouilles; Chauvac's behind it."

"And Sainte-Colombe, do you know that?"

244

"Yes, monsieur, it's in the same direction. But it's not much of a place. Nothing to shout about."

"Can we have a frank talk?" said Angelo.

"That depends," said the man. "Generally speaking, it isn't fatal."

"I'm going to buy five packets of your medicine," said Angelo; "with an extra écu thrown in, that makes a louis. I'll throw it down at your feet if you're not afraid of contagion."

"I have my formula," said the man. "And a louis never gave anyone cholera. Go on, but don't ask me about the moon."

"What are the soldiers up to hereabouts?"

"You've hit the bull's eye: they're a public nuisance."

"They seem to be everywhere."

"I'll give you your money's worth. Towards Chauvac, where you're heading, it's packed with dragoons, and even with infantry, because it's the highway and it's crowded with civilians. They put them through a sieve. They have to go through fifteen days' quarantine at the friars' school, which has been converted into a hospital. If you've got any cash, you run two risks: first they beat you up, to prove you tried to grease their palms, and then they pick you clean – confiscation they call it. Since they have to give it all back to you when you leave, they like you to leave feet first. And that's what happens."

"Then there's nothing to do except avoid the town."

"Nothing to do except avoid the town; you're right. But if you want to hear any more, it's time for another five-franc piece."

"If it's worth it."

"I'll say it is. Listen and you'll see. If you wait till you reach Chauvac before striking off, it's too late. They're tricky and they have horses with six legs that can climb anything – like flies. Don't try to outsmart them among the rocks; they'd catch you in no time They've blocked all the trails, even the smallest. This is where you have to know the ropes. And, for that écu, I'll tell you."

"There it is," said Angelo, "go ahead; but if you get me into that mess, I'd better warn you that I'm Italian and I know how to cast spells."

"Don't get carried away," said the man. "I wouldn't gain anything by getting you into a mess. You're in no danger. As for spells, I've been seeing all sorts for some time now. I don't need the help of an

Italian. It's as simple as pie: all that you need is to be a native of these parts. They don't catch any of us.

"Here's the story. When you start out, take the Sainte-Cyrice road. First it is level for a good while, then it begins to go down. Keep going down until you see the belfry. Then halt: it's bad ahead. It's a good spot to die in. They do that on the grand scale. There were six more last evening. On the right you'll find an earth track which goes to Bayons. Go that way. When you get to Bayons, watch out. You arrive by the wash-house. Don't go into the village; keep left and go straight on. It's plain sailing as far as Montjay. That's right, madame, write it down. Old Antoine's not the dumb bastard they take him for. Excuse my language. If I'm here talking to you, it's only because I slipped through the net.

"You'll be at Montjay by this evening. Wait till morning so you can make sure you're right at the foot of Charouilles. Instead of going full tilt up the main road with the hairpin bends, follow upstream along the path, straight to the top. From there a child of four would know how to avoid the town; it's already a good way off to the left. That's the story."

\* \*

They followed the directions point by point. The peasant had gone off down a side road, wishing them luck. His instructions were admirable. Within sight of the Sainte-Cyrice belfry they easily found an earth track. It led into russet grass, under a small umbrella pine. Thanks to it, they skirted the village of Sainte-Cyrice at a healthy distance. A significant silence reigned there.

"Without the mustard merchant's directions we should certainly have finished up in that charming stopover."

Indeed, since they had left the plateau and begun to descend the landscape had entirely changed. Friendly trees, especially golden limes and purple maples, ran in hedges and borders or swelled into groves among the fields, small vineyards, meadows, and grey fallow lands of a hilly countryside. Groves of forest pines covered the tops of the hills.

The little village below which they were passing was particularly attractive, clinging to the flank of the plateau by balustrades, eaves, pink-tiled gutters, vine arbours, ramparts, turrets, alabaster-white

246

stairways; and autumn was bronzing the elms in its little squares. The belfry's beautiful wrought-iron cage rose before the mullioned windows of a small country château, which topped the knoll with its simple battlements and the slender cypresses of its terraces.

"I should have been suspicious of the birds," said the young woman. "They've taken possession of the place. I can see thousands resting on the roofs. Look at those balconies laden with them. That's not black washing hanging on those wires, but crows, and no doubt the same as the one who threw himself on me when he thought I had at last consented to die."

Fortunately the country they crossed was empty as far as Bayons. They skirted a succession of low hills, each one prettier than the last. Every bend in the path brought them fresh views of those omnipresent pines surrounding the red autumnal groves in a decorum fit for a king's court. It made one literally laugh with pleasure. They made a brief halt for the sake of the horses, by a field of oats. They did not unpack the teakettle but ate some bread with a handful or two of sugar, in spite of the idea that this might cause their teeth to fall out.

They reached Montjay on the threshold of night. A few big drops of rain were beginning to spatter. They were tired.

The village, situated at a fairly important cluster of country lanes, seemed clean and well kept. There was lodging for man and beast, right as one entered.

The innkeeper did not seem to find Angelo very extraordinary. The infection, he said, was nonsense. Nobody was dying here: except the old, as usual. Obviously there are always people who get frightened, and that upset trade a bit, but on this side of the mountain there was absolutely nothing to fear. He added that he had rooms and they were very clean.

"I believe you," said Angelo, "but we'll talk of that in a minute. Show me your stable."

It had begun to rain. The horses were led into a huge building designed to shelter wagons and trains of merchandise. For the moment it was empty, echoing and full of shadows; the lantern only lit a part of it.

247

"Here's what I want," said Angelo, going to the corner of the mangers. "Pour two bushels of dry oats into this, and bring eight trusses of hay: five for the horses and three for me."

"You're not very polite," said the innkeeper softly. "You seem to think somebody has designs on your horses. Perhaps you even suspect me? It would be better to say so straight out."

And he came nearer. He was a thickset mountain-dweller.

"When I have suspicions I don't conceal them, and I have just spoken pretty clearly," said Angelo. "Do what I say, since I'm prepared to pay for what you do. I think as I choose. I do as I choose. And when I choose to change my mind, I shan't ask you for permission. Now, step back a bit and listen, if you want to earn your living like everyone else."

"You are a *sous-préfet*, perhaps, monsieur," said the man.

"That is within the bounds of possibility," said Angelo. "Next, put two chickens on the spit. And boil a dozen eggs while we're waiting."

"You don't do things by halves," said the man. "All this is going to cost you dear."

"I expect it will," said Angelo. "A *sous-préfet*'s salary can stand it. If you have a boy, send him to me for the saddlebags."

It was a young but sturdily built girl, well up to doing a man's work, who came to attend to the horses.

"How is the young lady upstairs?" asked Angelo. "Is she being looked after?"

"Is she your wife?"

"Yes."

"Did you buy her her big ring?"

"Yes, I did."

"You're generous."

"I'm extremely generous," said Angelo, "especially when people serve me well. Is there any cholera here?"

And he gave her a forty-sou piece.

"Not too much," said she.

"Not too much is how many?"

"Two."

"When?"

"Eight days ago."

248

"Do something for me," said Angelo. "Here are six francs. Go to the grocer's and buy me ten pounds of maize flour, two sous' worth of salt and one franc's worth of brown sugar. Put the lot under my saddle, here, in the straw. I'll see to the baggage."

Before going back into the inn, he made sure that there was no way out of the stable except by the carriage entrance, and that this was duly locked and bolted with an iron bar that couldn't be drawn without being heard.

The young woman was sitting by the fireplace, boiling the water for the tea.

"You're not cold?" asked Angelo.

And he glanced at her legs, which were beautiful without their boots, clad in cotton stockings with arabesque designs.

"Not in the least."

"Here's the baggage," he said, "and I'm going, if you'll allow me, to be a nuisance. Have you any woollen stockings in your bags?"

"I can answer 'no' without looking. I've never worn woollen stockings in my life."

"It's not too late to begin. There must be some at the grocer's: this village must certainly be very cold in winter. We'll buy some. Meanwhile put on these – they're mine and ten times too big for you, but it's important to keep your feet very warm."

"One could hardly resist such well-meant gallantry," she said. "Hold these garters for me, I'll put on your stockings. You are right. It's no use entering for a race if one doesn't train. But you, have you taken precautions?"

"I shall soon have been five months wandering about in this filth," he said. "I've won all the medals going. The contagion fears me like the plague, but I've taken precautions for the days to come."

He spoke of the purchases he had had made at the grocer's. He said that, from now on, they wouldn't be so foolish as to buy bread but would simply make polenta out of maize flour in the kettle, as in Piedmont. They must keep well fed; they could expect some hard stretches in the mountains; even today's stretch hadn't been within everybody's capacity. Whereupon he began to blush.

"You must excuse me," he said, turning crimson but not ceasing to gaze wide-eyed at the young woman, "but I absolutely must talk to you just as I would to one of my men. You ride astride. Aren't you sore, or bruised?"

"I'm surprised at this solicitude, so sure of itself, which you show towards everyone, myself included," she said. "Reassure yourself, I can do stretches like today's for days on end, without being anything but tired, which I am now, I don't deny it. I've been riding since I was a child. My father – I lived alone with him – was a country doctor, and I used to make the rounds with him, rain or shine, on my mare. For reasons it would take too long to explain, I've ridden as much if not more since my marriage. Besides, I'm very well equipped."

And she told him in a matter-of-fact way of the leather breeches she was wearing under her skirt.

"I'm very glad," said Angelo. "I don't see why we shouldn't be comrades, just because you're a woman and I'm a man. I admit that, several times today, I was embarrassed. For instance, this morning when I found you pistol in hand, I was tempted to slap you on the shoulder as I do with Giuseppe or even Lavinia when necessary. I restrained myself, which is a pity, for sometimes that says more than any words can at a critical moment."

He was on the verge of talking passionately to her about fighting for liberty.

"Who is Lavinia?" she said.

"The wife of my foster-brother, Giuseppe. She was my mother's maid in Italy. She went with Giuseppe when he had to go into exile; not long afterward I was reduced to the same extremity. Later they got married. But I can still see her, when she was ten or twelve years old, softening my mother's leather breeches with talc. Like you, my mother used to wear them under her skirts when she rode to our Granta estate."

And he described the forests of Granta.

The young woman greatly enjoyed the whole chicken he had ordered for her. She finished it off, as Angelo did his. They also ate the eggs, and finished their meal with a substantial plate of soup.

"You will now sleep in a bed," said Angelo. "I'm not going to leave the horses and baggage. It wouldn't take long to be robbed of them. You noticed how the mustard merchant eyed them too. At heart, I'm not a dupe except for the fun of it. When it comes to essentials, I can add and subtract like anyone else."

He advised her not to yield to the temptation of a warm bath; water thoroughly boiled was necessary.

"You must," he added, "cover yourself up very warm and keep my woollen stockings on while you sleep. Fatigue leads to shivering and, anyway, warmth relaxes one. Bolt the door and put your pistols under the bolster. At the least thing, even the least shiver, just fire your pistol, since you don't have a bell. We're in enemy country; it's silly to economize on powder. Anyhow," he added, "the main thing is that you shouldn't run any sort of risk and that you should be spared everything. The fact of setting the whole inn in a turmoil is of no importance and perfectly legitimate. I am here to make everybody understand that."

He then went and smoked a cigar outside the door.

It was still raining gently. The mountain was sighing above the village.

Angelo made his bed in the straw, beside the horses. He was just falling asleep when he heard the sound of wheels, and a moment later the small door communicating with the inn opened, the innkeeper hurried across the huge, echoing stable, and drew the bolt of the main entrance.

It was to let in a cabriolet. A man stepped down from it to whom the innkeeper kowtowed for all he was worth.

When the commotion subsided, the man came back with the stable girl and some trusses of straw. He too made ready to sleep beside his horse.

He was a man of about fifty, severely dressed in clothes of good quality; his stock was of choice cashmere. He spread a large Scottish plaid over his straw.

"I'm sorry to have disturbed you," he said, noticing that Angelo had his eyes open. "If I'd followed your example earlier I'd have saved myself a lot of trouble."

He described how, three days before, he had been robbed of a magnificent horse and carriage. He'd had to pay a stiff price for this one. He had come from Chauvac. He was trying to get to the Rhone valley where, with luck, he hoped to get a boat across the river and reach the Ardèche, where, it seemed, the air was putting up a victorious fight against the infection. He came from Savoy, where the cholera was raging beyond all belief.

Angelo asked him whether the soldiers were causing travellers much trouble at Chauvac.

"To tell the truth," said the man, "I'm more inclined to think now that they're not doing enough. They could certainly have found my robbers and got me back a lovely horse, which those peasants will only ruin without anyone being the better off. I must admit, anyone who's a little hotheaded has a hundred occasions a day for flying into a rage with those arrogant officers; they seem to believe you can deal with cholera by a military expedition, but actually they're (forgive the expression) pissing in their boots, figuratively, before the force of things brings them to do so in reality. As their orders are to stay put and they're scared, they've invented orders designed to give them as much company as possible, especially that of people like you and me. If you are going up into the Alps, monsieur, what lies ahead of you is not pretty."

He explained that the towns were at their last gasp.

"Do you know the stage things have reached in the biggest of them – towns where, with fifteen to twenty thousand inhabitants, you might expect there'd be some spirit left? The stage of absolute funk (they don't beat about the bush). The stage of masquerades, carnivals on the *corso*. People dress up as Pierrots, Harlequins, Columbines, clowns, to get away from death. They wear masks, they put on cardboard noses, false moustaches, false beards, they paint themselves ludicrous faces, they play at '*après moi le déluge*' vicariously. We're right back in the Middle Ages, sir. At every crossroads they're burning straw effigies entitled 'Father Cholera'; they insult it, they laugh at it. They dance around it and then go home to die of fear or diarrhoea."

"Monsieur," said Angelo, "I despise people who lack a sense of humour."

"That's an excellent rule of conduct," said the man. "If one dies at your age, it's perfect. If one reaches mine, one modifies it. So it gives no trouble in any case. It's been said again and again with variations that the best medicine against the cholera is a swift horse. And it's true. Result: here we are both lying in the straw at our horses' feet for fear of having them stolen; you from prudence, no doubt, for which I congratulate you; I from experience. It's no use pretending we have much love for our neighbours. You may say: 'I'm not doing anyone any harm.' Be careful: the opposite of love is not hate; it's selfishness that's opposed to love, or, to be more exact, sir, a sentiment you'll hear much talk of from now on, both good and ill: the spirit of self-preservation.

"But I'm preventing you from sleeping and no doubt you still have a long way to go, with many ambushes; so have I. And while I'm on the subject, I should tell you that people around here seem to have taken to robbery with violence, to holding up passengers on the roads, even to stripping the dead. I saw three thieves shot the day before yesterday with a great deal of ceremony. They were actually very humble-looking fellows. Thieves at a fair.

"Let's not be over-particular, let's be content, sir, with what we have this evening (and were certainly looking for): a raft at sea, just wide enough to sleep on.

"Good night, sir."

# I I

THE YOUNG WOMAN was up early and obviously in perfect health. Angelo had supervised with great care the boiling of the water for the tea. He also showed great personal satisfaction over the bag of maize flour, the brown sugar, and the dozen hard-boiled eggs he had had the wit to order.

"The news I have about Chauvac isn't good," he said.

He described the man who had slept beside him, who had left at daybreak.

"I think we're going to have a struggle getting there. In any case, this is my idea. Tell me if you agree. Let's stick to the wildest and most deserted part of the country. Let's keep away from the roads and towns, everywhere where there are people. It seems that not only have they the cholera, but they've gone mad as well. In the mountains we've only one thing to fear: brigands. Apparently there are some about. We shall see.

"Anyhow, from what Giuseppe told me, and according to his map, Sainte-Colombe is in an appallingly lonely spot. As soon as we've joined forces with my foster-brother and his wife, we can ride roughshod over all the brigands in the world. Giuseppe's a lion and Lavinia would die for her husband or for me."

"I agree entirely," said the young woman. "I've only one thing to add."

And she leaned towards Angelo to speak into his ear.

"Pay my bill, it will look more natural. I'll pay you back the money when we're alone. No, don't draw away. Listen: I know it's not important, but I haven't finished; I'm going to give you a bit of advice that concerns our safety in the highest degree: if it didn't I wouldn't ask you what I'm going to ask you, and it will cost you a lot. This is what it is: pay, but be miserly. Don't give a sou more than you're asked for. Even try to give a sou less. People will respect us like the Holy Sacrament. For the rest, I've as much confidence in you as you have in yourself, if not more, and I know we shall ride roughshod over all the brigands in the world, without help from either your Giuseppe or your Lavinia."

"You talk like the police officer at Turin who didn't dare arrest me. 'Ah! sir,' he said, 'why duel with the sabre when it's so easy to assassinate with the knife? In those cases we have the right to be blind.'"

"You see," she said, "you put excellent people in embarrassing situations. You come upon them without warning and demand of them courage, generosity, enthusiasm, or heaven knows what, things they're not capable of except after long reflection and much warming-up. They're family men most of the time. Be generous: give less. They wreck themselves wishing to follow you. Here, it's more simple. It's dangerous to show that we have money. People may take a shot at you from a window or put rat poison in your soup."

"You're right," said Angelo; "that would spoil everything."

Without actually trying to beat the man down, Angelo paid the bill like a bourgeois. He counted his change carefully and looked at both faces of the two-sou piece he gave the stable girl.

"We had rather sharp words last night," he said to the innkeeper, "but you must be used to excitable people these days. Do you know a place called Sainte-Colombe? We should like to get there without going through Chauvac."

"You're all the same," said the man. "What is there so terrible about Chauvac? It's only the sickest ones who die."

"That's my opinion too," said Angelo; "it's just the soldiers I'm worrying about. I'm not keen on them."

"Neither am I," said the man. "They've taken the bread out of my mouth by stopping people travelling. Just when I was putting a few pennies aside. Here's my advice. Leave the stream right where you are. There's been a guard post at the top of Charouilles since the day before yesterday. Go left through the woods. When you get through the trees, follow the valley. When you reach the other end, head for the Villebois windmill – it's as plain as the nose in your face. You'll come to a brook. Follow up it. It goes through a gorge. Your Sainte-Colombe is in there."

They climbed among the escarpments, then through a sparse forest. The day was dark blue. The trees were glistening from the night's rain. The branches were shaking off their water amid sighs. A thousand tiny rills were rustling like cats through the grass.

Beyond the scattered pines the mountain turned into pastureland already red-brown. One could also see the line of its crest and the enormous trees, beeches no doubt, that commanded its summit.

The route suggested by the innkeeper was easy to follow and kept the travellers completely hidden under the trees, in the hollow of the valley, and on the flanks of the hillocks. At the last, it even took them over the crest in a sort of natural trench, beneath gigantic beeches. At this point, the lighter air carried to their ears a sort of twittering or chirping, which might have been taken for that of certain birds. But Angelo, rising in his stirrups, saw and pointed out to the young woman some red blobs moving under the branches a few hundred yards to their left.

It was the soldiers, beyond any doubt. Indeed, a few moments later, a small caravan emerged from cover and began to descend the slope. Evidently some people had just been caught by the guards and were being taken back to town. Angelo counted five or six people in black and two red dolmans bringing up the rear.

Contrary to expectation, there was no deep valley on the other side of Charouilles, but simply a wide basin of heavy, almost mournful earth. Chauvac was clearly visible two leagues away on the left.

Angelo and the young lady judged it prudent to turn their backs on it and ride farther away. They covered at least two leagues more to the right, well concealed under the beeches, over easy terrain and in enchanting landscape. Marble branches supported the droop of thick golden fleeces. The gleaming russet foliage seemed to make its own sunshine under the grey sky. Avenues of springy turf led peacefully off on all sides, between columns, under arches white as snow.

Leaving the wood they came into a sad countryside. The unfleshed soil displayed its bones. There was no mill to be seen anywhere. They scaled a miniature mountain of black schist furrowed with ravines. All they could see from the top was a basin half a league wide, containing a few ancient stony fields and three stunted trees worn down by wind, rain, and frost. Advancing, they discovered a little house hidden in a hollow. But it was empty. It contained no trace of recent life.

They thought for a moment of camping there. In spite of their security and solitude, they contented themselves with eating two eggs, without dismounting, and all the time glancing furtively to right and left. Even the grass was uninviting: hard, dry, and grey, it rebuked even the muzzles of the animals. Flowerless clumps of lavender powdered with funereal ash the bony flanks of the hollow.

They climbed the other side, only to find a whole succession of similar hollows and crumbling dunes. A wild oat, small and bright yellow, which grew in thin tufts between the stones, emphasized the sadness of this region, throwing into relief by its colour the lividness of the rocks.

For several hours they followed the crests, looking for the mill in every direction.

"We're lost," said Angelo. "We should try to find a peasant to tell us the way; otherwise we shall wander till evening. Let's go down."

They entered a very sinister narrow defile, in which a waterfall sounded. The horses scrambled through dark mire. A slack, dirty stream hampered their passage and poked its way among boulders, deposits of mud, tree stumps, half-drowned bushes. Desolate slopes, sightless and voiceless, surrounded them on all sides. Rivulets of funereal silver stressed the coal black of the marly detritus hemming them in. The ravine widened a little, bend by bend, but without any life other than the muddy water that accompanied them and entwined itself about their horses' legs. At last they emerged into a sort of bay; here there rose a little brown field bearing a few leafless nut trees and clumps of box. There seemed to be a sort of path marked out with stones. After following this trail for some time they perceived, nestling in a thicket of old, split willows, a log cabin with an unhinged door. But there was fresh manure here and, under an iron ring driven into the wall, recent stable-litter. Two planks placed on stones bridged the stream. Beyond here began scrub of arborescent box, through which wound a shadow that might be a lane. It was a track marked by the ruts of a log sledge. A little farther on they found more droppings, fresher than those by the cabin, and the hoofprints of a mule heavily shod and evidently drawing a big load, for it dug with the forepoint of its hoof.

Yet even from the height of their horses, and looking in every direction, they could see no living soul. There was something stale and sickening in this monotony of greyness and solitude. The bitter sap of box steeped the air. The bramble thorns, the juniper needles, the brittle grasses clinging like spiders to every little crust of powdery green earth, irritated the eyes. Sadness was in the country like a light. Without it, there would have been merely loneliness and terror. It made perceptible certain possibilities – horrible perhapses of the soul.

"One should be able to get used to places like this," Angelo told himself, "and even no longer desire to leave them. There's the happiness of the soldier (his I place above all others) and there's the happiness of the wretched. Wasn't I sometimes magnificently happy with my nun; and often at the moment when we were pottering around with corpses everywhere? There's no degree in happiness. If I changed all my habits and even went back on all my moral conceptions, I could be perfectly contented in the midst of that tortured vegetation and that almost celestial aridity. I could enjoy the keenest happiness in the heart of cowardice, dishonour, and even cruelty. Man is just as much made for these feelings that seem to me from another world, as this place, which seems to me to be another world, and yet here is the trace of a log sledge and the hoofprints of a mule. Giuseppe does not reason like this. Were he here, he'd be calling everywhere through cupped hands or else, from sheer weariness, he'd sing a marching-song to enliven the pace. And yet maybe one discerns here the reasons for never having a revolution. When the people aren't talking, shouting, or singing, they shut their eyes. They're wrong to shut their eyes. I haven't said a word to that young woman for two hours, but I am not asleep."

Still following the tracks of the log sledge, they went along the bitter flank of a pale mountain, shapeless, like a huge sack. At each bend they rose slightly and at last came to drier ground. Here began a lane that led them still higher, across a small saddle, and started to descend the other side of the mountain, down a slope slightly more wooded but still overshadowed by sadness.

"I'm sorry," said Angelo stupidly to his companion, "I'd like to talk to you but I don't know what to say."

"No need to apologize, my head's completely empty as well, except, two minutes ago, for the thought – which I tried to cheer myself up with – that Chauvac and the soldiers are far away now."

The track wound through a squalid pine forest, worn threadbare by an invasion of caterpillars, which had hung grey rags from all the branches. There was no trace of human habitation anywhere. They could not even tell any longer whether the log sledge had passed that way. The rocky soil, pale and hard, showed no mark.

They reached a ravine bottom, only to ford another stream and climb the opposite slope. They entered a wood of small oaks, thicker, more robust than the fir plantation, and its dry leaves began to crackle as they passed. Although deserted, this region showed signs of having been used. Through the gaps in the branches and the network of bare twigs they kept seeing the pale empty space, the drab shape of the broken-backed, dismal mountain under the white sky; but they found by the roadside four lopped stakes planted in a rectangle at a place where faggots had evidently been stacked. There were also deep ruts made by cartwheels over the earth banks and crushed bushes. A team had been turned here and wood loaded.

The twisting road raised them gradually, flight by flight, up this slope to the bare crest, from which they could see a whole lacework of overgrown ravines, a confusion of slopes covered with rusted woods, a swelling sea with livid crests. The track wound all over the place without seeming to be really leading anywhere. It could be seen disappearing here, bobbing up again there, burrowing into a wood, entering a clearing, crossing a heath, folding round one crest, reappearing on another, doubling back, descending, rising, coiling, on the move but getting nowhere.

"We're lost," said Angelo.

"I'm not complaining," said the young woman. "After all, the danger's been avoided. It's a thousand to one the soldiers never come here, and as for the plague, what would it do up here all alone? Without company? Look at us, standing here on our pedestal: we've never been in greater safety. We are well out of reach. You've got maize flour, and you say what you can make with it is better than bread. There's wood enough to burn Rome. The streams are obviously pure."

They followed down the slope without resistance, and entered a wood exposed to the north. Half the trees, which were short besides, were overgrown with lichen. The carcasses of dead fir trees had collapsed on every side. Gnawed by damp, they were crumbling into dust and reddish stumps. Angelo pointed out that none of them lay across the little trail. There must certainly be, from time to time, some traffic along it. The sledge and mule must have come from somewhere to the cabin in the first ravine, and returned somewhere. There was no trace of it, but it must have passed this way. By continuing in this direction one could count on overtaking it or reaching some inhabited spot. It had barely two or three hours' start.

The ravine whose bottom they had to reach before climbing the other side was very deep. At every turning now they moved into thicker and damper shadow. Thick mosses and lichens hung from every branch. The deep fold of the valley was cluttered with a whole cemetery of trees. The skeletons of great firs and even of a few once-muscular beeches, now tightly hugging, crowded the narrow bed of a stream, which the track forded. Giant leafless clematis encorded these piles of dead branches and fleshless trunks with their white tendrils. Sturdy brambles, with blue leaves and thorns like knife-points, were peacefully battening on the remains. Held back by this dam, black water lay stagnating among horse tails and rushes.

On the other side, they climbed on to a flat heath, all starred with enormous thistles. The track, till then well marked and even in places wide enough for a carriage, was now reduced to two deep ruts. The two lines could be seen winding uncertainly as far as the eye could reach over this vast bare slope, leading finally to a strange rock with jagged edges. After half an hour's riding they realized that these were walls; and they headed straight towards them, to find a deserted and half-ruined sheepfold. Here, however, there was a smell of wool and of sheep's dung. In the yard outside the ruin, some flat stones were still powdered with coarse reddish salt.

"Aha! It rained last night," thought Angelo. "This salt would have melted. There were still sheep here this morning."

The little spring that fed the trough was well kept. Its wooden spout, stuck into the side of a bank, had been recently bound with an iron ring that was still bright.

From the crest nearby they would no doubt see new horizons. They went up to it.

They looked out over a maze of wooded ravines, a vast expanse of mountain rooftops. This canton seemed to be a little more wooded than the one they had just traversed, but it bore no trace of life anywhere. Bare heaths, noticeably grey, which must be covered with wild lavender, and great patches of red beeches alternated endlessly to the horizon, where the last beech groves, blue and hardly thicker than a pen-stroke, were pinned against the white sky. The track continued with its two wavering ruts across this whole stretch of country.

"I think I hear a dog barking," said the young woman.

Angelo listened.

"It's a fox," he said. "And it's a long way off."

From the crest a long slanting descent down the northern slope brought them to the first of those beech forests. Its deep red foliage crackled in the still air. The undergrowth was bare, desolate, strewn with big rocks. The thick branches smothered every sound; the horses seemed to be moving through the depths of some dark lake.

They emerged into a thin pasture. Immediately after, there began a stubble field of sparse rye. It had been carefully scraped with the sickle, flush with the stones. The track led on through ill-defined fields dotted with box and lavender.

"What can we do for the man who sows and harvests this field?" thought Angelo.

He had ceased to think of the cholera.

"If we must fight in the streets," he said to himself, "and kill soldiers who may perhaps be this poor peasant's sons but who have their orders, we must at least have for our excuse the possibility of changing the face of the globe. There is evil and good here that we shall never be able to reform, and which it's probably better not to reform."

He felt the need to talk with his companion. They both agreed that this field granted some hope of soon finding a farm. But they rode on for more than an hour without seeing anything of the kind, even from the top of a new crest that unveiled once more the expanse of deserted land.

"I suppose we must persist," said the young woman. "At the worst, we can camp again in the woods."

"These heights are not so cosy as the pine wood we camped in the night before last," said Angelo. "It must get cold up here. I'd like to come to a village with a real road leading out of it, and push on to some decent place."

"You need company, even if they have cholera?"

"I'm not specially fond of it but, in point of fact, I don't get on too badly with the cholera."

He told her of his adventures with the nun, after he had come down from the roofs of the town.

"I admit," he said, "that I can breathe easily here, and I don't have to fight. But what can I do with a beech after five minutes of its company? I tell myself that it's beautiful, I repeat this to myself two or three times, I take pleasure in its beauty; then I need to pass on to something else, something that concerns human beings. I can stay indefinitely in this wilderness – it doesn't frighten me, as you can see – but if I find a field scraped to the bone like that one just now, I have a feeling that I must do something about it. If only to say good-day to the man who came all this way to sweat among the stones."

"And yet," said she, "what can we imagine that's any better? To go where we want to go, in your case as far as Italy, since you have things to do there, along deserted roads; to my mind that would be perfect. Here there are no bad neighbours: no high towers, no deep river, no lord of the manor."

The track was taking them through the black woods and the pale heaths, bringing them slowly to the great solitary beeches. They had plenty of time to watch these rise and spread out in all their barbaric architecture; their salt-white frames lifted high into the sky the heavy fleece of foliage, sometimes russet and sometimes blood-red.

Angelo noticed that all these woods had geometrical shapes and resembled battalions of the line, with grounded arms, drawn up in fours or sixteens, held in reserve on a field of battle. Sometimes an isolated fir tree, standing on a knoll in its heavy cavalry cloak, completed the illusion; or the murmur of a company that has been too long awaiting orders came from a grove whose edge they were passing.

He was impressed, against his will, by those trees, standing mustered for centuries in solitude.

"Does the freedom of one's country," he asked himself, "count less than honour, for example, or all the trouble I've taken to keep alive?"

He saw here a countryside without cholera or revolution, but he found it sad.

At last, after an hour of silent and pensive riding, through a landscape of wide expanses, they saw in the middle of a denuded stretch a sort of pillar rising in isolation.

It was a wayside oratory surmounted by a small iron cross.

"Come," said Angelo to himself, "I've been dreaming. Man is here. You'd better come down to earth. This proves it."

"You must admit," he said, "that if there are people on these heights they announce their presence a long way off. It was barely midday when we found the hut, and now dusk is on the point of falling."

They quickened their pace but still had to cross a very long empty slope and pass through two wooded ravines before discovering a low house with its grey roofs flush with the ground. Even then it was only revealed to them by a thread of smoke rising from its chimney and a glow of yellow lamplight from its windowpanes.

Furthermore, it stood alone. There was no village.

They made straight for it at a jog trot, and were approaching its yard when the door opened. A man came out, carrying a bucket.

"Stop," he shouted.

He put down the bucket and flung himself on to a huge dog that had just risen from a heap of straw and was getting ready to jump evilly at the horses' legs.

"We've had a close shave," Angelo said to him with a smile.

"Closer than you think," said the man. "He's a lion. And when he obeys me – which isn't always – it's time to cross yourself with your elbow. You can't imagine how fond he is of biting. And when he does, monsieur, it's too late."

He was a small man, round as a ball, bursting with health. It was all he could do to hold back the dog by the collar: its enormous mouth hung open over jutting white fangs.

"Where are we?" said Angelo, manoeuvring his baulky horse between the young woman and the dog.

"Wait," said the man, "I'll lock him up first."

He dragged the dog towards a small stable.

"Look," said the young woman under her breath.

The bucket was full to the brim with blood, covered with pink foam.

The man returned after shutting up the dog and carefully wedging a stake against the door, at which the animal flung itself, growling.

"What's this place called?" asked Angelo.

"It's not called," said the man, "at any rate, I don't know. It's home."

He motioned all around.

"This is Charouilles."

He had little, short arms.

"Is there a village near here?"

"Here? Never has been. Down there in the valley, yes, but it's far from here and you have to know the way. Where are you from?"

"Montjay."

"That's no direction," said the man. "People never come from Montjay."

His hands were red with blood, and there were even remnants of meat between his fingers.

"We've been killing the pig," he said. "The little lady's horse doesn't like my pail of blood, I see. Wait, I'll put it out of sight. But you must have something on your mind? It'll be getting dark soon."

"We had no ideas ten minutes ago," said Angelo. "But we'd like to wait for daylight around here, if you don't mind."

"Why should I mind?" said the man. "Come in. Truth to tell, it's a long ride down to the valley, and it goes through woods. Well, it was a funny idea, coming here from Montjay."

The house, which seemed enormous from the outside, contained only one large room with an alcove; the rest was all sheepfolds and stables; sheep could be heard bleating, pigs grunting, and bits clinking.

The pig, split like a watermelon, was laid out on the cover of the salting-tub. Its head lay grinning in a basket beside it. By the hearth, whose huge fire was leaping at a cauldron, a stout woman, whiter than the bacon fat she was cutting up with a long knife, was melting lumps of lard. The table was piled with sausage meat and red shreds. The dull smell of blood and of chopped meat, and the intense heat of the fire with the cauldron of fat boiling on it, were heavy with oppressive images for anyone who had been breathing the air all day upon the heights.

"I'm going to vomit," said the young woman.

Angelo took her outside, gave her a little alcohol to drink, was alarmed to see her pale and shivering, covered her with his cloak, and decided not to go and tend the horses as he had planned.

He pulled some straw from a stack and arranged the saddles and saddlebags so as to make a well-sheltered and comfortable bed.

"Lie down in that and rest," he said.

He piled so many coverings on her that she was almost smothered. He raised her head with a bolster of straw. He was obliged to touch her hair, the bun at once firm and silky, and to support her neck.

"What small ears she has," he thought.

He lit a fire, made some tea, brought it to her.

At last she got up; her colour had returned.

"I nearly fainted," she said. "How could you manage to stand the sight of so much raw meat and that pale woman cutting herself into pieces and boiling her own fat in the witches' cauldron?"

He had the presence of mind not to confess that at that moment he had been thinking of the horses, which he was anxious to rub down.

"You frightened me," he said. "When I saw you looking whiter than a sheet, I thought at once of the infection, which had gone out of my head all day."

He talked for five minutes and with the greatest naturalness of the fright he had had and of the care she must take. He was sincere, besides.

Night had completely fallen. The house was watching them with its big red eye of an open door. Inside, the man could be seen circling with his long pointed knife around the pig, busy severing the hams.

They had set up their camp in the yard, facing the depths where the valley must lie. Protected by the angle of the sheepfolds and the main building, they did not feel the wind, which had begun to murmur like the sea over the whole mountain. They saw the sky split open and disclose a few stars: then a kind of lamp was lit above the clouds, and it brightened the fleecy fringes of the rent. The moon had risen.

They had built a fire for their tea between two stones, and the kettle was singing.

After another swallow of alcohol, the young woman was able to bring herself to eat two hard-boiled eggs, without bread. Angelo boiled the maize flour for a long time.

"This," he said, "will make a very thick polenta, sweetened with brown sugar. It'll cool all night and stuff us well and truly tomorrow morning."

He made some more tea and lit a small cigar.

Well below the mountains, in what must be the valley, they saw several lights twinkling, then the flames of what must have been a huge fire; from here it looked no bigger than a pea, but it throbbed. The man came and sat down beside them. He had filled a pipe.

"You mustn't worry about my wife," he said. "For ten years she hasn't uttered a word. I don't know why. But she's never done any harm. It'd be easy for her: we use the same bed, and I sleep. She's never budged. What are you drinking?"

"Tea."

"What's that?"

"A sort of coffee."

"Seems things are bad down in the valleys."

"Why?"

"You must know better than I do."

"If you mean the cholera, yes, it's doing some damage."

"I've seen a little," said the man. "I went down a month ago. It was turning a lot of people wrong side up. They were certainly taking it hard. I had sold some ewes to a valley fellow who died. Finding the heirs was a hard day's work. They'd been taken off to Vaumeilh to be camphorated."

"Who'd taken them off?"

"The soldiers, of course!"

"There are soldiers down there?"

"No, but they come when they're needed. There's been four of them flattened out, one after the other. They've got nasty since then ..."

"What's the valley like?"

"A fine place. It's restful, you'll see if you go there."

"Four soldiers flattened out? You mean, they killed them?"

"They sure did! It doesn't pay to poke your nose in where it's not wanted. Besides, they're liars. They've got colic like everyone else, so why should anybody go with them to Vaumeilh? That's what I think.

I'm not from the valley, I'm from here. But what have the Vaumeilh people got, more than the valley people? They die just as much, camphor or not; and so do the soldiers. The law's the law, agreed, but show me where the cholera makes exceptions."

Angelo asked him many questions about the soldiers. The man talked of them as of a disease even more terrible than the plague, but a disease whose injustice was clear and against which there were weapons. The name of Chauvac did not enter the conversation. It was the soldiers of Vaumeilh that were the trouble. Angelo concluded that there were soldiers everywhere.

He tried to find out about the duties of these troops and how they carried them out. He put these questions in military terms.

"You wouldn't be one of them, monsieur?" said the man, suddenly on his guard.

"Far from it," said Angelo. "This lady and I gave them the slip and even gave three of them a dressing-down. Now we're doing all we can to get through them. That's why we travelled all day through the mountains, by unfrequented roads, and are now here. Would I be with this young lady if I were a soldier?"

"Who's to stop it?" said the man. "You don't know what you're talking about. They have their canteen women. And the whores take what they can get."

The young lady protested, laughing, and assured him for her part that they were simply travellers with one pressing object – to cross this country as quickly as possible and reach home.

"I believe you," said the man. "Your voice doesn't sound like those wine-drinking women, and by God! soldiers don't accept excuses, they make you drink. You talk like someone who wants to get home. Now *he* makes me uneasy, he speaks officer's lingo."

"It's true," said Angelo, "I'm Piedmontese and I was an officer in my own country. I'm going back there, but to serve the cause of liberty."

He did not want to deny what he was. He told himself: "If the man's a complete idiot, if he can't see the difference between these dragoons, blindly carrying out orders whose principles one can't condemn, and me who am all love, I'll saddle the horses and off we go. The night be damned!"

He was very pleased to have thought of "love" to describe his feelings about human misery and liberty. He spoke with passion of the mean little rye-field.

"That's all very fine," said the man. "So you passed by there. The field is mine, actually. I sowed it because there was a fight about who owned it. You're right; everything would be better if there weren't any laws."

He was impressed by the little speech delivered with such fire. Angelo seemed to him a man of the world.

"What do you think," he asked, "of people who won't settle up for the thirty lambs they bought from me? Dragging cholera into the account."

Angelo described what the young woman and he had seen. He spoke of streets full of dead, deserted towns, people camping in the fields, corpses of dear ones thrown over hedges by night to avoid quarantine.

"I've had the cholerine, like everyone else," said the man. "You take your trousers down two or three times instead of the one: and that's that. People do die of it sometimes, it seems. It's just the double rations of weather. Nothing to call the police about."

He was obliged, however, to admit that certain things did seem queer, but it was not necessary to think that this came from little flies people swallowed as they breathed. His friend had told him that at La Motte, not five leagues from there, a dog had begun to talk; it had even recited the responses to the catechism for extreme unction. It was generally known that at Gantières, on the 22nd of July last, there had been a shower of toads. Those were facts. He knew a woman who had always been an upright family woman; she was ready to swear on the heads of her children that she herself had pulled out of the ear of her youngest, Julia by name, a little snake as thick as a finger and the length of a needleful of thread. A yellow one, stubborn as a mule, which she killed with her meat chopper, and it distinctly uttered the words "Ave Maria" before dying. He himself, not five days ago, alone on the heath you've just crossed, was minding the sheep one morning when he saw, rising up from the direction of Vaumeilh, a cloud that he first took for smoke, then for soot, and which was, monsieur and madame, more than five hundred thousand crows.

"They came right over here. They manoeuvred as if on parade and, since you're an officer, I can tell you they were in anti-cavalry formation. And there was a voice that came from the ground and gave them orders. That's not the end of it. I crossed the slope with my sheep and hid behind the crest. 'Halt and report,' said the voice. They came down. They settled. 'Who's eaten Christians?' said the voice. 'Me! Me! Me!' they answered. 'By the right, form fours,' it said; 'come get your medals.' They went in fours up to the big beech that stands all alone, and there, under its shade, there was some-body who spoke, out of sight, and said: 'I'm pleased with you. They'll learn what stuff I'm made of.' There's been great injustices, monsieur, with all these kings playing leapfrog over each other. Well, he sent his armies back to their posts. 'You to Vaumeilh.' And you should have seen that one set off at the head of his squadrons as fast as his wings could carry him, trumpets sounding. 'You to Montauban, you to Beaumont,' and there went the battalions on the move, drums rolling. Their runners came over to reconnoitre me, where I was hiding on my slope. But he just wasn't interested. He drew up his plan of battle as usual. And when I came back, when the crows were all gone, and looked under the beech, first from a distance, then going up step by step till I could touch the trunk itself, well, monsieur, there wasn't anyone, of course. Flies! They say it's flies! They make me laugh with their flies!"

With a certain Italian gravity, Angelo replied that they too had seen a lot of crows.

"It'll be ten or twelve years, monsieur," said the man, "that my wife has not pronounced a word. I don't complain; the work gets done, but this and all the other things show that cholera's nothing new. We've had to pay for things ever since there's been a world. They're not going to cover up with the cholera now, to do me out of the money they owe me. If they do, there's no answer but your liberty."

In the morning the sky was clear. The day promised to be brilliant. There was already an apricot glow upon all the mountains.

"You still look a bit pale," said Angelo. "Yesterday's journey tired you out, body and soul. Would you like to rest today? This man obviously hasn't got cholera."

269

"I feel strong as a Turk," she said. "I simply didn't get much sleep last night. If the Emperor Napoleon's crows haven't stolen our porridge, let's eat and have some tea, and then I'll be ready."

On the repeated assurance that there were no soldiers in the valley, they set out for the village. They rode for about two hours through landscapes similar to those of the previous day, before catching sight of a ravine full of willows and the roofs of about twenty houses clustered in the middle of the meadows.

A hundred yards from the entrance to the village, the track joined a little, very well-kept road along which Angelo and the young woman, in morning high spirits, started at a brisk trot.

They were moving at this pace, one behind the other, into a narrow alleyway between two barns, when they heard disturbing sounds ahead of them. But they were moving headlong, and before they could turn, emerged into a sort of small square full of soldiers and turned into a trap by means of carts upended across every outlet.

The young woman was already surrounded by five or six dragoons, who hemmed her in and hid her completely.

Angelo's one thought was to get near his companion. All he could see of her now was the little hat.

"Admit it's neatly set, boss," said the corporal holding Angelo's stirrup. "Make the best of a bad job. It's not poison. We mean well."

"Tell your men to get away from that young woman," replied Angelo in his best colonel's manner. "We have no intention of running away."

"You'd find it a job, Your Excellency," said the corporal. "We shan't eat your little lady. We're not hungry."

A tall lieutenant, thin and pale, who appeared to be shivering in his heavy cloak, was taking command of the situation. The soldiers stepped back and Angelo was able to move up close to his friend. She had not lost her presence of mind and was backing her horse with flicks of the wrist so as to place it back to the wall. Angelo did the same. Now they could face their opponents.

There were about twenty dragoons, six of them already mounted and drawing their swords. The others had seized arms and were holding their musketoons.

"Let's not touch our pistols now," muttered Angelo.

"Let's wait for a chance," said she.

The lieutenant was obviously ill. Around his mouth, with its black moustache, he was pale to greenness. His cheeks were hollow; his eyes glittering, widely dilated with that astonished look which Angelo knew well. He approached, huddling into his boots and mantle.

"Don't try any tricks," he said.

"We don't understand what's happening, monsieur," said Angelo politely.

"Where have you come from and where are you going?"

"We are from Gap," said the young woman, "and we are going home."

The lieutenant stared at her for a long time. He appeared to be studying her from head to foot, but in reality one felt that he was on the watch for things taking place inside him. He was puffing like a horse over dirty water.

"He won't last an hour," thought Angelo.

"There's no going home, madame," said the lieutenant. "All travelling is forbidden. Those on the roads must go into quarantine."

"It would be better to let us go home," said the young woman softly but very gently.

"It is not for me to know what would be better," said the lieutenant; "I don't question orders."

He wanted to make an impeccable about-turn, but he suddenly clutched his hand to his side.

"Eight men," he said to the corporal, without turning his head. "Dupuis in charge. Two groups of four; one for the woman, one for the man, five paces apart. Take them to Vaumeilh. It is not for me to know what would be better," he repeated, looking at Angelo.

He went back to a bed of straw that the soldiers had made for him in the doorway of a barn.

"Keep calm, messieurs-dames," said Dupuis, a huge sergeant-major, redder than his dolman. "Don't make things difficult for me. I admired your performance just now. Congratulations, little lady, you know how to place a nag ready to charge. You're no young recruit and neither am I. All the more reason for us to see eye to eye. An hour from now the lieutenant'll be far away and this place'll be full of flies. Come along with Papa Dupuis. I'll take you to the Hôtel du Roi d'Angleterre."

He began to draw up his men.

"Try nothing without being sure," said Angelo under his breath. "If you get a chance to escape alone, take it. I'll keep them busy. Hide your pistols."

"I could only hide one, they're too big. But it's done."

A cart was turned round to make way for them and they left the rustic redoubt with their escort.

Angelo rode ahead, flanked by four dragoons. When the little troop began to trot, he felt a great pleasure at seeing the uniforms dancing by his side. They were trotting over a plain of lean fields on which all the crops had turned black, but the morning was gay, drenched in yellow sunlight, and clouds of larks could be heard even above the hammering of hoofs upon the road. This peaceful bird-song, these soldiers, these broad expanses over which the light rebounded, this trotting rhythm to whose cadence he had so often listened before giving an order – Angelo exulted in them all.

Dupuis shouted that they were going too fast in front.

"Got to keep going," he said through his white moustaches, "but not going like this, my dear sir. And you four," he added to the soldiers, "haven't you seen that he's the kind who can tie you in knots whenever he wants to? Can't you see the way he sits his nag? In five minutes he'll have you charging, if he goes on with it. Why was I saddled with these f—g fools?"

The road was approaching a hill, in any case. They dropped to a walk. They climbed through yellow heath land, wholly barren, dotted only, at wide intervals, with tall leafless poplars, so white that the light made them invisible, substituting for them sheaves of sparks. Against the mild sky the mountains enclosing the horizon on every side raised their crests, iridescent in the sun.

Angelo was astonished to see multitudes of butterflies dancing. The road was bordered with centaury and those yellow honey-scented flowers that curdle milk. Swarms of little blue butterflies, which normally only fly near pools of water, were whirling above the flowers, together with others, yellow, red and black, white ones spotted with red, and huge ones, almost as big as sparrows, with wings like the leaves of the ash tree. He saw that, on the heath, what he had taken until now for the shimmering of the morning air was the fluttering of a vast throng of butterflies over the ground.

He used the excuse of pointing this out to the young woman to see how she was doing, five or six paces behind him. He felt sure she wouldn't try to escape in this open country, where anyone could pursue her or bring her down like a rabbit.

She was getting on very well and had started a conversation with her guards, who were playing the half-gallant.

"Amazing, eh, those filthy things?" said Dupuis. "You'll see a lot more of them. There's as many of those devils as there are flies. They eat human meat, pretty as they are. I wouldn't advise you to lie down in the grass, even if it was allowed. You'd soon have them even in your mouth. And what they like best, the dirty bastards, is the eyes, as usual. What the hell have we got in our eyes that makes animals so greedy for them?"

At length, round a bend, they saw the five or six zigzags of road that still lay ahead of them, and the town of Vaumeilh itself. This crowned the whole summit of the high, yellow hill, facing them on this side with windowless ramparts of grey stone. It bore no more trace of foliage or trees than the eminence on which it stood. It was surmounted by an enormous square tower, flanked by two thinner and taller ones, all three battlemented.

As they approached, they came upon more and more butterflies. They had invaded and covered the road; they floated between the horses' legs. Their colours, endlessly darting, tired the eyes, induced a kind of vertigo. They were soon mingled with swarms of blue flies and wasps, whose heavy humming urged sleep in spite of the morning.

The ramparts of Vaumeilh plunged down to wide moats, which the little troop crossed by an earth causeway. On each side, in the depths warmed by the sun, the butterflies and flies were so numerous that their flight rose and fell like the flames of a vast brazier. Angelo saw that these whirlwinds were rising from piles of jackets, dresses, sheets, eiderdowns, blankets, quilts, pillows, pallets, and mattresses thrown down at the foot of the walls.

They entered the town through a gate that breathed out a fearful stench. The cavalcade immediately set up a loud clatter on the cobbles, but the street remained deserted. All the houses were hermetically shut; some of them had their shutters barred with nailed-up planks.

After riding down a narrow street, crossing a square on which wide stairways converged, passing through alleys where the smell was abominable, and circling around a solitary fountain in a street of old and noble houses, they entered upon a ramp rising under arched vaults.

Through the openings pierced at long intervals to light this covered way, Angelo saw that they were mounting above the roofs of this treeless town, built all of stone (even the roofs of the houses were made of flat stones); without smoke, without a sound, except that of the horses' hoofs.

They came out on to a vast esplanade of dazzling whiteness, before the gate of a fortress. It was the square tower they had seen from the road. From here they looked out over the vast undulating circle of the mountains.

"You'll be in fresh air," said Dupuis.

They all dismounted in an inner courtyard of extraordinary bareness.

Angelo managed to approach the young woman and say: "Patience, I'm not asleep. We shan't stay here long."

The gate was shut behind them; the four walls rose to more than ninety feet and had no windows except at a level with the eaves.

"You've been angels," said Dupuis. "There are those who put on airs, or cry, or offer money (which I accept) for a drink. By the way, you'd make yourself popular if you stood a few litres of wine to these good soldiers. They lead a dog's life."

"I'm not seeking to make myself popular," said Angelo. "We've followed you here without any fuss. Now you'll have to justify your way of proceeding. I am waiting."

"Well, my dear sir, you'll wait for quite a time. Exactly forty days, if all goes well. That's the ruling. This way out."

He took them through a low doorway. They went down a long, sombre corridor. The sergeant-major knocked at a window.

"Two, sir," he said.

"Hand them over to the sisters with the rest," said a voice.

"In file, right turn."

They turned into another corridor as long as the first, but lit by barred windows giving on to a courtyard down below. This courtyard stood on a terrace, for beyond and over the wall scarcely three feet high could be seen the stone roofs of the little deserted town.

"I suppose," said Angelo carelessly, "they haven't already ransacked our baggage."

"It's within the bounds of possibility."

"Because I'm prepared to give a silver crown to the man who could get this lady's case and my own restored to me."

"With the saddlebags?"

"Let's say that, with the saddlebags, which contain only cooking utensils, I'll go up to eight francs."

"I knew you were a good fellow," said Dupuis. "I've got one vice: I can't bring myself to steal. I have too weak a stomach. I get a lot of legacies, certainly, but stealing's not in my nature. That won't stop me from being your sole heir if things take the usual turn. Go up to ten francs and wait a couple of minutes, for I think I shall have to look sharp."

"I've only got eight francs," said Angelo. "You'll find the rest in my legacy, but hurry up.

"I've been counting," he told the young woman as soon as they were alone. "There are twenty-four of them. The lieutenant out there has the dry cholera and won't live through the day; let's hope he brings luck to two or three of his men; that form of the plague spreads quickly in dirty bodies. This platoon is the worst disciplined I've ever seen. It has nothing to do but trap civilians, yet it smells of rotten leather as if it were on campaign. At the outside I shall have seven or eight on my hands this evening, including some who'll be scared silly, not of me but of sudden death. Now take a look at these corridors! I can manoeuvre so as never to have to face more than two at a time."

"I forbid you to fight like this," said the young woman gravely.

The cheeks of her thin, pointed face were pink with a certain confusion. Her lips were trembling. She was about to continue when a soft voice beside them said: "Why should he want to fight?"

275

It was a nun who had come up silently. Short and dumpy, she resembled a capable housewife with her long black sleeves rolled up to show dimpled, blood-red arms.

"He's a child, Mother," said the young woman, making a quick curtsy.

Angelo was still marvelling at that suddenly troubled face and those trembling lips.

"She is very beautiful," he said to himself.

The place where that face had been on fire remained as a white spot in his memory.

Dupuis arrived with the baggage. It did not seem to have been touched.

Angelo drew the huge sergeant-major into a window recess.

"Here are ten francs," he said, "and I'm going to give you something more precious than money. The officer who arrested us out there in the valley is dead by now. And I know why. You're clever enough to realize that civilians too sometimes know what's what. He's died of a very vicious sort of cholera they call dry cholera, which bowls them over like ninepins. Now, I have a remedy. I'm not asking you to take my word for it. Just wait till the patrol comes back. If I'm right, he won't be the only one to kick the bucket. In that case, come and see me, I'll give you something to protect you."

To himself he said: "It's impossible for a cavalryman, who's had a taste of power and got such pleasure out of being in command just now on the road, full in the sun, not to be frightened of dying between four walls, especially such high ones. And I took him by the arm. That's the way to make him think."

He was pleased to observe that he intrigued this apoplectic man, awkward in his humours, this bureaucrat of the horse, and had even driven out of him the desire to laugh.

Angelo was just beginning to find that this prison had a most agreeable complexion and allowed one to live royally, when he noticed that the nun was feeling, with signs of the most sordid satisfaction, the folds of a little cashmere shawl that the young woman wore knotted round her neck. He was shocked by this effrontery, this undisguised greed, and gently but firmly he pulled away the scullery-maid hand.

"You seem very sure of yourself," said this peasant woman who had given herself to God, "but we've seen others and it's better we should be frank from the start. I've seen you put your hand in your pocket; you'll have to do it again. We are a little sisterhood who have accepted martyrdom. But not for your sweet sake. Here board and lodging are paid for cash down and in advance. The ways of the Lord are impenetrable. All men are mortal and many are dying these days. We can't afford to be left with food on our hands. *We have our poor.* Your bill for the moment is six francs, and you'd be wise to pay me at once if you want soup for your lunch. You will also sign for me, both of you, a paper so that, in case of death, we can dispose of your things, at our own risk. Your natural heirs might make trouble, and we shall no doubt be obliged to burn everything that belongs to you."

Luckily Angelo found this speech immensely comic. He had the sense to feign great consternation and even slight cowardice. He paid with a certain studied munificence.

The nun led them to the end of the corridor, opened a grill, and made them pass through a vast, echoing, but dark hall, then other rooms lit by borrowed light. All this seemed designed for mortification and prayer. On the utter bareness of the walls the body of Christ, in wood, was crucified. In the shadowy corners tall upright chairs and stalls could also be seen. Finally, there was everywhere the glacial cold and the smell of worm-eaten wood characteristic of mountain convents.

As long as quarantine had been a town or village affair, run by local people who needed to devote themselves to something in order to keep sane, barns and outhouses had been used. Sometimes camps had even been set up under trees or in meadows. Everyone escaped: either by violence or by bribery. The guards made an income wandering around with old shotguns.

Then it was decided that the cholera must be blocked up. The patrols of bourgeois, artisans, and peasants were proving insufficient to police the roads. Travellers were tending more and more to impose their way of looking at things, pistol in hand. When the government took charge, it appealed to the authority of the prefects and their garrisons. The soldiers had their uniforms and an evident need to fire into the general confusion and twirl their sabres. They had been told that they must sacrifice themselves, which would not have been enough to give them a real interest in the business, but it was more amusing to dash about the roads than to stay in the barracks, where death was moreover very easy and very frequent. Fresh air always passes for a panacea; movement changed their outlook. It was, besides, extremely comforting to arrest people at odds of twenty to one, and to see that you caused fear, when you were frightened yourself.

The small towns possessing hospitals or leper houses crammed the travellers into them. Elsewhere church schools, convents, seminaries, sometimes even churches, were pressed into use. The Vaumeilh quarantine was installed in the château, a former commandery of the Templars bequeathed at the turn of the century by Baron Charles-Albert Bon de Vaumeilh to a small sisterhood of Presentines. It harboured eleven humble women from the farms round about, who had exchanged kitchens and annual childbirth for the rule of a master who wore no velvet breeches and left them in peace seven days out of seven.

After passing through more than twenty small arched doorways that bored their way through the thickness of the walls, then under high vaults that lost themselves in shadow, and close by steep stair-ways without handrails, cut in saw-tooth pattern in worn stone, leading to galleries, cells stuck under the roof like nests, balustrades beyond which shone the dusty rays of a yellow daylight, Angelo and the young woman were led to a grille through which the nun made them pass, closing it behind them.

They were in a stairwell that might have held a schooner in full sail.

"There you are in your new home," said the little fat nun from the other side of the grille, before departing.

Angelo said: "One would only have to tear off her coif and a little of her hair, box her soundly on both ears, and then take her bunch of keys, to turn her straightaway into a properly submissive country servant who'd reply 'Yes, madame, yes, monsieur,' to everything one said and might even prove devoted. But in that case, she'd be scared of everything, and just now of the cholera. Her teeth would be chattering. I don't think you should make mountains of these soldiers, either. They'll simply cave in before anyone who's got hold of the right end of the stick."

"Don't worry," she said, "I've been watching you examining the width of the doors, counting your paces and noting landmarks. They couldn't have picked a more exciting quarantine for you. You are bound to escape."

"Of course," said Angelo. "From now on, our hands are free. I don't intend to waste any time. I know what we're going to find here, and hell isn't very mannerly. I no longer need to take care of everybody."

While he was hiding their baggage in a dark corner he said some bitter things about the "little Frenchman" and his hopeless efforts with the dying.

"The only thing that counts is to get you out of this. Have you a good place to carry your pistols?"

"The best place is in my hands."

"They'll tire you out; besides you'll have to take along something to load them with. I've got mine in my pockets, but we ought to have a bag for the powder boxes, bullets, caps, your tea, the kettle, and some sugar. We don't know if we'll be able to get the horses back. At all events, when our escape's well under way, I'll tip the rest of the baggage out of a window, and if we've time we'll go and look for it. But here inside this seemingly vast place let's cling to our weapons. They're our viaticum."

He made a sort of haversack out of the saddlebags and managed to fasten it on his back without much trouble. He took the little sabre in his hand, and they began to mount the staircase, which seemed to lead towards bright light.

To judge from the size and shape of the building in which they found themselves, they must be in that big square tower they had seen from the road.

The shallow steps rose slowly in long flights turning at right angles. At a certain point there was, not exactly a second floor, but a sort of landing with a low door at either end. Both were bolted. Higher up, rays of sunlight coming through loopholes crisscrossed and, striking the walls, maintained a strong light. In the top of the tower wild pigeons were nesting; suddenly they all took to flight, making a torrential sound.

Immediately a door opened above them and three heads came and peered over the balustrade. One of them, belonging to a very dark man, bearded no doubt, withdrew hastily.

The Presentine nuns of Vaumeilh were all former farm girls or farmers' daughters. They knew how to keep chickens and rabbits, and how to shut doors. They had set up the quarantine in the part of the commandery originally designed to serve as a last bastion.

In the roof of the big tower there was a vast room running its whole width. The ceiling was simply the fabric of huge beams that supported the stone flooring of the defence platform. The light came from all sides through more than fifty openings pierced round the four walls, former arrow-slits roofed over in the Italian fashion and transformed roughly into windows by odd panes of glass.

It was in fact an ideal place for pickling suspects in healthy fresh air and full sunshine. There was also a fine view from it. One could take in the whole horizon of harsh, green-clad mountains, which carried roads in every direction. The wind (rough even in good weather) of this rude countryside, which makes everything, even springtime, an arid duty, kept the windows ceaselessly rattling, lifted the straw strewn over the floor, and boomed like the sea against the walls.

The four wooden kegs of drinking-water had to be covered with cloaks to protect it from the dust. An attempt had also been made to shield the corner containing the buckets used as privies, by hanging up horse blankets and more especially shawls, old petticoats, and other women's clothing. In the embrasure of an open machicolation they built fires on the bare stones for private cooking: tea, coffee, and chocolate for those who still could afford them. Naturally, if one didn't afterwards take the precaution of wetting the embers (usually with urine, since there was only one serving of drinking-water a day), the drafts would lift them and fling their ash all over the place.

Sickness was quite frequent.

"You see, it was quite right to stop you from roaming about," said the nuns. "Round here there are some villages that haven't yet had a single death. You'd have brought them the infection."

Which was a white lie, for the villages round about had been devastated like the other villages. And besides, their dead had died, after all, more comfortably than those in quarantine, sometimes with a doctor or at least with drugs to relieve them, at any rate in beds and often in dark alcoves that spared them the supplementary torture of the strong light, so painful to the retina of cholera victims.

More than twenty sick had already been lost. The survivors had had to be brutally subdued, especially the members of the afflicted families. Unlike what happened outside, the deaths led to displays of grief, doubtless sincere but always exceedingly noisy. Death did not come in the intimacy of the family, where to be oneself is possible and permissible; where, when the dirge is over, one must think of saving the furniture. Disaster struck its blow in broad daylight, in front of everybody, and they would all retreat and huddle at the other end of the room, like a flock of sheep who had seen the wolf enter. Because of the four very thick walls and the grille down below, known to be kept carefully shut, there was no hope of being able to use guile as elsewhere, as in the free world, as everywhere in times when death persists long in the same place. They were no longer losing their dear ones. They were reading the writing on the wall. They could not get away, so they wailed. Besides, that lent a certain decorum; appearances are a consolation for disappearances: in short, they now wept endlessly for themselves. After five minutes the indifferent were wailing as loudly as the afflicted; after five minutes there were no indifferent left.

"What the f— are you doing up there?" shouted the soldiers.

"What a shambles," said the nuns, rather proud of not dying.

The little community had been immune up until now. Yet they worked on the dead coolly and unconcernedly. The soldiers would come up with a stretcher. They would be very sympathetic, say a few words of comfort, pat the women kindly on the shoulder, make jokes. Their lips would be as white as chalk under their moustaches. They were very clumsy with the corpses. They handled them rather stiffly, preferring to take them by the feet rather than the head, and swore when (as happened nearly every time) the body, relaxing its muscles knotted by pain and the death agony, twitched in their hands and emitted those fetid juices, white like rice and similar to curdled milk, for the last time.

At first they had tried, after each death, to burn the befouled straw. But when burned in the embrasure of the machicolation, this straw, all damp with excrement, produced a thick smoke and an appalling stench, which infested the entire room in spite of its size and ventilation, poisoned the whole tower, staircase and all, and even seeped down the passages to the Presentines' and the soldiers' quarters. They contented themselves, after that, with piling this straw in one corner, where it dried. The necessities of a cloistered, communal life had moreover created legends designed to make that life possible and even endurable, since this was necessary. These legends were no sillier than others. For instance, it was evident here that the cholera was not transmitted by contact. If it were contagious, they said, we should all be dead by now. But we are not all dead (some added: "Knock on wood!"). Therefore it is not contagious. Therefore there is no need to burn the straw, which produces so nauseating and suffocating a smoke. And above all, it was not absolutely necessary to form a quarantine within the quarantine for those who had tended, or had to do with, the person who had died. At the time of the sickness, during the agony and death throes, people moved away to the other end of the room: it was never a very entertaining sight, but one need no longer move away for reasons of chicken-heartedness or cowardice, so hard to admit in company, but on the contrary out of tact, good breeding (that good breeding so indispensable, so dear to the mediocre) – all the sentiments on which the bourgeois way of life is based.

To be locked up in quarantine (people blamed only themselves, accused themselves of having been clumsy or rash; they never went so far as to accuse the government that had called out its troops), confined to a straw litter, did not prevent one from being what one was. One still had a house of one's own, with one's name on the list of property holders; one still had possessions; was still a notary, a bailiff, a draper, a father of a family, a marriageable daughter, and even a liar, a hypocrite or jealous, or a celebrity in one's market town, or a figure of fun. At liberty, one would have been able to take refuge in the woods, hunting-lodges, farms, country houses (and was in fact trying to do so when arrested by the soldiers). One would have saved one's face. Here, one must continue to save it. It was essential to maintain one's position. Which purpose was served by all the new folklore and, in the first place, by the dogma of non-contagion, which once accepted, oiled the wheels considerably. It even gave one courage, or at least an attitude that was a counterfeit of courage. Up to the moment when suddenly one had that astonished look which Angelo had seen on the face of the officer on patrol, and became absorbed in watching things just then starting to happen inside oneself. But then one was quick to lose consciousness and barely heard, if at all, the sound made by the rest of the company as they politely moved away from one.

Newcomers to the quarantine under the roof of the tower would remain for a whole day, sometimes two, close by the door. They never mingled at once with the old hands, who had been there from ten to fifteen days. Everyone understood this (one realized that it was difficult to accept this change of existence: one had been through that disgust, that recoil, oneself. To start life again on a fresh basis is not done on the spur of the moment). Nobody took offence. One let them find their feet. One swaggered a bit before them to encourage them to come forward, to incorporate themselves more easily, to make them lose that feeling of no hope short of escape. One took great pleasure in assimilating two, four, or ten more; one congratulated the soldiers. "The more the merrier," one said. One was glad to have proof that one's own was the common lot (it was most consoling). That one was not the only rash or clumsy person, that there were others, that the soldiers were very clever, letting no one escape, that in the end everyone was bundled into quarantine, that one wasn't an exception. That is what people tried to impress upon the newcomers who stayed by the door, not daring to accept the situation and still convinced that being shut up in this vast room, rumbling with wind, light, and fear at the top of the tower of Vaumeilh, was altogether exceptional.

Angelo and the young woman paused, likewise taken aback, at the threshold of the great room. The noise of the wind had an unchallengeable quality of pathos. The dazzling light, which pierced the quarantine from end to end, leaving nothing in shadow, burnished even the sickly yellow of the straw and drew gleams from both the fine cloth of the riding-coats and the filth that soiled them, from both the watered silk, the satin of certain dresses (one pale, fair-haired young girl even had an organdy skirt), and the filth that soiled them. All these crumpled garments, in which people slept, sprawled on the

283

straw for siestas of private despair, or fetched water and cleaned the latrines, clad members of a society that still owned opera hats, ringlets, travelling-caps, and a false forthrightness of gesture.

There were also four or five bewildered people near the door: a stout grey-haired woman of about fifty, dressed for a walk in a demi-crinoline of purple faille; a squat, sturdy peasant with his head sunk between his shoulders who crouched, curled up into a ball, in a brand-new russet velvet suit (put on for the first time, no doubt, for the journey that was ending so unexpectedly here); a young man-about-town with a waisted jacket, Cronstadt hat, knobbed cane; a group of three bourgeois, evidently bachelors, well-to-do in mustard-coloured frock coats bordered with black, very "sporty" in appearance but with their arms dangling and their mouths open ("You've just come?" they said stupidly to Angelo. "As you see," he replied); and a little girl between ten and twelve, well dressed, who seemed to belong to nobody, but at whom the stout woman kept casting stealthy glances.

These were the passengers from a contraband coach, arrested the evening before: infallibly rich, for it cost a lot to bribe a coachman. But the coachman was not there: he must have escaped, or paid the soldiers a percentage, or simply betrayed his customers to spare himself the journey, and pocketed his money without earning it, perhaps even taken money from both sides.

"*Continua la commedia*," said Angelo to himself. "And not one of them thinks of making a fight or a bolt for it. If I bide my time, it'll be easy."

"Don't be upset," he murmured to the young woman, "and take care not to think too deeply, as these are all doing, so far as their nature allows. It makes one look an idiot, as you can see, and then one is lost. You've more shrewdness and courage than all of them put together, but you have more heart and you'd get too depressed."

"I feel exactly the same," answered the young woman, "but those are wise words: with all the wise words in the world, one can't stop oneself shivering when it's cold."

"We'll get out of here, even if we have to climb down the walls like flies. That's the only thought I'll allow you," said Angelo.

"Beg pardon, monsieur," (it was the short young man in the waisted jacket), "but what does one have to do to get one's baggage?"

"The same as everywhere else, monsieur."

"We have been here since yesterday evening and no one has bothered about us."

"Then you bother them."

One of the bourgeois asked him what was that weapon he was holding.

"It's my umbrella," said Angelo.

In fact, he tucked the little sabre under his arm like an umbrella and led the young woman across the quarantine to a wide window, through which the wind blew freely, and from which everyone kept away.

"In our bags," he said, "I've got the tea, the sugar, the maize flour, the chocolate, your pistols, your powder, mine, your bullets and mine; my own loaded pistols are in my pocket. Our cloaks and your little case are down below, hidden under the stairs. We are resolute, and we'll get out of here tonight. All you see here is a lot of dirty people, half dead with fear and putting on airs because, to them, revolt is in bad taste. It isn't to me."

And he talked for more than five minutes about social revolution and liberty, but he had the wit to use short, simple sentences that contained at bottom a good deal of sense and were a hundred leagues away from the cholera. He had also in his favour his stiff little beard from three days' travelling over hill and down dale. The window was filled with that landscape of mountains which is more exalting than the sea when seen from a height; over them it breathed a calm, warm wind, for it was close to noon.

A most handsome man, looking like a horse dealer and smoothing his side whiskers with a tiny comb, approached Angelo.

"I see you're having quite a conversation," said this man bluntly. His eyes were framed with attractive, malicious little wrinkles. "You're new and you're wondering how we live. It's easy. All the new ones prefer to do their own cooking on little fires, which they light in that corner over there. If you want a bundle of faggots that I've cut myself out of a plank, I'm ready to sell it to you for six sous. If you smoke, I've trooper's tobacco for sale. I have also at your disposal a small flask of *eau de vie*, always useful if the lady doesn't feel well. In short, ask, and, if you've the wherewithal, it shall be given. For three sous I can also find you a man who'll replace you when it's your turn to fetch the water or empty the stink buckets. It'll be three sous for the lady too: by our laws she's liable like everyone else."

"You are exactly the man I was looking for," said Angelo. "If you hadn't presented yourself I should have been put to a lot of trouble. I've already done some business with your friend Dupuis . . ."

"You know Dupuis? He's an old rascal. He takes all my profit off me, but I'm a philanthropist and . . ."

"Where money's concerned," said Angelo, lowering his voice, "we shall always understand each other. Hold out your hand between madame and me so they can't see what I'm going to put in it, and here, to begin with, are twenty sous for the wood, the fatigues, and the pleasure of knowing you."

"As I always say, monsieur," said the man, "people who are well brought up can get on anywhere. Now hold out your hand, I don't want to be left behind you. Here's a little tobacco. My apologies, it's not very good; I'm obliged to keep it on me, in my trouser pocket, because here everything gets stolen, and the heat of a man's thigh isn't good for tobacco. Such as it is, though, one mustn't spit on it, as you'll see when you've been here a bit."

This personage gave them all the news of this singular spot, that is to say, news of the world. Vaumeilh had been bled white. Out of two thousand inhabitants, over six hundred had gone to their reward in the most complete anarchy of bedroom and cemetery ever seen. Upon these mountain-dwellers, austere through neglect, to whom *fresh air* was the chief justification of existence, isolated in a countryside that till then had been considered healthy, the presence of death imposed what one was forced to call deaths by conviction. This went back, moreover, to the first outbreak of the plague. Reason had resumed control. Before the establishment of quarantines almost all survivors had gone to camp in the woods, visible from here on the slope of a black mountain, where they had made a sort of Indian village. They were there still. They had trusted nothing but the winter, which in these parts freezes everything. If flies there were, as some claimed, they could not live through it. In the town there remained only about a hundred res-olute men and women, who were trading with the quarantine, competing with each other, and leading a gay life, as they would see that evening; they would hear them shouting.

In the tower itself there were not, for the moment, too many deaths, but they had been through one bad stretch. This man had been there fifteen days.

"I sell sewing-machines," he said. "I was doing my best to get back to Valence on the quiet when I got caught stupidly by the roadside, where I'd fallen asleep under a tree." He had been shut up here with six others, who had gone off to join the daisies, one after the other, in the following three days. "I was put in charge of the room because I'm the oldest inhabitant, because I'm tough and order is needed. I've kept a list. The soldiers have brought a hundred and twelve persons here. There are thirty-four of us today, counting the ones who arrived last night and yourselves. Anyhow, for the moment, instead of getting fewer, we're increasing, and with people like yourselves. We ought to have more."

He considered this a fine day.

Six men on fatigue had gone down to the grille to fetch the three cauldrons of bread-and-cabbage soup prepared by the nuns, and were now bringing it in.

"Wait," said Angelo, "I've something serious to say to you, since you have a head on your shoulders. Look out of the window. Isn't that the patrol coming back on the road down there? Look at the horses they're bringing back riderless: four of them. And if I'm not mistaken that's Dupuis who's taken command of the column. When we were arrested this morning, the lieutenant was in the first throes of a fine attack of dry cholera. I have an impression he was only the first. We may expect them to get fewer still. Enjoy your meal. We two are going to get along on tea today, even though we've paid our share."

"Look here," said the man, "I won't intrude on you. I know a husband and wife have things to say to one another that aren't anybody else's concern, especially in a situation like this. Give me a bowl of your tea and a little sugar, I'll go and drink it in my corner and leave you in peace. But I don't want any of that soup either. Take care not to mention dry cholera in here, or else look to your sabre. I've already seen some ugly scenes. It's no good trusting their opera hats, you know, monsieur. Underneath them there's what I won't name in front of Madame, but it doesn't smell nice."

The sewing-machine salesman returned to his corner with his bowl of tea. He had also been given a slab of chocolate, a lump of brown sugar, and a handful of maize flour. Angelo showed him how to mix the sugar and the uncooked maize flour so as to get a sort of mash, rather unpleasant to chew but very nourishing, and preferable in any case to that more than doubtful soup. The soup, however, was having a great success. Someone even had to be posted to defend the cauldrons from the attacks of respectable ladies and gentlemen. Even the young girl in the organdy dress (had she been arrested on leaving one of those costume parties that were all the rage these days? Had she, after the ball, wandered through the countryside in a fresh fit of terror? Had she fled blindly and finally run into the soldiers?) – even the girl in the organdy dress was demanding rather less soup and rather more bread. Yet she was quite pretty, almost a thorough-bred, with just a touch of hosier's blood in the rather pronounced bridge of the nose. She was trying to push her way through the sturdy men and women who, standing firmly by their rights, were laying close siege to the cauldrons. Not having very strong arms, she was using her body, as if in a dance, demanding bread in a shrill voice. Finally, a man who was backing out straightened up suddenly and sent her bowl flying out of her hands.

It was the hour when the wind calms down. Outside there was that apricot light of the last warm days of autumn. The mountains had disappeared in the sunlight; in their place there were waves of sparkling and translucent mauve silk, weightless and almost shapeless, invisible except for the undulating line of their crests scarcely marked against the sky. The billowing yellow heaths, rising in hills to support the town and the castle, vanished under an iridescent fluttering like that which shimmers deep in overheated air; but here it was caused by real butterflies flitting low over the ground. It cost Angelo an effort to imagine that monstrous swarm. "There's not a single flower," he thought, "not a single tree with sweet sap in the whole countryside. Where will they find all the sugar they need?" His throat contracted and he hastily swallowed his saliva. Some crows crossed the sky, followed by a few pigeons, flying less fast but beating their wings violently in order to keep up with them. As the birds passed over the iridescent heaths, a whirlwind of insects rose, split into the sunshine like a blaze from a strange brazier, whose flame stretched out, blackened, became like a hanging cloud of soot, darted towards them and began to unfold in the sky a brilliant, black streamer, glittering like faille or paste jewellery, floating in the wake of the flock and flying after them. The crows were making for the blue smoke clouds that oozed from the insubstantial side of one of the mountains.

The patrol entered the courtyard. Not four, but five horsemen had left their saddles empty. Five horses were led in by the bridle, five sheathed sabres, five muskets each hanging from an empty saddle-bow. As he set foot on the ground, one of the soldiers fell. He got up by himself.

"I'm not afraid of death any longer," said the young woman.

"What are you afraid of instead?" said Angelo after a silence.

"Of the cauldron."

He smiled thinly.

"We have our pistols," he said.

"I shan't have the courage."

"If that's courage, then I confess I shan't either – but one can always take refuge somewhere; no need to jump into the water to avoid getting wet. If only you could bring down one of those filthy gluttons and see him begin to look human again in the process of dying a violent death, in blood instead of muck, that would restore you. It isn't ourselves we ought to shoot, after all, but them. The sewing-machine salesman is looking out for himself. He's been taking a commission up until now. We must look out for ourselves."

"You'd do it?"

"I don't know what I shall do. We've tea, sugar, and maize for five days. In five days we shall be far from here, but if we weren't, we should be at the point where we'd have to choose between becoming like them or remaining as we are. Is that a good enough reason for you?"

"You don't need to give me reasons. I was thinking just now that if the sill of this window weren't so high, one could just lean out rather too far, which is easy to do. Your own weight carries you along. When you get to the bottom, everything's settled for good. I'm amazed they haven't thought of it."

"Perhaps they have, but prefer the cauldron. Perhaps some people have jumped, but they haven't mentioned it to us because they think it's an act of lunacy. They're not frightened about catching it, so it doesn't occupy their minds. They're only terrified, they only talk, of those who've died properly (as they put it to themselves), wallowing in filthy straw. Which is what they're doing already, in good health, without a scruple."

"I know that five days from now, I shan't lean out of the window. I know that this evening I shall lie down in the straw without thinking of the window or the pistols, that my pistols are now worthless tools, which now have no more power to save me than a St Christopher. I know that night is coming, as is only natural for it to do, that I shall make my bed as is natural for me, in this straw, filthy or not, that tomorrow I shall be like them, that I shall lead my life here, with what I can get, as it is natural and easy for me to do, until I die of cholera. You see? I'm no longer afraid of this death which makes one vomit."

"And what if you don't die? . . . for you may escape it. Are you sure you'd forget what you'd been for a while, that you could believe again in yourself? They don't have this trouble. They weren't anything before. I can still see you, with your torch, in that lonely house, that rotting town, facing a man who must have been pretty terrifying as he rose up out of the shadows. Considering what I'd been through on the roofs, I didn't look very sweet, did I? I remember that the flames of your candlestick were steady and stiff as the prongs of a pitchfork. And the hand that made me tea that evening knew how to do its job without trembling. And your big pistol was hidden under a shawl, near the stove where you were heating me the drink I needed. It must have taken some self-confidence to act like that. The woman whose hand did not tremble then had never been a coward, otherwise she'd have had some cowardly thought right away (it was then or never), and the flames would have quivered. There is somebody one can never deceive: oneself, because one always agrees with one's acts. It's not a trifling matter to eat at the cauldron, or even to bed down in that straw. You'll never be able to fool your-self and tell yourself stories later on, saying to yourself that you were forced to do it. Whatever happens, people like you will never be able to do that. And you'll have to live with the thought that you yielded because you had agreed to accepting the cauldron.

"I don't know who you are. I only know one thing about you: in exceptional circumstances, you stand up to them. That's why I spoke to you by the barricade. With the others, I was alone against the soldiers; with you, I was no longer alone. When we had our first skirmish, I might easily have received a jab from behind; the dragoons weren't joking. If I'd had to fear that, I'd have needed to wheel my horse round in a far from elegant manner to parry it. But I didn't worry because I knew you were there (even though I had shouted to you to flee and save yourself); that allowed me the *brio* which is such fun. And, *naturally*, there you were, with your little hand aiming the big pistol at the poor corporal."

"But the next day I shot a crow because he was cooing like a dove."

"Well! is a crow that coos like a dove a trifle? One should always shoot at things like that. I'd have done the same and my eyes would have been as big as yours. Just dying is a tiny thing. Do you know what is destroying your soul here? It's this smell of dung and urine, all those skirts that stink like barrels of codfish. It's not iron bars of walls that keep prisoners in prison: it's the stink of their latrines, which they have to smell for months, then years, on end. With debased senses, what sort of a world can they have inside them? The most intransigent, the most nostalgic, end up by doing what I said just now: they slit one of their fellow prisoners' bellies open to breathe the smell of blood, to see a red colour once more, as people eat the moss off rafts to get a little meat between their teeth. Come, let's lean out of this window, not to lose our balance but to get it back."

The sun had already lowered its light. The mountains were beginning to take on substance again. Angelo and the young woman were looking out over a part of the little town's roofs and one whole side of the castle. They stayed there for over two hours, watching the sky deposit its lees and become a beautiful pearl-grey. The sun was at a season when it withdraws quickly; all the flat stone scales of the roofs with their piping of shadow passed from grey to a soft green. Some of the lower roofs were spotted with great patches of yellowed lichen. The wind that had come up gave this whole countryside a suggestion of ocean, an odour of the open sea.

The butterflies sparkled like sand. The mingled crows and pigeons spurted up like spray from tall houses, towers, and belfry, at each pulse of the sea.

Angelo passed those two hours in the most absolute serenity. He had avoided smoking one of his little cigars, in order not to rouse envy among those in the quarantine who had no tobacco. Before deciding on this, he had glanced once or twice over his shoulder to see if there were any smokers; there were none. After eating their soup, the people had lain down. Evidently the sewing-machine salesman was not generous every day. Angelo suffered from this privation for five minutes at the most. He counted the columns of smoke rising from the chimneys: there were seven. Seven fires in a town where, before the plague, at about four o'clock in the afternoon more than eight hundred must have been lit. He followed the activities of the soldiers in the courtyard. He saw one of them cleaning the glass of a saddlebow lantern: he supposed they were preparing a night patrol. Not long afterwards this was confirmed by an order of which he caught a few words. He wondered what he would do if he were in the captain's place. From time to time he shifted his weight from his right leg to his left. He looked for the position of the various roads. He saw two deserted ones leading towards the mountains. The part of the castle he could see was not encouraging. The tower descended sheer, without any footholds, to the soldiers' courtyard. Beyond that, there was a wall forty or fifty feet high, and the roundway visible on top of it must, to judge from the distance of the roofs, be at least sixty feet above the town. He let his imagination play. A perfect peace stole over him. He thought of the nuns. He told himself that they must certainly be afraid of noise and blood. He knew how people behave when a pistol goes off suddenly under their nose in the middle of the night. Soldiers were a different matter. "But these ones aren't warmed up. Arresting bourgeois puts men to sleep. Even at the beginning of a campaign a soldiers needs five or six days of adjustment before he can face a volley or even isolated bullets. It's only in novels that people treat them like wasps." Once the battle began, he knew he would have to do, as quickly as possible, all the harm he could. It is the first four killed that make the difference, provided one gets one's sword swinging as soon as they go down.

"I'll give her all the time she wants to reload," he said to himself, thinking of his little sabre and the young woman.

He glanced at her. She did not look very well. He asked her anxiously if she was feeling ill.

"Only what's natural," she said; "I'm going to have to go to those vile latrines."

"No," he said; "come."

He shouldered the saddlebags and put the sabre back under his arm. They went down the great staircase, plunging into gloom, towards the grille. Angelo stopped on the little landing.

"Would you go and look for the cases?" he said. "They're down below in the corner, under the first flight of stairs. I'll wait for you here."

He went and tried the doors giving on to the landing. One of them was unshakable, firmly gripped in its frame. The other had some play. Its wood was less massive and fitted loosely. Angelo slipped his sword through the slit. The door was not locked. Where the latch was, the sword-blade had free passage, but above and below it was stopped by the bar of a bolt. He tried to slide this bolt back but had no success.

"I suppose," he said to himself, "it's one of those bolts with handles that lower on to a mortise and that you have to raise to open the door."

He estimated the length of the bolt and the approximate position of this handle. He tried to cut into the door with the point of the sabre. The wood was not very hard.

"What are you doing?" asked the young lady.

"Trying to make a hole here, just to pass the time."

He made one, in fact, half an inch deep. The wood was solid and flaked away in splinters. It was an ashwood panel about three inches thick, but it had lost substance with age.

"Give me the powder box. Spread out the luggage and lie down. If anyone comes up or down, I shall say you're ill. I shall talk brutally about dry cholera and they'll leave us alone. Keep an eye on the staircase and give me warning."

He poured some powder into the hole he had made and set fire to it. The red flame went out at once, but a little blue glow clung on at the back of the hole, creeping round among the splinters, gnawing, finally leaving embers on which Angelo blew.

At last, after considerable manipulation but no setbacks, he managed to push back the two bolts, and they entered a large, dark room.

They shut the door behind them at once, slid back the bolts, and blocked up the holes, each the size of two écus, with strips of a black shawl.

"That will take them in till tomorrow morning. Perhaps longer," said Angelo. "I know them – they'll look first in the corners where animals go to die. They have no idea what stout hearts we have inside us."

With the door shut, it was hard to form any definite notion of the place that they were in. The light seeped in parsimoniously through the stones blocking up a tall Gothic window.

When their eyes got used to the darkness, they perceived around them a vast hall, entirely bare. The floor was springy, as though made of trampled earth that time and solitude had reduced to dust. On the wall at the far end a black spot seemed to be an opening. It was in fact a doorway with neither door nor hinges, simply a sort of tunnel cut through a wall over six feet thick and leading to a narrow spiral staircase, within which there seemed to be a sort of sleepy grey light . . .

They descended towards this light, step by step. Angelo was very happy and quite unconcerned about cholera. Step by step they drew nearer to a light that became gradually more golden. They emerged at length on to a gallery running almost level with the vault, around a vast deep hall lit by tall lancets and a rose-window of yellow glass. Here, too, there was nothing but stone: no furniture, no woodwork, and the floor down below also made simply of earth, as though out in the fields. In spite of the rose-window and stained glass, it had never been used as a church; there was no trace of an altar site.

They went all round the gallery. They passed by a window, some of whose panels had fallen out of their leading. Outside they could see below them a large, barren garden entirely planted with grey thyme, divided by two paths that crossed in the middle.

Angelo glanced at the young woman and smiled. She smiled back. He remembered to ask if she felt better. Didn't she, for instance, feel a vague pain here? And with the tip of his finger he touched the pit of her stomach.

She said she felt perfectly well, and apologized.

"There's nothing to apologize for," he said. "You're not responsible if something starts to rot inside you and destroy you. I don't believe in the flies. However small they're said to be, I believe one would feel them as one breathed. I believe there's a place in the stomach or the bowels that suddenly starts to go bad."

He described how he had massaged the little Frenchman through out a whole night but all to no effect because he had started too late. You mustn't wait till you're *astonished at yourself*, like the lieutenant of the patrol. As soon as you feel a slight, sharp pricking in the side, you must cry for help. It's worth while, going on living.

"If you really have a pain in the place I've just indicated, you must show me your stomach at once. When it's caught in time and you're massaged, you've ninety-nine chances out of a hundred of surviving."

At the end of the gallery they discovered a little passage, narrow and very dark, which seemed to run through the thickness of the walls. They had difficulty in dragging their baggage along it. This passage was warm and smelt of dead stone. After turning sharp right they saw a ray of pale light ahead. It came through a narrow slit. Through this could be seen, facing them, the huge tower and the windows of the quarantine, against which the wind thundered.

"We must be on the other side of the soldiers' courtyard, unless those are not the windows we were leaning out of a little while ago."

It was impossible to look down through the slit; they could just make out the row of the quarantine's windows, the crown of battlements, and the sky, bright blue and dappled with little clouds exactly like daisies, lit by a slanting sun.

Farther on, the passage grew so narrow that Angelo was obliged to remove the bags he was carrying on his back. They had to step over rubble and even bend double to pass through places where it was half blocked.

Again a ray of pale light pierced the darkness ahead. This slit, which, like the one before, seemed to be a watchman's loophole, looked out this time on to open space. Again they saw the bright blue sky, dappled with pink, and had a glimpse of the mountains lit by the setting sun.

Beyond, the passage was more and more in ruins. They advanced on all fours, hampered by the cloaks, case, and saddlebags. They made slow progress, in total darkness, over a real rubble-heap. At last Angelo's out-thrust hand touched a sharply chiselled stone and he felt a cool draught coming from below. They had found the opening to something. By the light of sparks from his tinder, then of the wick on which he blew, Angelo saw that they had just emerged into a corkscrew staircase, as narrow as the passage but in good condition. A few turns down and they met daylight again and finally, cautiously, they reached a door that opened on to the thyme garden they had seen through the broken window in the gallery.

The autumn twilight was beginning to fall. They remained hidden. The garden looked as if it were regularly used. There must be other, easier ways into it. The place where Angelo and the young woman were hiding was moreover used as a toolshed, and two spades, a rake, and a big coarse straw hat like those worn by harvesters had been left there.

In the garden there was nothing but thyme and stones. It was clearly a terrace and must overlook a defence platform, a street, a bank – Angelo wondered which, and at what height. But it would have been too rash to go and see. They must wait till evening had really fallen. It was certainly a place loved by the nuns, to judge from those touching garden tools placed ready for tilling a terrace of white earth as dry as salt.

Swifts and swallows began to dart past the door-opening. Following the birds' new custom, as soon as they perceived the motionless figures of Angelo and the young woman, they approached and even flew right in under the vault, wheeling round them with cries and violent wingbeats.

"This could easily give us away," said Angelo. "Let's go back up the stairs a bit and hide."

They were hardly settled in the shadow when they heard footsteps in the garden. It was a nun, not at all the red-faced sister with big bare arms, but a tall, thin sort of shopkeeper whose ample black skirt forced upon her a certain look of nobility. She took off her coif, revealing a tiny head and an extraordinarily unpleasant face with quite small and very active black eyes. She came to fetch the rake and began to rake the paths. After which, she fumbled under her skirt, took out of her pocket a horn knife and, crouching down, meticulously weeded around the tufts of thyme. She threw herself with a sort of passion into this useless work.

At last it began to grow dark. The nun having withdrawn, Angelo ran to the edge of the rampart, leaned over, and returned.

"It's only ten to twelve feet high," he said, "and there's a clump of wild laurel growing in the wall."

They tied all the luggage together in a bundle.

"I'll carry it," said Angelo. "We'll have to forget about our horses. Unless you'll agree to a fight. That, I confess, would be balm to my heart and I think you too would get a good breath of fresh air out of it. But it wouldn't be wise. Still, I'd give a lot, and in particular a lesson in fencing, to hear you talk as you did this morning to the soldiers who brought you here. All the time I had the feeling that at some more banal remark than usual you'd show a clean pair of heels and leave them gaping. If you haven't thoroughly understood that in reality we did not surrender, I propose a little battle in the soldiers' courtyard, when we'll make all we have to tell them perfectly clear. Otherwise, we only have to throw the luggage overboard and jump twelve feet, making use of the laurel stump. There's a grass bank on the other side, and it slopes straight down to the fields. We'll walk as far as we can during the night, and tomorrow we shall be far away. I still have over three hundred francs. We'll buy nags of some sort. Would you like to go to that little village near Gap, where you told me your sister-in-law lives?"

"That's exactly what I must do. Besides, have you thought that even if you did give the soldiers a beating, it wouldn't count, seeing that they've certainly got cholera and you haven't? It interferes with swordsmanship, I imagine."

"You mean it would interfere with mine?" said Angelo very obtusely. "It's possible. We're still a bit stiff and it's no joke to leave this place by slithering on all fours through the walls. A twelve-foot jump isn't much, after all. And there's the laurel stump. I'd have liked to put sense into the heads of those sheep shut up there, but that would mean a song and dance."

In spite of everything, before they left their shelter, Angelo went to make sure that the other door leading into the garden was shut.

He said to himself: "How different it would all be if I were alone. (Then I don't think. And what a pleasure that is!)"

Five minutes later they were on the slope. The young woman had jumped without fuss and had even made most clever use of the laurel stump. Everything had been extremely easy. Angelo, disappointed, was watching the shadows set up by the rising moon. They were feeling very tranquil. He would have liked some sort of fight, he did not quite know what. He had hoped to find at least one soldier at the foot of the wall, a sentry whom he would have had to disarm. He had had visions of himself struggling and overthrowing his adversary.

A few frogs were chanting in some cisterns that were no doubt half empty and echoed loudly.

"This is great fun," said the young woman: "it reminds me of an evening when I jumped out of the window to go and dance in the square at Rians. My father hadn't forbidden me to go out, far from it, but any stolen fruit – what a joy! And after all, jumping out of the window!"

"Women," said Angelo to himself, "are incomplete creatures."

He wondered why she was suddenly so lively after having been so downcast during the afternoon. "I too enjoyed crawling on all fours through the walls, but I knew how serious our position is. And it wasn't so extraordinary to expect a sentry at the foot of this wall; there should have been if the captain whose voice I heard was doing his job."

At length Angelo slung the bundle on his back and they set off down the glacis, gently sloping, muffled with grass, and ending in fields of lavender, wide open to freedom on all sides and even faintly scented.

They walked for about an hour through the fields, then found a track leading in the direction Angelo had decided to take. It soon began to climb. The moon, which had gradually taken its place at the highest point in the sky, was shedding a bright light. It revealed the muscular back of a treeless mountain studded with small rocks gleaming like silver.

The night was truly gentle. The crickets, restored to vigour by the heat of that Indian summer's day, were now making their metallic grating sound, which seems like an intoxication of the air itself. The sluggish wind blew warm gusts.

Angelo and the young woman made good progress along this track, which headed vaguely northward. On the other side of the mountain, towards midnight, they crossed a fairly wide road lined by tall poplars, in whose long branches the moonlight played seductively. All was peaceful and reassuring. They even heard the wheels of a carriage in the distance and the jog trot of a horse that seemed to feel at ease in the softness of the night.

They hid behind some tall broom bushes and finally saw a cabriolet pass close by with its hood folded back, carrying a man and woman in calm conversation.

The road from which the cabriolet had come led eastward, along a valley bottom. The company of the poplars, leafless but glazed with white light, was very comforting. Judging from the two who had just passed, that part of the countryside must be agreeable.

"What we need," said Angelo, who found his bundle absurd now that he had seen the well-sprung cabriolet bowling along behind its horse, "is a carriage like that. It would make up for our horses ten times over. At any rate, it would give us that well-to-do air which intimidates the soldiers. The man and woman we saw talking just now were not fugitives. Seeing them, it's almost impossible to imagine there's a quarantine at Vaumeilh, and yet it's barely five leagues from this road. Let's go and see what there is over there. Especially as it's still more our direction than the one we've been following until now. Let's forget about the rendezvous with Giuseppe. He's big enough to find his way by himself. What matters for us is to get as quickly as possible to that village near Gap where your sister-in-law lives."

"What is your name?" said the young woman. "Yesterday in the quarantine I needed to call you several times, though I was near you. After all, I can't go on calling you 'monsieur'. Besides, it's not such a help as a Christian name in delicate situations. Mine is Pauline."

"My name's Angelo," said he. "And my surname's Pardi. That's certainly not my father's name. I'm rather proud of its being simply the name of a large forest owned by my mother near Turin."

"Your first name is very pretty. Will you let me carry my share of the baggage, now that we're walking on a comfortable road?"

"Certainly not. I have a long stride and I don't feel the weight. The cloaks are very soft on the shoulder. Your little case and our bags are properly wrapped up. It's quite enough that you should be forced to walk in riding-boots. That's not too easy. Riders without their mounts are always a bit absurd, but the cabriolet that passed us – which was, I admit, the very image of tranquillity and peace – doesn't reassure me. The only thing that reassures me is the distance we've been putting for some hours between ourselves and that quarantine where you lost your courage for five minutes. Aren't you tired?"

"My boots are excellent and I used always to wear them for my walks in the woods. They were very long walks. My husband is an expert on boots and pistols. It was he who taught me to double-load. He also took care to have boots as pliable as gloves made for me. We live in a country of brushwood and hills where one has to go leagues to distract oneself with the spectacle of nature."

"That's the way we lived at Granta, before I joined the Cadets. And every time I went home, before I left for France, every day it was some endless ride, or even a road march on which you had to drag your horse by the bridle if you wanted to get out of the forest to see a fine sunset, a beautiful dawn, or simply the open sky my mother loves so much."

The road had risen little by little on to high land where it wound between woods of ilex. The moon, half buried in the west, was casting that strange light, tinged with yellow, which creates dramatic realities. The horizon into which it was sinking seemed to have burst into silver dust amid which there floated the misty phantom of the mountains. The night was at once dark and brilliant; the trees, etched black against the brightness of the moon, stood out sparkling white against the shadows of the night. The wind no longer knew in which direction to blow; it swayed like a warm palm tree.

Angelo and the young woman had been walking for nearly hours. They were no longer spurred on by dread of being pursued and captured. These woods were quite different from Vaumeilh, this light far removed from any in which one could picture ordinary patrols.

Twenty paces from the road they found under the ilexes a thicket of tall broom that encircled, as though by design, a little room of warm springy earth. Angelo put down the bundle. It was useless to deny it, he was limp with fatigue and, in spite of the moonlight, had been secretly in a vile temper for the last hour of walking.

"I don't like carrying baggage," he had kept saying to himself.

He unrolled the cloaks and made a comfortable bed.

"Lie down," he said to the young woman, "and if I may give some advice, take off your breeches. You'll rest better. We can't tell what's ahead of us, except that, judging by what we've already seen, it won't be easy sailing. Let's try to be ready for anything. If we reach a town, ten to one it'll be putrid and full of soldiers. We don't have horses any more. We're going to have to hoof it. I now think those two bowling along so charmingly in the cabriolet must have been fools. Walking isn't at all the same as riding. If you get blisters, your wounds don't heal and you can't walk any more. It would be absurd to die stupidly where you are from having neglected your thighs."

He spoke to her as to a trooper. She was too tired to give any other reply than: "You're right." She quickly did as he said. Besides, he *was* right. She slept deeply for twenty minutes, then roused herself and said: "You've nothing over you! You've put my cloak under me and yours on top of me!"

"I'm quite all right," said Angelo. "I've slept on the hard ground in the bitterest cold with nothing to cover me but my dolman. And that's not much. Now I've got my good velvet jacket, I'm in no danger, but since you're awake, wait."

And he gave her some brown sugar to eat and a small tot of alcohol to drink.

"We've empty stomachs. The tea we drank in the window recess and the little handful of maize flour are a long way back. A sleep's not always as good as a dinner, especially after a march like the one we've just done. We should have lit a fire and cooked some polenta, but I confess I'm tired. This'll keep us going for at least an hour or two."

Angelo did not fall asleep at once. His shoulders were aching. He had never carried a pack; he was worn out.

He wondered whether the road they were on really led to a town, and whether that was to be desired or dreaded. Were there garrisons and quarantines everywhere? The two travellers in the cabriolet had not seemed to be worrying. Perhaps they were archbishop's children with passports of the kind that get saluted. He remembered the dry cholera that had leapt upon the captain in the open countryside and unhorsed him. There was a certain equality, after all. He was seeing the black side of things.

He reckoned that for the past six days they had been travelling blindly. There was no clear reason for supposing that the village near Gap was to the northwest of the spot where they now were. He told himself that the cause of liberty had nothing to do with that village near Gap. He recognized that it was now impossible to return to the place of rendezvous Giuseppe had fixed, but he saw himself on a horse, or he did not see himself at all. The foot-slogging and, above all, the pack, had made him melancholy. He was not very sure, either, of having made a real escape from the quarantine at Vaumeilh. Burning a little powder in the wood of a door was not a sufficient event to make one sure of the thing and of oneself. He thought, too, of Dupuis, who had neglected to take the pistols from the baggage, and had even let him keep the little sabre: all for ten francs, perhaps indeed for nothing and from indifference. The soldiers had not even searched him.

"Everybody is becoming an official," he thought, "and I don't see what place there is for me in such a world."

The moon, however, now almost at the end of its descent and half buried in the mists of the horizon, was sliding long pink rays under the ilex branches. The young woman was sleeping steadily and heaving faint, charming sighs.

Angelo thought of his little cigars. He smoked one with such pleasure that he lit a second from the stump of the first.

If Giuseppe had been there he would at once have been pleased to explain to him that things were not so stupid as people thought. No one was guarding the quarantine at Vaumeilh. People were picked up, packed into four walls. They stayed put. There was no need to bother about them. They guarded themselves. The able ones even did a little business.

"I blundered," Angelo thought: "all I need have done was to go down to the grille and say: 'Open up, I'm leaving.' 'This is rather a surprise,' they'd have replied, 'but yes, no doubt you don't belong here.' Now, one can easily die simply through lacking that simple sort of initiative. I don't die, but I do make three times the gestures necessary. If Giuseppe were here I'd say: 'I know exactly what to expect. You'll rob me of my horse legally and make me carry a pack.' He'd get angry and reply: 'You're not stupid, but what can we do for the people, then?' For he doesn't believe he's one of them. And that's what he's proud of. They make revolutions to become dukes. I do too, but they'll rob me of my horse. Only the cholera is genuine."

Ever since they had taken to the country roads, they had seen very few dead, except for that arrogant captain whom they had found on the road, curled up like a child in its mother's lap, with his stripes and his spurs. But Angelo remembered Manosque, and his horror on the roofs when he could not close his eyes without finding himself immediately covered with birds who knew what they wanted. He remembered, too, the infernal heat, the braziers where the corpses were being burned, and the droning of the flies.

Despite the coolness of the morning (dawn was not far off) and the utter silence of the forest, asleep over its vast expanse, he saw in his mind's eye with great precision the agonies and the deaths that must be still laying waste the inhabited places.

# 12

THE TEA WAS MADE and the polenta cooking on a magnificent fire when the young woman awoke.

"Don't move," said Angelo, "you're still exhausted."

He gave her some boiling hot, very sweet, tea.

"I've been on my little patrol," he said; "fifty yards from here, there's a crossroads with a signpost. According to this, we're five leagues west of Saint-Dizier. Don't you remember passing through a place of that name on the journey you told me about? It does seem to be our way."

"No, I don't remember Saint-Dizier. But let me get up and help you."

"You're helping me by staying where you are. If you get up, in five minutes you'll be in the absurd position of having to lie down again. I haven't told you everything. Immediately after the crossroads, the road goes down into a valley, and just on the slope, a hundred yards at most from where we are, there's the most charming hamlet of four houses one could hope to see. What's so extraordinary, the people there are behaving quite normally. Just now, a woman was feeding her chickens. A man started harvesting a field and is still there. If it weren't for the rim of the valley and these trees, you'd hear him speaking to his horse. I shouldn't be surprised if there were children playing outside. In any case, I didn't show myself, but an old woman put a chair in the sun outside her door, sat down, and is knitting. There are also at least three quite old men smoking their pipes and talking about rain and fine weather, standing with their hands in their pockets."

"It's incredible!"

"I had my eyes mostly on the chickens," said Angelo. "Still, you'll see for yourself how the land lies presently, when I allow you to try your knees. But take my word for it, you'd better lie still and keep warm. We're going to need our legs. We're on a hilltop with the finest view in the world. I'll tell you why I had my eyes mostly on the chickens. Now that you've drunk your tea, stay nice and quiet. This is what I'm going to do. Here are your pistols, put them by your head, but there's nothing to worry about for leagues around. I'm going to buy a chicken and some vegetables. I shall borrow a pot. We're going to stew a chicken. That'll put some heart into us. We're famished: at least, I am."

The people of the hamlet were very hospitable. They wanted to make some coffee for Angelo, but he, seized with qualms, talked to them frankly about the cholera and how unwise it was to let strangers into their houses.

"You wouldn't be the first to come in and drink from my bowls," said the woman to whom he had spoken. "We don't see so many people on the roads these days because of the soldiers, but a while ago we had swarms of them. We've always done what we should and no one's died of it. Don't leave your lady in the woods; bring her here. If you really insist on staying out of doors, come and set yourselves up on the green. Then I can keep a closer eye on the pot I'm lending you. It's worth more than the chicken you're buying."

Angelo returned with this good news to the camp under the ilex. He found the young woman up and ready. She had tidied herself a bit, undone her bun, and braided her hair. This made her look like a little girl. Her face, framed in black tresses, now had the perfect shape of a lance-point.

Angelo and the young woman stayed two days in this hamlet, sleeping out near the houses, eating chicken and potatoes baked in the ashes. After the recent orgies of maize and brown sugar, nothing could have been better than the rock salt. Angelo still refused the homemade bread, though its cheapness was tempting, and the wine, which, being drawn from a cask, one could not be sure of.

"Let's boil everything," he said to the young woman, "and eat nothing that hasn't been boiled under our eyes. The question is whether we want to profit from all the remote tracks we've taken, or whether we're going to be at the mercy of this bread, which, I admit, makes my mouth water too. I've heard it repeated a thousand times, as you have, that neither the cholera nor the plague – so they say – gets into bread. But when one's been through all we have, and especially six hours on foot, one doesn't want to get fooled by putting the wrong thing in one's mouth."

The countryside had a majestic vastness. It was a gently undulating plateau (what Angelo had called a valley, where the hamlet's four houses stood, was just a depression, barely perceptible, like the hollow of the hand). The land, sulphur-yellow or tender green, extended to infinity, bearing on its rolling back lopsided trees and bushes as light and transparent as foam. It was at the fullness of that heat which lingers into autumn. The wind was languishing, yet, across these open spaces, it had the voice of the sea, even in its faintest sighs. A pale light gilded the vast circle of mountains all around the horizon.

Angelo pointed out that there was not a single bird to be heard. Normally, during these Indian summers, the thrushes sing, the tits go mad and hurl splashes of blue at the sun. Here there was nothing of the kind; only the wind brushing its peaceful surf over the tiles of the houses and the bare branches of the trees. Sometimes the dust rose from some dry heath and enlivened the expanse with its floating columns.

The man living in the house nearest to the road came and sat down on the green. He was an old man of over eighty. He said he looked after all his own needs.

"Do *you* believe in this cholera?" he added.

Double chins of long standing hung in scarves about his scrawny neck. His face was shrivelled like a nut. His black lips moved as he chewed his quid.

He stared at the cloaks.

"That's good cloth you've got there, monsieur. Is it tartan or what? Or maybe it's navy stuff?[1] know Toulon. I was a carpenter at the arsenal. Where do they make cloth like that? Winter's on its way up here. People say there's too much dying. Where do they get that idea? It isn't a very new one. Now they're in a panic. Are you on the run too? What've you got in those bags? That's real leather if I ever saw any. There's been more than one went down this road! A regular parade! Where did they go to? It must be twenty years since I set foot in Saint-Dizier. Do you know Saint-Dizier?"

"No," said Angelo, "we were just wondering if it's big and if it's on the road to Gap."

"What's Gap?"

"A place we're heading for."

"No, it can't be. Saint-Dizier isn't on the roads. There's the one that goes in and the one going out. Full stop. And that's all, and it's enough. It's not the Toulon road. I've been there. Look at that crooked almond tree; it was the size of my finger at the time. It was growing out of an old stump. I walked by it at four in the morning one summer. I said to myself: 'What's he up to here, the little bastard?' He's grown. I was young. First-rate carpenter and sawyer. One knocks about the world. You haven't got three sous?"

He had slid his behind across the grass to get near the cloaks and feel their cloth between fingers that looked like iron.

"It's the devil's own job getting a bit of tobacco; they've made a plug cost its weight in gold. Vices cost money. And in the end we all wind up the same way! That's for sure. The fat fellow who came every year in March to buy the kids, you'd have given him a hundred years with cheeks like his. He's as dead as a doornail, like the others. You should see this country in March, it's a fair sight. Some times we have twenty kids. The breath he'd waste for a sou! He's kicked the bucket. It's bound to happen. What do you expect? He was getting on!"

Angelo gave him a little cigar. He broke it in two and stuffed half of it into his mouth at once.

"You must be rich to smoke these," he said. "They cost a sou apiece."

He kept on trying to find out what was in the bags, squinting also at the case, and ceaselessly fingering the cloaks. Finally he became too familiar and Angelo was about to make him move off when a man came out of the house behind the little chestnut tree, just at the right moment, and called the old man, who hastened to obey. Angelo and the young woman thought afterwards that this man must have been there a long time, watching them. Perhaps indeed he had arranged it . . .

"This place seems queer to me," said the young woman several times. "Believe me, we're not safe."

"They claim that soldiers never come this way, and we've every reason to believe it."

"It's something else," she said. "We're being watched. I can feel it; something presses on my shoulders whenever I turn my back on the houses. The little boy who was there just now hitting the euphorbia with his whip wasn't doing it naturally. I've whipped euphorbias like everyone else. I know what it's like. It doesn't fit in with the sly glances he was throwing in our direction. He was watching us."

"It's just that we're strangers, and further we're bound to behave differently from the people of Saint-Dizier, or anywhere else, after our recent adventures. I've never seen eyes as big as yours."

"Well then, I must tell you what happened to me this morning. I'd gone into the bushes. On my way back I met the woman who sold you the chicken. She had obviously been waiting for me, without wishing to show it. She said: 'Show me the ring on your finger.' I assure you it didn't sound like a joke. I showed it to her. 'Will you give it to me?' she said. I said: 'No,' very firmly. One doesn't go into the bushes with a pistol, but she didn't scare me. And now there's the old boy and the one who called him at the right moment. And the little boy. And a face I just saw now, watching us from behind the pillar of the barn – don't look – on the right. It's just gone."

"I hadn't noticed that ring. You weren't wearing it these last days?"

"No, I put it on yesterday morning, under the ilex, when you were on patrol."

"I saw the man hiding behind the pillar of the barn, sure enough. He does indeed seem to be following all our movements. It's the young man who was drawing water from the well this morning. How many are there altogether in this hamlet?"

"I've counted nine: four women and five men, including the old man and the boy. The women are sturdily built."

"They'd better have their hearts in the right place too, if it comes to a fight. I intend to shoot straight into them and not at their legs. We won't attack but we'll take our precautions. Let's pack. You're not afraid?"

"I'd gladly crack the head of that woman who noticed my ring before you did," said the young woman. "Trust me, I've a steady hand and I'm not boasting. We've fallen among a bunch of those brigands we've been hearing about."

"No," said Angelo, "we've fallen among worthy people who no longer fear the gendarmes. That's worse. They'd cut off your head with an ear-pick, even if it took them a hundred tries."

They made up the pack. Angelo watched the houses out of the corner of his eye. He rejoiced in this slight atmosphere of war, with nothing to fear but gunshots. "If there's something behind all this," he thought, "our packing up will bring it out in the open."

In fact, a door opened, and a man took a few swift steps in their direction. He was holding a gun. The other doors had opened and the men and women came out, even the old man. But there was only one gun, and even before it was levelled, Angelo had turned to face them, holding his two pistols well aimed. They all stopped in their tracks.

They could hear the surf of the wind.

More than the pistols (and the young woman had hers raised too, but she was hardly noticed) Angelo's attitude had disconcerted and frightened them. These peasants could see that he was bursting with joy. He was not on the defensive, he was attacking, and with a far from ordinary vigour. He had the little sabre under his arm.

"Stand behind me," he said loudly to the young woman. And, taking two paces towards the group of peasants: "At the slightest movement, blow in the faces of those two freaks with the sticks, over on my right. I'll take care of the ones in front. Throw down that gun, you; throw down those sticks. And step back to the wall."

He continued to advance on them, and they retreated. But they didn't throw down either gun or sticks. And suddenly the young woman's pistol thundered. It made so extraordinary a noise that in a flash the weapons were thrown down and everyone was lined up against the wall, except for a young man who had fallen. He got up and ran to line up with the others. He had his right hand riddled with buckshot, perhaps even a finger blown off. His blood was dripping on to the grass.

"Reload your pistol," said Angelo coldly; "I'm holding them."

And he held them, in fact, without a glance at the wounded man and without a word.

"They'll have to get it into their heads . . ." he said to himself.

"It's done," said the young woman quickly.

"Whose is the horse that was harrowing the other morning?"

"It's a mule," said the man who had had the gun.

"Saddle it and bring it out," said Angelo. "Pauline, keep an eye on him while he does it. Until we're gone, and in our own time, no one will touch that hand. That fellow's bleeding like a pig, hurry up."

The saddled mule was quickly brought out, and the young woman loaded the baggage on to it. Angelo was in heaven. At last he could forget the cholera, which was always in his thoughts and was so mystifying. Here, the peasants were simply like urchins caught in some mischief. They clearly still had their hearts set on it: that could be seen in their eyes and furtive looks. The unexpected business of the mule was on the point of giving them courage. Angelo gripped the butts of his pistols with great conviction.

"Here's a remedy and I know how to use it," he thought.

He made a little speech.

"I'm not a thief," he said. "And yet, what is there to stop me? We were friends. I paid you for the chicken, the vegetables, even the salt. I gave your spy a cigar. It's you who are responsible for what has just happened. And if I choose not only to take away your mule without paying for it but also to slaughter the lot of you, it would be easy and I'd be within my rights. We have four shots to fire and, as you've seen, this lady knows how to use her weapons. After that, look what I've got under my arm. It could chop you into little pieces and, at the slightest movement, I shan't hesitate to do so. I shall pay you thirty francs for the mule; that's a reasonable price. Anyhow, you've no choice but to accept it. What's more, let me tell you I'm the cousin of your *préfet,* and, if I'm not satisfied with you, I'll send the soldiers. That's why I wasn't worried and you couldn't frighten me. I shall add ten francs for the gun, which I'm taking away to avoid all risks. That makes exactly two louis. I shall throw them to you as soon as we are on the road. My pistols carry fifteen yards perfectly well. You have been warned."

The young woman took the mule's bridle, and the little troop retired in splendid style. Nothing was left to chance. Angelo walked backwards and kept the peasants in view. They had been impressed by his speech. No one had ever spoken to them at such length, looking them in the eyes and, after all, using valid arguments. They were also keen to see the two louis. At heart they were interested in any number of things that no longer demanded assaulting any one. They were wondering if it would be easy to find the gold coins in the grass where that thin person with the eyes of fire would surely throw them.

Angelo was naturally cunning enough to throw the money some distance, and well away from the road. At the same time he set his troop at the double and so gained some ground.

"Let's stay on the road," he said. "There it goes, straight over the plateau. However much they feel like following us, we shall see them a long way off. And we've got their gun. Let's go towards Saint-Dizier: evidently it's a town, and they won't like that because there must be soldiers there, or at any rate the sort of men they're afraid of – notary, bailiff, wholesalers. They wouldn't risk murdering anyone in their presence, you may be sure. Anyway, we've gained a half-mount. Walking's easier when there's an animal to carry the baggage. When you're tired, you can sit on the crupper."

It was three in the afternoon and still fine weather. After forcing the pace for a league, they slowed down. They had the plateau to themselves.

"We still have an hour of daylight and two hours of dusk. That's enough to bring us to the outskirts of this Saint-Dizier without hurrying. We'll see what it's best to do about the place: avoid it, as I think, or sample it cautiously. At any rate, I have an idea the cholera isn't so strong around here."

"I don't know," said the young woman, "I don't agree. The boldness of those peasants seems to prove the contrary."

"My congratulations on just now. You reloaded your pistol disconcertingly fast."

"I wanted to disconcert: I didn't reload at all. The most important thing was to make them believe we were wonders. That's often more useful than a charge of powder. Who could imagine I was lying?"

"Even I didn't," said Angelo. "Nevertheless, although that trick isn't beyond me, it's wiser for me to be warned. In war, I like to do my own lying."

They were still walking too fast for any consecutive conversation. Angelo accused himself of having perhaps spoken rather sharply.

"It's true, Christian names are very convenient under fire," he said, after some time. But he lacked sincerity.

The sun had disappeared behind the mountains. Evening was falling. The warmth, the gold of the day, the peace, all that had made its glory lingered on faintly in spite of the shadows. The road led over the plateau. Tall lilac mountains, till then hidden under the light, were rising on all sides. The depths of distant valleys rumbled at the least movement of the air.

The mule was docile and sturdy.

They saw, quite a long way off, a man walking ahead of them. Gradually they caught him up. He was well-equipped for the road, with gaiters, a haversack, and a stick. He was also wearing a charming straw hat like a harvester's. Seen up close, he had a grey beard, bright blue eyes, and an expression of great charm. One might have given him about sixty years, but he strode vigorously like the Wandering Jew himself.

"Are you going to Saint-Dizier?" he asked, after greeting them. "I hope you don't mind my asking, since we seem to be in the same boat and I've heard bad things about that place."

From what he said, it was a town of two or three thousand inhabitants, and had been decimated by the plague in a particularly beastly way. Apparently it lay in an unhealthy hollow, beside one of those little streams that dry up in summer. Having barely enough drinking-water, Saint-Dizier was even in normal times a heap of filth. The latrines streaked its walls with hieroglyphs easily deciphered by the nose. The people had vied with each other in dying. Only a quarter of the population, it seemed, was left – completely dazed and yet contriving, so he understood, to recover the enjoyment of a day-to-day, animal existence.

"It's far from funny, it seems. I was advised to give it a wide berth. Seeing a lady, I took the liberty of speaking, to warn you."

His manners were easy. He also kept, with marked discretion, to his side of the road. Angelo judged him to be brave and to belong to the category of clear-visioned misanthropes.

"We've just had a foretaste of that," Angelo told him.

He described their adventure at the hamlet.

"That doesn't surprise me," said the man. "But for your presence of mind and your pistols, you'd have been in the soup, that's certain. I'm like you: I know what decent people are made of. It seems that in normal times they welcome you here most hospitably. That's quite possible, but the question remains whether what they call normal isn't what we are seeing now. I once knew a monkey that had been trained to smoke a pipe. You can do anything with a whip; even make decent people harmless."

"If you don't mind my asking," said Angelo, "have you come a long way?"

"I don't mind in the least," said the man. "What are we doing, you and I, on the roads? There's no need to ask, it's plain to see. We're beating it. And inevitably, in that case, one comes from a long way off. I've been tramping the roads for more than two months. I've come from Marseille."

It had been quite an expedition. He had left the town towards the end of August, at the moment when the flames of the plague were raging at their height. From eight to nine hundred people more than usual were dying every day. Food changed hands at fantastic prices under the counter. "Crows", gravediggers, and even medical attendants had been recruited from the prisons, as elsewhere. Besides the cholera, all sorts of deaths were possible. Looters were shot. It was very easy to be a looter. The solid citizens killed seven or eight fountain-poisoners each day. Bourgeois had been discovered sprink-ling doorways and even shop windows with green powder. They had been dealt with in a jiffy. The number of loose women openly selling their charms on the cours Belsunce increased along with the number of deaths. There was such a confusion of limbs of every kind, sugared over with rice powder, that, in defiance of all reason, fits of irresistible lust came over one. It's easy to say: "Get thee behind me". In short, the towns, and Marseille in particular, never places for choirboys, had done nothing but strengthen and adorn the cholera. The survivors took it on themselves to carry out, over and above their own duties, the crimes and lubricities abandoned by the dead.

This man had played solo clarinet at the city opera. He described how he had spent two months of terror and chattering teeth over trifles. He had, like everyone else, been through everything. No one who had not experienced it could ever know what it was like to live in streets hemmed in by houses on every floor of which people were dying. One searched for rat-holes to burrow in. One caught oneself straining to use one's muscles like a grasshopper, dying with desire to leap towards that little strip of pure sky above the streets. Dying was the exact word – one was dying to do almost anything. Besides, just then, it was calm weather, the most calmly crushing weather there could be, the most sumptuous, the most magnificent, with cloth of gold, lapis lazuli, carbuncles on the smallest wrinkle of the sea.

Obviously, the opera had closed its doors; everyone had a far stranger opera going on within himself. The clarinetist (after much darting around in that town rotting at the roots) had asked himself what on earth he was still doing there. In the end a brutal pain right in the stomach (what they call colic) had decided him. He had collapsed on his bed, weeping, groaning, crying out. Cries were also coming from the other side of the courtyard that his bedroom window faced. Finally he noticed that, by virtue of crying out, he was no longer in pain. On the other hand, people were still crying out on the other side of the courtyard, and even giving those raucous appeals, rather like the roaring of a lion cub, that cholera victims uttered in their death agony. That cured him altogether. He got up in fine form and with ten times his former strength. He realized that the cholera could be invented; that that was what he had been doing; that it was better to take to the roads and find something less frightening to invent. A bachelor has all sorts of rights.

The question of health certificates did not trouble him. He had never had any intention of going to cool his heels at the town hall with legal-minded fugitives who, most of the time, died while they were still waiting to be interviewed. He went out through the working-class streets, which, since people were dying like flies in them, were free as the air.

"Here's a point," he said; "you spoke of murderers just now; there are never any murderers except in quiet places. One's never safer from being murdered than in a room where there's just been a murder. The warmer the corpse, the less the risk. One ought to look for victims behind whom to shelter."

He had gone up through the pine woods by Saint-Henri-les-Aygalades, without meeting either gendarmes or sentries. In the narrow alleys between the houses and gardens, he had merely had to step over corpses. Many were also dying in the coaching inns at Septêmes. People were passing through like letters through the post; in every direction. No controls. Nobody around; only free people. If you want to die, die; if you want to go through, go through. He had

had no trouble except at Aix, where he had had to turn off to the right by Palette, and as far as the foot of Mont Sainte-Victoire. But it's a pretty road in summer. On foot, you can get through anywhere. In the dry hills the dead don't smell bad; don't really smell at all; or sometimes they smell of the thyme and savory in which they are lying, always in very noble postures because they have died facing a grand landscape. Sight of the free horizon, generally periwinkle-blue, gives the muscles a fluidity that makes them unclench after death. He had observed that, in the pine groves, where the scent of the resin joins with the sun to create an atmosphere like an oven, the corpses he encountered (one of them was a game keeper's) had above all the *mal du siècle*: a certain nonchalance of style and melancholy in their attitudes, a look of ennui, a sort of well-bred contempt. The woods above Palette, when you approach the rocky spurs of Sainte-Victoire, look out over a billowing of hills, a network of little plains, valleys, copses, vistas, and aqueducts as Roman as could be. You are forced to think of the geese of the Capitol, of the Cimbri wrapped in the Nordic mists like processionary caterpillars in their cotton nests. A man dying, especially of cholera and shaken by electric discharges of pain, no longer sees the present, he sees the past and the future through a magnifying glass for several long minutes. Time enough to compose on his face either a convulsion or a smile, according to his character.

He enjoyed talking as he walked. He had had no company for two months, or else only that inconsequential company with whom one must above all never speak one's mind. Death isn't everything; he was realizing that at this instant. It was a great pleasure at last to come upon two young people who had such style and had just vanquished a hamlet. Now he could chatter, provided he wasn't boring them.

Angelo protested. "I like this way of talking," he said to himself. "Every sentence is a story. That's how it is where I come from; what does truth matter? Italy, mother of the arts, all you lack is liberty! He's like Felice Orsini, who is my age but wears a beard and looks old."

"It's to Madame, above all, that I apologize," said the man. "Ladies like us to gild the pill. I'm just an egoist; it's the only thing I am really good at. Actually I get frightened more often than hurt, so I can afford to joke a bit."

"Don't worry about me," said the young woman. "I'm even more of an egoist than you are. I make volumes of French history out of my own adventures, even when I'm dozing in an armchair. Judge from that whether I enjoy listening to you."

The day had been so fine that night fell with infinite slowness. The glints of reddened light that lay along the rough grasses of the plateau moved only with reluctance and took a long time to disappear. They could be seen slowly preparing the delayed leap that would bear them off into the sky. They stretched out until they were like those strands of pale hair that certain spiders hang on the wind, and before disappearing, they wrapped themselves one last time round the naked branches of the trees from which, thread by thread and cautiously, they were picked off by still-burning shadows. The west was sighing with regret.

This man seemed to be at home on the road. He had filled a small clay pipe and started to smoke without slowing his pace. He cast long looks at the landscape and seemed to get something out of everything.

Angelo asked him if he had any idea of the direction to be followed to reach Gap.

"I've something better than an idea," said he, "I have a map."

They stopped for a couple of minutes to look at it. It was no longer light enough to make out the route in detail. At all events, they must go by Saint-Dizier, then Les Laures and eventually Savournon; after that, to judge by the remaining distance to be covered, they had only to ask for Gap.

"Besides," said the man, "by then you'll already be in the mountains."

The cholera fly, apparently, did not rise above a certain altitude. People took refuge on the heights when they could. That was what he himself was doing. He was not going to Gap, there were nearer mountains. He would try to find a village, the smallest possible: two or three houses at the most. There he would wait till it was all over before going down again. He could live on milk. He still had a few sous. He knew he could go without tobacco without becoming too bad-tempered. Anyhow, mountain people don't pay much heed to bad temper; they even consider it a sign of strength. One must always do one's best not to die.

He, too, must have had his troubles with the soldiers.

Not a great deal. It's never amusing to be arrested. They demand all sorts of papers. The first two or three times, one always wonders how one'll get out of it. One never has the right papers, of course. In the end, with practice, one slips away. He had, however, spent eight days in a quarantine in the Haut Var; for after passing around Sainte-Victoire, he had found himself with the Haut Var before him. He had thought that that region was essentially a desert, and that he would be able to walk through it undisturbed; but it proved quite the contrary. When in danger of sudden death, people always have a strong taste for desert places, and these were densely populated. Everyone had had the same idea as he, and the fly had had the same idea as everyone. He came to roads littered with dead. He counted seven lying across his track in less than a league. He took to paths, he walked over hills and fields. He got lost. He went to the outskirts of a small town and was picked up by the soldiers.

Soldiers are like everybody else. At heart, they hate death. This is only natural. But there's the uniform.

He said several things that made Angelo redden. "If he weren't so nonchalant (and yet such a good walker) I'd answer him," he told himself. "But he doesn't think half the things he says. In reality, he's never stopped being frightened. That's where his irony derives from. For all his fear, he's covered almost a hundred leagues on foot, through all this filth which I've only been through, up to now, on horseback." (He was forgetting, very generously, the roofs of Manosque and the nun.)

He had been locked up in the quarantine at Rians.

"When was this?" said the young woman.

"The first days of September."

"You came to Rians by the Vauvenargues road?"

"I passed by Vauvenargues but I didn't come by a road. At a little place called Claps, where there were three houses and a fountain under an oak tree, I was disgusted by the sight I saw. There were four or five corpses there (I didn't count them) in most unpleasant attitudes. It was hot and they must have been lying there at least two days, paying no attention to either the sun or the forces that had been busy on them. That's where I took to the woods."

"I know Claps very well," she said. "You went through the woods of La Gardiole."

"I didn't bother about the name of the woods. I tried to get away as quickly as possible. The cover is fine. It's pines. I whistled a little tune and was glad to get lost: the main thing was to have a view that would take my mind off things."

"Didn't you meet anyone who told you you were passing near the Château de la Valette?"

"I didn't meet anyone, and that's how I wanted it. I did in fact see a château. The house was shut up. There were cocks crowing a little farther on, around a big building that looked inhabited. I didn't take a close look at it. I can only tell you one thing: there wasn't a soul; just the cocks, that's all. But usually where there are cocks crowing there are people living."

"There are sometimes dead people too," thought Angelo. But he could not remember whether the cocks had been crowing in that totally devastated village where he had encountered the cholera for the first time.

"I left that place in July," said the young woman. "It was I who closed the windows of the château. A servant died suddenly after eating some melon. You saw La Valette from the south; to the north there's a little hamlet hardly any bigger than Claps. The next day three people died there. I was alone. I went to take refuge with my aunts at Manosque, which is where we've come from, this gentleman and I."

"You did well to leave," said the man. "Both places. The best would be to leave them all. That's what's hard. It's why I'm walking now, and smoking my pipe."

He described some of the horrors of the quarantine at Rians, which the sunlight he depicted tinged an unbearable red.

"We're in the habit of associating the sun with ideas of joy and health. When we see it in reality acting like an acid on flesh just like our own (and therefore sacred), under the simple pretext that this flesh is dead, we suddenly get a true idea of death, and one which it is most unpleasant to have. And new ideas about the sun, the golden colour it gives to everything, which pleases us so. The blue sky is wonderfully beautiful. A blue face has a queer effect, I can tell you. Yet it's the same blue, or near enough. In any case, similar in every

318

way to the blue that slumbers over the deep places of the sea. In a sandy place, a quarry where I went burrowing for shelter from a storm, I found dry corpses, not an ounce of rottenness; gilded from top to toe. This is very ugly."

He had discovered a curious fact about egoism. "The egoist loves everybody. He's even a glutton. That's my own case, I confess; it's the case with everyone. Now, though, the egoist goes to the desert. Like the saints. But when one's alone, one finds oneself. One becomes a glutton for oneself. And then what happens?" Excesses and basenesses he would rather not mention.

They walked for some time in silence. Night had at length come, black and nearly starless. They saw some fluttering red lights ahead of them. The road began to descend. In a valley two huge braziers had been lit on a sort of apple-green carpet that must be a meadow. The flames illuminated the walls of a little town close by.

"There's Saint-Dizier," said the man. "I was told they had private feuds that one mustn't stick one's nose into. But I see they've been having other feuds, even more private, with the fly."

"I know those pyres," said Angelo. "If they're still busy burning their dead, we haven't progressed a step since Manosque, where this smell of burnt fat has already put me off cutlets for the rest of my life."

Gradually, indeed, a faint odour of burnt fat was replacing the plateau's sharp scent of stones and dry trees.

The young woman had placed her hands over her eyes.

"They're roasting rotten Christians," said the man. "I confess it's almost a sight to gladden the heart, when one knows what bestiality people have sunk to, just because of fear. They must have a talent for it. Who'd have suspected that this little mountain village was actually Sodom and Gomorrah? Who but the fly? I have a feeling that it must be having a good laugh. If you daren't look at that sight, madame, I think you'd do better to put your eyes out. That would spare you the fatigue of holding your hands over your face. Once the cholera's over, there'll still be mirrors to face."

Despite his love of liberty, Angelo was on the point of losing his temper. But he was sufficiently on the side of those who saw rottenness everywhere.

The young woman let fall her hands. She was hardly visible, save in the delicate and tenderly pink reflections of the distant flames. In their doubtless deceptive and in any case very confused light, she looked nonplussed, anxious, somehow caught in the act.

As they drew near, they saw in the darkness the bulk of the town. It was probably a market town: it had the pot-bellied ramparts of an important centre. Though darker than the night, one could make out above its crown of roofs two massive belfries like the horns of a young bullock.

If they kept to the road, they would have to go through the town. Angelo refused.

"We didn't leave Manosque, where they'd already got past burning the dead," he said, "to land once more in a place where they are still reduced to doing so."

"For myself, with no precise goal and travelling light, it's child's play," said the man. "But I expect I'll be obliged to go through kitchen gardens. On foot it's easy to clamber over fences, but with your mule you'd be in a fine mess. Now here, from what I've been told, the cholera's the last thing to worry about. The dead are dead, they're burned, and that's that. The people have got over their fright (which was excessive) by realizing that the plague was a business proposition; that thanks to it they could first make easy money and then allow themselves a good time. They need customers for all that. When people try to avoid them they consider the bread's being taken out of their mouths. And God knows how nasty they turn then! Do you want to know what I think? We ought to go around by the pyres: that'll be the side they aren't watching. If they have an ambush, it's in the dark. They tell themselves that everyone instinctively keeps away from that kitchen – and it doesn't smell very good, to be sure. Let's hold our noses and go that way. Dead people, roasted into the bargain, can't harm anyone. Whereas live ones have all sorts of ideas, such as putting men and women into two different quarantines."

Angelo stopped for a minute to load the young woman's pistol himself. She let him do so. He handed the weapon back to her without a word. He wanted to behave perfectly, and it was very difficult.

The pedestrian seemed to be right. They drew near the pyres, which seemed to be burning by themselves, without seeing anyone or anything but the meadows, made greener by the red brilliance of the flames. They even found an earth track along which the mule walked easily, though with ears pricked towards the greasy smoke rolling low over the grass.

Angelo had taken his little sabre in his hand, but felt himself absurd. "And yet," he thought, "a naked blade, with which I'd strike immediately, will make a much greater impression on these runaway bourgeois than a pistol. For it's easy to press a trigger, and they know it, being themselves capable of such a pretty exploit, which brings its man down without any necessity for courage. At the moment, I feel pretty small myself. That's why I feel stupid with this cabbage-chopper in my hand. But the moment danger comes, it'll be a sabre again: and I know that with such a weapon I can be very frightening."

Thus he did not pay undue attention to the sickening stench from the pyres. Often, without knowing it, he escaped much more general causes of disgust in the same fashion.

At last, after wandering for some time through the tangle of sometimes sunken tracks leading to the different blocks of land belonging to the suburbs, they set foot on a small hard road that climbed up the wooded slopes on the other side of the town.

Quite soon they were in a sparse fir forest, which was purring like a cat. The moon was rising in a murky sky.

"In half an hour's time she'll be out of the clouds and it'll be almost as bright as day. We passed the ticklish spot at the right moment. I confess your little sabre cheered me. When we were walking in the light of the braziers I thought, watching you, that I was at a romantic opera. I had the impression that at any moment you were going to burst into an aria, and I wasn't frightened. Mind you, I trusted you and perhaps you would have used the thing. But anyhow the danger's passed; it always reduces me to such a jelly that afterwards I have to joke. Then I can breathe again. What's more, I'm going to leave you. I'm not going to Gap. And this road's yours, but it takes me out of my way."

Angelo and the young woman bade him good-bye rather coldly. He set off through the woods. He seemed to know what he was about.

"I think we've walked enough for today," said Angelo. "I'd never have believed you were so strong. But let's not overdo it. We shall have to do as much again tomorrow. I like this district less and less. I want to get out of it as quickly as possible. You march like a foot soldier. But in a short while it won't be your head but your knees, your ankles, and your hips that take command, and with these things there's no arguing. If you strain yourself too far, all of a sudden you'll drop like a sack and be unable to put one foot before the other. And suppose we again have to hurry past people who are burning their dead ..."

He even added a certain tenderness to his following remarks. "If I'm not nice to her," he thought, "she'll be obstinate, and I shall end by being stupidly tied to a young woman who can't walk a step and whom I shall feel bound to protect through thick and thin. That wouldn't be funny."

"I am tired, you're right," she said, "and since the road started to climb I've been dragging. You've been kind to act as if you didn't notice, but in five minutes' time I'd have had to tell you that I'm not altogether up to certain circumstances."

"No one can exceed his physical strength. There's nothing to be ashamed of. I'm tired myself."

"You couldn't tell me anything more cheering. I just felt all the heart go out of me, seeing our companion go off gaily on his way, as if he'd just jumped out of bed. He's walked as much as we have."

"He hasn't gone far," said Angelo. "I bet he's simply gone down into the valley to sleep. I know the ways of his kind, especially when they reach a certain age. They'll never let go of anything while you're watching. They're only themselves when they're alone. He hasn't taken his road. He's looking for a corner to lie down in."

Now and then the moon freed itself from the dappled clouds rising from the south. Then its milky brightness gave the theatrical architecture of the beeches the lightness of vapour.

They left the road and moved into the undergrowth. The soil was springy and covered with crackling leaves. They chose a tall beech on the edge of the valley and retired under its cover. Facing them they had a great slab of curdled sky; the edge of each cloud glittered like salt; low on the horizon of black mountains a few stars shone, veiled and confidential; from the wooded valley hollowed out at their feet emerged high branches frosted with moonlight, the way submerged forests rise again from a lake that is drying up. The air was

322

warm and still. Alone in the sky, the slow rising of the clouds gave life to the night, opening and closing over the woods a fan of gleams and shadows.

Angelo pitched their camp at the foot of the beech, where the dead leaves were thick and warm. He hobbled the mule, which immediately dozed off on its feet, and then, sure that they were staying there, lay down peacefully without ceremony.

"Try to sleep," said Angelo.

He again referred to the leather breeches, without the least self-consciousness.

Under the circling beacon of the moon the forest became laden with shadows and mystery, then through its white branches opened up vistas in which the stripped trees assumed tragic poses. Saint-Dizier, hidden by the shoulder of the mountain, threw up occasional red glows into the sky.

"Did you notice," said the young woman, "that the man who's just left us never came close to us while we were walking with him, but took care to keep to his side of the road?"

"It seemed to me quite natural," said Angelo. "Nowadays it's preferable for people to keep away from each other. I dread the death that lurks in the coat of the passer-by. And he dreads the death that's in mine. If he had been too familiar with us, I should have said something about it out loud and he'd have gone back to his place."

"And yet for six days now we've been together, you and I," said the young woman. "I've never seen you shrink from approaching me. And I sleep in your cloak."

"Naturally. What is there to fear?"

"The death that may lurk in my skirt, as in the coat of the passer-by."

Angelo didn't reply. She asked if he was asleep.

"Yes," he said. "I was dropping off."

"Peacefully, by my side?"

"Of course."

"Without dreading the death I might give you, the same as anyone else?"

"No, not just the same. I'm sorry," he added. "I was asleep when I answered just then. That's not what I meant. I meant to say that we are companions and have nothing to fear from each other, because on the contrary we protect one another. We're travelling together. We try not to catch the plague but, if you were to do so, do you suppose I'd make a bolt for it?"

She did not reply and almost immediately after gave the deep sighs of sleep.

The night was one of vast, motionless peace, except for the sky, where the clouds were soundlessly moving; but even this movement, powerful, slow, and regular, added to the serenity of the silence. The mule's nostrils snorted; racing field-mice ruffled the dry leaves; from time to time the big branches stretched and groaned. A faint rumble, like the one that comes out of deep wells, filled all space.

Down in the valley a wood owl began to hoot. Then it uttered a long, composed phrase. It was not an owl but a clarinet, peacefully playing a sad and tender tune.

"He didn't go very far," thought Angelo. "He talked a great deal but he said nothing of what he really meant, nothing essential. Like all of us. He waited till he was alone."

The rather absurd warble of the clarinet became transfigured by the swelling echoes, the white décor of the forest, the ceremonious prologue that the beeches rounded out slowly and ceaselessly into noble gestures beneath the moon.

"Those are Mozart's 'German Dances'," said the young woman.

"I thought you were asleep."

"I wasn't asleep, I had my eyes closed in peace."

Day came with a dirty and sombre sky.

"We must move on at once," said Angelo, "and find shelter. It's going to rain."

They quickly boiled the tea, encouraging the fire with dry beech leaves that flared up briskly. They ate some cornstarch, but without much appetite.

"I am thirsty for cold water," said the young woman. "This weather, heavy with rain, slows me down."

"The plague has a predilection for organisms that are tired and cold. It's unpleasant walking in the rain, and where we are going there are heights where in cloudy weather it's very cold for people with wet clothes. I'm afraid of houses, but I'm also afraid of rain, indeed that's perhaps what I fear most on your account. We have to choose. And above all, we must get on our way. We may have the luck to find a hut by this forest track or, better still, a cave. I would love a drink of cold water too. I dream so much of unhealthy drinks that I've only to close my eyes to hear fountains flowing. But let's think of keeping alive."

They walked through hilly woods under an increasingly overcast sky that made threatening gestures. The gusts of warm wind smelt of water. Rain scampered like rats among the leaves. From the top of a knoll they looked out over the great forest through which they were passing. It was thick as fleece. It covered a humped, dark blue country, without much hope. The trees were selfishly rejoicing in the imminent rain. These vast vegetable expanses, living a well-organized life, perfectly indifferent to anything that was not their immediate concern, were as frightening as the cholera.

There were no longer even any crows. They saw a falcon searching for something quite other than corpses.

Fortunately the track was clearly marked. Though not a carriage road, it sufficed for the mule, and above all it showed signs of having been kept up. It clearly existed for some reason, and led to inhabited places. At all events, very remote ones. Though Angelo and the young woman forced their pace, they saw nothing but trees and undergrowth the entire morning. The clouds had finally resolved themselves into a fine drizzle that barely seeped below the pines but spread the sound of the sleeping sea over the whole countryside. The indifference of it all was such that Angelo found a distant roll of thunder most attractive. He much preferred to be assaulted directly. At last, as they were crossing the donkey-back of a ridge, they saw at one and the same time the black workings of the sky, and about a quarter of a league ahead, the reddish patch of a clearing and the front of a large house.

The autumn storm, indolent but brutal, struck two or three heavy blows in the neighbouring valleys. Dense curtains of rain fell all around in the woods. The sound made the mule prick up its ears and step out more vigorously. The young woman held on to the strap of the pack-saddle. They ran. The downpour caught them. Yet they had time to see that they were crossing a sort of park before they were in shelter under the porch of the house's front door.

"Dry your hair quickly," said Angelo. "Don't catch cold in your head. We've got here just in time."

After a mild flash and a rumble that shook up echoes like cauldrons, the rain began to fall with violence. The enormous house, deserted and acting as a drum for the rain, increased their sense of solitude.

"This is a curious place," said Angelo. "The box bushes have been trimmed and the trees planted in avenues, more than a hundred years ago, to judge from the thickness of those maple trunks that form the drive. What's this barrack doing in the woods? Can't you smell sulphur?"

"Yes. But if you're trying to frighten me, it's no good. I'm not thinking of the devil. I remember this smell of rotten eggs. It woke me up in my closed carriage the first time I passed through this district. According to my husband, there are four or five villages about here with sulphur springs, and people bathe in them. This barrack must be simply a sort of hotel used in summer during the watering season."

"I only thought of the devil vaguely," said Angelo, "and merely because the devil's better than nothing. So you think we're in the right direction, since you've already smelled this smell on the way to Gap?"

"If we're on the outskirts of one of those villages, we've only ten or twelve leagues left before reaching Gap, and Théus is three more beyond. I remember too that we went through woods. But it was night. I was riding in a carriage and not worrying. I was a long way from supposing that one day I'd have to find my way on foot through these forests."

For conscience's sake, Angelo knocked on the big door against which they were sheltering. His blows echoed down empty corridors. The rain had settled in. The thickness of the clouds was bringing twilight before its time.

"We should be able to get inside," said Angelo, "light a fire in a fireplace, and spend the night under cover. Stay here. I'll scout along the walls. There's sure to be an easier door to force than this one."

He found one that led into a storeroom, and there they unloaded the mule. It was a harness room; the stable was behind; one could enter it freely. They scraped up from the racks enough oats and dry straw for their beast.

"This looks too good not to explore it further, don't you think?"

"Provided we keep our pistols handy," said Angelo.

He greatly enjoyed listening to all the suspicious noises of the deserted house and exaggerated their strangeness.

Three steps led them into a corridor. It was long and ended at a glass door full of phantasmagoria. It connected with offices and a great kitchen like a torture chamber with its spits, wheels for dumbwaiters, coppers, and smell of burnt fat. Somewhere the rain was drumming on skylights, making stairwells echo.

The glass door was merely on the latch. Beyond there broadened out a rather pretentious hall. The daylight filtering through the chinks of the shutters was only just enough to reveal on the walls the faint gleams of what must be the colours and gilding of painted panels, doubtless hunting-scenes. Groping his way forward, Angelo touched the edge of a billiard table set in the middle of the hall.

"I've found something very interesting," said the young woman.

"What?"

"A candlestick with candles."

It took a little time to get the wick to light – it was old. At each spark of the tinder the hall and its colours opened out in the darkness like a flower. And indeed, when the candles were lit, they saw that they were in a vast room with every square inch gilded in a bourgeois and banal style. Chairs stood in rows along the walls, under Pomonas, Venuses, trophies of fruit and game, all far larger than life.

"Here you are again with a candlestick in your hand," said Angelo, "like the first time I saw you, at Manosque. But that evening you were in a long dress."

"Yes, all alone. I used to dress in the evening. I had even put on some rouge and powder. It was a way of giving myself courage. But when I took the plunge, to end by meeting you and arriving here, I only brought my riding-skirt and pistols. One finally knows just what to do about the cholera."

"You impressed me."

"That's because I was frightened. I impress even my husband then."

The hall gave on the entrance hall, out of which there rose a wide, curving staircase, with the rain drumming above it.

Going upstairs, Angelo advised caution.

"For me," he said, "cholera is a staircase that I go up or down on tiptoe, to find myself before a half-open door that I push open, and I have to step over a woman of whom there's nothing left but hair, a corpse in a nightcap, or linen that's not pretty to see. Stay behind me."

There were no corpses. In all the rooms the bedding had been carefully rolled, beaten, folded, and camphorated. The floors were clean, the seats and armchairs under dust-covers. The tall pier-glasses reflected the light of the candles and the two anxious faces.

"We shall be able to sleep in beds."

At the end of the corridor they entered rather more boldly into a large room used as a *salon*, less overloaded with gilding than the hall, but florid enough with its scrolls and cupids.

"All we have to do is light a fire in this fireplace and stay here."

They even found a tall pressure-lamp half filled with oil, and three more candlesticks complete with new candles.

Angelo remembered having seen a pile of firewood near the kitchen. They returned downstairs to fetch some. The wood had been carefully stacked against a door, and they moved it aside. When tapped, the door sounded hollow. It was locked, but not firmly, and Angelo sprang the bolt with his knife.

"Here's something funny," said Angelo.

He had just discovered some steps down to a cellar.

"Come along."

They descended five or six steps and found themselves on a floor of soft sand, under cobwebbed vaults and facing standard racks of empty bottles. But in a corner the earth seemed to have been raised as though by a group of moles, and by scratching the sand, they uncovered a whole nest of full bottles, carefully sealed. There was red wine and white, and even some liqueur, too transparent and fluid to be marc; it must be kirsch. At any rate, there were more than fifty bottles of wine there.

"It's perhaps the only chance we'll have of a cool drink without risk," said Angelo. "This wine's been sheltered from the flies for over five years, if the date on the labels is to be trusted; and why not? There was no cholera then. What do you say to it?"

"I'm even thirstier than you," said the young woman. "I was think-ing of our daily maize with horror. See if there's a light red wine."

328

"There is. But we must eat before we drink. We've been marching with just a little tea inside. Be thankful we've got the maize. Besides, I'm going to make the polenta with white wine. That'll take away fatigue."

There was a very handsome corkscrew in the drawer of the kitchen table and glasses on the dresser. But Angelo was adamant. He lit a fire in the drawing-room, set the glasses to boil in a saucepan of water, and began to stir his polenta with wine.

"You're old as the streets," said the young woman. "Much older than my husband."

He was sure he was acting as one should; he did not see what he could be blamed for. Naïvely he replied: "That surprises me. I'm twenty-six."

"And he's sixty-eight," she said, "but he takes more risks than you."

"I'm not running a risk if I let you drink on an empty stomach. It s you who take the risk. It's easy to take such a responsibility if you are indifferent."

The *polenta au vin blanc*, very sweet and as liquid as soup, was appetizing to swallow. Afterwards it lay on the stomach like red lead.

"You think you're stronger than one of my old hussars," thought Angelo. "They eat polenta cooked with wine when they're in a tight spot. It's stupid things like that that give one strength of character."

He uncorked a bottle of red wine and pushed it towards the young woman. He drank, in quick succession, four or five glasses of a thick, very strong and dark wine, which resembled *nebbia* but had a more delicate taste. She emptied her bottle as quickly. They had been wanting something besides tea for a long time.

"My husband is not indifferent," she said.

"Then where is he? Dead?"

"No. If he were dead I wouldn't be here."

"Where would you be?"

"Certainly dead."

"You don't do things by halves."

"You don't understand me at all. I'd have nursed him and have died from the plague; if you must have everything explained."

"Then it's not so certain. I've nursed more than twenty cholera victims; I've washed corpses, any amount of them. I'm still on my

329

feet. So you might be on yours, and here, even if your husband had died with all the honours due to his rank."

"Don't argue. I should be dead. Or at least I should long to be. Let's talk of something else."

"Of what?"

"I don't know. We've found plenty of subjects for conversation up to now."

"Yes, pistols and sabre, then sabre and pistols."

"The subject is inexhaustible and full of instruction. As a body-guard you're certainly first class, I admit. As soon as the situation becomes hair-raising, you come into your own."

"That's my trade."

"Before I met you, I little imagined such a trade existed among men."

"I'm not forced to be like everyone else."

"Don't worry, you're not. Indeed, I wonder how one should take you."

"I don't want to be taken. On the contrary."

"And you like that?"

"Very much."

"You're not French?"

"I'm Piedmontese. I told you, and it's obvious."

"What's obvious has four or five names, all very fine ones. Is that Piedmont or your character?"

"I don't see what you call very fine. I do what suits me. I was happy when I was a child. I want to go on being so."

"You had a lonely childhood?"

"No. My mother's only sixteen years older than I. I also had my foster-brother Giuseppe, and his mother, who was my nurse, Teresa. She'd be astonished if she knew that I stir polenta for ladies."

"What does she suppose you do to ladies?"

"Something grandiose; to ladies and the whole world."

"Is she capable of knowing what this is?"

"Very. She does it herself, all the time."

"Doesn't that get in the way?"

"No. The house demands it, and has done so for a long time."

"Who are you? You've told me your first name: Angelo, and perhaps your surname –"

"My surname's Pardi."

"– without my being much further forward, except to call to you more easily for help when I need it . . ."

"I know that your name is Pauline."

"Pauline de Théus since my marriage. My maiden name was Colet. My father was a doctor at Rians."

"I never knew my father."

"I never knew my mother. She died when I was born."

"I – I don't know if he's dead. No one knows; no one cares. We've done very well without him."

"Tell me about your mother."

"She wouldn't appeal to you."

"All mothers appeal to me. Mine, it seems, was very pretty, very gentle, very delicate, and she wanted me. I've had plenty of time to love a ghost. Smiling at my father never altogether satisfied me, even in my cradle, if I can judge by the unfulfilled desires that have remained in me. And yet my father was an easy man to love, he could be happy with nothing at all: that's to say, with me all his life. But a poor doctor's house in Rians! A big white village, among rocks, where two worn valleys intersect, bare as a hand, down which rolls the wind, and only the wind, all the time. A big village worn away by the wind; the angle of every wall gnawed like a bone by a winter fox. Much wilder country than any we've crossed, and I know nothing sadder than its sun.

"I was alone most of the time, or with hunchbacked Anaïs; a woman of pure gold. Everyone was of gold. My father was of gold. No one ever hurt me: on the contrary. Everywhere I was caressed, cajoled, worn down, scraped by hands, lips, beards, just as that tense, restless countryside is by the wind. I was restless; I loved my little felt slippers because they let me move without a sound, straight as a die, step by step, and steal up to the creaking window, the groaning door, and listen to them from close to. I had to be sure; it was far more important than fear. Sure of what? Sure of everything.

"When I heard your stealthy steps in the house at Manosque, where I was alone in the middle of the cholera, I took a candlestick and went to see what it was. I always have to go and see. I can't run away. I've no refuge anywhere, except in what threatens me. I get so frightened! Boldness is the lap I turn to. I think I'm a bit drunk."

"Don't let that worry you. Drink. We need wine. But take some of this dark one. It's like a wine from my country and it contains tannin. That's what you want when you're facing a long march."

"You know too many things."

"I know nothing. The first time I had to command men (and I had a thousand advantages, especially the plume on my helmet, gold on my sleeves, and the walls of the Pardi palace seated on the horse with me) I asked myself: 'By what right?' Before me I had fifty moustaches that one could have grasped in handfuls; and Giuseppe, my foster-brother, in the ranks, at attention. He and I had had another fight the day before, like dogs, and with sabres. But there I have the advantage. When we were little, his mother wanted him to call me 'My Lord'. When Teresa wants something, and particularly if it's to do with me, she sees that she gets it. He used to call me 'My Lord', and add what he had to between his teeth. We used to fight. We slept in each other's arms in the same bed. He's my brother. He was stiff as a ramrod on his horse. I said to myself: 'If one day you order him to charge, he'll charge.' I'd taken a slice out of his forearm the day before and we'd spent part of the night weeping together. It was a good three days before we went for each other again. He was my orderly. I put the captain in charge of the parade, called Giuseppe, and we went off for a walk in the woods."

"I never believed you were an officer."

"I'm a colonel; commission bought and paid for."

"Then what are you doing in France? – in these peasant's clothes?"

"I'm in hiding, or rather I was in hiding. I'm going home now."

"Drunk with the desire for vengeance."

"I've nothing to avenge. I'm drunk this evening like you, but that's all. It's the others who want to avenge themselves on me."

"Followed by the faithful Giuseppe?"

"Followed by the faithful Giuseppe, who must also be roaming about the roads and woods now, after waiting for me at Sainte Colombe and sending me to the devil."

"– and by Lavinia."

"The hatched girl."

"Why the hatched girl?"

"My mother christened her that. 'One might say I'd hatched her out like a hen,' she said. Lavinia came to the Pardi palace three apples high and because she was three apples high. The rest is too delicate to tell."

"Delicate for whom?"

"Delicate for everyone."

"You daren't tell me what your mother employed Lavinia to do? And why she christened her 'the hatched girl'? And why she had to be only three apples high?"

"You're very rash," said Angelo. "You don't know me. Suppose I'm a brigand. There are people at home who have good manners and even courage. They're all republicans besides. But there always comes a moment when they think of themselves. Then, look out! Now, I've been drinking and you give me an excuse for losing my temper. How can you imagine that I daren't? It's a childish story, that's all. My mother used to stand and make Lavinia burrow under her skirts. The little girl had to push her hand under my mother's stays and smooth out her petticoat. That's why she was hatched and brooded as though by a hen. It wasn't very terrible, and Lavinia was still performing her task just before she left with Giuseppe. And about that too there's a lot to be said. She didn't go off with Giuseppe for love. The women at home like love, it's true, but they'll get up in the middle of the night joyfully to take part in some secret and heroic deed, especially if it's clearly established that their only interest is in the adventure, or in the pleasure of brushing against, touching, some sombre anxious man with great Brutus-like gestures, listening to his talk and serving him. We belong to a country where people like to have hobnobbed with the man being shot in the main square. Our political executions are morning spectacles much sought after, because everyone has a little bit of his heart involved in the ceremony.

"My mother does nothing unfeelingly. She's the Primavera. She constantly has her finger under my nose to make me raise my head and look up in the air."

"You were right. I don't like your mother."

"Because she's not here."

"Perhaps: but above all because you are."

"It would have been easy to give things a different turn, if I hadn't had that finger under my nose. Had I been prepared to look downward, I had a silver spoon in my mouth all right. Giuseppe reproaches me often enough on that account. But I don't believe revolutions are murders, or if they are, I give up. People know that. That's why I get shot at with red-hot bullets from both sides. I once killed a man. An informer. Is it an illusion for me to say that an informer's a man like anyone else? Reasons of expediency are always bad. Believing that there can be two weights and two measures is bad too. It would have been easy to settle his hash at some street corner. Put out the street lamps and skewer him. Just take one's hand out of one's pocket. With a couple of louis I'd have had as many petty assassins at my beck and call as there are men, or even women, in Turin. It would have been enough to wave my arm, as they say: then stay cosily in my bed while the thing was being done independently of me. That's what they call saving oneself. But it happens that there's another little difference between me and them. I'm a good orator only when talking to myself. If one must follow great examples, if that is the price of the liberty and happiness of the people, I should despise myself for not being the first to be guilty of it. One kills, perhaps, but one doesn't acquire a soul vicariously."

"So you are one of those people who provide food for conversation and make such a stir by hiding in the forests on the other side of the Alps? But why talk of Brutus? Everyone more or less has killed a man. If modesty has any charm, therein lies its greatest. Will you believe me if I tell you that I was courted with a corpse devoured by the crows and foxes? Did I tell you my husband was sixty-eight? That usually makes people open their eyes. You never batted an eyelid. That's because you're indifferent to me, but –"

"I'm not indifferent to you at all. I've been making fires and polenta for you for ten days, and instead of going about my own business, I'm pushing on with you to Gap –"

"Where I shall, I hope, find my husband again. For I love him. That doesn't seem to move you very much either."

"It's quite natural, since you married him."

"One comes upon a certain gallantry often, in what you say. It's true, in spite of his great name and fortune, if I hadn't loved him I wouldn't have married him. Thank you. The fact remains, he is nearly forty-five years older than I. And that still doesn't astonish you?"

334

"No. What does astonish me is your way of harping on his age all the time."

"It's one of my weaknesses. Would you like an Amazon? Perhaps I am one indeed, and precisely over this. It's not his age I harp on, it's his handsomeness. Marriages like mine are always suspected of having some sordid interest. Is it really a weakness to want to clear oneself of that at all costs?"

"Let's say, to reassure you, that as far as I'm concerned you're merely insulting me. I know how extravagant all my worries are: they make me look a simpleton. But you shouldn't be so sure. I recognize the worth of people very quickly. The idea that you could behave in a vulgar way would never enter my head."

"With you I find myself constantly being abashed," said the young woman. "And it's far from disagreeable. I've suddenly forgotten what I was going to tell you for the sake of what I'd like to say here and now, if you promise not to answer."

"I promise."

"No one has any but blind hopes. Be less candid. And now here's what I meant to tell you first. By dint of being a lonely little girl in a poor doctor's house at Rians, the day came when I was sixteen. From door to door the world had grown up around me. I sometimes used to go dancing under the limes. I had seen girls get married and even become pregnant. The young bourgeois of the place courted me, that is to say, they spun round before me like plums in boiling water.

"The country, as I told you, is rough and has no springtime. My father never had a carriage. We weren't so poor as all that, but the carriage would have been no use to him on the hill paths. He went his rounds on horseback. He bought me a mare so that I could accompany him. So I came to know the happiness of trotting and even galloping over those uplands. They're so vast that one can easily believe one is fleeing, and even getting away.

"One evening, after a storm, returning down the valley, at a bend of the stream which had suddenly swollen, we found a man who had been thrown from his horse and hurt. The water was half over him. Though unconscious, he was clutching the mud and gave the impression that death itself could not stop him from fighting. His chief injury was a pistol wound in the chest. Naturally, we took him home. I had been hardening myself with my terrors and still more, for several years, with my desires. That abandoned body which had to be saved, and which for that very reason let itself be taken in one's arms, that unconscious face which still wouldn't relax its frown, touched me more than anything else ever will. Back at home, my father laid the wounded man out on our kitchen table. He boiled some water, took off his coat, and rolled up his shirtsleeves. The man's first movement, when he came round, was a menacing gesture. But he recovered his wits with amazing promptness; he understood at once why my father had that little, gleaming knife in his hand, and he gave a beautiful smile, spoke a few words of apology, and submitted courageously.

"I don't expect you will be either surprised or roused to indignation when I tell you that the bullet, once extracted, turned out to be from a musket. And more, from one of the regulation police muskets, my father said. The man's clothes, though soiled with mud and blood, were plainly of fine cloth and very well cut. That sprang to the eyes of peasants like us. Under his spotless silk shirt he wore an emblazoned cross, attached to his neck by a gold chain so supple, so delicately woven that I thought at first it was made of a woman's hair.

"To be brief, we installed him in a room on the first floor, where he remained in seclusion. I looked after him alone. He quickly regained his health. My father was quite astonished. 'This man is at least sixty,' he said, 'and he's picking up like a youngster.' I remembered then that I had seen his chest covered with thick grey hair, and that this had had to be cut with scissors to apply the dressing.

"He had been with us for about a month without anyone knowing. I was simply thrilled about this situation. In the early days his alert eyes kept watching my father. His look then was hard and even cruel. I knew that, most rashly and at the cost of painful effort, he had got up in spite of his dressing, and that he had a loaded pistol under his bolster. But he never mistrusted me. I could go into his room at any hour of the day or night; he never jumped. That meant he could recognize my step, even at its lightest, and that I had his confidence. I found happiness in a thousand tiny details of that nature. At length, after two weeks, he simply declared to my father that he offered him his apologies a second time. 'And this time for good,' he added. He had the gift of putting much grace into few words.

"One evening when I was taking the air under the lime walk, I saw a stranger leaning against a tree, watching me. He was awkwardly clad in his Sunday best. I hurried indoors. I saw that the man had followed me and was approaching the house. I ran upstairs, two at a time, to our guest's room. 'Don't worry,' he said, when I had described the man, 'ask him in and bring him up here. I was expecting him.' And indeed, the man immediately took on the manner of a servant. When night had fallen, he went to fetch his mount from where he had concealed it and brought a trunk with clean clothes. He went away, no doubt with orders. Two weeks later, he returned openly and in livery. He brought with him an extremely handsome horse with an English saddle.

"We never knew how he had managed to let his servant know the first time. He kept it even from me, and if I now have some ideas on that subject they are purely and simply ideas. We were equally surprised, about then, at the stories running round Rians. Monsieur de Théus had apparently been our friend for a long time, and if he had honoured us by visiting and staying with us, it was purely out of friendship.

"There remained, however, that ball from a regulation police musket, which nobody mentioned and which I kept in a little silk bag hung around my neck.

"Monsieur de Théus was soon able to stand and even to eat at our table. He treated me like a lady, with the greatest attention. I was enchanted and expected even better. He did not disappoint me.

"He begged for my company on the rides my father had prescribed for him. We went only once. We returned to where I had found him. But he insisted that I push on further into the scrub. We walked our horses for a good quarter of an hour along a narrow earth track.

"'I've only seen this bit of country in a storm and a flash of lightning,' he told me, 'but I'm looking for a tall ilex and I think that's it in front of us.' The solitude of that countryside is never paradisiacal; but on that day it was. He made me dismount. He pulled back the bushes of clematis that were choking the trunk of the ilex.

337

"'Come and see,' he said. I went up to him. He put his arm around my waist. At the first glance I saw a musket beside some torn shreds of uniform. There was the fleshless corpse of a sort of soldier with red facings. Finally he showed me the man's skull: the forehead was blown in.

"'That's my pistol shot,' he said. 'I was blinded by the rain and the lightning when I took aim, and I already had his bullet in my chest. Must I tell you it's a gendarme or can you see it well enough? I shouldn't like you to believe that I can be shot down easily or without risk,' he added. This was said so tenderly that it was almost like cooing.

"When we had found this wounded man in the mud of the stream, I had not connected it with an event that had occurred a week before on the road from Saint-Maximin to Aix. Monsieur de Théus put all his grace into making me do so. He reminded me of the stage coach that had been attacked on the Pourrières slope and plundered of all the money it was transporting for the Treasury, in spite of its police escort."

"Those attacks on coaches, especially the ones transporting your government's bullion, seem to be quite a local industry," said Angelo. "When I was at Aix last year, I remember the thing happening three times in the space of six months, both on the road you mention, on the Avignon road, and on the one that goes up to the Alps."

"So you've lived at Aix?"

"I spent two years there."

"We were neighbours," said the young woman. "La Valette, where I've lived since my marriage (it's our home), is only just three leagues to the east, in that part of Sainte-Victoire which turns pink at each sunset. We might have met. I often used to come to Aix, sometimes on quite social occasions."

"In which I never took part. I lived rather like a savage. I only visited the fencing-masters and knew a few of the officers at the garrison (from a distance and simply as opponents). But I used to go for long rides in the woods, precisely in the part where the mountain turns pink in the evening. I may have been on your land. I said so to myself yesterday when you were talking about the Château de la Valette with our clarinet-player. I remember seeing, through the pines, the front of a big house that seemed to me to have a soul."

"If it had a soul, it was ours. Don't think I'm just being silly. If you'd merely said it was beautiful, I'd have been less sure. All the big country houses around Aix are beautiful, but soul – that requires something more, and I think we have it. If you've seen the celebrated face of La Valette, that self-assured nobility which confirmed me in my feelings, you can't possibly have forgotten it."

"I did in fact wonder what they could be like, the passionate creatures capable of living in such a place."

"One of them is before you. Have you looked at her enough? Where did you live, in Aix?"

"Away from home: and that's saying everything. An exile, an outlaw, has to grow accustomed to possessing nothing of value but himself. I at least had the consolation of not having fled. How often have I blessed the folly that forced me to leave my country! A murder, even in legitimate self-defence – as was the case – would never have left me any peace in any surroundings. The man I killed was selling republicans to the Austrian government, and his victims were dying in prison. But there are never good reasons for cowardice; precisely because he was ignoble, it was essential for me not to be. I killed him in a duel. He had a fair chance. I've been reproached for risking my life. The defenders of the people haven't apparently the right to indulge in nobility. Really, I believe every one was delighted; for me the choice lay between prison and flight. In the first you kick the bucket, usually from colic, which isn't very glorious; and flight means *squaring your shoulders* and becoming a rat. You see, I was above all embarrassing my friends. I left my home in full uniform and at a walk. As I was going up into the mountains, near Cezana, I heard galloping behind me. I dismounted and picked a little bunch of the daffodils with which the fields were covered. I was wearing my plumed helmet and gold-braided blue uniform, and all the trimmings. The *carabinieri* gave me a regular salute. I realized that my friends had reckoned poorly. We are ultimately a daffodil-loving people.

"That made it possible for me to live at Aix, in the house of a good woman who professed, I think, to keep house for a priest. It was a house with two doors, three if you count the one into the garden. But I preferred to use this garrison town to keep my wrist supple. My mother sent me money regularly through

Marseille. I bought what I needed. I took a fencing-master and went to the school.

"I imagine you've kept your musket ball in its silk bag, so you won't laugh if I tell you that in my purse I have an old envelope containing some bits of dried grass, like tea: they're my little bunch of daffodils from Cezana. I like that."

"So you didn't move in good society?"

"I moved in excellent society, particularly that of Alexandre Petit – they called him 'Alexander the Little'. That was their nickname for a lanky old stick who handles a sabre like a god. He and I taught each other a lot of things."

"*Good* society would also have taught you some very curious and useful things, especially about the Gordian knot that strangles men of liberal sentiments. Often it's not a bad thing to entrust it to cool fingers; they dispatch more swiftly than the sabre. There are some very pretty women in Aix."

"I sometimes took part in fencing matches in front of them."

"You must have been their darling . . ."

"Yes, they made a fine tapestry. I like tapestries. I've often dreamed of being condemned to death by a potentate in a ceremonial chamber with walls tapestried from, say, the cantos of Ariosto. The assassins are behind the door and as I advance towards them I gaze at the woollen smile of Angelica or the tender eyes of a cross stitch Bradamante. But the sentence of death is the essential thing."

"We've drunk too much," said the young woman. "Another five minutes and we shall be talking in verse. Don't you think we should try to sleep?"

They chose two rooms with facing doors.

Angelo used his drunken energy to make a square bed in his room as in barracks.

He woke up in the middle of the night. The rain was raging; he heard the rattling of the windows and the tumultuous stir of the woods. Thunder rolled in the distance. He remembered the young woman.

"We got into this house easily," he thought, "and others may do the same. We're not the only ones on the roads, and in weather like this people take shelter anywhere. They might come ferreting in here. If

340

she saw a man come into her room, especially one got up like the clarinetist, she'd be frightened."

He unmade his square bed, dragged the mattress into the corridor without a sound, and lay down outside the young woman's door. Once sure he was properly across it, he fell asleep.

# 13

ANGELO HAD THE WIT to remove his paraphernalia very early. When the young woman entered the room in which they had spent the evening, he had already made the tea and some polenta, this time salted.

They found the mule still in the stable. The animal was in a good temper. It was no longer raining, but the weather remained threatening and bent on every sort of caprice. The clouds were rolling up from the south in tremendous haste. The woods, stripped of many of their leaves, were almost transparent, as in winter. It was rather cold.

"Let's go," said Angelo, "but let's get this clear first: you're to obey me. Put on my cloak and get on to the mule. In an hour's time you'll walk for a bit, and so on. Chilled sweat means instant cholera. Believe me. You must take care of yourself."

The young woman seemed preoccupied and almost ashamed. She made no bones about wrapping herself in the big cloak and mounting the mule. Angelo took its bridle.

The track climbed up some rather steep slopes and finally emerged at the edge of the woods, on to a wide dark plateau over which the clouds were brushing closely. Here the wind blew in gusts through an icy mist. Only the clouds of spray chased by the squalls over the scrubland gave any life to these desert wastes.

Angelo turned up the collar of his velvet jacket. His thick clothes covered him well.

"Long live Giuseppe and Lavinia," he thought; "they foresaw everything. That's true love."

For a heart like his, smitten with liberty, these inhuman solitudes had a certain charm. Neither was he unaware that the fine rain was giving his handsome brown hair the heavy, tumbling look of acanthus leaves.

"How *satisfied* a cold character would be in my place," he added, "but I have a crazy soul, I can't help it. I need Ariosto. There, yes, I'm at my ease."

They walked for over three hours before reaching the end of a stony track that wound among box and juniper bushes, and a whole vegetation contorted by long subjection to the wind. The horizons, smothered by the low sky, revealed nothing but the ceaseless assault of the clouds. They went through several showers, rapid but dense and as if studded with splinters of ice. The young woman had covered her head with the big hood and let herself docilely ride along, without a word.

The track descended into a little valley, forded a stream swollen by the rain, turned a shoulder of grey rock, and suddenly entered a hamlet of about ten little grey houses hidden under dusty grey clouds. In spite of the smell of fires, the peacefully smoking chimneys, and the nice warm windows, Angelo urged on the mule. But at least there were evident signs of health here.

"We must go as far as we can," said Angelo. "You're sensible to let yourself be carried quietly. Stay as you are, leave everything to me. Let's push on. There may already be a fall of snow at any moment on these heights. Let's hurry and cross them."

The track took them along a ravine, and climbed through small potato-fields, almost bare but well cared for. Then it entered some thickets of Russian oaks, quite tall and well grown, still covered with their golden leaves, in which the wind and the rain made a considerable clatter. Gradually, sliding from side to side of the broadening ravine, it reached once more the region of box bushes, of wild scrub, and the raised desert overrun by the marble-dust of the rain.

The weather grew more and more alarming. The clouds dragged along flush with the bushes, in spite of the sharp cold. The thunder snarled several times on the left. The mule showed bad temper. The young woman suggested getting down.

"Stay where you are," said Angelo. "This brute will walk; if I need to, I'll even make it run."

He employed the method used by mountain artillerymen: with soldierly promptness, he got busy on one of the animal's ears, and it immediately stopped its acting up.

Heavy showers and squalls now came in uninterrupted succession. The whole sky was enveloped in black clouds. At length, with a quivering flash of lightning, even before the thunder crashed, dense and continuous rain began to fall.

Angelo was so busy goading the mule and running ahead to look for any kind of shelter, perhaps a big tree in this welter of water, that he only noticed the path was ascending when he stopped for lack of breath. Without realizing it, he passed some ruined houses, then afterwards recollected that he had just caught a glimpse, through the rain, of a sort of vault. He turned the mule back and plunged with it under an archway. He had entered the remains of a cellar or vaulted barn. Outside, the flood was drowning the ruins of an old village.

Hampered though she was by the huge cloak, the young woman sprang down with agility.

"You're soaking," she said, "and it's you who will catch that fatal chill you spoke of."

"I'm going to make a fire," said Angelo.

But there was no wood in this cellar, and besides, the rain was now so headlong that water was already seeping through the vault.

They had been there for some time, almost struck dumb by the violence of the storm, when they heard an odd noise. It was the noise made by the downpour on a large blue umbrella.

This apparatus, astonishing in its colour and dimensions, seemed to be struggling all by itself against the squall, so completely did it conceal the man who was carrying it. And yet he was a big, jovial man, tightly belted into a peculiar-looking riding-coat.

"I've been waving to you for over five minutes, shouting at you and banging against my windows," the man said to them with bluff cheerfulness. "You look like two chickens that have found a knife. Come into my house opposite. This is no moment for larking about. Come along."

Through the density of the rain and clouds tearing through this high place, the village appeared to be in complete ruin; only the stumps of walls were left. The man in the riding-coat led them across a sort of square cluttered with bushes and grass; he manoeuvred his enormous umbrella with a sailor's skill. He opened a stable door and they pushed the mule inside.

"We'll attend to him later," he said. "Come in here."

Angelo and the young woman saw, to their amazement, shelves full of books in the midst of an indescribable disorder of many other objects. It was very warm, and Angelo shivered.

344

"Mademoiselle can study this little engraving – it represents Moscow," said the man, "(count the domes and the spans of the bridges, it's most instructive) – while this young man will please strip down in front of the fire and give himself a thorough rubdown. I detest pneumonia. For twenty years I've been saying velvet's idiotic stuff to wear, at least in these parts. As soon as it's wet it smells like a dog, and it takes the devil of a time to dry. Rub hard. Give me that towel."

He took it away from Angelo and began to rub him really hard. He was a powerful and determined man. Angelo lost his breath and turned scarlet from head to foot in no time.

"Wrap yourself up in this blanket and sit down, not by the fire but in it. I want to see you roast. And drink this: it's rum, and not from the grocer's. Bottoms up. This young lady's clothes are dry as salt! How many domes and spans are there?"

"Thirty-two," said the young woman.

"You're astonishing!" he said. "That's correct. She really did count them! Thirty-two. The joke is that there are thirty-three. See that little thing there? When I get bored, I count it in. You can't quite tell if it's a dome or an arch, pork or bacon, but it makes thirty-three and it's good to find something new at these moments."

The room was lit by the great blaze in the fireplace. The tall window looking out over the ruins did not admit much light: its small panes were misted over on the outside by the clouds rushing past at ground level, and inside by a thick border of dust. The flames, leaping powerfully from enormous logs, lit up the huge clutter of furniture; it was sumptuous but badly worn, and every piece was weighed down with fat tomes and piles of papers, on top of which were precariously perched jugs, cans, bowls, basins, bottles, pans, ladles, pipes of all sizes, all shapes, and even drawers full of kitchen utensils. Shelves loaded with rows of books sagging like grain in the wind ran all along the walls. The round, square, and oval tables, the commodes collapsing under the weight of old papers and leaning to right and left, the chests, writing-desks, and stools set all over the place, with a sort of path winding between them, did nevertheless leave in front of the fire a fairly large space, in which stood two armchairs face to face and a pretty card table, as delicate as some beautiful little girl. The table bore an oil lamp and an open book. Everything except this table, lamp, book, and one of the armchairs, was powdered with white dust. Large heaps of cinders cluttered the fireplace and raised the fire a span above the heads of the firedogs.

There was no cooking to be seen in progress. Yet there was an exquisite smell of something being jugged or stewed; in any case, of a wine sauce simmering.

Angelo was deeply affected by this smell. "That does it," he thought: "everything has changed." He could well imagine how with a little stew at the right moment all the heroes and heroines of Ariosto could be brought down to earth and reality. "And," he added stupidly, "one is confronting reality most of the time." He also felt humiliated at squatting there naked in a blanket by the fire, and that *he had to do so if he wanted to stay alive*. After all, there was liberty, and this young woman to be taken to Gap. He spoke of the cholera.

"It's comical," said the big man in the riding-coat. "We're having an epidemic of fear. Right now, if I were to call a yellow armband 'cholera' and make a thousand people wear it, the thousand would die in a fortnight."

Angelo, who could not reconcile himself either to nakedness or to the blanket (even though the attitude of the young woman crouching by him and warming her hands, and of the man in the riding-coat, who was filling a pipe, were exemplary), began a solemn discourse on chlorine and chloride, and how the towns were short of them. He thus expressed his thought completely, which was: "This situation I'm in, this blanket, these bare protruding feet, are most humiliating. I should dearly like to get some sort of clothes on."

"It isn't chloride the towns are short of," said the man, lighting his pipe. "They're short of everything; at all events, of everything necessary to resist a fly, especially when that fly doesn't exist, as is the case. Look here, my young friend, I know what I'm talking about," he went on, wedging himself into the armchair adjoining the little card table. "I've practised medicine for over forty years. I know perfectly well that the cholera isn't the outcome of pure imagination. But if it spreads so easily, if it has what we call this 'epidemic violence', that's because by the continual presence of death it enhances everybody's huge congenital egoism. People die, literally, of egoism.

Please note what I say: it's the result of numerous clinical observations, extending the term to cover the streets and fields and the so-called good health that is enjoyed in them; I've spent much more time in streets and fields than at bedsides. When it's a matter of plague or cholera, the good don't die, young man! I know – you're going to tell me you've seen good people die. My answer is: 'That's because they weren't very good.'"

Angelo mentioned the little Frenchman.

"A relative immunity always leads to complacency," said the man. "That's a weakness the gods have taken advantage of at all times, and the famous fly doesn't lag behind. My dear sir, death to the man who believes he is innocent: that's what the gods say. And it's just. One can always find the best reasons in the world for thinking oneself perspicacious when one succeeds in seizing the bull by the horns. That isn't enough. You cite the case of a country doctor, or myself, or the *vulgum pecus*: they all die, of course . . ."

Angelo, who in his position had need of corpses, described how the little Frenchman had dazzled him with his unselfishness and devotion.

"Granted," said the man; "in that case he was *too* good. There has to be a mean in everything. But give me simply someone who *forgets himself*. That's the word I was looking for: someone who isn't thinking of himself, and who therefore doesn't look for the moribund in heaps of corpses to give himself the pleasure of saving them, as you've just told me your little doctor did. Give me someone who forgets his liver, his spleen, and his gizzard. *He* doesn't die. At least, not of cholera. Of old age, no doubt; but of cholera, no."

He added that the region was volcanic and consequently preserved from the noxious miasmas; that within a radius of seven or eight leagues (and his field of observation must be extended that far in order to mean anything in this unpopulated place) there had not been a single death from cholera since the start of the epidemic.

"We have here a substratum of lava from which warm and sulphurous emanations rise. In short, we live at minimum expense." Upon which he freely admitted that Angelo's chloride was not really so stupid, and that chemistry might well replace philosophy and ethics in the towns.

He had practised in Lyon, Grenoble, and even Paris. That was the origin of his melancholia, he remarked, his lips gilded with the most delicate of smiles. Melancholia, but not misanthropy, as they could plainly see. Moreover he treated it with the domes of Moscow. It was an extremely powerful method, and so stupid that it worked like a dose of iron easily assimilated by an organism grown anaemic. "Do you realize that this is a highly important discovery?" Up to then there had been no cure for melancholia. Medicine was powerless.

"Now melancholia, though less theatrical (and its hypocrisy multiplies its poison tenfold) is claiming more victims than the cholera. Let's pass over the fact that it kills – that, of course, is a commonplace – and kills on a scale people never realize, because its victims don't display green bellies all along the streets but pop off with great decency and modesty in secret corners where they are held (perhaps rightly) to have died a natural death. But apart from these basic conclusions, melancholia turns a certain part of society into a company of living dead, *a cemetery above the ground*, if I may put it that way; it removes the appetite and the sense of taste, makes you impotent, puts out the lights and even the sun, and in addition produces what one might call a *delirium of uselessness*, which moreover tallies perfectly with all the aforementioned deficiencies; and, even if it is not directly contagious in the sense we unconsciously give that word, does at any rate drive its victims to *excesses of negation* that may easily infect, reduce to idleness, and consequently destroy an entire country. Not forgetting the great enterprises to which in the end melancholics of the sanguine type almost always devote themselves, which drag whole populations into carnage no more savoury than that of the plague or cholera."

His little trick with the domes of Moscow wasn't bad, if they would consider it carefully. He was now perfecting it. But did they know what he had turned to in the meantime? Victor Hugo – no more, no less.

And he brought down the palm of his hand on the open book beside him near the oil lamp.

Thereupon, by a natural transition, he turned to gaze at the window, clouded and streaming with water, which shook with the assaults of the wind, and declared that it was extraordinary weather.

Angelo's boots, shirt, and suit were dry. He went off to dress in a dark corner.

"The devil take modesty," said the man, "stay here by the fire. You're well built, what risk do you run? D'you think Mademoiselle was created and brought into the world *per studiare la matematica*? All the young are North Poles, Swedenborgs, Cromwells! And what about the infectious warmth of banquets? What do you do about that? Be Greek, my young friend! Just look at his face and those big eyes. '*It's Greece, my mother, where the sky is so kind!*'"

Angelo would have given a sharp retort, but, to his stupefaction, it was all he could do to swallow his saliva, which was copious and salty. While speaking, the man in the riding-coat had crouched down beside the young woman; he pushed aside the ashes in the hearth, uncovered a cast-iron stewpot simmering there, and raised its lid. For one who had lived on polenta and tea for a week, that powerful smell of game and wine sauce was irresistible.

"Will you act as hostess, my dear? In the sideboard – it's all right, it's on the opposite side from where our mother's darling is pulling on his breeches – there's a clean cloth, plates, and all that we need. Please set the table. We will now do honour to this hare, the product of my ancestral skill. Now that for once I have guests, I'm going to allow myself one of those Belshazzar's feasts that are milestones in a man's life, especially in the life of a hardened, solitary, and let's admit it, ageing bachelor.

> '*Woe to the prince who, drunk at festal board,*
> *Mocks th'oppressed and the prophet of the Lord!*
> *Ev'n as Belshazzar, blind to fate that lowers,*
> *He sees not on the echoing walls*
> *The words a flaming finger scrawls*
> *In letters all of fire 'twixt knots of flowers.*'"

Angelo was glad to feel the stiffness of his velvet jacket on his back once again.

"To be booted and spurred," he thought, "is perhaps the root of all power." But the smell of cooking carried everything before it. He even forgot to wonder if it were wise for the young woman to eat in this strange house – and eat what was clearly a heavily spiced meal. He was prey to an irresistible temptation. "Can't be helped," he told himself happily. The boots were no longer of much use.

He went to look after the mule. He rubbed it down with wads of straw. It was one of those times when the smell of stable dung did him good. He thought regretfully of his fine uniform. He would have enjoyed giving some orders.

The violence of the storm, which thundered in every echo, drew him to the stable door. It was a deluge such as he had never before seen.

The young woman came and joined him. They were both subdued and depressed, and gazed at each other sadly.

"Still," she said, "I liked the polenta very much. You make it so well." She even added: "You put so much into making it."

"Of course," said Angelo, "it helped us out, but . . ."

"It's impossible to leave here," said she.

"We mustn't offend the man; he's certainly very kind," said Angelo.

They ate with very powerful appetite, and without avoiding any-thing, neither the bread, which, through prudence, they had not touched for a long time, nor the very plain wine that the man in the riding-coat served them generously.

Angelo noticed that the young woman devoured the food brutally and could not even restrain one or two little moans. She also kept closing her eyes.

In short, it was a depressing meal for both of them, but not for their host, who kept quoting Victor Hugo on the slightest pretext.

Angelo was happy to find his little cigars quite dry in their case.

"I've still got twenty-five. My handkerchiefs much have protected the box from the rain," he thought with sudden but keen delight. "No pleasure is ever small."

Still, now that he was no longer hungry, he could have wished he had not eaten. He blamed the young woman for having abandoned herself to these joys as supinely as he had. He was not prepared to forget the little moans of satisfied greed that she had instinctively uttered. He saw everything in its worst light. He spoke of what was on his mind.

"That fellow's phenomenal," said the man. "He's absolutely deter-mined one should take an interest in his cholera. I can talk to you about the cholera and plague *ad libitum*. But, believe me, it's better to sit and look at the spring flowers in the shape of this charming person."

"This person will only stay charming if she doesn't die of cholera," said Angelo primly.

"You have your own way of looking at things, young man, I don t deny. But its real value is a moot question, if an old doctor may say so. Experience enables me to state that we are incapable of discerning, in the nexus of events, that which will engender good or evil. I've seen inflammation of the lungs cured by a monstrous, revolting, cancriform anthrax.

"*'Lord, Thou hast filled the world with mystery.'*

"Perfect discernment, definite, concrete, never failing while we are concerned with the senses. For the senses work in the immediate present. Hence, my humility. Why must you keep worrying yourself with *future diplomacy* in which a sow may not be able to find her piglets, and wondering whether Mademoiselle will remain charming, just because she is so now. In short, what exactly do you want of me?"

"It's very simple," said Angelo. "You're a doctor, you must know some remedy. Perhaps you even have one or two in a cupboard? We are on the road, with no resource but our desire to live. And that, I fear, isn't enough in these times. I believe that calomel, or even paregoric elixir – "

"Fudge! Calomel, paregoric elixir! What is – "

"But," said the young woman, "in this nexus of events, which, if I understood rightly, seemed to concern me, and the obscurity of which you so pertinently emphasized, if I may put a word in, it's to ask that I may live to be a hundred, like everybody else."

"A profound error, a profound error," said the man . . . "but your interruption has already saved me from two or three rude words I had on the tip of my tongue: far be it from me to speak them here, my children!

> *'Fair, simple foreheads bent to hear my sigh,*
> *Sweet mouths, enamel teeth forever asking 'Why?''*

Let's cheer ourselves up with this rum, which, mark my words, is worth all the calomels in the world."

"Yes," said Angelo, very seriously, "alcohol is excellent."

"Everything is excellent," said the man. "If I get started on the cholera you'll be astonished. You've seen it advance through the countryside and it's given you quite a lot to hide (you'll manage that easily because you're young); but to see the cholera invade a human body – that's a spectacle which induces frankness. All the same, to have even an approximate knowledge of these sumptuous Panathenæa one must first familiarize oneself with the terrain in which these festivities take place. The liver, the spleen, and the gizzard, of which I was speaking just now; it takes no time to say their names, but what are they? Above all, what are they before they're spread out on the marble for autopsy? Once they get there, they're not much use; just little bouquets, subjects of chitchat; they help mould public opinion, and satisfy convention. But at this moment, for you and me for example, and for that immense quantity (don't forget) of men and women fully alive and destined to go on living – what are they? I'm not going to give you a lecture; it's not a question of anatomy. It's a question of penetrating to where passions, errors, sublimity, and fear are concocted. An adult liver, just where it belongs in an upright, healthy lady or gentleman, is a beautiful thing! We don't need Claude Bernard in such a case. He only tells us that the liver produces sugar. Are we better seamen for knowing that the sea produces salt? If we want some idea of the human adventure, it isn't Claude Bernard we need here, it's Lapérouse, Dumont d'Urville or, better still, the real collectors of trophies! Columbus, Magellan, Marco Polo. I've cut up the human liver, lots of them, with my little knife. I've settled my glasses on my nose and said: 'Let's have a look', like anyone else. I've seen – what? That it could be either clogged or putrid, inflamed or obstructed, that it sometimes adhered to the diaphragm. And a lot further that got me!"

He was ready to assert, then and there, that the liver is like an extraordinary ocean whose depths cannot be sounded, leading to Malabars, Americas, sumptuous navigations through expanses hung with double blue. He had naturally been treated as unscientific, even as a downright ass, by clinical gentlemen who, like anyone else, entertained their bad temper and indignation in their livers, without for a moment trying to see that, if this lack of logic was the product of sugar, it was in any case a sugar with which it was hard to sweeten one's coffee.

Certainly he would not advise anyone, given the objective paths that experimental science was bent on pursuing, to speak of monsters, Easter Islands, tempests, sea breezes, calms, wigwams, bougainvilleas, cassia, gold, thunderbolts, albatrosses, in a word, everything that is needed to change skies and dreams, in connection with the liver. Unless they were prepared, like him, to endure sarcasm and forge ahead.

"For give me a liver and a carcass, man's or woman's *ad libitum*. I stuff one into the other, and that's enough to set off, win or lose, all the vaudeville of the contemplative or social life. I'm murdering Fualdès[1] or Paul-Louis Courrier.[2] I'm selling Negroes into slavery, setting them free, making them into sausage meat or flags for consultative bodies. I'm inventing, I'm founding the Society of Jesus and making it work, loving, hating, caressing, and killing, not to mention giving my sister in marriage to the Zouave who assures the perpetuity of the human race."

He drew their attention to the following point: these examples were not selected at random. They were meant to show that what we had here was not the generator of raw deeds, but of all the combinations and embellishments: the barrel organ to drown the victim's cries; the adulterous woman full of nocturnal forests, shots and the reading of wills; in short, the whole comedy, including the one played, not in people's heads but, he had the honour to point out, in their beds.

All that remained for him was to coil up beside it a few yards of guts, not forgetting the rectum, which gives space and a lyrical quality, to set out kidneys, a spleen, and one or two intestinal accessories, and he would be able to provide the whole scale of the passions with all the flats and sharps necessary to the magnificent two-legged animal, the pre-eminent liar. Need he add that he did not attach any pejorative sense to the word "liar"? Far from it. He could be as objective as father or mother on occasion.

A parenthesis. He wished to bring out the cogency of his way of seeing things. Cholera is a disease with great depths; it does not spread by infection but by *proselytism*. Before going further, there was a most important point to consider. "Here you have a man (or woman) opened up from head to foot like an ox at a butcher shop and there, leaning over him (or her) with all his implements, the artist. He may know quite well what the man (or woman) died of. But "why", in its deeper sense, is another matter. Another matter, which, to be brought into the open, would require knowledge of the "how": how this man (or this woman) had lived. This man (or woman) has loved; hated; lied; suffered; and enjoyed the love, hatred, and lies of others. But no trace of all this at the autopsy. This man (or woman) has loved and I know nothing about it. Has hated, and I don't know whom, or in what way. Has enjoyed and suffered: dust! Who can assure us that there is no connection, close or remote, between that greenish bile filling the bowels, and love? (When it is genuine, deep, everything it should be, and has lasted for ten or twenty years, even if directed at different objects, I grant you.) Who will certify that hatred and jealousy have no part in those livid purplish spots, those internal carbuncles I discover in the mucus glands of the intestines? Who will maintain that the blue thunderbolt of rapture, full of wild peacocks, has swooped down several thousand times on this organism without leaving any traces behind? Aren't they the ones I see? Close the parenthesis.

"No, mademoiselle, I have not mentioned the heart; a lady's handiwork. It is a lion we wear embroidered on our shirts. In the remains before me, there is nothing resembling it. In the place to which you point, I find a combined suction and forcing-pump that does its little job, and when it ceases one knows it. Leave St Vincent de Paul and Co. in peace. In any case he's coming. He's coming up from the violet ocean. He's emerging from the deep, all shining with that strange sugar so dear to Claude Bernard. It's a variant of '*Vénus toute entière à sa proie attachée.*' I can synthesize for you the mercy of Augustus, more than you'll know what to do with, by means of a little gastric juice; and all Don Juan needs from me is one second of negligence as I measure out my ingredients. Free will is a chemistry manual."

He had expected from them a burst of injured pride. None came, no, really none? "Note that your so-called humility is simply digestive sloth, by a good fire, after a lunch, in extraordinary weather (which is continuing, if I'm not mistaken; is getting more furious and beautiful)." And also – he would not conceal it from himself or from anyone – the obvious pleasure always to be had from listening to talk on this subject. "But in yourselves you are convinced you have nothing in common with these chemical compounds. You surreptitiously stroke the lion embroidered on your shirts. Besides, there's the flower of your breast underneath, and that, in both sexes, is very sensitive."

Ah well! He would not hold it back from them any longer: "Cholera is not a disease, it's *a burst of pride*." A burst of pride worthy of the great deeps, the vast spaces of which he had just spoken; equal to the strange possibilities of these spaces and abysses; a hypertrophy of embellishment (if the term may be used); a barrel organ worthy of an unbridled chemistry; the embroidered lion that leans on the flower of your breast and suddenly assumes substance and antediluvian dimensions. Everything ending, moreover, in ineluctable chemistry. But what lovely fireworks!

"Do you know what is the best anatomical table going? It's a map, a map of Tenderness with East Indies shown *to the life*. At one and the same moment it is noon in Paris, five in the morning in Ceylon, noon in Tahiti, and six in the evening at Lima. While a camel lies in its death throes in the dust of Karakorum, a shopgirl is drinking champagne in a café, a family of crocodiles is descending the Amazon, a herd of elephants is crossing the equator, a llama with a load of borate of soda is spitting in its driver's face on a path in the Andes, a whale is floating between Cape North and the Lofoten Islands, and it's the Feast of the Virgin in Bolivia. The terraqueous globe revolves, heavens knows why or how, in solitude and shadow.

"Another parenthesis; let's digress for a moment; let's look around to right and left. Have you ever closely examined a pin wheel? What is it? Quite simply cardboard, powder, strips of wood, and some wire. The cardboard will take twenty years, a hundred years, a thousand, to live its cardboard life. A sad thing, the life of cardboard! Whether it's blue, yellow, red, or green (colours don't bother me, I like them all) or grey, the life of cardboard isn't worth a fig. Now Champollion found cardboard in Egypt that had been living that life for three thousand years (it's still living it now in a glass case). The loves and joys of cardboard, the sufferings and woes of cardboard: can you imagine them? But set fire to the cardboard cartridge in the village square. What a sight! Everybody cries: 'Ah! Ah!'

"*A burst of pride.* At that moment, nothing counts but the burst and the pride; everything explodes: family and fatherland. Tristan has set fire to himself, he literally bursts in his skin, and Juliet too, and Antony and Cleopatra, and the whole caboodle. Each for himself. I love you and you love me; it's very beautiful, but who will give me reasons for persisting in these compromises, these half measures and *little deaths* when, from the abysses of my liver, are emerging the best reasons in the world for *becoming.*"

An end to joking! They had paid him the honour, he believed, of asking him about cholera; he was now ready to reply.

"Enter, let us enter into these five or six cubic feet of flesh about to become cholera-stricken, flesh prey to the symptoms of that *cancer of pure reason*, flesh tired of the evasions imposed upon it by its grey matter, which with the aid of its mysteries suddenly starts to reason and to work overtime.

"What happened in the beginning? Nobody can tell us. No doubt, later on, a solitary wave, fifty to sixty feet high, seven to eight hundred miles long and advancing at the rate of two knots a second, has traversed the dead flat ocean. Before and after it, April rests blossoming on the waters. No boom, no foam; there are no breakers or ripples in these vast, fathomless expanses, which *nothing can surprise*. Just water moving over water, and no consciousness to perceive it.

"Up till now, everything's beginning, nothing has changed. Adolphe, Marie, or François are still at your side, loving you (or hating you). It's a matter of three seconds."

He wanted, he said, to give a description, "even an approximate one, if, alas, I can't do more," of how human consciousness finally felt when stripped of all its joys. Even the memory of them was effaced. He compared these joys to birds. The migrants first and foremost, those that delight the most diverse lands according to time and season, and especially the wonderful wild peacocks. High-flying peacocks, able to speed their fleeing arrowheads more swiftly than the grebe, the plover, the woodcock, the green duck, and the thrush.

"All this bird life, fleeing not towards the horizon but towards the zenith, fills and overflows the sky. There are so many that it is jammed with them, its high places are choked, it suffers pain.

"That is the moment when the cholera victim's face reflects that stupor said to be characteristic. His debilitated joys are terrified today by something other than their own weakness; by some unknown thing from which they flee far beyond true north and are lost to view. Heavens, Adolphe! or Marie, or François, what's wrong with you? What's wrong is that he's dying, to put it politely, *dying of pride*. Little he cares, from now on, for the flesh, or for the flesh of his flesh. *He is following his notion.*

"Sometimes, though, a hand still clings to the apron, the lapel, of a friend, of a lover. But the sedentary birds: the passerines, the sparrows, tits, nightingales (think of the nightingales! What a lot of people enjoy them, especially during nights in May), all the feeders on filth, on decay, on worms and insects to be found everywhere just by hopping about – *all the sedentary joys knock off*. They find out in an instant how to organize themselves into high flying wedges. Fear gives wings and wit. The day darkens. The stupor is not enough: one has to stagger, fall on the spot: at table, in the street, in love, in hate, and attend to far more intimate, personal, and passionate things."

He considered Angelo an all but perfect specimen of the most attentive and charming cavalier. "You have succeeded in interesting me and even, I may say, in charming me, if only by your struggle with your breeches, and not everybody could do that." As for Mademoiselle, he had always been at the mercy of those little lance-point faces. But what was the formal end of all that? The pericardium suffused with sanguinolent fluid, the cellular tissue covered with a varicose network of veins filled with liquefied black blood, the abdomen distended, the bile black, the lungs white, the bronchial tubes red and foamy – these teach their brain more in one flash than a thousand years of philosophy. Now that is precisely the condition in which we shall find the insides of Adolphe, Marie, and François, emptied of birds. Or your own, if it takes your fancy.

"If that were all, the truth would be within reach of every purse, at the mercy of a miracle; but one can't burn just half a pin wheel, once the powder's been lit."

Third parenthesis: Had they ever seen a volcanic eruption? Neither had he. But it was easy to imagine the moment when, daylight

357

having been abolished by the ashes, smoke, and poison-clouds, a new light arises from the burning crater.

"Here we have the first glimmers of that light which, little by little, will reveal the other side of things. The cholera victim is no longer able to avert his gaze from it. Jesus, Mary, and Joseph themselves wouldn't wish to miss a scrap of it."

Some details must be gone into. Had they any notion, even an elementary one, of human flesh? That wasn't surprising. Most people shared their ignorance. "It's all the more strange since everyone is continuously consuming human flesh, without even knowing what it is. Who has not seen the world change, darken or bloom, because some hand no longer touches yours, or because certain lips caress you? But they're exactly like you, they do it on faith. Not to mention one's own flesh, which one burns in shovelfuls, day in and day out, for a yes or a no.

"It's so small a matter that it's nothing." He had only to recall how pettish they both looked out in the storm, when he caught sight of them under the ruined arch of that cellar, to be convinced that they were ready to sacrifice themselves each for the other. Come now, that leapt to the eye, and they needn't affect irony, especially Mademoiselle. "Admit you were afraid for him. People never frankly admit those things, and it's a pity, but it's a matter of habitual compromise, of half-tints, half-tones, flats and sharps." The fact remained that they were quite simply ready to sacrifice themselves for a certain quantity of salt and water; for a plumber's job of pipes and bell-wires.

Nor would he go now into interminable considerations. This sufficed. The vanity of people and things was well known to all. Yet people continued to be surprised at the indifference shown by cholera victims to those around them and to the courage and devotion often spent upon them. "In most illnesses, the sick person takes an interest in those who are looking after him. Patients on the point of death have been seen shedding tears over their loved ones or asking for news of Aunt Eulalie. The cholera victim is not a patient: he's an *impatient*. He has just understood too many essential things. He's in a hurry to know more. That's all that interests him, and if you both caught the cholera you'd cease to mean anything to each other. *You'd have found something better.*

"I regret to say this to you, in spite of the obvious signs of your deep attachment. And here we cannot avoid speaking of *jealous* care for the sick. The loved one is leaving you for a new passion, and one you know to be final. Even if he is still in your arms, he is shaking with shudders and spasms, groaning in an embrace from which you are shut out.

"That's why I told you a little while ago that your little Frenchman wasn't altogether good, or else he was too much so. I should have added that in any case he lacked elegance. *He wasn't facing reality.* He was clinging on. To everybody. What for? To end by following their example.

"But this, as always, is a matter of temperament. Let's return to our pipes, bell-wires, and other gewgaws."

If all this had no feeling, it would be heaven. There'd be no curiosity, hence no pride; we should be truly eternal. "But lo and behold, vast balls of fire slop heavily out of the crater, incandescent clouds take the place of the sky. Your cholera victim is prodigiously interested. His one aim from now on is to know more.

"What is it he's feeling? Banal things: his feet are cold. His hands icy. He's cold in what are called the extremities. His blood is receding, rushing to the site of the spectacle. It doesn't want to miss anything.

"Well, it's nothing much. Generally, there's nothing to be done. Poultices for wooden legs – as you can imagine, there's an infinite variety of them. Calomel is one. No, I haven't got any. What should I do with it? Syrup of gum perfumed with orange blossom is another. We have a choice between leeches at the anus and blood-letting – one doesn't need much erudition to think of these in such cases. We can pass from clysters to cachou, from ratany to quinine, mint, camomile, lime, balm. In Poland they give a grain of belladonna; in London two grains of subnitrate of bismuth. Some try cupping the epigastrium, or mustard plasters on the abdomen. Some administer (it's a pretty word) hydrochlorate of soda or acetate of lead.

"The best remedy would be to make oneself preferred. But, as you can see, one has nothing to offer *in exchange*, to replace this new passion. That's to say, we keep on looking for a specific capable of neutralizing the toxic attack, according to the formula of learned persons, when what is wanted is to make oneself preferred, offer more than is given by that burst of pride: in a word, *to be stronger, or more handsome, or more seductive, than death.*"

He would tell them something in confidence – or rather, no, the confidence should stop there. He wouldn't say a word more on this subject. "Prayers, appealing looks, and all your charm are no help. If you knew me better, you'd know that when I've decided to be silent I never yield to the temptation to talk."

On the other hand, they had wanted a description of the cholera. He had agreed; they should have it. "And no stopping up your ears, if you please. Just now this young man seemed disposed to eat me alive if I didn't humour his desires. He shoved his pretty lady under my nose; he shoved you under my nose with the excuse that you must be saved at all costs. Why must you? That's a question he doesn't even ask himself. Above all, why should I and the rest of the world share his opinion? And, I repeat, save what?"

He wasn't in the least scared by loftiness: "Sit down and take some more rum, it's more sensible." He was an old gentleman. He had shot his bolt long ago. "Sabre, pistol, the duel you considerately offer me with such amusing ardour – what good would they do? *Was it I who made the world?*

"If I inflict my confidences on you, it's precisely because I think I'm in the presence of reasonable persons, having regard to their pleasant faces and notwithstanding that awkward age which so easily drives one to extremes. Be thankful for youth, which permits one to approach death without mistrust or terror.

"The cholera victim no longer has any face: he has a *facies* – a facies that *could only mean cholera.* The eye, sunk deep in its socket and seemingly atrophied, is surrounded by a livid circle and half covered by the upper eyelid. It expresses either great agitation of the soul or a sort of annihilation. The sclerosis, now visible, is smitten with ecchymosis; the pupil is dilated and will never contract again. These eyes will never have tears again. The lashes, the lids are impregnated with a dry, greyish matter. Eyes that remain wide open in a rain of ashes, gazing at haloes, giant fireflies, flashes of lightning.

"The cheeks have lost their flesh, the mouth is half open, the lips glued to the teeth. The breath passing through the narrow dental arcades becomes loud. It's like a child imitating an enormous kettle. The tongue is swollen, flabby, rather red, covered with a yellowish coating.

"The chill, first felt in the feet, knees, and hands, tends to invade the whole body. Nose, cheeks, ears are frozen. The breath is cold, the pulse slow, extremely weak, towards the decline of physiological existence.

"Now in this condition the victim answers with lucidity if questioned. His voice is hoarse but he doesn't wander. He sees clearly, and *from both sides*. When he chooses, it is with full awareness."

He pointed out that all this takes longer to describe than to happen. "It is all seen in a flash as one cries out, rushes forward, takes Jacques, Pierre, or Paul in one's arms and asks: 'What's to be done? He's lost!'"

So he felt; but, as he had remarked at the beginning, he had never been present at any volcanic eruptions. Nevertheless, he could imagine them quite well; and there must be in the spectacle of these convulsions a deeply tragic moment, doubtless of hypnotic value – the moment when the festival of fire sprang from the entrails of the earth and flung itself roaring upon life. Without having read anything on the subject except the Ætna and the stories of the Cyclops, it was easy to imagine those gigantic brayings, those brutalities incandescent, cindery, mephitic, and probably containing electricity. One had to be struck with such surprise, facing so clear a demonstration of our nothingness, that all the salt and probably all the sugar of Monsieur Claude Bernard turned into a statue.

"Some of my colleagues, who aren't all blind, have spoken of 'choleric asphyxia'. I even thought for a moment that they were capable of understanding and expressing a little more than science whispers into their ears, when they added this charming remark – and how true! – 'The air still reaches the blood, but the blood doesn't reach the air'. I should have liked, after that (I repeat) most intelligent observation, to hear them pronounce the name of Cassandra, immediately after, and to show that they had really understood.

"I have spoken of proselytism; I mean that people cannot resist the need to proclaim the future, that is to say the truth, the truth in the egg.

"I've often thought that there is perhaps a moment when the cholera victim suffers, suffers horribly, not in his pride as hitherto (that's what is pushing him on) but, at last, in his love, and this might hold him back on our side.

"Here I open another parenthesis. Soon to be closed, don't worry, but necessary. It should be noted that the cholera, as you know, strikes everyone without distinction, and without warning. People take the decision to have cholera suddenly, in the midst of other fixed and firm decisions engendered by all the force of habit. And those most above suspicion are forthwith susceptible: the mother just as much as the girl in love, the housewife, the bourgeois, the soldier, the house-painter and the painter of battle scenes. Mediocrity does not exclude it; happiness (as is right) provokes it. Let's now close the parenthesis and keep its contents well in our minds. We are really much more than we think.

"It is maintained, then, that the cholera victim suffers horribly. It is said that nothing can compare with the torture of these living corpses who appreciate all the horror of their position. This obviously happens, as you will understand, in a state without dimensions or duration; let us place this horror: when they are among the cones of fire, the waves of sparks, the octopus lava, the fans of light. Their bodies are deaf, blind, dumb, *insensible*. That is to say, they no longer have hands, feet, back, nails, hair, or hide. And yet they are lucid. They continue to hear and see those around them, the noises in the street, the pot simmering on the fire, the flapping of the washing on the line, the groans, the red of a dress, the black of a moustache, the buzzing of the flies.

"If there is suffering, now is the moment. I say 'if'; for what proof have we of this suffering? The spasms? The convulsions? The hiccups? The cries? The grinding of the teeth? Are we so sure we know the true outward manifestations of joy?

"But – a flash of pain, real horrible pain, that I believe in; and if it is possible, this is the moment for it. I say 'if' because I am trying, like everyone else, to be objective, not to take a short cut, leave anything to chance. It comes at the moment when, under the rain of ashes, the victim wonders if *all this* is worthwhile, if it wasn't better to be eating one's stew and not thinking of Charlemagne.

"The invalid is in an extreme state of agitation. He tries to rid himself of every covering, complains of unbearable heat, feels thirsty; forgetting all modesty, he flings himself out of bed or furiously uncovers his sexual parts. And yet his skin has turned cold and soaked with an icy sweat, which soon becomes sticky and gives to anyone touching it the disagreeable impression of contact with a cold-blooded animal.

"The pulse becomes more and more faint but it is still very rapid. The extremities take on a bluish tinge. The nose, ears, fingers suffer cyanosis; similar patches appear on the body.

"The emaciation we have noted in the face has extended all over. The skin has lost its elasticity, and *retains the crease if one pinches it.*

"The voice is extinguished. The patient now speaks only in sighs. The breath has a sickening smell, impossible to describe but unforgettable once one has smelled it.

"Calm comes at last. Death is not far off.

"I've seen some come out of this coma, sit up and for several seconds *look for air,* put their hands to their throats and, with a pantomime as painful as it is expressive, indicate to me an appalling strangling sensation.

"The eyes are turned up, their brilliance has vanished, the cornea itself has thickened. The gaping mouth reveals a thick tongue covered with ulcers. The chest no longer rises. A few sighs. It is over. He knows what to think of the outward marks of respect."

1 Local official, murdered round about this time at Béziars. While his throat was being cut indoors, a barrel organ was played outside to drown his cries. [Translator's note.]

2 The well-known writer. Supposed to have been murdered by a gamekeeper who, like a D. H. Lawrence hero, was his wife's lover. [Translator's note.]

# 14

ANGELO AND THE YOUNG WOMAN spent the night in armchairs by the fire. In the morning the sky was clear.

"You're ten leagues from Gap," the man in the riding-coat told them, "and you can't miss it. As you go down from here, you'll find seven or eight houses, which make up what the people call Saint-Martin-le-Jeune, and in the middle of these houses a crossroad, where the track you were following yesterday joins up with a fair-sized trunk road. There's nothing to worry about. Follow this road to the right for five leagues through country as healthy as a baby, and you come to the edge of the plateau. From here, you will see a hundred yards below your noses the main road to Gap. Go down and sit by the side of the road; the *diligence* was still running two days ago. And there are no barriers anywhere. Or, if you've got the money, push on to the little hamlet you'll see among the poplars. There's a post house there."

He made them take a flask of rum and a handful of coffee beans.

Things were just as he said. The people of Saint-Martin-le-Jeune were going about their normal business. One was sitting on the ground, sharpening his scythe; another was observing the weather and told Angelo it would be sunny for three days.

It was warm – one of those autumn days that seem like spring. The tough-leaved vegetation of the plateau, bright from the recent rain, sparkled like the sea. A bland smell of mushrooms was rising from under the junipers and box bushes. A light wind, flecked with cold, gave the air an unparalleled vigour and virtue. Even the mule was happy.

The young woman walked along gaily and, like Angelo, kept exclaiming over the clarity of the sky, the beauty of the camellia-coloured mountains lost in morning mist, towards which they were heading.

They saw timid crows again, passed a pedestrian returning to Saint-Martin with a sack of bread. The solitude was joyful.

Even after several leagues, when all trace of human life had vanished and they were passing through a little forest of stunted pines, the light, the air, the fragrance of the earth still kept the two travellers in high spirits. For the first time they were tasting the pleasures of travel.

"We are going to get there soon," said the young woman.

"I'll need at least two more days," said Angelo, "before I reach the other side of those lovely mountains."

"You will stay a good two days at Théus, I hope. I still have to thank you for your help. And you've never seen me in a long dress, except for that evening at Manosque when I had dressed up for reasons quite unconnected with you."

"I'll stay for the time it takes to buy a horse," said Angelo. "Don't take that for rudeness or indifference to what you are like in a long dress when you put it on for someone. But I am not my own master. I really have to fight for liberty."

His gaiety infected his old passion and he spoke of sacrificing his life for the happiness of mankind.

"It's a noble cause," she said.

He had enough wit to look up, to see whether she was being ironical. She was serious, even a little too much so.

She spoke of her sister-in-law, who was, it seemed, very eccentric and kind, an old lady formerly tortured by a charming husband. The Château de Théus, though countrified, was full of charms, and its rustic terraces overlooked the Durance at its most torrential point, facing an extravagant setting of mountains. He would be able to find suitable horses at the village of Remollon nearby. He would have plenty to choose from.

Angelo apologized: he would certainly be the first to beg hospitality of Madame de Théus.

"That's my name too," she said.

Well then, he would beg the hospitality of both Mesdames de Théus, and would ask the younger one to do him the favour of appearing in a long dress and all her finery.

"I shall have to choose my horse with great care," he thought. "On it I may have to perform some grand exploit as soon as I've crossed the frontier. So it can't be settled in an instant."

They halted at noon in the sunlit solitude. They made tea and rested for about an hour. They were sitting at the foot of a pine, on a knoll of soft, warm needles, before the miraculous spectacle of the plateau all bathed in light. The vaporous mountains seemed to contain it like some golden liqueur at the bottom of a blue bowl. The young woman closed her eyes and dozed. She was asleep, and snuffling in the most touching manner, when Angelo woke her.

"I'm sorry," he said, "but we must reach that road before dark. We'll go to that post house and you shall sleep in a bed. Come on, it's the last lap."

He suggested she should again ride on the mule. She vehemently refused and stepped out, still half asleep but with an enchanting smile.

Shortly before nightfall they reached the edge of the plateau. Everything was as the man in the riding-coat had described it. The main road lay a few hundred yards below them.

"And there's the little poplar wood," said Angelo, "with its cluster of houses. And the post haste."

But she was looking at him stupidly. Before he could cry: "What's the matter, Pauline?" she gave a sort of reflection of a still charming little smile and dropped down, slowly, folding her knees, bending her neck, her arms dangling.

As he rushed to her side, she opened her eyes and plainly tried to speak, but belched out a small flood of white, clotted matter, like rice paste.

Angelo tore the pack off the mule, spread his big cloak on the grass, and wrapped the young woman in it. He tried to make her drink some rum. Her neck was already as hard as wood and yet it shuddered, as if from tremendous blows struck deep inside her.

Angelo listened to those strange appeals to which the whole body of the young woman was responding. He was empty of ideas. He was only conscious that evening was falling, that he was alone. In the end he thought of the little Frenchman, but as of something minute. Then he dragged the young woman's body further away from the road, more into the bushes. This place where the infection had as yet claimed no victim would be liable to every excess of egoism at the first sign of attack, and he remembered the man with the sack of loaves they had passed the same morning on this road . . .

He pulled off the young woman's boots. Her legs were already stiff. Her calves were trembling. Her straining muscles protruded from the flesh. From her mouth, still plastered with its flow of rice, came little, shrill moans. He noticed that her lips were curling back over her teeth and that the young woman had a sort of cruel, almost carnivorous laugh on her face. Her cheeks were fallen in and palpitating. He began to massage her icy feet with all his strength.

He remembered the woman he had treated on the doorstep of the barn at Peyruis. He had needed the old gentleman's skill to undress her. He had to undress Pauline. He had also to light a fire and heat some big stones. He dared not stop massaging her feet, which remained like marble.

At length he told himself: "If I think about it, I'm done for. Let's do things properly." He had suddenly lost hope. He stood up and unpacked all the heavy garments that might give some warmth. He found enough twigs and even a thick pine log. He lit a fire, heated some stones, set a sort of cushion under the head whose face he could no longer recognize and whose weight astonished him. The hair, flowing over his hands, was harsh and as though tortured by a desert heat.

Angelo had placed some large pebbles in the fire. When they were very hot, he wrapped them in some linen and laid them close to the young woman's stomach. But the feet had turned purple. He began to massage again. He could feel the cold fleeing from his fingers and climbing up the leg. He raised the skirts. An icy hand seized his.

"I'd rather die," said Pauline.

Angelo gave some answer, he knew not what. That voice, though a stranger's, put him in a sort of tender rage. He shook off the hand brutally and tore out the laces binding the skirt at the waist. He undressed the young woman the way one skins a rabbit, dragging off the petticoats and drawers bordered with lace. He immediately massaged the thighs but, feeling them warm and soft, he withdrew his hands as though from live charcoal and returned to the legs and knees, which were already in a grip of ice and turning blue. The feet were snow-white. He uncovered the belly and studied it attentively. He felt it with both hands, all over. It was supple and warm but traversed with shudders and cramps. He could see it was inhabited by bluish shapes, swimming about and rising to strike the surface of the skin.

367

The young woman's groans now came rather loudly with each spasm. They made a continuous complaint, betraying no very great pain but accompanying the deep workings of some sort of ambiguous state, which was waiting, even hoping (or so it seemed), for a paroxysm when the cry would become savage and, as it were, delirious. These spasms that shook the whole body recurred every minute, making Pauline's stomach and thighs crack and arch each time, leaving her exhausted under Angelo's hands after each assault.

He never stopped massaging. He had thrown off his jacket. At each cry he could feel the cold make a fresh advance in its climb up the legs. He at once attacked the thighs, which were beginning to be peacock-patterned with blue spots. He renewed the little nest of burning-hot stones around the stomach.

He suddenly noticed that it was pitch dark, that the mule had gone. "I'm alone," he thought. For all his fear of egoism, he called out. His voice made a little insect noise. At one moment he heard, down on the main road, the rumble of a tilbury, the trotting of a horse. He saw the lantern of someone going on his way, a hundred yards or two below him.

He had massaged with such vigour and for so long that he was broken with fatigue and aching all over, but after feeding the fire he returned to those thighs and stomach. Pauline had begun to foul herself below. He cleaned everything carefully and placed under her buttocks a draw-sheet made of embroidered underclothes that he had taken out of the little case.

"She must be forced to drink some rum," he thought. With his fingertip he unblocked the mouth, choked with fresh vomitings of rice pudding. He struggled to unlock the teeth. He succeeded. The mouth opened. "The smell isn't nauseating," he thought, "no, it doesn't smell bad." He poured in the rum, little by little. At first it was not swallowed, but then the alcohol vanished like water in sand.

He automatically raised the bottle to his own lips and drank. He realized in a flash that he had that instant been holding the neck of the bottle to Pauline's mouth, but said to himself: "And so what?"

The cyanosis seemed to have settled in above the thighs. Angelo energetically massaged the folds of the groin. The diarrhoea had ceased. The young woman was breathing feebly, first hiccuping, then panting heavily as though after a struggle that had left her breathless. Her stomach was still shuddering with memories. The moaning had ceased.

She continued to disgorge clotted, whitish matter. Angelo noticed a frightful stench spreading. He wondered where it came from.

For some hours on end he had been asking himself: "What have I got in the way of remedies? What must I do?" All he had was a little case full of feminine underwear, his own case, his sabre, his pistols. For a moment he thought of using gunpowder. He did not know for what. But it seemed to him that there was some power in it, what power did not matter, that might reinforce his own. He thought of mixing this gunpowder with the *eau de vie* and making Pauline drink it. He told himself: "This isn't the first time I've tended someone with cholera, and I'd have given my life for the little Frenchman. There's no doubt about that. This time I'm out-matched."

He could only massage without stopping. His hands ached. He massaged with *eau de vie*. He kept renewing the hot stones. He carefully dragged the young woman as close as possible to the fire.

The night had become extremely dark and silent.

"This isn't the first time," thought Angelo, "but they've all died in my hands."

The absence of hope, rather than despair, and above all physical exhaustion now made him more and more frequently turn to gaze into the night. He was not seeking help but some repose.

Pauline seemed to be slipping away. He dared not question her. The words of the man in the riding-coat were still too recent. He remembered the lucidity of which the man had spoken, and he dreaded lucidity from this mouth, still discharging its whitish mud.

He was amazed, even rather terrified, by the emptiness of the night. He wondered how he had managed not to be frightened till now, especially of things so menacing. Yet he never ceased to labour with his hands to bring back warmth to that groin at the edges of which the cold and marble hue still lurked.

At length a whole series of little, highly coloured, brightly lit thoughts came to him, some of them absurd and laughable, and, at the end of his tether, he rested his cheek on that stomach, now shuddering only feebly, and fell asleep.

A pain in his eyes woke him; he saw red, opened his eyes. It was day.

He could not think what the soft, warm thing was on which his head was resting. He could see he was covered to the chin by the folds of his cloak. He breathed deeply. A cool hand touched his cheek.

"I covered you up," said a voice. "You were cold."

He was on his feet in an instant. The voice was not entirely unfamiliar. Pauline was looking at him with almost human eyes.

"I fell asleep," he thought, but said it aloud and in a miserable tone of voice.

"You were at the end of your tether," she said.

He asked some incoherent questions and made several futile journeys between the pack-saddle and Pauline's pillow, not knowing either what he wanted to fetch or what ought to be done. At length he had the sense to feel the patient's pulse. It was beating quite strongly and its speed was on the whole reassuring.

"You've been ill," he said emphatically and as if it were necessary to find an excuse for something: "you still are; you mustn't move; I'm very glad."

He caught sight of the naked stomach and thighs, and turned purple in the face.

"Cover yourself up well," he said.

He fetched all the contents of his case and made the young woman a nicely banked-up bed with plenty of hot stones. He placed several at her feet and as high as he dared up the legs, almost to the knees. In doing so he could not help brushing the back of his hand against her flesh. It seemed to have recovered some of its warmth.

The morning was as joyful as that of the day before.

Angelo remembered the maize water Teresa used to make him take when he was small: apparently it cured everything, particularly dysentery. He had never once thought of maize water since he had dedicated himself to the fight for the good of mankind. This morning, everything spoke of it: the air, the light, and the fire. He remembered that sticky, insipid but very refreshing infusion.

He at once set some water to boil and made an excellent infusion, concentrating solely on what he was doing.

The young woman drank greedily, several times. Towards noon the cramps were plainly over.

"I'm only exhausted," she said, "but you . . ."

"I'm fine," said Angelo. "It's enough to see that shy pink beginning to come to the right place in your cheeks. Just there it never means fever. Now let me feel your pulse."

It was clearly much stronger and more regular than two hours before. The afternoon passed in ever renewed attentions, in quickly dissipated alarms. It was warm, and although not sleepy, far from it, Angelo received the images of the world's splendour in a head quite empty but ready to seize on anything with drunken joy.

He renewed the hot stones ceaselessly.

At length the young woman announced that she now felt as warm and soft as a chick in its egg.

Evening fell. Angelo made coffee with the handful of beans given him by the man in the riding-coat.

"Did you disinfect yourself?" said the young woman suddenly.

"Of course," said Angelo. "Don't worry."

He drank the coffee and a generous bumper of rum. He lay down, wrapped in his jacket near the fire.

"Give me your hand," said Pauline.

He held out his hand and the young woman put hers in it. He was already half asleep. Slumber seemed to him a sure and peaceful refuge.

"But the hot stones are no longer necessary," he told himself.

"You've torn my clothes," said Pauline next morning. "You've wrenched off the fastenings of my skirt, and look what you've done to these pretty lace drawers. How am I going to dress? I feel quite well."

"That's out of the question," said Angelo. "I'm going down to the road – it's no distance – to watch out for some passer-by who'll take a message to the post house. Our mule's gone. And I insist on your lying where you are. You're going home in a carriage. This evening we'll be at Théus."

"I'm anxious about you," she said. "I've had cholera, there's no doubt about that. It's not my skirt fastenings and drawers that have made my stomach so sore. I must have been horrible! And you, haven't you been rash?"

"Yes, but in these cases the infection shows at once. I've got a night's start on death," said Angelo, "and it won't catch me up."

He had not been five minutes by the roadside before he saw a small, empty hay cart coming from the direction of Saint-Martin. He advanced to meet it. It was led by a peasant who at first glance seemed rather stupid. Between its side racks, along with pitchforks and tarpaulins, was an old woman in a red petticoat.

Angelo told them straight out that over in the bushes was a woman who had been ill; now she had recovered, he asked them to be so good as to transport her as far as the post house. Moreover, he would pay for it. This made no impression either on the stupid man or the old woman.

They stopped the cart and followed Angelo stolidly into the thicket.

"But it's Madame la Marquise!" said the old woman.

She had been daily woman for a whole winter at Théus. She was now living with her son-in-law, the simpleton. Proudly she gave orders. At length, towards three in the afternoon, Pauline was lying in a big, soft bed in the postmaster's house, asleep in the midst of hot-water bottles.

"No one's scared here," thought Angelo. Indeed everyone spoke to him with all the respect two gold pieces he had distributed on arrival could procure. They kept calling him "Marquis", and he had to be extremely firm in order to avoid this tiresome misunderstanding, which made him blush each time. He did not altogether succeed. They saw him leave the dining-room hourly and go upstairs. He would open the bedroom door, look at Pauline as she slept, and even feel her pulse, which was still excellent. And, well, you know, here a bed was a bed, especially with a young woman in it who did not appear very ill. They were making a lot of fuss about nothing down in the plains and by the sea, if that was what the sick looked like in the end. The carters there had in any case decided that it wasn't plague at all; that this woman with such lovely hair and such a friendly smile for everyone was indeed ill, but simply with the vapours. A Marquise, in their opinion (and the old woman of Saint-Martin had done all she could to see that no one forgot who Pauline was), was subject to vapours. As for the Marquis, they said, he was young. He'd learn. "He'll end by drinking his punch quietly like everyone else, if he doesn't come to a bad end." "You'll accompany me to Théus?" said the young woman.

"I shall certainly not leave you one yard before," replied Angelo. "I've hired, booked, paid for and even – to conceal nothing from you – placed under the guard of a boy, who's only fifteen but as tough as they come and my devoted servant till death (or, rather, till the bottom of my purse, which I showed him) – the most agreeable, most comfortable, fastest little trap I could find here. It's ours, it's awaiting us. I shall drive you right to Théus. You will lean on my arm to mount the steps, if there are any, and I shall stay two days," he added, so happy was he to see the colour returning to her face. "Remember the long dress."

"I was afraid you were busy buying yourself a horse," she said. "I heard you having a long talk in the stables. I can easily recognize the sound of your voice in spite of the walls."

Finally, new tapes were sewn on the skirt, the petticoat, and even the little embroidered drawers. The material itself had been torn and even holed by Angelo's nails – which had grown very long during his travels for want of scissors – and had needed big stitches to darn it.

He was rather worried about having let a cholera victim sleep in an inn bed, and he imparted his qualms in veiled terms to the postmaster, a man with a round sanguine face like a March moon.

"I'm used to all sorts," was the placid reply.

"It is," thought Angelo, "a case of cholera, of course, but a cured one."

It was impossible to picture any kind of infection likely to attack with any chance of success these simple, ruddy, slow-eyed men and women, living in the poplar wood by the roadside.

They reached Théus two days later, in the evening. The village overlooked the deep valley from very high up. It was inhabited by even simpler, placider, and ruddier people. The château dominated the village. There were numerous flights of steps from terrace to terrace, all of them rustic, without trimmings, indeed very severe and much to Angelo's liking. He did not back out of his promises. He gave the young woman his arm. The Marquis was not there. There was no news of him.

"He certainly won't have thought of me," said old Mme de Théus.

"I expect he's up to some folly somewhere. They say life's strange down there."

Angelo was about to undress in the comfortable room he had been given, complete with a four-poster bed, when there was a knock on his door.

It was the old Marquise. She was plump and ruddy too, in spite of her age, like the peasant women of the village. Her eyes were of that very clear blue which generally denotes a heart tender but free of superfluous pity. She had only come to enquire after the comfort of her guest, but she sat down carefully in an armchair.

Angelo was at last between walls like those of La Brenta. In the corridors he had recognized that smell which large and very old houses always have. He talked at great length to the old Marquise as he would have to his mother, and exclusively about the people and liberty.

It was after midnight when the old lady left him, wishing him good-night and telling him to sleep well.

A horse dealer from Remollon came to the bottom of the terraces and displayed four or five horses, among them an extremely proud animal, which Angelo bought with enthusiasm.

This horse gave him matchless pleasure for three days. He kept thinking of it. He saw himself galloping.

Every evening Pauline put on a long dress. The illness had made her little face sharper than ever. It was as smooth and pointed as a lance-head and, under the powder and rouge, faintly tinged with blue.

"How do you think I look?" she said.

"Very beautiful."

The morning that he left, Angelo right away gave free rein to his horse, which he had himself, every day, fed with oats. It had a swiftness he could be proud of. He saw galloping towards him those rosy mountains, near enough now for him to make out the rising larches and firs on their lower slopes.

"Beyond is Italy," he thought.

He was beside himself with joy.